THE UNDEAD. DAY EIGHTEEN

RRHAYWOOD.COM

RR HAYWOOD

QUOTES

"It was an organic transition of events that allowed the present situation to develop to its current system"
- Big Chris

"He who ceases to learn may well cease to know"
-Reginald

"Who stole Clarence's socks?
-Paula

CHAPTER ONE

'JAGGER...' he shouts the warning over and over, screaming with every ounce of his strength but his voice is weak and his movements are slow. Arms and legs pumping but no motion is gained. He tries and tries to run, forcing his legs to move but the bullet soars across the distance and slams into Jagger who falls with a look of intense hurt etched on his face. 'JAGGER...' still he screams but there is no point now. The death shot is given and Jagger lies dying on the ground. Now he can move. Now he can run and he looks down at the face of his friend and cries real tears. 'Jag...don't die...Jag...' He weeps and the pain in his heart is greater than he can take. 'Jag...bro....' he begs and pleads but the blood runs from Jagger's ears onto the rain soaked ground and big drops land on Mo Mo's cheeks to roll down his face. He wipes then away but his hand is weird. Soft and warm and wet. He wipes again but there is a course feel to the softness. He wipes harder and harder with his hand moving from chin to eye and then the other side from eye to chin. He can't stop wiping the tears but his hand isn't his hand.

She licks the boy's face. In the quiet of the dawn she felt his heart soaring and heard the whimpers from a sleep disturbed.

Rising silently she crosses to his bed and can both see and smell the salty tears coursing down his face and sensing the turmoil she whines softly in her throat with her own distress at the pack suffering.

His eyes open and she watches the pupils retract as he adjusts to the low light coming from the weak dawn. He swallows, exhales and blinks the silent tears as the sadness of the dream show true. His hands reach up into the soft fur of her neck and she lowers her weight gently until her head rests on his chest and his fingers run through the velvety hairs of her ears.

Quiet now. The pain eases and his heart slows from the dream. Just a dream. That's all. Just a dream. Sleep now. I watch.

She stays put until his breathing slows and he succumbs back to the sleep his young body needs so much. The fingers on her ears stroke softer and slower until the hands go still then gently slide down to his sides.

Only when she's sure he sleeps does she rise, turn and then stop at the sight of the small man watching silently from the door. She makes her way towards him. Past the two new pack members who sleep close together. One of them grinds her teeth and makes fists as though ready to fight. She also makes smells from her backside but she doesn't blink when she's asleep.

The other one also whimpered and cried in the night and Meredith was there to give comfort when the pain of the dream awoke the girl. She wept too. Silent and deep and she clutched the dog to her chest like the little one used to do. Meredith didn't mind. They were pack.

She moves past the other three, the laughing one whose emotions are so obvious. The hard faced one who sometimes takes the pack leader role and the special one she reserves extra attention for. They sleep sound and deep but they too whimpered sometimes and twitched from the motions from within their dreams.

The two that make a den together. The pack within the pack. The man is quiet but the woman has an energy that makes

Meredith think of the alpha female in her old pack. The mother to the little one she used to protect.

The big pack member snores with a deep but strangely soothing rumble and even in that sleep he protects with an aura that stretches round to envelope them all.

Close to him lies the scared one who sleeps curled up like a little one. Full of fear and confusion and Meredith senses the weakness about him. He is the runt of the pack. Defenceless and relying on the others to protect him. He brings nothing to the pack and she is disinclined to show affection to one so weak.

The other female who stayed with the leader to watch the pack while they first slept and she saw when the pack leader led her back into the den and helped her lie down in her bed. She used to smell wrong, not like the things that hurt the little ones but different and that smell has now changed again, almost normal, almost.

She stops at the den of the pack leader and watches carefully, ready to show submission should he wake and look at her. Just a dip of the head and a flicker of her ears that will pull back to show she serves and accepts his leadership. His energy is charged and different to all others. A thing of such brutality of violence that it should be dark and sinister yet it is filled with a pulsing love that drives into all of them. Round him they work. Round him they run and fight and round him they kill the things that can hurt the little ones.

Then there is the other one and she trots away from the pack with her tail wagging at the man waiting in the doorway. He drops down to a crouch and gives a rare show of his teeth as she pushes into his chest. A hand, firm yet gentle sweeps down her back. He is not like the others of his kind in the pack but something between them and her. He lacks the emotions of the others yet his emotions and energy are not animal. He could lead yet he chooses not to. His power is greater than anything she has known yet there is no hunger to that power. Only submission to serve the leader with a loyalty that makes her own look paltry in comparison and she knows he would kill them all if it was needed.

He too heard the new female pack member cry out and moved into the shadows of the room with one hand holding the thing that helps him kill so quickly. She sensed him watching, always watching, and only when the new female pack member went back to sleep did he move away.

They move to the main door and she waits while he pulls the bolts back and pushes it open. Together they step out and together they sniff the air but the heavy rain still coming down dampens nearly all smells. Smoke from a fire but it's far away.

Together they listen. Ears straining to hear past the drumming patter of the water striking the flat surfaces.

Dave waits and watches. Letting the senses of the dog work to sniff the air and hear what he cannot. She shows no alarm and walks further away to squat down and piss on the ground. She then moves further out and after finding a suitable spot she squats and defecates to relieve the pressure in her bowels.

It's early. Dawn only just rising and even that is weak and hidden by the incessant rain still coming down from the heavy grey clouds hanging low in the sky.

The pack will sleep for longer and an image of the warm beds in the room fills the dog's mind. The big pack member snoring noisily and the blinking girl making smells from her backside. She pushes past into the foyer and with a last glance at the small man she noses the main door open and trots back into the snug warmth of the room and over to stand in the middle of the mattresses of the young ones but there is an urge building. An instinct to do something that is so strong it cannot be denied. She has to do it and to not give way to the urge is unthinkable. The long hairs on her body protect her undercoat from the rain. The droplets slide down to drip on the floor but if left, they will work through those long hairs and into the undercoat. This is the urge she has now. To rid those droplets and prevent the undercoat from being made wet. She does not know this, she only knows she has to shake and, being an exceptionally big dog, she shakes well.

With legs planted wide it starts with a swing of her head from side to side as the muscles bunch and release with an explosion of energy and force. Every inch judders with an incredible motion that has the lips of her mouth swinging up to reveal her teeth. Eyes clamped shut and the vibration goes down the neck to the shoulders and further down her long back to the tail that swishes.

Droplets start spraying off, tens that become hundreds that become thousands and with the force generated those droplets go high and wide. A cascading waterfall of rain that sails up into the air of the room made warm by so many sleeping bodies. Those droplets reach the apex of their graceful rise and start to fall and like frozen pins of acid they pummel down onto every inch of exposed skin.

'OH MY FUCKING GOD...' Cookey is up and bursting to his feet with a wide eyed look of shock specially reserved for those who have gone from deep sleep to awake in a split second.

'SHIT,' Blowers follows and rolls heroically from his mattress in a desperate attempt to be away from the danger. He rolls into Nick's bed and clutches at the covers to protect himself.

'FUCK OFF,' Nick roars at the sudden removal of his cover and the exposure to the cold water striking his naked upper body.

'AARRRGHHHH,' Cookey went to bed topless. He, Blowers and Nick all choosing to sleep in their trousers but without tops. Of course this was done because of the warmth and the presence of Charlie had no bearing on that decision making process and he cries out trying to cover his body with his arms but too sleepy to think of moving away.

Meredith shakes. It has started now and cannot be stopped. Blowers and Nick scrapping to secure the victory of using Nick's cover. Blowers wins and rolls himself over and over while Nick cries out and lunges to grab Mo Mo's but the young lad is fast and rises to his feet with the cover held tight. He tries to run and flee the danger but the covers are round his feet and he goes down with a strangled yelp.

Charlie gasps with a sudden wakefulness and tries tugging her cover up but one of Meredith's back feet trap the end and it won't come. She pulls and tugs but the dog is heavy and there is no give. She scrabbles away, twisting onto all fours in a doomed attempt to crawl to safety.

Blinky farts and rolls over with a low muttering of threats to the other hockey player that has the ball.

Marcy snaps awake and her days of survival have served her well. She can see the danger and knows what action must be taken. Without hesitation she flings her cover back at the sight of Charlie trying to crawl to freedom and yells across the rapidly drenching gap, 'HERE...' Charlie clamps eyes on the place of safety and crawls faster as the raining droplets slam into her form. Marcy shuffles to make space and holds the cover open until Charlie makes the desperate dive for safety and lands on the soft warmth of the mattress. Marcy covers them both as they shiver and judder from the cold shock.

Blinky farts again and gets the ball from the other hockey player and, seeing as he referee is looking the other way, she punches the other hockey player in the face.

Clarence roars. A bear awoke from his hibernation and all shall suffer from this breach of etiquette. On his feet with a wild look and he looks over to see Nick and Blowers fighting for a duvet then Nick lunging to Mo Mo who tries to run away but trips and falls. Charlie crawling to Marcy and a foul smell from someone farting. 'WHO LET THE BLOODY DOG OUT?'

Reginald whimpers from the fright at being woken so brutally. This new world is beyond him and the ever present danger is too much. Death everywhere. Suffering. Blood and pain and now this. Getting soaked with cold water when he was happily dreaming of doing a crossword in a nice dry café. He rolls deeper into the cover and cowers from the danger.

Paula gets walloped by a direct hit full in the face and draws a sharp breath of shock into her lungs as her heart surges to flood her body with adrenalin. She sits up and without knowing it she reaches for the assault rifle as her eyes take in the sight. Roy was protected by Paula, snuggled into her back and safe but now exposed and the water strikes his also naked torso. A grunt and he tries grabbing the cover but it's wrapped round Paula sitting up.

'WHO LET THE BLOODY DOG OUT?' Paula snaps her head over to see Clarence on his feet raging into the room and anyone that was still asleep now wakes. A foul smells hits her nose. Someone farting and she gags from the stench and blinks from next direct hit of water on her face.

'NOT FAIR!' Blinky was seen punching the other hockey player and is not only being sent off but the referee has a hose. She shouts her frustration and sits up to sniff her own farts with a look of distaste.

'PAULA!' Marcy cries out at seeing her friend being so brutally assaulted, 'IN HERE...'

Paula makes an assessment of the threats and the risks. The dog is still shaking. The water still cascading. Roy is fighting to gain the covers and protect himself. Clarence raging. Mo Mo falling over. Cookey standing there trying to cover his upper body with his arms. Marcy offering refuge as the side of her cover raises with the promise of an opening into a dry place of safety.

Decision made and she goes for it. Abandoning Roy she lunges to roll across the gap and takes Clarence's cover as she goes. Into the opening and the three women create a fort with soft walls and giggle at the sounds of the others suffering so clearly.

Howie comes awake with a rush from sleep to conscious. Feet gained. Axe in hand and he's up, ready for the danger and cries out in pain and agony as the water strikes his also naked torso. He tries to turn away but the rate of fire is too much. He starts going down, unable to compute the need to run and flee. Cold water strikes again and again as he sinks to his knees and the axe falls from his hands and he surrenders to the devastation being wrought against them all. Sinking to his knees then over into the foetal position, 'ARGH IT HURTS....'

'It's just water,' Marcy calls out from the safety of her fort.

'We're doomed.....doomed I tell you...' Cookey wails on the spot with pathetic attempts to block the water with his hands.

'Was that meant to be a Scottish accent?' Blowers calls out from the depths of Nick's cover.

'You bastard,' Nick turns back to dive on Blowers as Mo Mo goes down again, 'that's my cover...'

'Fuck you,' Blowers grips the cover harder as Nick starts trying to tug it free.

'Blowers you prick...'

'Take it for the team,' Blowers shouts.

'He's got my cover,' Nick cries into the air as he gets rapidly drenched.

'Use mine!' Charlie shouts from the fort.

Two people hear the words. One standing while trying to protect his body. The other gripping the cover held so tightly by Blowers. Nick and Cookey clamp eyes on each other then slowly over the vacant bed of Charlie.

'FUCK YOU,' Cookey goes for it.

'She said it to me...' Nick lunges.

Blinky is fast. Years of training and she can see that two covers will give greater protection than one and still holding her own cover she also goes for Charlie's empty bed.

Mo Mo rolls to the side and away from the rainfall. He comes to rest facing the battle for Charlie's bed and watches as the three land at the same time. Arms and legs tangling as covers get pulled back and forth. Cookey gets a good grip but he shouts out in victory too early as Blinky rolls bodily on him and forces the air from his chest. Nick takes the advantage and tries to rip Blink's cover from her grasp but she grips hard and fights two fronts.

Mo Mo gets to his feet while still wrapped in the duvet and

starts hopping away from the battle but snags and again goes down with another strangled yelp.

'Stop pissing about,' yells a grumpy bear.

'Oh God...make it stop...' Howie wails.

'It's only water,' Marcy says again with a tone of smugness from the safety of her fort.

'Only water?' Clarence leans down with one huge hand that grips the double cover and pulls it easily from the prone bodies of the three women so snug and warm, 'only water?'

'Clarence!' Marcy yells in alarm, 'we're naked!'

Cookey, Nick and Blinky instantly stop fighting and as one they rise up at the suggestion of seeing naked ladies.

'You're not naked,' Clarence says, 'and it's only water...'

'Roy...save me,' Paula shouts.

'No chance,' Roy says from the security of his own cover, 'you deserted me.'

'Come on,' Clarence says holding the double duvets away from the reaching girls, 'it's only water.'

'Are they really naked?' Blinky asks.

'No we're not!' Charlie shouts, 'and she's finished shaking,' she adds then looks up at Clarence with a face that morphs into an expression of pure pity, 'please,' she says meekly, 'can we have the covers back?'

'Of course,' Clarence complies immediately at the perfectly delivered request.

'Clarence,' Howie shouts, 'don't fall for it...'

'Please,' Charlie asks meekly again with wide eyes looking up, 'we're ever so cold.'

Clarence huffs and hands the cover back to the sound of victorious cackling coming from the mattress, 'well done, Charlie,' Marcy says.

'So?' Cookey asks, 'just to be clear...they are *not* naked?'

'Pervert!' Charlie shouts.

'Yep,' Cookey says with a proud nod.

'Can I come into your bed?' Blinky asks.

'No. You've been farting all night,' Charlie shouts back.

'Was that you?' Nick asks with a look of horror at Blinky.

'Yeah,' Blinky chuckles, 'probably.'

'I didn't fart,' Cookey says, 'so...'

'No.'

'Fine,' he huffs and looks over at Blowers, 'coward,' he tuts.

'Fuck you,' Blowers mutters, 'standing there bloody crying...I stole Nick's bed.'

'So you're sleeping in Nick's bed?'

'Yep.'

'In Nick's bed?' Cookey asks again as Blowers looks up with a look of suspicion, 'in Nick's nice warm bed made warm by his naked body...that warm bed...is that right?'

'Fuck you,' Blowers growls, 'it's not...'

'So is,' Cookey laughs with delight.

'Gay,' Blinky says the word the other two were holding back from saying, 'so gay.'

'Coffee,' Clarence stomps about his bed area gathering clothes and his bag, 'I need coffee and Mr Howie needs coffee...do you need coffee, Mr Howie?'

'You never call me Mr Howie...you always say boss...but yes, Cookey? Are you still on brew duty?'

'Er no?' Cookey replies, 'Dave said I was now forgiven for all past sins due to my heroic efforts yesterday.'

'I did not say that, Alex,' a voice calls from the reception.

'How!' Cookey exclaims, 'how did he hear that?'

'I hear everything,' Dave says pushing the doors open as he walks into the room, 'and you two can make the brews,' he says with a nod at Cookey and Nick.

'HA!' Blowers says in delight, 'you got Daved.'

'And Simon will be assisting you,' Dave adds, 'Mohammed, why are you over there?'

'I tried running but fell.'

'Good evasive manoeuvre but poorly executed. You will assist making the brews.'

'Yes, Dave.'

'Charlotte and Patricia,' Dave looks round to see Charlie's head poking out from the covers, 'while the brews are being made you will work with me to strip and clean all the rifles before we commence a live firing exercise.'

'Yes, Dave,' Blinky jumps to her feet with an attempt at standing to attention.

'Can I go to the toilet first?' Charlie asks politely.

'You may use the ablutions,' Dave says before turning to face Howie still curled up on the ground, 'Mr Howie,' he says formally, 'it is still raining.'

'No shit,' Howie mutters slowly sitting up.

'She did.'

'Eh?'

'Meredith, Mr Howie.'

'What about her?'

'She had one.'

'What? One what?'

'Outside.'

'Huh?'

'That's how she got wet.'

'Oh my god...it's too early...Dave,' Howie groans and rubs his face, 'what did Meredith do?'

'She had a shit,' Marcy says, 'Dave is telling you she had a shit outside.'

'Yes,' Dave says.

'Oh,' Howie blinks in understanding, 'got it...so I said *no shit* and you thought I was asking if there actually was no shit but the response was as in a turn of phrase used when someone states something very obvious...'

'Yes, Mr Howie. She did. Outside.'

'Yep,' Howie says getting to his feet, 'got it...but er...I wasn't actually asking if she had a shit. I was replying to your statement when you said it was raining and I said no shit as in *yeah I can tell it's raining* seeing as Meredith is soaking wet.'

'She got wet outside, Mr Howie.'

'Yes, yes I can...I know that...'

'Cookey!'

'Yes, Paula?' Cookey calls from the kitchen.

'Mr Howie really needs that coffee.'

'Coming...'

Howie pauses as though ready to resume the conversation before shrugging and reaching down for his bag and rifle, 'I'm going to the bathroom to get dried.'

'Good idea,' Clarence follows suit as Roy heaves himself up from the bed and takes his own bag and rifle after the other two.

'Reginald,' Roy pauses at his mattress, 'you coming?' He waits as Reginald pushes his covers back and gets to his feet, 'you okay?' Roy asks and gets a shallow nod in return. 'Sleep okay?'

'Fine, thank you,' Reginald says quietly earning a worried glance from Marcy as he says it. He walks after Roy with the same slumped appearance as the day before. Head down, shoulders low and his steps as heavy as though he'd walked a great distance.

'You worried?' Paula asks as the room empties with everyone either in the kitchen or using the bathrooms of the hotel.

'The life's gone out of him,' Marcy says, 'he's not even moaning now.'

'Bad sign. Do you think he's jealous?'

'What from?' Marcy asks, 'Howie? God no...' she says with a smile, 'Reginald isn't like that.'

'Sure? Maybe he is but doesn't show it.'

'No, definitely not that. I know Reggie and he doesn't think like that. He's just overwhelmed by everyone here.'

'He can go with Roy when he gets a van,' Paula says, 'will that help?'

'Hope so,' Marcy says with a quizzical look, 'so you're not going with Roy then?'

'Leaving? We said yesterday...'

'No I mean when Roy gets a van, you're not going in his van with him?'

'Oh I see...yes, yes maybe I should.'

'Should?'

'I like being in with everyone else,' Paula says carefully, 'but...I don't know if Roy will be offended if I don't go with him in his van.'

'Do both,' Marcy says, 'we can use the second van for anyone that needs a quiet time out.'

'Ah, good idea,' Paula says approvingly.

'So you can stay with us,' Marcy says, 'or we can use it as a sin bin for Cookey,' she adds with a laugh.

'You'd put Cookey in with Roy and Reggie?' Paula asks with a chuckle.

'Okay, maybe not.'

'So, you okay?' Paula asks with a glance loading with meaning and rolls onto her side to face the other woman.

Marcy laughs and rolls to face Paula, 'fine thank you, and you?'

'Fine.'

'Good. I'm fine too.'

'Good,' Paula grins, 'anything happen in the night?'

'Now why on earth would you ask that?' Marcy asks with a bright smile.

'That won't work on me,' Paula laughs, 'you went out with Howie last night...to the reception.'

'Oh you saw that then?'

'I did. So?'

'Nothing happened,' Marcy says with the smile easing gently away, 'we held hands and sat on the desk...then I fell asleep on his shoulder and at some point he brought me back in here.'

'Oh,' Paula says as though disappointed as Marcy chuckles at the tone.

'And he ravished me,' Marcy adds with a grin.

'Ooh that's better,' Paula replies with malicious delight, 'what happened?'

'Er,' Marcy pulls a face, 'er...he led me outside into the rain and we made wild love on the er...the golf sandpit?'

'No?' A shocked Paula asks.

'Oh yes,' Marcy nods seriously, 'and there were roses and candles and...'

'Sod the roses,' Paula chuckles again.

'He was a wild animal,' Marcy continues, 'ripping my clothes off and growling like a beast.'

'A beast?'

'A wild beast?'

'A very wild beast,' Marcy says, 'dominant and strong...like a... like a....caveman.'

'Caveman?' Paula bursts out laughing.

'I don't know! I couldn't think of anything else. No, we just held hands and I dribbled on his shoulder.'

'Bless.'

'I wouldn't do that,' Marcy says seriously, 'Lani only died yesterday.'

'Yes,' Paula says slowly, 'but these are different times.'

'Different how?'

'Time is magnified. I've only just met Roy and would never have slept with him so quickly but it's different now. Everything happens so quickly and it's like everything is sped up? So things happen faster. I've only been with this group for a few days but it feels like weeks...months even.'

'Yes it does,' Marcy says thoughtfully, 'it kind of feels like that now.'

'It will for Charlie and Blinky too. My point is that yes Lani only just died but remember that Howie only knew Lani for a few days. I adored Lani, we all did. The same as I adored everyone else I knew before this happened...but like I said, Marcy. These are different times. Listen, what we're doing is special. We all know that...you and Reggie were turned but now you're not...if anyone else knew what you did they'd kill you instantly but this lot accept you for you and who you are now and they do that because of Howie. We're all here because of Howie.'

Marcy listens intently, watching Paula speaking and noticing the intense look in her eyes.

'What I'm saying,' Paula drops her voice, 'is that if you and Howie can take comfort from each other then do it. Take it. Take it as much as you can. You know what we're doing today right?' She watches Marcy nodding and hanging off every word being said, 'we're going to find them and kill them...and no matter what happens Howie won't stop...so,' Paula hesitates before proceeding, 'so if you, *or if Howie,* needs that comfort...' She trails off, not needing to finish the sentence as Marcy nods with understanding.

CHAPTER TWO

I n the bathroom of a small hotel room and after pissing in the toilet I start brushing my teeth while casually looking about at the clean sterile shelves and the gleaming taps. My hair is getting a bit long and needs a trim. I shaved yesterday and could do it again now but sod it, I can't be arsed.

Christ my body is covered in bruises and cuts. I drop my hand holding the toothbrush and stare at the discoloured patches of skin and the bite marks on my shoulders and arms. The cuts from fingernails across my chest and the livid welts of skin. The contrast from the room to me is stark. White, sterile and clean against bruised and dirtied by death. I twist round and use the mirror to look at my back and the scars and marks all over it. Barely a few inches of clear skin anywhere that doesn't have a mark of some kind on it.

Every picture paints a thousand words and every mark is from a fight against those fucking things and represents a life taken and a life lost. Each bruise is from a person that had hopes and desires who loved and felt love. I'm not a naïve fool and I know many would have been nasty bastards that probably deserved it but so many didn't. So many were taken from their beds and consumed in utter terror while watching their loved ones get torn apart, or worse, they were taken by those loved ones and suddenly my mind fills with the images of the children that stalked Marcy and I down the garden and that consuming energy is back.

I get dressed. New socks. Boots tugged on and laced up. My top is shaken out and pulled down over my head and I re-pack my new bag and head down the corridor to the reception and the local maps and guidebooks on display. I gather them up and go inside the main room to find tables have been pulled together with fresh cups of coffee being brought out.

Charlie and Blinky work to one side with Dave talking them through how to strip and clean the weapons again and Blowers helping. Reginald sits quietly at the far end of the table, withdrawing himself from the main group. Everyone else is gathering kit and belongings, drinking coffee and talking amiably.

'Any?' I ask Cookey with a hand stretching out towards the coffee mugs.

'Er, that one is yours,' he slides one over.

I take a sip from the mug and feel the instant psychological boost at the taste of the strong bitter liquid, 'spot on, mate.'

'What you got there?' Clarence asks with a glance at the books from reception in my hand.

'Mm,' swallowing the mouthful I put the books on the table, 'maps...to work out our cunning plan...and...'

'Tourist guides?' Clarence picks one of the books up, 'we going sightseeing?'

'Just grabbed what was there.'

'English Heritage...' he reads from the front and flicks through the pamphlets and books, 'castles...stately homes...places to visit...country walk anyone? Oh yes!' He holds one up with a grin, '*the real ale guide to the south of England...*'

'We should do that one,' Roy says.

'You like real ale?' Clarence asks.

'Of course.'

'Me and Roy just bonded,' Clarence announces.

'Guinness,' Blowers calls out from the other table.

'You a Guinness man, Blowers?' Clarence asks, 'I thought you'd be lager and fighting down the boozer after doing tequila shots.'

'Yep,' Blowers says with a broad grin, 'and Guinness.'

'Now Cookey,' Clarence says with a smile, 'is a lager man through and through, so is Nick...'

'Racist,' Cookey says.

'Mo Mo...hmmm, what's your tipple, Mo?'

'I don't drink alcohol,' Mo says seriously.

'Shit sorry,' Clarence sputters his coffee in the rush to apologise, 'is that because of your religion?'

'Nah I'm sixteen innit,' Mo grins, 'too young to drink bro, you get me?'

'Little shit,' Clarence tuts.

'You're sixteen?' Charlie cuts in.

'Yeah,' Mo Mo says turning round.

'You're older than that,' Charlie says, 'I thought you were at least eighteen.'

'Nah, sixteen,' Mo Mo replies lifting a few inches from the ground and his head threatening to split in half from the wide grin.

'So what is your favourite drink then?' Cookey asks him.

'Dunno,' Mo says with a shrug, 'I drank beer once but I was stoned and puked up.'

'You smoked cannabis?' Charlie asks with genuine shock, 'but that's illegal.'

'Oh my god!' Cookey jumps up quickly with his hands waving in the air and his best posh accent, 'you smoked drugs?'

'Very funny,' Charlie says drily, 'I do not sound like that.'

'You so do,' Blowers says.

'I do not,' Charlie says primly, 'not that extreme anyway. But really, Mo. Did you smoke cannabis?'

'Er yeah.'

'But...but who gave it to you? You're only sixteen. Did the police know? What's so funny?' She asks at the lads all laughing, 'he is only sixteen and should not have been smoking drugs.'

'Yeah Mo,' Nick says, 'where did the drugs come from?'

'Oh my god!' Cookey goes for it again, 'you smoked drugs?'

'I really do not sound like that,' Charlie says again, 'Blinky, do I sound like that?'

'Yep,' Blinky says focussing on the task of re-assembling an assault rifle, 'posh as fuck.'

'You speak very nicely,' Paula says.

'But where did Mo get the drugs from?' Cookey asks aghast with his hands pressed to his cheeks.

'Where *did* you get the drugs from?' Charlie asks with a frown.

'From me,' Mo laughs, 'was a dealer.'

'Oh my god!' Cookey bursts to his feet again, 'you were a drug dealer?'

'And a burglar?' Nick asks with the same shock.

'And you stole cars?' Blowers asks.

'Oh my god!' Cookey shakes his head, 'did the police know?'

'Really?' Charlie asks.

'Yep,' Mo Mo says and despite the grin I detect a flicker of uncertainty in his eyes.

'But he's our burglar and thief now,' Clarence says in his deep assuring voice, 'and those skills are good skills.'

'Mo's fucking awesome,' Nick says with a nod at the younger man, 'he got in this place and got the fuel from that truck yesterday...'

'And he'll be like Dave if he gets any faster with those knives,' Blowers adds.

'Yeah,' Cookey says slowly while leaning back in his chair with his hands interlinked behind his head, 'I was a male escort before this...'

'Fucking twat,' Blowers laughs.

'Very successful,' Cookey nods and adds a wink, 'let's just say there was high demand for my services...'

'Such a dick,' Nick groans.

'I was committed to it...took it seriously...worked hard and then I met April and...'

'Oh for God's sake,' Paula sinks her head onto the table, 'Dave...tell him...'

'Alex.'

'Aw but I didn't say it.'

'Don't say it.'

'Aw, Dave...'

'No.'

'Okay, sorry, Dave.'

'Oh let him say it,' Paula groans, 'Dave...can he say it once before he sulks?'

'Dave?' I look over with a grin at the sight of Cookey's bottom lip pouting out.

'Once,' Dave says in his flat voice.

'And no punishment?' Cookey asks quietly as though hardly daring to believe it.

'Once.'

'But Dave cut her head off and I was heartbroken and knew the love of my life was gone forever and that's when I decided that being a male escort wasn't for me anymore...' Cookey rushes the words out to his grinning audience, 'I thank you,' he adds.

'Right, on to the serious plan of making serious plans,' I say.

'Serious cunning plans,' Clarence slides one of the maps over and starts opening it out.

'Proper serious cunning plans,' I slide one of the maps to me and start opening it out.

'Full on intense serious properly thought out cunning plans,' Clarence says turning the map round while squinting at it, 'but not with this...this is a map of golf courses...'

'And this is a map of country walks,' I cast mine aside and grab another.

'Ah,' Clarence says opening his next map out, 'we've got country walks...' that one gets pushed off the table.

'This is the map for the real ale pubs...I think it goes with that guidebook you had a minute ago.'

'Keep that one,' Clarence reaches over to fold it back up.

'Right,' I open the next map and stare down for a few minutes amidst a table of silence.

'It's upside down,' Marcy says quietly.

'I knew that,' I say quickly, 'I was showing Clarence.'

'He was showing me,' Clarence says from opposite me and leaning over to see it.

'He wasn't showing you,' she says then looks at me, 'you weren't showing him.'

'Was,' I say with a nod, 'so was...er...where are we?'

'In a golf hotel,' Clarence says looking at me blankly.

'On the map, where are we on the map?'

'I don't know, where are we?'

'That's what I said.'

'That's what I'm asking. Where are we?'

'I don't know. Look at the map.'

'I can look at the map all day long but until I know where we are there isn't much point.'

'Find it on the map then.'

'Find what? Where? What's the name of the place we are at? As in the name of the place?'

'Oh...er...' I look round at the dining room, 'some golf hotel...'

'Got it,' he says and starts tracing a finger across the spread out map, 'some...golf...hotel....hmmm, doesn't seem to be here...'

'Jesus this is painful,' Paula reaches over to pull the map over, 'someone find out the name of the hotel.'

'It's some hotel,' Cookey says helpfully, 'Mr Howie just said it.'

'How the hell do we work out where to go if nobody knows where we are?' Paula snaps.

'Do you know where we are?' Clarence asks.

'That. That is not the point,' Paula says while avoiding looking at him.

'We're here,' Roy leans over and places a finger on a wide green section of the map, 'I saw the sign on the way in.'

'Thank God someone has some sense round here,' Paula says, 'thank you, Roy...now...so...what's the plan?'

'Er, we go places and kill things,' I say with an air of confidence.

'That it?' Marcy asks.

'Sounds cunning to me,' Clarence says.

'So why the map?' She asks me.

'For the plan,' I reply.

'The plan of going places and killing things?'

'That plan, yeah.'

'Great plan.'

'Thanks.'

'I was being sarcastic. Paula? Can you devise another plan?'

'What's wrong with our plan?' I ask.

'It's shit,' Marcy says, 'it's the worst plan ever.'

'No,' I draw the map back over and look down, 'bollocks... where are we again?'

'Here,' Roy leans over and places his finger back on the green splodge.

'Right so we're here...' I tap my finger, 'so we go from here...to these other places,' I sweep my hand round the map, 'and kill stuff.'

'Great plan.'

'Cheers, Clarence.'

'Shit plan.'

'Er, I'll stop you there,' I hold my hand up to Marcy, 'Clarence was in the army and he says it's a great plan.'

'Awesome plan.'

'And Cookey was in the army too and he said it was an awesome plan.'

'Love the plan, boss.'

'And Blowers was in the army and he loves the plan.'

'Best plan ever.'

'And Nick thinks it's the best plan ever.'

'Dave,' Marcy stands up to look round for Dave at the table with the girls.

'Yes, Marcy.'

'See,' she nods in victory.

'Oh no...that was Dave responding to you calling his name and not saying yes as in yes I agree with you Marcy.'

'Dave,' Marcy says again.

'Yes, Marcy.'

'Is Howie's plan a good plan?'

'Any plan is better than no plan.'

'Yes!' I claim the victory back.

'Good answer, Dave,' Clarence says manfully.

'Not an answer,' Paula says taking over from Marcy, 'Dave... could the plan be better?'

'Any plan could be better with greater intelligence and under- standing of the objectives to be achieved and the opposition faced by those seeking to...'

'No,' Paula sighs, 'could this plan...I mean the plan that Howie suggested...the way he suggested it...'

'Having fun?' I look over at Paula.

'Keep going,' Clarence smiles.

'Give me strength...Roy,' she turns on him with a glare, 'what do you think of the plan?'

He shrugs and looks round the table, 'to be fair it's not far off what we've been doing anyway.'

'Roy!' Clarence booms, 'brilliant answer...' He leans back to look round Paula, 'we should get some real ale.'

Roy leans back to answer, 'loads of old pubs round here I should imagine.'

'Excuse me,' Paula says with a huff, 'that is not a plan...and we're not doing it.'

'Not going places and killing stuff?' Cookey asks.

'No we're going places and killing stuff but there'll be a bit more direction than that.'

The table falls to an expectant silence as we all look to Paula who deigns to ignore us and stares at the map, 'sod off the lot of you,' she mutters to a round of grins and chuckles that die off at the serious look spreading across her face, 'problem,' she says.

'Go on,' I lean forward to listen.

'The infection is evolving right? It split us up yesterday so it's learning new tactics and gaining greater intelligence, is that a fair assumption?'

'I'd say so,' I reply with a glance round at everyone.

'We're here,' she places a finger on the green splodge, 'and I guess we're going to be attacking these places,' she motions to the urban grey splodges on the map, 'but the problem is that if we hit this one first,' she says with a finger held in the closest grey section, 'then the infection will know we are here...and can pull in resources to the other towns nearby...'

'But it won't know which one we'll hit,' I say.

'It will see the direction we leave,' Paula says.

'How will it? We'll kill them all,' I say but realise the flaw as soon as the words leave my mouth, 'how did they know where we were yesterday?'

'Crawler in our garden,' Clarence says, 'Dave cut its throat.'

'It has a hive mind,' Marcy says, 'so it only needs one pair of eyes to see where we go and it will know the direction...'

'We could leave a false trail,' Clarence says, 'leave one way but then veer off toward somewhere else.'

'The risk,' Paula says, 'is that we'll form a pattern...and once we do that we're at risk of being caught out again.'

'Go random them,' Clarence says, 'we'll just pick a town and go for it...then bug out and choose another one.'

'Sounds good to me,' I say after a moment's thought, 'stay random and don't let the infection know where we're going.'

'Okay,' Paula says staring down at the map, 'we hit the first town, do what we can then leave via whatever route is available then...then we stop and choose another location at random.'

'Perfect, everyone happy?' I look round at the faces nodding in agreement, apart from Reginald who has gone from being morose to looking like he wants to say something with a pensive expression and leaning slightly forward, 'what's up?' I ask him.

'Nothing,' he says quickly.

'Sure?'

'I am sure, thank you,' he replies with a tone that makes Marcy look over with concern.

'Right, we'll head outside and do some live firing with Charlie and Blinky...Marcy can have some practise and...'

'Reggie,' Marcy says sharply, 'I know that face.'

'My name is Reginald,' he says stiffly, 'and...'

'And nothing,' she cuts him off, 'you've been sitting there with a stick up your backside for the last five minutes. Spit it out.'

'I beg your pardon!'

'Reggie,' she says firmly, 'I know you and I know how intelligent you are. Say it, everyone will listen...'

'Say what?' I ask.

'Whatever he needs to say,' she replies, 'he's got something on his mind.'

'Mate,' I glance over at the look of thunder on his face as he glares at Marcy, 'what's on your mind?'

'There are many things on my mind,' he stammers with a glare at Marcy, 'but having a stick up my backside is not one of them. Really, Marcy.' He looks away with distaste.

'Ten minutes and we'll move out,' I say into the awkward silence that follows, 'Dave, do you want to take Blinky and Charlie outside now to live fire?'

'Yes, Mr Howie.'

'Lads,' I say as they all start to rise with drool hanging from their mouths at the prospect of standing close to Charlie and no doubt show her how to hold the rifle nice and snug, 'get ready to go...take your kit bags with you now,' I add to the girls.

I follow the three of them out into reception and stare through the doors to the heaving rain still pelting down outside.

'Everything okay?' I ask them both once they've put their bags down and with Dave standing to one side.

Blinky nods and blinks.

'Fine, thank you,' Charlie says politely.

'You've had a night to think things over, any change of mind? You can say at any time you know.'

Blinky blinks and stares at Dave.

'I'm okay, I think Blinky is er...settling in very well,' Charlie says.

'Fuck yeah,' Blinky snorts.

'Right, well...you did practise yesterday so now is about getting used to the rifle being fired...Dave...'

He unbolts the doors and pushes them open, 'Patricia come here, insert the magazine and make the weapon ready for firing...' he watches mutely as she quickly pulls a magazine out from her pocket, slams it into the hole, racks the bolt back and checks the safety.

'Loaded, ready and the safety is on,' she snaps the words out.

'Select single shot,' he says.

'Single shot selected.'

'Shoulder the weapon in the approved manner. Good. Finger on the trigger and do not snatch but squeeze...breathe as you do it and fire once...'

The rifle booms with a single shot as she aims far into the golf course.

'Good,' Dave says, 'relax and do it again, single shots...go...'

She fires one after the other and you can see the visible change as her body relaxes the tension held in her stance and posture. The flinching from the initial recoil is soon gone and the last ten shots are delivered smoothly.

'MAGAZINE!' She booms with a habit from yesterday's drill already ingrained.

'Good,' Dave says, 'Charlotte, replace Patricia please.'

'Can you call me Blinky, please,' Blinky asks.

'No,' Dave says shutting down any further conversation on the topic. 'Charlotte, make the weapon ready for firing please,' he orders in that dull monotone of his.

She goes through the same actions and shoulders the weapon ready for firing, 'ready.'

'Have you selected single shot?'

'I have,' she says in a confident tone and without a tremor showing in her hands or voice.

'Proceed,' Dave says.

She fires and even with my lack of knowledge I can see the girl is a natural. The shots are squeezed, the recoil absorbed, the first shot induces a natural flinch but after that they quickly reduce until she is firing at a steady pace and adjusting her own stance to increase her comfort.

'MAGAZINE,' she shouts not quite as loudly as Blinky.

'Good,' Dave says, 'Patricia come forward and both step outside doors...burst fire...this is achieved by a controlled depressing of the trigger to release several rounds into the target without having to fight for control of a weapon on automatic fire. Do you understand? I will show you,' he steps smartly between them and brings his own rifle up to his shoulder and aims into the rain, 'burst,' he says and holds the trigger down for a second or two, 'burst,' he does it again, 'burst,' he repeats the action with a burst fire rate that is so perfectly done he could be doing videos on youtube.

'Patricia first,' he says and moves to her side.

'Burst,' she says and fires a single shot, 'fuck it!' She curses and turns the weapon to change the fire mode, 'sorry, Dave.'

'Mistakes are part of learning,' Dave says parrot fashion.

'Burst,' she says it again and fires a short burst into the golf course, 'it lifts,' she says.

'It does,' Dave says, 'you have to compensate but not over compensate. Burst fire is used to prevent a loss of control of aiming, do it again.'

'Burst,' she fires again and works to keep the weapon steady, 'burst,' she says.

'You do not need to say burst each time,' Dave says.

'Sorry, Dave,' Blinky says and fires through the remainder of the magazine.

'Charlotte,' Dave says, 'burst fire please.'

She selects the fire mode, shoulders the weapon, adjusts her stance and fires a controlled burst, pauses then repeats as she works through the rounds.

'You're so fucking good,' Blinky says when she lowers the weapon.

Charlie shrugs self-consciously and looks to Dave.

'Change magazine and burst fire please,' Dave says to both of them.

They do it again and although the difference between them is slight it is also noticeable. Blinky is competent and fearless in her approach but lets her natural aggression show whereas Charlie is composed and almost cold in her delivery.

'Cease fire,' Dave says and heads back into reception to take up a plastic display stand that he carries out into the rain and away to a decent distance so it's only just visible through the rainfall, 'single shot,' he moves to the side away from danger and we both watch as they select single shots, shoulder their weapons and aim for the plastic stand. They both miss the first few shots but once the adjustments are made the stand starts getting blown to bits until the fourth or fifth shot has it smashing to the ground, 'can you still see it?' Dave asks.

'Yes, Dave!' Blinky snaps the words back.

'Burst fire on the target.'

They adjust and do as bid with controlled bursts that steadily pulverises the poor stand to bits.

'Both of you will change to fully automatic and fire into target...on my command....FIRE'

I drop back from the sudden booming noise of two assault rifles letting rip. Blinky goes all out with determination but Charlie stops after a second or two and goes back to burst firing.

'CEASEFIRE,' Dave shouts from the rain, 'good, Patricia your aim is slightly off but time will rectify that. Charlotte, you stopped fully automatic because the weapon was becoming unwieldy and you reverted to burst fire.'

'Was that wrong?' Charlie asks with a worried frown.

'Not wrong,' Dave says, 'control must be maintained at all times...Mr Howie I would like to try Charlotte with a sniper rifle.'

'Eh? What now? Have we got one?'

'We do not have one.'

'How the hell we gonna try her then?'

'We should find a sniper rifle.'

'Yeah add it to the list, Dave. We'll get a van from the van store, some radios from the radio store and a sniper rifle from the bloody sniping store...'

'Okay.'

'Okay,' I say back at him.

'Charlotte is capable of being a marksmen.'

'Markswoman,' Charlotte says politely.

'Markswoman,' Dave says.

'How can you tell?' Charlie asks.

'Control and the manner in which you are firing,' Dave says, 'Mr Howie, we also need to give consideration for hand weapons for Patricia, Charlotte, Paula and Marcy.'

'Want an axe,' Blinky says.

'Axes are heavy,' Dave says then stares for a minute at Blinky's muscled frame, 'axe will be fine for you.'

'Add it to the list,' I say, 'I'll get the others ready...five more minutes?'

'Yes, Mr Howie...CHANGE MAGAZINE AND COMMENCE SINGLE FIRE ON MY COMMAND,' he surges towards them with that drill sergeant voice booming into the air.

'Armoured van,' Roy greets me as I walk back into the main room.

'A what?'

'Mo Mo's suggestion,' he says with a nod at Mo, 'he suggested we try for a cash in transit van.'

'Well done, Mo,' I say to the young lad, 'where do we find one? There's one in Boroughfare...I saw it on the night it happened, some bloke drove past my house beeping the horn and making them all chase him.'

'Who was he?' Marcy asks turning round to look at me.

'No idea, saw him a bit later when he got surrounded but when I went back he was gone...'

'What sort was it?' Mo asks.

'Sort?'

'Yeah, boss. Like...transit or...'

'Dunno, er...I can't actually remember...I think it was rounded edges so yeah, must have been transit based chassis I guess.'

'Square Mercedes ones are best,' he says, 'stronger...much harder to break into.'

'Good to know,' I say, 'so where we going to find one from?'

'There's a storage depot outside Portsmouth,' he says, 'or we's find a bank with a secure yard.'

'We'll find a bank,' I say, 'I hate Portsmouth...'

'MAGAZINE!'

'Is that Blinky?' Paula asks with a look of surprise.

'Yep, Dave said Charlie is a natural and we have to find a sniper rifle for her...and he also said we have to get you ladies some hand weapons as axes are too heavy.'

'Sexist,' Paula says automatically, 'but alas very true.'

'Right, load up...we're moving out...'

CHAPTER THREE

D*ay Eighteen*

I AWOKE this morning to a landscape changed by precipipitatio by prepicipiatio damn that blasted word. It has rained and the rain has changed the landscape. Water is everywhere shimmering with newly formed lakes that ripple with motion caused by the incessant rain. Yesterday was a day of days. That group I observed in the town of Finkton and the sheer numbers of infected marching against them and the way those infected moved too. To see a thing of that nature is truly terrifying but worse for the actions taken by that bloody horse.

She attacked them. My horse attacked the infected. A horse does not attack people. They are docile herd animals that give flight when in fear. They do not attack. I understand that Jess was trained in riot tactics and therefore a mass of noisy people would not, by itself, cause her fear. I also understand that Jess was "retired" from the police service due to displaying an overly aggressive nature in that she was happy to bite and kick. Which apparently is a bad thing for horses to do when policing peaceful events and demonstrations.

Jess perhaps possesses a higher degree of aggression than normal horses but to charge and attack screaming howling people is incomprehensible. That she did it to seemingly protect that strange dark haired man is even more troubling for it means that she had capacity to understand not only that he was at risk, but what actions to take in response to that risk.

Now she is eating oats and behaving distinctly horse-like again. If she could talk I would ask her what on earth possessed her to respond in that manner. However, she cannot talk. She is a horse.

HMMM, perhaps I have spent too much time in my own company. Perhaps I am losing my ability to rationalise and hold normal cognitive function. Ah yes, perhaps yesterday did not happen and it was simply a figment of my imagination brought about by prolonged exposure to fright and stress. Yes. No. It happened.

THAT DARK HAIRED man was cut and appeared to have bite marks. He was under a large mound of infected hosts that were clearly all targeting him. He must have been bitten and cut but he survived so therefore he must be immune.

THE LIST I have in my possession contains names of those believed to have immunity. That list was compiled during my time in The Facility and was taken by me when I escaped and started my preparations on learning the true purpose of the infection.

WE HAD UNRESTRICTED access to data in The Facility and those included medical records. Those medical records were examined to find those that had a chain of DNA that matched to the immunity.

Every person who ever had a medical procedure, gave blood or was subject to a blood test. Those who were screened for sexually transmitted diseases. Every person arrested and taken into police custody. Every member of the armed services. Every member of the emergency services. They all had their DNA taken and stored. Consent was not gained and the whole process was most unlawful. To store the essence of people without their consent or knowledge is an absolute invasion of privacy.

BUT THANK God it was done. It enabled us to find out who had immunity and it enabled The List to be compiled which in turn prompted me to escape and commence this absurdly dangerous undertaking.

ON THAT NOTE, I will record clearly here within my diary, should it ever be found, that I am not suited to work of this nature. I am not a soldier nor a person of bravery or courage. Jess has more bravery and courage in the hairs on her tail than I possess in my whole body.

THAT SAID, The List is the fundamentally most important document in existence. I have to find those who are immune and take steps to take what they have to end this. That dark haired man is immune but I do not know which one he is. I do not have photographs or images of the people on The List. Given time I could have cross-referenced the names against the driving license and passport agencies databases and matched the last obtained image. But there wasn't time. I have only names and last known addresses.

SO MY MISSION, for now at least, changes. Instead of working through the list I will try and find that man and his group. If they have survived yesterday that is. If I find evidence of their deaths I will continue with my originally intended plan.

I MUST GO BACK *to Finkton and commence my investigation. In the rain. Did I say it was raining?*

NB
   Neal Barrett.

CHAPTER FOUR

'First town ahead,' I call back. On the motorway and the sight is biblical. Like the floods that made that crazy man build a boat to save a few pigeons and a goat. Maybe that was a zombie apocalypse too. Everyone became brain eating fucktards and it rained for ages and some mad bloke made a boat. New bible right there.

Using the central reservation as a guide I build the speed up and get a gratifying sensation at pummelling through the water until the waves at the sides are spraying against the door windows.

Fortunately the next junction is on an incline and stretches up and across the lanes on a flyover to a huge roundabout poking up like another island and this time I follow the signs for whatever the name of the town is. Names don't matter now. Place names are gone, road names are gone, famous landmarks mean nothing and each town now only represents foraging and points of danger.

As we get closer so we start to see houses and structures at the sides. Some built higher and safe from the floods. Others, mainly the newer builds, are already flooded with water getting through the broken front doors.

With the closer proximity to urbanisation so too we start to see the flotsam and jetsam picked up by the water and floating along on the surface. Litter and debris mainly but larger items hidden from view and the first corpse almost goes by without notice as just the rounded back shows until we're bumping it away and the thing rolls onto his back to reveal a face torn away but washed clean so the bones and sinew show clear. Rags of clothing, paper, crisp packets and all manner of things floating or caught in the hundreds of whirls and rip tides.

Closer to the town centre now and every street has red, white and blue bunting hanging from the buildings and lampposts. Some torn and hanging but mostly still in place from whatever festival or event was taking place. The signs of damage are horrendous and plentiful with nearly every window smashed and every door broken. From a roundabout we head towards the High Street and a sea of corpses floating grotesque and bloated. Broken market stalls show stark with red and white stripes and this town was in full swing of a local event when the infection struck. A scaffold and plank built stage in the middle of a large car park and the amplifiers and drum kit are still on view surrounded by dead bodies bobbing in the shallow waters.

The High Street is actually away from the town centre and being on an incline the water level is less so there are fewer bodies littering the ground. Quiet now as we watch the macabre view go past and start working on the task at hand to find a bank. We see several but they're just shop fronts in amongst the clothes shops, opticians and cafes.

'There...Lloyds,' Clarence points off to his side at the large Victorian façade sitting squat on a junction of a side road. I aim for the opening of the side street and manoeuvre down to see the long side wall of the bank giving way to a razor wire topped solid concrete wall and a high metal gate fitted with security cameras and signs warning of security patrols and to keep access clear at all times. 'Pull up by the gates and I'll check,' he says.

He jumps down and runs through the rain to pause at the

crack in the centre where the gates meet, a thumbs up and he runs back with a big grin, 'three in there.'

'No way,' I reply not expecting it to be this easy.

'What did he say?' Roy calls out.

'There's three armoured vans in the yard,' Clarence shouts, 'pop the gates open with the Saxon,' he pats the front wing and backs away as I reverse to gain a run up.

'Once we're in the yard everyone out the back and guard the perimeter, hold on...' I don't go fast as the Saxon doesn't need speed to batter things down. The torque and power of her engine just needs forward momentum. I aim for the middle of the gates and push the accelerator down as the vehicle connects. A wrenching metallic sound that screeches followed by something snapping and the gates burst open as the Saxon surges forward with the sudden cessation of resistance at the front.

The second the vehicle comes to a halt the doors burst open and we drop down into the rain with weapons up and raised and I don't need to give any orders as Blowers takes his group onto the street and the rest of us fan out into the puddled yard while Roy runs to three dark blue armoured vans.

Square looking with riveted windows and doors. Thick tyres, robust and they look almost military in design. I was expecting the rounded Ford Transit style things but these are far more modern Mercedes with bull bars across the grille giving a sign of the already dangerous times we lived in where greater security was given for the transit of cash than the health and well-being of the average person. It annoys me instantly, that these vehicles, so capable of protecting life were left locked in here while everyone out there got chomped and killed. Even the bank itself is like a fortress with one rear back door that looks like it belongs on some hidden American mountain base.

I shake my head to rid the excess drops falling from my hair and see Roy shaking his head as he motions the vehicles are all

locked and he turns to face the back of the bank as I walk over
to him.

'Keys'll be in there,' he says.

'Bloody hell,' I take in the sight of the thick walls, the barred
windows and the solid metal featureless door that is devoid of
anything to attach a chain to, 'Dave,' I call him over and the others,
apart from Blowers and the younger lot outside the gates, all walk
over to me and Roy, 'can we blow that door?'

He shakes his head, 'no, Mr Howie, we need shape charges for
a door like that.'

'Ram it then?' I suggest, 'like I did with that wall in the munitions factory...'

'We could,' Roy says hesitantly, 'but do we want to risk
damaging the Saxon?'

'Not really, what else do you suggest?'

'Find something else,' he says, 'like a truck and use that.'

'Could do,' I reply.

'Sledge hammers,' Clarence says, 'we'll beat the wall out round
the door.'

'Can we blow a car up?' I ask, 'you know, like park it by the
door and set fire to the tank...would that do it?'

'The blast wouldn't be enough,' Dave says.

'Sledge hammers,' Clarence says again, 'there'll be a diy store
round here somewhere.'

'Maybe there's roof access, like a skylight,' Roy says, 'Mo Mo
could get up and try and find a way in, if we get him some rope he
could climb down on the inside.'

'If we're getting rope we might as well get sledge hammers,'
Clarence says.

'We've got rope,' Roy says, 'in the cupboards in the back.'

'Mind out,' Paula calls as the Saxon starts edging forward to
turn further into the yard.

We step aside without giving it any thought, 'not a bad idea for
Mo Mo,' I say to the men standing round me as we stare at the back

of the bank like builders sizing a job up, 'they would have been relying on alarms to protect any skylight...'

'Er, who is driving the Saxon?' Clarence asks as it reverses past us. We all watch as the front draws level with Marcy behind the wheel leaning out the door as Paula guides her back, 'what are they doing?' He adds with a frown.

'Fuck knows,' I say as Paula shouts for Marcy to stop. She gets to the back doors and starts pulling the thick chain free, 'what on earth?'

'There's nothing on the door to attach it to,' Clarence says.

Holding the hooked end of the chain, Paula drags it over to the back wall of the bank and reaches up to hook it through the bars on the window. With the other end already attached to the Saxon she gives a thumbs up as Marcy pulls away gently to lift the chain off the ground then punches forward. A wrench of metal, a dull thud and the whole barred section pops free of the window frame and clatters noisily to the ground as Marcy brings the Saxon to a stop, 'did it work?' She asks jumping down.

'Perfect,' Paula shouts, 'get Mo in.'

'Mo Mo,' Marcy shouts, 'can we borrow you please.'

'Sure thing,' he runs in and straight towards her, 'what's up?'

'Can you get in that window?' Marcy asks pointing at the now unbarred window.

'Yeah,' he slings his rifle and scouts round for a second before finding a lump of concrete on the ground. He hefts it up, stalks at the window and throws it up and through the glass that shatters in the frame then using the butt of his rifle he reaches up and rakes the glass out, 'you want that door open?' He asks Paula pointing at the solid metal door.

'Yes please,' she says.

He gets up and over the frame, pauses to look then drops down out of sight. Less than a minute later the solid metal door swings outwards and he strolls out, 'anything else?'

'You're a star, Mo,' Paula smiles at him, 'thank you.'

'Thanks, Mo,' Marcy beams at him as he jogs past towards the gates.

'Well,' Roy breaks our stunned silence, 'it appears the bank is now open.'

'We should just go back to the hotel and leave them to it,' I reply.

'Why are you just standing there?' Paula calls over, 'I do not want to hang about in the pouring bloody rain...'

It stops raining with a suddenness that stuns us all. Not a petering off or a reduction in flow of water falling from the sky but an abrupt finish as though a tap has been turned or a button pressed.

'It's stopped raining,' Cookey shouts from the street.

'Are you God?' I ask Paula with sudden deep suspicion.

'Not God,' she says with a look at the sky, 'just godlike,' she adds with a grin, 'couldn't have timed that any better really.'

The reduction in noise is weird too. That incessant drumming sound now gone and only the individual noises of water pouring from roofs and flat surfaces left.

'Oh wow,' Marcy says at the first shaft of sunlight streaming through the rapidly thinning cloud. A thick beam that seems to glisten and glitter as it strikes the ground, then more appear as the sun's rays gradually get through. Like bars of light and a visual display playing out all around us.

'The sun's coming out,' Cookey shouts from the street.

I've never seen anything like it. A real tangible changing of the weather happening right in front of our eyes. It's always bloody raining in England so that wasn't altogether weird, the force and volume was strange but not the actuality of rain. But to see and hear the rain end and then the rays of sun peeking through and then growing in number is like something from a movie.

'Keys then,' I say quietly and stare around at the glinting sunlight reflecting off the puddled standing water.

'Yes,' Roy says equally as muted, 'I'll get them.'

Dave goes with him, the only one of us not seemingly stunned at the striking change happening around us.

'I'll check the street,' I say and move round the Saxon and through the broken gates, 'everything okay?' I ask on seeing the group outside fanned out with rifles raised and aimed so all angles are covered.

'Fucking weird,' Nick mutters, 'weird as fuck.'

'You got a smoke, mate?'

'Sure,' he lowers his rifle and drags the packet from a pocket.

'It's so quiet now,' Charlie says from a few metres away, 'it's beautiful.'

'What is?' I ask turning round to face her.

'All the waterfalls, listen,' she turns to look at me and Nick as we stay motionless and pick out the individual sounds of water pouring from the roofs. Some thick and they sound like bath water, others are spraying and pattering gently. More further away and she's right, it's like listening to a hundred waterfalls all at different tempos and speeds.

'Makes me need a piss,' Blinky states.

'Charming,' Charlie replies.

I light the smoke and stare up at the street, at the windows of the shops and doorways and the hundreds of places they could be hiding in or watching us from, as that thought hits so does the sensation of being watched grows and creeps up my spine. Nick pauses with his hand about to put the cigarette back in his mouth, his eyes wide and staring first at the ground then up and about.

I look round for Meredith and spot her off to one side near Cookey. She's standing still too, with her ears pricked and her alert eyes flicking around the view.

'Mo,' Nick asks softly, 'you feeling that?'

'Fuck yeah,' he whispers back as I cast a questioning look at Nick, 'they's here somewhere,' Mo adds.

'Do what?' I ask Nick and glance at Mo Mo.

'He did it yesterday,' Nick says in a soft voice, 'right before they attacked...before any of us heard anything...in the square and again at that house...'

'Did what?' I ask.

'Kinda reacted,' Nick says with a shrug, 'like he knew they were coming.'

'Mo? Seriously?'

'He did,' Blowers calls over just as softly, 'sorry, Mr Howie, I forgot to say...'

'Yeah me too,' Nick says with a wince, 'sorry.'

'No it's fine, Mo? Is that right?'

'Dunno, Mr Howie,' he says, 'like...s'weird but...like...a feeling, you get me?'

'Meredith seems okay,' Cookey says while looking at the dog.

'You said she can smell them,' Charlie says, 'this water will wash the smells away terribly so she might not be able to pick the scent up...'

'Will it terribly?' Cookey asks.

Meredith is our best way of having advance warning and Charlie's words hit home with a realisation that they could be anywhere in this street watching us. 'Stay alert,' I walk back through the gates and motion for Dave to come over, 'they're in the street somewhere,' I whisper when he gets close, 'can feel it but Meredith can't smell them...'

'The water will ruin the scent.'

'You knew that?'

'Yes, Mr Howie.'

'Could have said something, Dave.'

'I just did.'

'No, before...you could have said something before. Listen, the lads said Mo reacted before they were attacked yesterday. Like he knew they were coming but before there was any noise or anything...keep an eye on him.'

'Do you think he is infected?'

'No, not that,' I reply and pause for a second, 'Meredith is fine with him...just worth watching him to see if does it again.'

'Okay, Mr Howie,' he says with a curt nod.

'Keep watch with them, I'll get Roy moving. Has he got the keys yet?'

'He has, he was checking each vehicle for suitability.'

'They're all the bloody same,' I say with a glance at the three identical armoured vans.

'I don't know. I can't drive.'

'We should teach you.'

'I don't have a licence.'

'You don't need a licence now, Dave. We'll just get some L plates.'

'L plates?'

'Yeah, the magnetic things they put on cars to show the driver is learning.'

'Oh, okay, Mr Howie.'

'I was joking. We don't need L plates.'

'I haven't done the theory test.'

I stare for a second and for once let my mind catch up with my mouth before I speak, 'it's fine, mate. We can bypass the theory test.'

'Theory is an important facet of any learning experience, Mr Howie.'

'Yes, it is but...no good point, we can do a theory input if you want... but er, for now just keep an eye on Mo and I'll get this sorted out.'

He nods smartly and marches outside and straight to Mo Mo who he stares at until the young lad looks up and smiles nervously. Subtle as a house brick.

'How are you getting on?' I ask at joining the others.

'Roy's checking the last one now,' Marcy says, 'like there's a difference...'

'Reginald?'

'With Roy,' Marcy says, 'I don't know what the hell has got into him,' she adds darkly.

'Give him a break, he's shitting himself and hating every minute of being with us.'

'He's always shitting himself and he hates every minute of everything but he's gone all sulky and...any good?' She switches instantly to bright and breezy as Roy and Reginald appear walking up the side of the last van.

'I think we'll take the middle one,' Roy says, 'less wear on the tyres and the interior is cleaner.'

'Praise the lord,' Clarence mutters, 'he's made a decision. Have you seen inside?' He asks me.

'Only that one I told you about...can't imagine it's that different.'

I follow him between the vans to the rear of the middle one where Roy is waiting to give the guided tour.

'Rear door, solid and armoured,' Roy swings the single door a few times, 'hinges are hidden and protected, the seals are tight...double skin panels,' he reaches out to tap the back end of the vehicle, 'inside we have a desk, bolted to the floor as you can see and a chair also bolted but on runners so the position can be adjusted. Then on this side we have shelving units all coded with numbers that must have been used to store the cash bags from each premises they visited. The roof has an escape hatch sealed from the inside and there is another door leading to the front cab which is also locked from the inside. Air flow comes from vents but the vents on the outside are hidden to prevent anyone pumping gas inside I guess...and er...' he pauses to look round then points at a fire extinguisher attached to the wall, 'fire extinguisher...oh the windows,' he says with a look of love in his eyes, 'they're sealed and riveted and not even glass but a high density polycarbonate I would suggest,' he taps the Perspex and nods as though expecting us all to make appreciative noises, which we do.

'The best thing though,' he says, 'is this...' with a flourish he presses something on the desk and a flat screen monitor lifts up enough for him to prise it into an upright position, 'security camera feed,' he says tapping the screen, 'oh, actually I haven't tested the electrics on all of them yet...'

'Roy, we need to get going,' I cut him off, 'test this one and if it works we'll use it.'

'Yes, yes of course...hang on...' he climbs through the open door into the cabin and settles in the driver's seat. A few seconds later and the engine thrums gently to life with a slight vibration through the frame.

'Sounds good,' Clarence calls out from next to me, 'been idle for over two weeks so...'

'Is the screen on?' Roy calls out twisting in the seat to stare down the back.

'Er...no, mate,' I say leaning in to look at the monitor, 'Reginald, does it need turning on?'

'Ah yes,' Reginald moves from the side by the shelves and presses the bottom corner of the monitor. Immediately the screen comes to life with four images showing in high definition on a split screen format.

'Bloody hell,' I say in genuine surprise at the clarity of the live feed, 'where are the cameras?'

'Light clusters?' Clarence says moving to the rear passenger side lights and bending down to stare close so his big face looms on the bottom left quarter of the screen.

'Yep,' I say, 'Reginald? This okay for you?'

'Yes, thank you,' he says politely, 'as long as Roy doesn't mind having my company.'

'Fine with me,' Roy shouts from the front, 'you don't talk that much do you...so...'

'Oh he bloody does when he gets going,' Marcy says under her breath.

'How many seats in the front, Roy?'

'Two, and that one in the back...but then we can carry more if they sit on the floor.'

'What about that shelving?' I ask, 'takes up a lot of space.'

'It's in three sections,' Roy says climbing back into the rear, 'I was thinking we could remove two sections and keep one for storage.'

'Perfect, can you do it now?'

'I can,' Clarence says heaving himself up into the back, 'which one do you want to keep?' He asks gripping one end as he braces to rip it free.

'God no!' A look of panic crosses Roy's face, 'do it properly... undo the bolts and...'

'We don't have time for that, Roy,' Clarence says.

'Roy,' Paula leans into the back, 'we can't stay here for long... they could be watching us right now.'

'Okay okay, fine,' he says with a worried look, 'just try not to break anything.'

'But I am breaking it,' Clarence says, 'I'm breaking this...'

'We'll unload the Saxon,' I walk towards the back of our vehicle, 'Dave, send a couple of the lads in to help move the kit over.'

I get in the back and stare down in dismay at the sheer amount of ammunition cases and bags of gear littered everywhere then smile at the first splintering wrenching sound comes from Clarence smashing shit up. I pass boxes out to the lads who stack them on the ground while we sort GPMG ammunition from assault rifle and pistol rounds. Grenades, bags of clothing, spare equipment taken from the shops yesterday.

'Nick,' I call out from the inside of the Saxon, 'Roy's van will have a radio, can you make it connect to ours in here...'

'What's the frequency setting?'

'What's the what what?'

'I'll go and look.'

'Good God we've got some shit in here...who let it get this messy?'

Roy's van, minus the shelving ripped out by Clarence and cast aside in a heap, backs out of the space and manoeuvres so the rear door butts up close to the Saxon.

We unload, load, re-load, stack and sort through everything until the Saxon and the new van slowly start getting put in order. Nick runs between the two checking the radios and looking intently happy with screw drivers and wire strippers in his hands.

I leave them to it and go out the gates to see Charlie, Blinky and Dave scanning the area, 'everything okay?'

'Feels like we're being watched,' Charlie replies softly.

I stop next to her, 'we probably are. In fact, I would guess that right now there's some rancid fucker staring right at us and listening to every word we say. Some ugly. Rancid. Disgusting. Putrid. Filthy. Horrible. Vile. Contagious. Diseased...did I say putrid?'

'You did,' she says.

'Er...Filthy. Warped. Twisted. Weak....Er...Help me out...'

'Oh gosh,' she says and pauses to think, 'I would say, yes...I would say they are a nauseatingly repulsive foul abomination of creatures...'

'Nice,' I say appreciatively.

'Or,' she adds after another second of thinking, 'a villainous vicious monstrously demonic fetid group of...er...'

'Cunts?' Blinky suggests.

'Yes...that word,' Charlie says.

'They'll be gathering,' I look down and speak low, 'or massing somewhere nearby...We'll get the...SHIT DAVE!' I drop down as the gunshot booms right behind me, 'what the fuck?'

'Got it,' he says lowering the rifle, 'up there...third floor window on the far right.'

I twist round while my heart races from the fright of the unexpected gunshot to see him still aiming down to the left side of the street and up at the windows of a building.

'Which one?'

'The bakery,' he says.

'Yeah I see it,' I say and start looking at the windows above the bakery.

'Next to that is a shoe shop.'

'Yeah...'

'Next to that is a clothes shop.'

'Yes,' I say slowly.

'Next to that is a café.'

'Yes, café.'

'Next to that is a chemist.'

'Chemist. Yes, Dave.'

'Next to that is a...I don't know what that is...'

'Betting shop,' I say at the sight of the posters in the window.'

'And next to that is a travel agents shop.'

'Yes...'

'And next to that is another chemist.'

'Yes, Dave...'

'And next to that is a pet shop.'

'Dave...'

'And next to that is a book shop.'

'Dave...which...'

'And next to that is a Spar convenience store.'

'Right, yes...' I rub my face.

'And next to that is Santander.'

'Yep, Santander.'

'...'

'Santander?'

'Yes, Mr Howie.'

'We got to Santander and you stopped.'

'Yes, Mr Howie.'

'Which bloody...'

'Do you mean the windows above Santander?'

'Yes, Charlotte.'

'The third floor...the window on the far right...'

'Yes, Charlotte.'

'Dave.'

'Yes, Mr Howie.'

'You could have just said Santander.'

'I did.'

'No, I mean instead of saying all the other shops you could have just said Santander...'

'A process of thought,' Charlotte says, 'that was clear and understandable.'

'That's fucking miles away,' Blinky says in awe at the window down the far end of the street.

'Yes, yes it was clear but...'

'What's going on?' The rest come running from the yard with rifles ready.

'Dave saw one in the window above Santander,' I say.

'Where's that?' Clarence asks scanning the street.

'Down there,' I point to the left.

'Er...'

'Next to the Spar,' I say.

'Spar?' Clarence says shielding his eyes from the sun.

'Fuck me...next to the book shop.'

'What book shop?'

'Next to the fucking pet shop!'

'Can't see it.'

'Oh for fuck's sake you are shitting me...'

'Chemist,' Charlie says.

'Yeah I can see the chemist's,' Clarence says, 'got a café next door.'

'Oh my god...'

'Not that chemist,' Charlie says, 'the travel agents?'

'Travel agents...' Clarence says, 'yep, I can see that...'

'Travel agents?' Marcy asks.

'Next to the betting shop,' Clarence says helpfully.

'Above the betting shop?' Paula asks.

'No...above Santanfuckingder,' I groan.

'Where's Santander?' Blowers asks shielding his own eyes to stare down the street.

'Next to the fucking Spar!'

'They're both red,' Marcy says, 'which one is Santander?'

'The one further away,' Charlie says, 'the closest one is the Spar which is next to the...'

'Howie?' Paula says, 'are you okay?'

'Fine! Is Roy finished?'

'Roy will never be finished,' Paula says without a flicker of expression, 'but yes, he's finished enough for us to go.'

'Thank fuck, we're moving out. Nick, did you get the...where's Nick?'

'Doing the radios like you asked him,' Marcy says.

'Right,' I stomp back in the yard, 'Nick, how you getting on?'

'Er hang on,' he shouts from somewhere, 'the radio from the new van is encrypted.'

'Where are you?'

'In the Saxon.'

I get to the open passenger door to find him fitting a new radio into a set of stripped wires. 'What's that?'

'Hang on,' he turns his head and spits the screwdriver from his mouth, 'radio from one of the other vans. This one,' he taps the Saxon's original radio, 'doesn't work with this one,' he taps the new one, 'so we wouldn't be able to talk to each other...so I took a radio from one of the other vans and split the antenna wire to our old radio to feed into this one so...we...shit, Roy? We using yellow as the live?'

'Yes,' Roy shouts from somewhere else.

'Yellow is live,' Nick mutters to himself and pushes a yellow wire into the back of the new radio, 'so we took a radio from one of the other vans,' he repeats with a glance at me, 'and yeah...and er Roy is taking the radio from the last van and we'll put that into the back of the Saxon.'

'Why?'

'The back of Roy's van has a radio, and the front...and the front of this one will have on and the back too...so we can all talk.'

'Awesome, how long will it take?'

'Five minutes, Mr Howie.'

'Okay.'

'What was the gunshot?'

'Dave saw one in a window about ten miles away.'

'He get it?'

'Yep, but they know we're here.'

'Understood. Right, let's see,' he pushes the radio back into a cubby hole and presses a button on the front, 'got power,' he says as the front lights up, 'Roy, what's your preset?'

'Seven is displayed on the front.'

'Seven,' Nick mutters pushing a button to cycle through numbers until the display reads 07, '*Nick to Roy...Nick to Roy,*' he says pressing the button on the side of the handset.

'*Yep, got you loud and clear...*'

'Result,' Nick beams, '*loud and clear, Roy.*'

'Fuck me,' I mutter, 'well done, I'm impressed. What's the range?'

'Should be very good,' Nick says, 'they had to reach the base.'

'It worked then?' Roy appears by the driver's door.

'Spot on,' Nick says, 'we'll do the other one later, boss wants to get going.'

'Load up,' I step back and call out, 'Paula, you going with Roy?'

'Yep,' she says running in with the others, 'for now but not all the time...unless anyone else wants to go in there?'

'Not now,' I say before another discussion can commence, 'Roy, Paula and Reginald in the new van, everyone else in the Saxon.'

'Plan?' Paula shouts as the rest head for the Saxon.

'Town centre' I say keeping my voice low, 'we'll see if we can draw them out...from here on we're armed, loaded with bags on and hand weapons in reach...'

'Boss,' Blowers says with a wince, 'Charlie and Blinky don't have hand weapons.'

'Nor do I,' Marcy says, 'or Reginald...who isn't carrying his rifle by the way.'

'I saw, it's up to him. You've got knives? Use them for now until we can find something else. Nick, up top and keep a look for them.'

'On it, can I smoke up there?'

'Crack on.'

'Thanks, boss.'

'Dave and Blowers take the last seats either side of the back doors,' I say much to everyone's surprise, 'they're your seats from now on so you can direct the team as they get out.'

'Got it,' Blowers nods firmly as he swaps seats with Mo Mo to sit opposite Dave who was already in place.

'Nick, don't use the GPMG until we really need it, you're up there to keep watch.'

'Okay,' he shouts down.

I get round into the driver's seat and climb up with relief at finally being able to move off and grab the handset for the new radio, '*Saxon to van.*'

'*Is that what we are?*'

'*Yes, Paula, you're the van.*'

'*Okay, er...van go ahead over and out.*'

'*We'll go first, stay behind...where's Clarence?*'

'*Pardon?*'

'In the back,' he says from behind me, 'I can stretch my legs out now.'

'*Clarence should be with you.*'

'*Yeah sorry, Paula...I didn't mean you.*'

'Do you mind me being up here?' Marcy asks.

'*No course not.*'

'*Pardon? Howie, are you talking to us?*'

'*No! Hang on...*No, it's fine...*yeah Paula, stay behind...we'll move out now.*'

'Did you find Clarence?'
'He's in the back.'
'Who's up front then?'
'Marcy.'
'Cosy...'
'Over and out, Paula.'

CHAPTER FIVE

D*ay Eighteen*

A BRIEF UPDATE.

Finkton is a war zone of the like I have never witnessed with corpses everywhere. The death given here is staggering but thankfully the rain washed most of the bodies clean and removed the worst of the awful rancid stench of rotting flesh which in turn enabled me to examine them visually.

The vehicle that was in the village square is now gone. It was a military looking thing with big wheels. It is now gone which suggests the group that were under attack somehow escaped and have left his area.

From that area I followed the bread crumb trail of dead infected hosts into the housing area of the village which finally led me to a large mansion house sign boarded as being Finkton Sports Academy.

Again the bodies are everywhere. Littered from the road down the driveway and clustered dense around the main entrance doorway and several deep within the lobby of the house. The stench within that lobby – so protected by the rain – was gag inducing to the point I was forced to make use of my protective breathing equipment and safety eye glasses, that is after I emptied my stomach on the ground while Jess stared at me with contempt.

The injuries inflicted to the fallen infected hosts are most severe and it is obvious that a mixture of weapons have been used. Some were shot. Many had neat surgically precise cuts given to their necks and within the groin area. Many were butchered by large bladed weapons and some were clearly beaten to death by someone very large and very strong. What I also observed were many of the bodies had what I can only describe as ragged throat wounds that is suggestive of some kind of animal, and some of those who suffered the ragged wounds had deep claw marks down their chests and stomach.

It was macabre. Frightening. Sickening and deeply unsettling.

My conclusion is that there was a very large group of highly professional and trained soldiers armed to the teeth (possibly Special Forces) who fought a retreat into this house and slaughtered hundreds of infected hosts. Within that conclusion there is an assumption that the dark haired man is one of that group.

Finkton is bordered by towns and villages in every direction. From the debris left I think I can work out the exit route they took.

NB

CHAPTER SIX

This is it. Everything we have done has led to this point. Every fight, every battle, every death given and every loss taken has been training for now. An armoured personnel carrier loaded with gun toting badasses and an armoured cash van loaded with a hypochondriac, a terrified ex-zombie and an accountant. Even so. This is it. We're ready. We have a huge arm-loving dog and a Dave and a Clarence. We have a Blinky who is practically frothing at the mouth at the prospect of a fight and has already puked with the anticipation. We have guns. Lots of guns with lots of bullets to throw about. We have axes and knives. We're dressed in black and we have a Marcy, who I suspect chose a top a size too small to accentuate her curves, but she does look sensationally amazing and it's actually really quite hard to focus on the road with her sat next to me. Even so. This is it. Dave and Blowers are at the back doors ready to charge out with voices roaring into the air. Nick up top looking like a double hard bastard with a cigarette hanging from his mouth like a nonchalant *French Resistance guerrilla fighter,* all he needs is a beret. We should get berets. We'd look awesome in berets. Marcy would look sexy in a beret. Just a beret.

Even so. This is it. The moment of truth. The pinnacle of all we are and every path taken has led to this moment. We are taking the fight to them. Today. On this day. On this now gloriously sunny day we are taking the fight to them. A gloriously sunny day that is reflecting the sun's rays of every pissing puddle and blinding the shit out of me.

Even so. We're ready.

'I need a piss,' Cookey says.

'How do I use this?' Marcy asks.

'Press the button on the side.'

'Which one?'

'That one.'

'Doesn't help when you say *that one* without actually indicating which one...'

'The bloody button on the side, press it in and talk.'

'I am pressing it in...nothing is happening.'

'What do you expect to happen? You talk and they hear you.'

'Why aren't they saying anything back then? Hello? Paula? Paula it's Marcy...they're not there...'

'No you...you have to let go so they can talk back.'

'What? But you said it works by pressing the button in.'

'Yes! You press the button and talk and that transmits and then you let go and they push their button and they talk and then you press your button and you talk...'

'So it's not a power button then?'

'Eh? No! No it's a bloody press-to-talk button.'

'Alright, no need to get shirty. You should have just said it was a press-to-talk button.'

'Really need a piss.'

'Okay, Marcy it's Paula shit! No, I'm Marcy. Paula, it's Marcy are you there? So now I let go?'

'Yes...fucking let go and let them talk.'

'Oh my god I'm in another bloody van and can still hear you two bickering.'

'Hi Paula, it's Marcy.'

'Did you press the button?'

'Yes, Howie! I pressed the bloody button.'

'She did press the button, Howie...and then she held the button so I...what? What, Roy? I am talking to Marcy. Yes I am talking to her...what? What's wrong with saying Marcy? Oh apparently I am not allowed to say names now.'

'Why can't you say names?'

'Roy said...yes Roy I am telling them...Roy said in case the infection is listening.'

'But the infection knows our names, what difference does that make?'

'Roy, Marcy said the infection knows our names so...oh you heard her...yes okay, Roy. I know it's not a phone call and everyone can hear it...'

'Roy, they already know our names so why bother hiding them?'

'Marcy, Roy said he thinks it's more professional.'

'Okay er...should we have codenames then? What do you want to be?'

'Oh how funny! I'll be er...oh I don't know...you can be Big Tits.'

'Did you say Big Tits? That's great!...okay I'll be Big Tits and you can be Nice Arse.'

'Nice Arse?! Brilliant. Love it, over Big Tits.'

'Received, Nice Arse.'

'I need a piss, Big Tits.'

'Alex!'

'What? That's her codename.'

'Big Tits to Nice Arse, Cookey needs the toilet.'

'Nice Arse to Big Tits, all received...and Roy said we're pissing about.'

'You are pissing about.'

'Yeah Howie agrees with him...are we pulling over? We're pulling over so Cookey can have a piss.'

'Roger roger over and out.'

'Did you hear that?!'

'Er yes? It's a radio and like, it's on loudspeaker.'

I pull over on a suitable bit of high ground so Cookey can jump down, run behind a wall and relieve himself just as Roy's van draws alongside and Paula waving through her window past me to Marcy.

'Actually,' Nick drops down, 'mind if I go too?'

'Carry on, mate...anyone else?'

A mass exodus as they file out from the back and head over to the toilet wall, I twist round to watch Blinky walking with the lads and disappearing out of sight behind the wall.

'Is Blinky going with them?' I ask Charlie.

'Won't bother her one bit,' she says with a roll of her eyes.

'Might bother them,' I chuckle.

'*Hey Nice Arse,*' Marcy says leaning forward to wave at Paula.

'*Hello! Why does Howie look grumpy?*'

'*I don't know, Howie, why do you look grumpy?*'

'I'm thinking about berets.'

'Berets? You mean the hats?'

'Yeah,' I nod amiably, 'you ever had one?'

'Don't think so,' she says, '*Paula, have you ever had a beret?*'

'*Oh God, years ago I had one. It was red, looked quite nice actually. I had a matching scarf that went with it.*'

'*Where did you get it from?*'

'*From Next I think.*'

'Next do some nice things.'

'*Charlie says Next do some nice things.*'

'*Tell Charlie I thought she was more a Laura Ashley woman.*'

'*She's too young for Laura Ashley.*'

'I am not too young for Laura Ashley.'

'*She said she's not too young for Laura Ashley.*'

'*I heard her, Howie, Roy asked if you're enjoying our chat as much as he is.*'

'Er...yes?'

'*And he just moaned about using names again.*'

'That was fucking gross,' Cookey says getting in the back, 'I just saw Blinky taking a piss.'

'I saw you pissing too.'

'Yeah but I was standing against the wall.'

'So? I was squatting against the wall surrounded by men holding their cocks...'

'Now you don't hear that every day,' I mutter as Marcy bursts out laughing.

'Gave me bloody stage fright,' Cookey moans, 'I've never seen such a thing...I'm scarred for life...'

'You're scarred? I saw your todger.'

'I saw your...'

'Alex!'

'I was going to say foofoo.'

'Foofoo? What the hell is a foofoo?'

'Your lady bits...I saw them.'

'I saw your man bits.'

'Urgh you shouldn't be looking.'

'You looked at my...'

'Patricia!'

'I was going to say foofoo.'

'Enough.'

'Yes, Dave.'

'Sorry, Dave.'

'That was weird,' Blowers says laughing as he gets in, 'Cookey and Blinky staring at each other while pissing...'

'I was not staring!' Cookey shouts.

'I was,' Blinky snorts.

'Oh God,' Clarence groans, 'right separate toilet breaks from now on.'

'We all in?'

'Yes, boss,' Blowers says slamming the rear door closed.

'Right, try again...'

. . .

SO THIS IS IT. Thirteen battle hardened...Twelve battle hardened killers and Reginald and a dog. No, I should count the dog. Yeah so thirteen battle hardened killers and Reginald hiding in the back of Roy's truck.

Even so. We're ready and we're coming for you. You saw us taking a new van and yeah, you know our names and who we are and maybe Roy is being a bit too worried about the whole names thing on the radio but even so, we're bringing the fight to you. Right to you and for making Jimmy Carr shit on my chin I will spank you up and down every bloody town centre, starting with this town centre. This one right here.

'We're here, everyone ready...I said EVERYONE READY?'

'FUCK YES!' Blinky roars.

'That's more like it...everyone out, weapons up and be ready...'

'Fan out into a circle, Blinky next to me, Charlie stay close to Nick...' Blowers gives the orders as we jump out. Axes shoved down between our backs and our bags. Knives ready to be drawn. Rifles being cocked with the metallic noises of bolts being drawn back. Roy's van coming to a halt and he jumps down in the spirit of the adventure with a hardened gleam in his eyes and armed to the teeth with his rifle in his hands, his sword down his back and his bow looped over his shoulders with the arrows poking out the top of his bag. Fuck yes. This is it. Try picking a fight with us now you pricks.

We go out into a wide circle. Everyone facing out and scanning. Always scanning. Watching. Always watching. Every window, every door, every recess and every road, path and alley that feeds into the square is monitored and watched. Meredith senses the energy and paces with her ears pricked, tail high and mouth panting.

I get next to Marcy who stands next to Paula who stands next to Roy. On my other side is Dave. Always Dave. His rifle is lowered but his aim never misses. They know we're here. They'll come charging and screaming and my God we'll fuck 'em up.

'Stinks,' Marcy sniffs the air.

'Water's heating up from the sun,' Paula says, 'it'll get worse. Looks like they were having a party here.'

'Yeah I saw the stage,' Marcy says turning round to look at the scaffolding and plank stage, 'must have been a mid-summer thing.'

'Focus,' I say in a low voice.

They fall silent and we wait. We watch and we wait. We wait for the undead voices to come screaming down the roads to be cut down by our many bullets fired from our many guns.

We wait. It's hot and with so much water around the humidity is staggeringly high. We sweat with beads that form on our focussed and intent faces. It does smell. Marcy was right. It smells damp and like everything is going off and the sun is reflecting off the standing water and dazzling us all.

'Contact,' Cookey mutters low and dangerous.

'How many?' I tense and look to the view ahead.

'One...he's wading through the water towards us.'

I turn to look at the single undead forcing his way through waist deep water of a sunken section of the deepest part of a side street.

'His mates will soon join him,' Roy says, 'stay sharp.'

'Cookey, keep eyes on him,' Clarence says in a growl, 'let's see what he does.'

'Will do.'

Time passes. We wait.

'What's he doing?' Clarence asks.

'He fell down twice and now he's back up and wading again.'

'Just the one?' I ask.

'Er, yes...just the one, Mr Howie.'

'Where are they?' Clarence mutters darkly.

'He fell down again,' Cookey says.

We all turn this time and watch the undead male floundering pathetically in the deep water. Arms flailing and splashing down and now I'm watching I can match the sounds to his movements.

'Can zombies swim?' Cookey asks.

'No idea,' Nick shrugs.

'Don't ask,' Marcy says as everyone looks round at her, 'I have no idea.'

'He's not swimming very well,' Nick says, 'er...Mr Howie?'

'Go ahead mate, we might as well.'

'Cool, want one?'

'Yeah why not.'

He hands them round and we light up to smoke with our weapons resting across shoulders or held in the crooks of arms while we watch the single undead.

'He's back up,' Paula says exhaling smoke away from Roy who still tuts.

'Maybe,' Marcy says after another few minutes of watching the undead slip and slide back into the water, 'maybe they used them all from this town yesterday?'

'Ah,' I look at her with a fresh surge of hope.

'Good thinking,' Clarence says with a slow nod, 'yep, I can see where we've gone wrong.'

'Too close to Finkton,' Roy says.

'Makes sense,' Blowers says drawing on his smoke, 'they threw a shit ton at us yesterday.'

'We used them all up then,' Cookey says, 'apart from that one,' he adds motioning towards our flounder now back on his feet, 'Oi shithead,' he shouts, 'did they leave you behind?'

'Perhaps he's on watch,' Charlie says, 'like the one Dave shot above Santander.'

'Santander? Where's that?' Marcy asks.

'Next to the bakery,' Clarence says.

'Don't fucking start.'

'It wasn't next to the bakery,' Dave says, 'it was next to the Spar.'

I huff and sag on the spot then idly flick the cigarette butt into the nearby flood water.

'Bollocks, next town then,' I get an idea and stare up and over to the undead, 'I SAID WE'D BETTER GO TO THE NEXT TOWN THEN...'

'What are you doing?' Marcy asks.

'GOOD IDEA MR HOWIE,' Clarence booms, 'THERE ARE NO...THINGS HERE FOR US TO KILL.'

'I LIKE THAT IDEA,' Cookey joins in, 'OI...DO YOU WANT SIMON BLOWERS TO COME AND HELP YOU?'

'Cookey,' Blowers groans.

'HE'S A BIT EXCITED RIGHT NOW AS HE SAW SOME WILLIES WHEN WE HAD A WEE WEE.'

'Such a dick.'

'I THINK HAS AN ERECTION.'

'Twat,' Blowers laughs which cuts off with a round of cheers as the male finally gets free of the deep water and starts making a proper concerted effort to get towards us. He even lets out a growl buts ends up gargling with dirty water spewing from his mouth.

'Get the dog!' I shout as she starts towards it with a bark. Clarence lunges forward and grabs her to guide her back. 'So,' I say loudly, 'to the next town...which is,' I turn round trying to get my bearings, 'which way did we come in?'

'That way,' Clarence points to the now obvious road we used.

'Then we shall go that way,' I point the other direction, 'to the next CLOSEST town.'

'Should we be really taunting it like this?' Roy asks seriously.

'Fuck 'em...Dave...'

Holding his rifle with his left hand and his right moves at frightening speed as the pistol is out, aimed and firing before I finished saying his name. The shot is a perfect head strike that blows the back of the skull off with a pink mist still hanging in the air as the body slumps into the water.

'Oh my fucking God,' Blinky whispers to herself, 'I love him...I actually love him.'

'Not appropriate, Patricia,' Dave says dully.

'Load up, we'll try the next one.'

Back into the vehicles we go. The Saxon loads up and Marcy takes the front to let Clarence stretch out in the back. I take the lead and pull away in a wide circle round to face the exit road and drive through the deep puddles with Roy staying close to make use of the wake of displaced water formed by the Saxon. Back down the High Street and past the side road leading to the yard where we found the van. Squinting through the now streaked and smeared windscreen from the dazzling reflections on the water on the ground. Still more of it pours from roofs and drips from broken drains but already it's lessening and in this heat it will soon evaporate. The heat is stifling, really close and muggy. I glance over to Marcy and the sheen of sweat glistening on her face as she checks her own reflection in a small compact mirror taken from her bag.

'They're getting better,' she says staring into her own eyes, 'look,' she looms at me with her eyes overly wide.

'Bloody hell,' I remark at the now mostly white iris streaked with a faint red colour, 'they look so much better. How do you feel?'

'Normal,' she says with a shrug, 'don't feel any different now.'

'Did you ache this morning?'

'Ache?'

'Yeah from all the running and stuff yesterday, did you hurt from that? Like your muscles and...'

'Yeah I get it,' she cuts me off, 'and no, no I didn't...is that bad?'

'Dunno, Cookey, Blowers, either of you aching from yesterday?'

'Not me,' Blowers says.

'My eyes ache,' Cookey says.

'Your eyes?' I ask in alarm as Marcy twists round.

'From seeing Blinky's ladybits.'

'Dick,' I chuckle, 'seriously though, any pain at all?'

'The bruises hurt,' Blowers says, 'when you touch them...'

'You like being touched.'

'And got a few new cuts that are a bit sore but not like they should be.'

'On the bum. You like being touched on the bum.'

'My bum isn't bruised.'

'You wish it was.'

'You do.'

'Your mum does.'

'Cookey?' I call out, 'what about you?'

'I don't like my bum being touched, Mr Howie.'

'Not your arse, your bruises.'

'Same as Blowers,' he says, 'are we infected?'

'Fuck knows, I'm the same as you. We should be hurting after all that running and fighting...like muscle fatigue at least. Nick?'

'I don't like my bum being touched either.'

'Not your bloody arse!'

'No, Boss. I'm not aching anywhere really. Got a few knocks that are a bit tender but...not really.'

'Mo?'

'Same, don't want no one touching my arse.'

'Fuck's sake!'

'Nah I don't ache, same as them. Sore where I got hit.'

'Clarence?'

'It depends on who it is.'

'Eh?'

'My arse, depends on who is touching it. A nice woman then yes.'

'Give me strength.'

'No I don't ache but we can't read anything into that. We've been running non-stop for days, fighting too. We could just be getting fitter naturally.'

'Yeah I suppose, Charlie?'

'I like my backside being touched.'

'Really?'

'Seriously?'

'What like...actually real?'

'No,' she laughs at the lads, 'well, same as Clarence. It depends on who is doing the touching of course but...'

'Oh my God.'

'Cookey, calm down,' I call out.

'Best day ever,' he says wistfully.

'In response to the question, Mr Howie. I do not ache but then both Blinky and I are used to extreme periods of intense exercise.'

'Fair one,' I say.

'You're so posh,' Nick laughs, '*in response to the question...*'

'Thank you,' Charlie says taking the compliment.

'You alright?' I ask Marcy quietly as the back descends into chaos of the lads all trying to speak posh, 'you look worried.'

'I'm fine.'

'What? What's up?'

'Nothing,' she waves her hand at me, 'just remembered something.'

'What?'

'How far off are we?'

'No idea, what did you remember?'

'Does it matter?'

'Er yeah?' I say with a laugh, 'I hate it when people do that.'

'Do what?'

'You know what.'

'It's where Darren bit me.'

'What the next town? I thought he bit you on the Isle of Wight.'

She gives me a withering look, 'on the arse, Howie. He bit me on the arse.'

'Oh...oh shit...Sorry.'

'It's not your fault.'

'Yeah no, I mean sorry for mentioning it. Does it hurt?'

'My arse, not at all.'

'Oh.'

'Scarred though.'

'Oh,' I say again trying not to think of Marcy's arse.

'Right on the cheek.'

'Cheek yeah?'

'Yeah, fucking cunt.'

'Marcy!'

'What?'

'You can't say cunt.'

'I can say what I like and he was a cunt.'

'Good point, yeah he was a cunt.'

'Were you thinking of my arse then?'

'When? When you said about it…no no, not at all.'

'You were.'

'Wasn't.'

'Do you want to see it?'

'Your arse? What now?'

'The bite mark.'

'Er, not right now no…I'm er…like driving and there's floods and things and…'

'Okay, I'll show you later.'

'Er, right…that's er…like…'

'Are we going to be on watch again?'

'Um, I don't know. It depends where we end up I guess.'

'Can we do the first watch again? I liked it.'

'Okay, yes I…' I swallow and navigate the debris floating in the flooded road.

'I'll show you tonight then.'

'I er, right. Like…weird.'

'So don't die today.'

'Eh?'

'Don't die.'

'I wasn't planning on dying today.'

'Good. Don't die and I'll show you if you want to see it.'

'Your arse or the bite mark?'

'Up to you.'

'Oh my fucking...Marcy...'

'What?'

'You can't just offer to show me your arse.'

'Why not? It's my arse. I can offer to show it to whomever I please.'

'Of course but...'

'Stop trying to control me.'

'What?'

'Joking,' she laughs, 'actually, you might not want to see where Darren bit me, it's not exactly a nice thing to remember.'

'I'm...lost for words.'

'I'm only teasing,' she chuckles and reaches over to pat my thigh, 'sorry, focus on the road.'

'I will...I am.'

'And seriously,' she fixes me with a warning look, 'don't die today.'

'Stop saying that. You don't die today.'

'I won't, I've got you and Dave and this lot behind me...' she says thumbing the rear of the Saxon, 'right now this has got to be safest place in the entire world.'

'When you say it like that...'

'I do feel safe with all of you,' she says softly.

'Ah no worries, this lot adore you so yeah, you're pretty safe I reckon.'

'Really? Do they?' She asks looking at me with surprise and a hint of hunger in her face.

'You love compliments don't you?'

'Narcissist,' she chuckles, 'and vain remember.'

'So vain.'

'So vain,' she echoes and fixes me a dazzling smile.

'You don't even deny it now!'

'I am vain,' she laughs, 'so vain.'

'I knew it and stop using that smile on me.'

'What smile? This smile?'

'Yeah that smile.'

'Paula is very pretty.'

'Where on earth did that come from?'

'Just saying,' she says, 'and Charlie is gorgeous,' she adds in a whisper.

'Yeah she is a pretty girl.'

'Don't you go looking at her,' she says with a mock narrowed eyed look. I laugh but don't reply. 'I mean it,' she says holding the narrowed look, 'I'll get jealous.'

'Okay, Marcy.'

'Don't you Marcy me, Mr Howie. I'm the one you hold hands with on watch.'

'Okay, Marcy.'

'Got a rifle now,' she says nodding at the weapon by her feet, 'I'll shoot anyone trying to hold hands with you.'

'Okay! I won't hold hands with anyone else on watch.'

'Or other times?'

'Ah you never said other times.'

'I am now. I am a very protective woman.'

'Protective or possessive?'

'Both.'

'So we held hands once and now you're saying that only you and I can hold hands from now on?'

'Yes. That is exactly what I am saying. And you kissed me so... you can't kiss anyone else either.'

'Oh right,' I burst out laughing at her serious delivery but give thanks for the humour in her eyes, 'not a stalker then.'

'Such a stalker,' she says with a nod, 'and I'm watching you,' she points her own fingers at her eyes then at me, 'I'll boil your bunny.'

'You are actually scaring me.'

'Good,' she gives me the dazzling smile again, 'remember that fear if you ever feel tempted.'

CHAPTER SEVEN

F ields and pasture land flooded on all sides with water still
pouring down the banks into the road that gathers speed into
fast moving streams. It looks dirty too. All the filth and dust from
the last few weeks of hot weather all picked up. Fluids from vehicles leaving oily streaks. The Saxon makes light work of it and once
again I give thanks that we have such a capable vehicle.

The pressure to be going somewhere and doing something is
unrelenting and I have to keep reminding myself the day is still
early.

We crest a hill road and start sweeping down to a view of
houses and buildings stretching into the distance and the shiny
surface of standing water throughout the roads and laying across
the fields on all sides and the first prickle of adrenalin. A tiny flick-
ering of my heart rate increasing at the sight. A big town, bigger
than most we've seen so far. Church spires, factories and office
blocks. A vista of concrete, glass and old England all giving
promise of streets full of undead to be cut down. The only downside is the town looks like it's nestled into a long sweeping valley
creating a flood plain. There must be a river running through it but

with the sheer amount of surface water about there's no way of picking it out.

'Can you let Roy know we're about five minutes out, five minutes in the back,' I add with a shout, 'be ready.'

'Hey, you there?'

'Yeah, we're here.'

'Howie said we're about five minutes out.'

'Got it, five minutes…'

We head down and hit the town proper with no gradual transference from countryside to urban. The town boundary is a wall and beyond are streets, housing estates and shops. There must have been a reason why the town never grew out past the wall, maybe a landowner refused to sell up or a rare butterfly was once seen taking a shit on a tree. Either way we're here and navigating the flooded roads at a lower speed with Dave up top and Roy right behind us. It looks the same as ever, broken, looted, damaged, wet and empty. From the outer sections we go along the main road aiming for the centre. A few small industrial estates here and there but nothing obvious to be seen.

What I didn't realise, and something that only becomes apparent now we're here, is that the middle area of the town is slightly higher than the immediate surrounding plains. Almost like a plateau within the valley and the standing water, although still present, gets shallower the closer we get to the centre.

Some English towns are thousands of years old. Centres of habitation that have changed hands from prehistoric to Romans to the Saxons and onwards through the years until what's left are confusing winding roads feeding from perfectly straight old Roman roads. Churches are built where places of worship have always stood and the town built round them and the other old buildings. With the onset of vehicular traffic so the town planners developed a mish mash of fucking one way streets designed to confuse the shit out of anyone visiting and so we have to rely on actual sign posts to find the town centre.

The end of days. The end of the world and we're still having to rely on bloody and bloodied signs showing which way to go.

We still get lost and end up down a dead end side street facing the entrance to a huge old multi-storey car park but I'll be fucked if we're getting trapped in one of those again and due to the size of our vehicles we're forced to reverse out, swing round and head off again in search of the elusive town centre.

In the end we find it by accident with Marcy pointing to a road on the right while listening to something being relayed by Paula from Roy and Clarence leaning over the seats saying we should turn round and go back down the road he said about five minutes ago and everyone else offering helpful hints and tips at how not to get lost.

What greets us snaps every word off. Marcy stops talking. Clarence falls silent. The radio ceases to squawk. I come to a sudden stop with Roy coming round to pull up next to us.

I take the radio from Marcy's hand and press the button just as Meredith starts to growl, *'Roy, you seeing this?'*

I glance over to see him doing the same as me and taking the radio from Paula's hand, *'Yes.'*

The centre is a wide plaza bordered by shops, office buildings and a church on one side. Bars and restaurants that were open when the infection hit and the signs of damage being the strongest at those points. It's wide and deep with the main road feeding round the edges. A fountain in the middle with a statue in the middle of that. Benches everywhere and in normal life it must have been a lovely spot full of life.

Now it's covered in a thick carpet of bodies that fills every square inch of the ground, like the scene of a terrible massacre. Men, women and children.

'Everyone out,' I mutter the words and instead of roaring out with shouts we ease the doors open and slip out into a wall of steaming air that hits us all hard. Like breathing the air in a sauna, hot, humid and instantly bringing sweat out on our foreheads.

Paula and Roy do the same as us and we gather at the front of the vehicles to stare at the amazing sight while Meredith goes low to the ground and growls deep in her throat.

'They must be close,' Clarence says quietly scanning the sides of the plaza. I look over at Meredith to see which direction she's staring but she's face on towards the plaza and fixed intently.

'Must be opposite us,' I say shielding my eyes and staring across to the other side. We're still on the road and several metres away from the edge of the plaza. I start walking forward, slow and careful. My axe wedged down my back and the assault rifle held ready. The others stretch out into a line with everyone staring round as we cover every direction.

'What happened?' Paula asks, 'this isn't...it's not...something is wrong.'

We all feel it but it takes time for the eyes to absorb the detail and then feed that into the brain which dissects the information and passes the conclusions to the mind. What we see are bodies and we're used to seeing bodies, so our minds expect to see bodies. It's Charlie that makes the connection first.

'No blood,' she says quickly.

'It's been raining,' Blowers replies softly.

'No,' she says urgently, 'no flies either...they're not dead...' she blurts and her words bring us all to a sudden stop.

'What?' I ask snapping my eyes down from the doors and windows at the sides to the bodies on the ground and it's like looking at one of those magic pictures that you stare at for ages until it suddenly morphs into what you are meant to be seeing. Bodies but not human bodies. Decaying bodies but not from the natural decay of being dead and in the sun and elements. Grey skinned bodies with mottled scalps and straggly hair and as I spot the first clawed hand so my mind makes the connection at the same time as everyone else does and suddenly our weapons are pointing down and not up.

Undead. All of them are undead. Clawed hands and the eyes that we can see are red and bloodshot.

'What the fuck?' Cookey mutters, 'they alive?'

None of us answer but remain still and silent with hearts racing from the sudden shock.

'Dave,' I whisper down the line, 'are they dead?'

'None of them have visible injuries consistent with causing a fatality,' he says.

'So like...are they breathing?' Mo Mo asks squinting from the brightness of the sun.

'Roy, stick an arrow in one of them mate...everyone else be ready in case they rise up,' I keep my voice as low as possible and watch as Roy slings his rifle, pulls his bow over and lifts his hand over his shoulder to draw an arrow. Watching him is like watching Dave draw his pistol, every movement is a fluid as water and so well practised he makes it look effortless.

'Big male, top off...see him?' Roy asks.

'Got him,' we all lock eyes on the big man lying close to the edge of the plaza.

He notches, pulls, lifts and aims all in one motion. A slight noise as the arrow is released and it embeds deep into the stomach of the male who doesn't flicker an inch. Not a groan comes from his lips, not a twitch from his muscles.

The second arrow strikes his chest. The third goes into his neck, the fourth into his meaty right thigh. The fifth hits his left shoulder. The sixth gets his left thigh. The seventh gets him in the right bicep.

'How many?' I lean forward to ask Roy.

'Just being thorough,' he says loosing the next arrow.

'Thorough? He looks like a hedgehog.'

'That's so fucking cool,' Blinky says watching Roy work the bow, 'have you got a crossbow?'

Roy freezes with a look of utter distaste etched on his face, 'No.

I do not have a crossbow. I have never fired a crossbow. Crossbow's have nothing to do with archery.'

'Okay,' she says with a huff, 'only asking.'

'And I am only answering that crossbows are not the same as firing a bow...they share a word...bow...that's it.'

'They both fire arrows,' Blinky says.

'They fire bolts, not arrows,' Roy says with a slow shake of his head as though this is the most ridiculous thing he has ever heard.

'Look like arrows, sharp and pointy.'

'My sword is sharp and pointy, is that an arrow?'

'So's his dick,' she points at Cookey and shrugs.

'What?' Cookey sputters, 'what did you fucking say?'

'And back to the matter at hand,' I say, 'the huge pile of undead bodies pretending to be dead...'

'They're not piled,' Marcy says, 'more like spread out.'

'Arranged,' Paula says, 'they look arranged.'

'Either bloody way it's creepy as hell...do you think they were trying to trick us?'

'No! Really?' Marcy looks at me aghast, 'the dirty rotters.'

'Very funny.'

'What will they think of next?'

'My dick is not sharp and pointy.'

'So is.'

'Right, everyone start shooting something,' I lift my rifle and aim at the closest head of a body within the carpet of undead. A second later and every gun is firing with single shots that boom into the quiet air. Skulls bursting apart sending fragments of bone pluming into the air with grey streaks of brain mixed into the pink and white colours.

A couple more seconds and they rise up going from prone to standing in one synchronised motion and suddenly the plaza is full of voices howling. They charge but they left it too late. We'd already killed loads and started with the closest bodies so the ones rising up have further to travel and have to navigate the obstacles of the corpses ahead of them.

Burst firing with sustained rounds being laid down and it's like shooting fish in a barrel, or zombies in a plaza. Twelve rifles firing and with each magazine holding thirty rounds it means we unload three hundred and sixty bullets into that plaza at a fire rate of over six hundred rounds per minute.

'MAGAZINE,' Blinky moves fast, ripping the old one out and remembering to pocket it before ramming the new one in.

They shout out in turn as they change magazine and our small line dominates their mass. Intelligence and preparation over sheer weight of numbers. They charge like the cavalry of the light brigade into the Russian guns that withered them remorselessly, and like those poor soldiers so long ago, these too are driven by an order than cannot be disobeyed and ultimately leads to their deaths.

It's not a battle but a slaughter and it's exactly what we came here to do. Cull the numbers, reduce the threat and be seen doing it. We fire and fire. Fingers holding triggers as hot lead spews deep into fleshy bodies and sends human forms spinning and slamming down. They howl and keep coming but we've done our job and made sure we had sufficient spare magazines and we change, make ready and continue to fire until the last few remain.

I take aim on a female off to one side and blink as she drops down with a stick poking out of her head. Another one a few feet away from her gets struck by an arrow next.

'Cease fire,' I call out, 'all yours, Roy.'

'Thanks,' he aims and fires with a speed that increases the more he does. His left hand holding a bunch of arrows ready while he grips the frame of the bow. His right hand pulling, loosing and deftly taking the next from his left hand before repeating the action. Arrows sail true, straight and silent and each one finds the target with a perfect shot.

We all watch and truth be told, I could watch Roy doing this all day long. The culmination of years of dedication and obsessive hard work. The speed is incredible. The rifles could never be matched for speed of fire rate but my god it's bloody good.

The arrows are so fast it's impossible to track them with the eye as they fly through the air and no sooner have I gained sight of the one that just landed and another one is in the air. The distance is long and because of the distance and speed of Roy's movements he even gets two in the air at the same time. One just landing with one just leaving. A look of serene contemplation on his face. Not overly focussed or furrowed with concentration but calm and peaceful. Paula is mesmerised by him, we all are. He can be such an annoying prick sometimes but right now every flaw of his character is forgiven for being able to do something so special and extraordinary.

He releases the final arrow, exhales slowly and lowers the bow and never before have I seen someone so perfectly composed within themselves. Except it doesn't last. Perfection can never last. With the bow lowered and no more arrows to be fired so the reality of the world comes flooding back and that subtle change spreads across his face and he twists gently to the side with a grimace, 'think I pulled something,' he mutters and the Roy we know is back.

'You left three,' Blowers says and I look round in surprise to see three still coming across the plaza.

'For the dog,' Roy says as though it's the most obvious thing in the world. Blowers makes to reply with a glare but gets cut off by Blinky bending double to vomit on the ground with a loud retching noise.

'Fuck that was good,' she says standing upright and wiping her mouth with the back of her hand, 'like totally fucking awesome.'

Nick reaches down to gently push the dog and she bounds away, streaking across the plaza and using a downed body to gain height as she leaps high and locks her jaws on the face of the first one she reaches. A vicious rag as she drops and it's done. One dead and the other two are dispatched with the same brutal efficiency and as the last one is killed so she turns round and starts working through the corpses to kill the crawlers.

'Know what,' I announce proudly, 'that was our first attack. The first time we've gone after them...all went rather well if I say so myself.'

'Very good,' Clarence booms with a grin as he looks round the plaza, 'happy with that.'

'Bit weird they were all lying down though,' Paula says thoughtfully, 'but having said that we've still killed a couple of hundred by the looks of it.'

'And it's still early,' I reply, 'this could be a good day. Where we going next? Anyone got any suggestions or are we doing the random thing?'

'Next town?' Clarence suggests as he replaces his magazine, 'might as well.'

'That's not random,' Paula says, 'and we'll get caught out if we do it like that.'

'Okay then, we go straight through the next town and attack the one after that,' I say, 'then we find another one like that and eventually come back for the ones we didn't do.'

'Perfect,' Clarence says.

'Everyone happy?' I look round at the faces all nodding amiably, 'Reginald still in Roy's van?'

'He is,' Marcy says with a frown.

'Ah, leave him alone. He can stay there if he wants. Load up and we'll move out.'

'Water,' Dave says dully, 'you are all losing fluids in this humidity. Take water on now.'

'You heard the man,' I say cheerily, 'I think we should have some music on the way to the next one, Cookey? Care to sort us out?'

CHAPTER EIGHT

H e frets but then he's always fretted. He worries too, but then he's always worried. He's scared and that would also be quite normal if the type of fear he was feeling was the same type of fear he used to feel, only it isn't. This is a different fear and one that is steadily growing into a consuming terror and just when he thinks the pinnacle of fear has been reached it gets worse and stronger and deeper until his stomach tightens into a ball of knots that flips and sinks.

His hands tremble. His knees knock together. Eyes darting from left to right, up and down. He rubs the back of his neck then his face as his body desperately tries to ease the tension. Constantly adjusting position and twitching at the uncomfortable sensation of the clothes he is so unused to wearing and his hands keep straying to the base of his neck to adjust and fiddle with the tie knot that isn't there.

He takes his glasses off and wipes the lenses before patting his sweaty face. The inside of the van is cooler than outside and Roy was nice enough to run the air conditioning but now with the van stationary the air conditioning has shut off and the temperature is creeping up.

It was different when he was turned. His natural fear of everything was still there but it was suppressed to a much lesser degree, and the control exerted over his mind was more powerful than the unique characteristics that made Reginald the person he was.

He should feel angry and embittered against Marcy for turning him and for everything that happened after but that same intellect that he prides himself on also makes the connection of knowledge that it was the infection working through Marcy. Marcy was the manifestation of the virus and not the cause. She was as much a tool as he was, as Darren was, as they all are. The infection is a hive mind of collective intelligence and it's that fact that strikes the greatest fear in Reginald. Howie can kill them now but that collective intelligence is growing by the day.

The human mind is a powerful instrument of evolution and still in its infancy of growth. The exceptional will become the norm and that excellence will continue to forge a path into the future until their race reaches the whole point of existence. What one can do all can do, they just don't know how to yet. Terrence Tao was formally recognised as the most intelligent person in the world with an IQ of two hundred and thirty in comparison to an average of one hundred and fifteen. Reginald knows that, given time, mankind would evolve to an average of two hundred and thirty and the exceptional will still be leaps ahead, but that would take time, hundreds of years. The rate the infection has shown is equivalent to a caveman becoming a tax inspector within a week and if that growth continues how long will it be until the tax inspector becomes Terrence Tao? What then? Howie can fight human forms but he cannot fight something he cannot understand, something that can outthink his every move.

He watches the monitor on the desk in the rear of the armoured transit van and that gnawing growing fear increases again. The cameras fitted in the light clusters give a commanding view of the plaza and of the bodies all lying prone and that connection that takes the team so many minutes to make is made almost instantly by Reginald. They are pretending. They are not dead but pretending. A clumsy, paltry and stupid thing to do but an act that, in the manner of what it represents, is wholly frightening. The infection has taken hundreds of host bodies and rather than attacking full on it has made them hide in plain sight. Play dead. A trick used by prey and predator alike. Bait. Lure the victim. An idea formed and executed and one that shows that the infection can grasp complex trains of thought.

He rubs his face at the danger being presented and the time it takes for the team to realise the trick seems to stretch for eons until Charlie makes the connection then all eyes are down and Roy starts firing his arrows into them. Whimpering into his hand Reginald watches as Howie fires first followed by everyone else and suddenly the air is once again filled with the thunderous roar of assault rifles that is soon matched by the howl of the undead as they rise and charge.

Every shot seems to invoke a wince. Every step closer the undead take seems to increase that fear and then it's over

and the silence that follows is broken by the raucous voices of the team celebrating a false victory.

Don't they know what's happening? Don't they realise the folly of their actions? Ignoring the next town to attack the one after is not a random selection. It is a choice made by the human mind which the infection is learning to understand and this, this hamfisted attempt at trickery by playing dead is laughable now but what it represents is terrifying in suggestion.

'...and it was a good start but what on earth were they doing?' Paula says getting into the front of the vehicle mid-conversation with Roy.

'Doing? I don't think they were doing anything,' Roy replies.

'Playing dead? Like that would fool us,' she scoffs with a glance at the mangled bodies in the plaza, 'Reginald, are you okay?' She twists round in her seat to look through the open access door to the rear, 'you must be hot in there, we'll put the air-con on...Roy, can you put the air-con on for Reginald, he looks very hot.'

'Will do,' Roy says obligingly, 'did you watch through the cameras, Reginald?'

'Yes, yes I did.'

'It's a top system they've put in here, the cameras must be wide angled lenses and high definition too.'

'Yes, yes very clear.'

'They were playing dead.'

'Yes, I saw that,' Reginald says politely.

'God knows what that was all about but Howie's plan is working so far...I think we must have killed a couple of hundred right there.'

'Indeed.'

'Well, we're skipping the next town and hitting the one after that...to keep it random.'

'Yes, indeed. I heard that.'

'Oh did you. I wasn't sure if you heard it and I wanted to keep you in the loop.'

'Thank you, Roy but...' Reginald falters, he was about to say it, to voice his concerns but what's the point? He can't fight. He can't shoot or wield an axe or stab with a knife. What right does he have to play a part in the decision making process.

'But what?' Paula asks in that overly kind voice that sends a ripple of irritation through Reginald at the perception of being patronised and treated like a child.

'Nothing,' he says keeping his tone polite and clipped.

'Sure?'

'Yes, yes I am sure, thank you, Paula.'

'Okay, do you want some water?'

'I er...I have water, thank you, Paula.'

'Make sure you drink plenty, it's so hot and humid today. Are you hungry?'

'No, not hungry. Thank you, Paula.'

'If you need anything just say.'

'Of course, indeed. Yes, yes I will be sure to say something.'

She turns away as Roy pulls the vehicle into the slipstream of the Saxon as they navigate the roads out of the town and back onto the main road towards the next. He thinks back to the morning and the map laid out on the table. Every symbol on the map represented a defining feature of the landscape. A town. A forest. A road. A lake. A village. The coast line. The gradient of the land. Campsites. Rivers. Streams. Footpaths. Bridleways. Map reading is a science, not an art. Maps are made by experts devoted to their profession and the fact the rest of the group paid such little attention to the map is staggeringly incompetent to Reginald. Every choice, every decision could mean the end to their lives. What kind of planning was it to glance at a map and stab the end of your finger at green and grey splodges and work out the future of mankind from that?

What scale was the map? A scale of 1:50000 would mean each centimetre on the map represents 500 metres in real life which does not leave a lot of space for the finer and finite details to be shown. Clarence was in the army, Dave too. Why didn't they pay attention to those facts? They must have studied map reading as part of their training, surely? No. They were soldiers and effectively they are the modern day equivalent to the enlisted man, the generalised infantry sent to do the dirty work at the front line. The officers would be the ones taught to make sure of the scale maps and work out the defining features of the locality to assist and aid in their campaigns.

Oh god. What were they doing? What were they thinking? The first town attacked would always have been a safe venture, well, as safe a venture as attacking hordes of deranged virus riddled monsters could be. The second will also be a safe venture. Howie's fighting skills and his ability to kill and walk away unscathed will see him and the rest through. The third might be lucky but by the fourth, the fifth...maybe the sixth they'll be outwitted, outmanoeuvred and out-planned.

Why didn't they bring the maps with them? Did they bring the maps with them? He turns round ready to call out the question to Roy and Paula in the front then stops before any sounds can be uttered. Who is he to ask for maps? He plays no part in this group but is merely tagging along as, for the present, it is far safer to be with them than without them. That, however, will end very soon. That safety will be over within a few hours.

His hands tremble as his body floods with fear inducing chemicals. It's like his blood is running cold in his veins. Like his stomach is flipping and churning. It's so hot in here too, oppressive and sticky. His hands go to adjust his tie knot that isn't there anymore. On the monitor he watches the quadrant split screen display from the cameras fitted on all four corners of the vehicle. Water spraying against the front from the flooded roads and deep puddles they power through. The Saxon glimpsed through the streaks in front of them. At the rear the wake left and the sides of the road, hedges, lanes and trees.

'*Next town coming up,*' Marcy's amplified voice fills the air.

'Are we still going through?' Roy asks Paula, 'ask Marcy to ask Howie if we're still going through to the next town.'

'*Marcy...*'

'No names!'

'Oh for god's sake, Roy. I don't think it makes any difference now.'

'But they could be listening to us.'

'And what if they are? They don't know where we are or what we're doing...*Marcy, Are we still going straight through to the next town?*'

'Now they know we're going straight through this town,' Roy says with a groan, 'you're giving our plan away.'

'I am not giving our plan away, Roy. They don't know what town we are at or...'

'Of course they do! They saw us leave the last town and could be watching us right now.'

'Then what....'

'Paula, Howie said yes.'

'Then what should I have said?' Paula asks Roy.

'You should have just asked if we were sticking to the original plan?'

'Right, yes but you asked me to ask if we were going straight through the next town so I just repeated what you asked me to say...'

'Paula? You there?'

'Yes still here, straight through. Got it.'

Roy was right. It could be listening and it could have seen the direction they took and it could be watching them right now. All it would take would be to place individuals in key places on the main routes to monitor the roads. Again Reginald forces himself to suppress his natural instinct of saying something with the belief that he doesn't belong here and therefore has no right to impart his views.

Through the monitor he watches the town come into view as Paula and Roy descend into a bickering match over what should have been said and the fact that Roy told Paula to say something and she just did as asked and Roy saying that Paula should not have taken it literally. Their voices fade into the background noise of the engine and the tyres on the surface of the road. Of water being sprayed and the view on the monitors. Streets and junctions that go past. Houses and shops. Cars parked up and signs of storm damage and looting everywhere. Bodies too. Dead and decomposing and either slumped in festering mounds or floating in the murky flood water which is exactly what they will all be by the end of this day, well the ones that cannot be turned that is. Howie, Blowers, Cookey, Marcy and himself for sure. The rest will be bitten and if they don't turn they will be torn limb from limb. Why did he turn then turn back? Howie is right, Marcy is the key to that. It was Marcy that turned him and the variant of the virus that she passed that infected Reginald. That variant was different to the main as it turned them and now it is going. Similar to Lani who was turned but recovered then eventually succumbed. Which also means that Lani did not rid her own body of the infection but carried it, which in turn means by default that he and Marcy and both carriers and could also succumb. That thought extrapolates as he once more thinks through the whole of the sequence of events. Howie will be a carrier. Blowers and Cookey and Reginald determines that more members of this group will also show immunity while still being carriers.

That train of thought shifts gear until he's back at the same question that continues to dog his mind. Why are they together? How does a group of seemingly unconnected people find each other and gain that connection while being in an apparent very low percentage of the population that is immune to the virus. Why them? Why did they find each other?

Science is one thing. The science of the infection. The virology of the transmission and the way it affects each person. It's different to anything ever known but yet not totally alien. There are plenty of viruses that act as parasitical entities in the way they infect a host body, and science could ultimately show how a virus could gain a conscious and awareness of life. What science cannot answer is how the bloody hell a bunch of crazy strangers all find each other amidst the carnage of the world falling apart, unless of course, that is a random act and one of them is the primary host for the variant gene within the infection that causes them to be immune.

The scenery passing by on the monitor causes an almost trance-like state that eases the troubles in his mind to allow the natural thought processes to flourish and meander. So many problems, so many things he thinks about but with the drone of the engine and the low voices of Paula and Roy in the background and the live feed on the monitor all working together so his mind starts to prioritise them into matters of urgency and the first priority is staying alive. Which will end if Howie continues on this same course of conduct.

'Paula, it looks like we're coming up to something...'

Marcy's voice filling the van and it jars him back to the present. The second township is coming up.

'Looks like a village,' Marcy adds, *'we're slowing down...Howie said to shout if you see any movement.'*

'Yep, will do,' Paula replies, 'Reginald, can you watch the monitor for movement.'

'Indeed I will,' Reginald says quickly, too quickly.

'Are you sure you're okay?' Paula asks leaning round to stare into the back.

'Yes fine,' Reginald says trying to give a tight smile, 'all good back here,' he adds with a nonchalant wave followed by a nonchalant nod and instantly curses himself for the strange look he gets in return.

On the monitor he stares blankly at the village coming into view. A main road running through a selection of tea gardens complete with thatched roofs and olde worlde signs displaying hand-crafted teddy bears and dolls. A chintzy craft village of stereotypical wares being peddled under the guise of everything being homemade and the mere suggestion makes Reginald lean away from the monitor as though the tiny increase in distance might prevent the tackiness from touching him. Homemade? Who wants homemade? Reginald certainly doesn't want anything homemade. Reginald hates anything with the label homemade. Goods should be designed, crafted and engineered by professionals in a professional workplace, not some overweight stay at home mum with a penchant for jams and keeping bees with her brood of snotty nosed children poking their bogey covered fingers into every bowl and jar. God no! The thought of it makes him wince and groan in disgust and Teddy Bears? They should be made in factories by persons presented by a union and paid a decent wage with healthcare benefits, not knocked up by some doddery old codger from the WI with a needle and thread. And who has thatched cottages these days? The whole ambience is one of a trite play on the senses that somehow, because the wares are made by bogey covered children and half-blind WI women under thatched roofs that it's all more innocent and clean.

Thatched cottages are not renowned for their energy conservation and are no match for modern materials constructed by professionals. The energy bills must have been huge and they probably all run off coal and log burners which only add to the gases pumped into the environment let alone the whole argument of fossil fuels being depleted but hey, it's okay because everything is homemade so just ignore the fact the wood is probably stolen by some little oik running about with a chainsaw.

'*Oh it does,*' Marcy's voice fills the van in reply to a comment made by Paula, '*it looks so...so...what's the word? Yes twee! Charlie said it looks twee...*'

And what on earth is happening to Marcy? She has gone from a woman possessed with a belief of changing the world by showing what the infection can be used for to running about in Howie's shadow shouting that everything looks twee. Yes, admittedly, Marcy was also once a genocidal maniac tearing whole streets apart with a blood lust that would make Genghis Khan vomit but nevertheless, she was a somebody doing an important thing and it was those experiences that shaped her into the woman he chose to follow even when their bodies were purging the infection. Even when his mind became wholly his own again he chose to stay with Marcy as she was driven full of determination to use those same experiences and herself for that matter, to rid the infection as it has become to be known. Leaving Marcy was just not an option.

Oh god they're here, wherever here is. The vehicles have stopped and everyone is piling out with their weapons held up and aimed ready. Reginald watches them on the monitor. At the way they all move and scan the area, at the supreme confidence they exude. Even the two new girls, Charlie and Blinky, or Patricia as Dave so rightly refers to her, even they now match the others in the way they step and turn. They do look good. That is without question. They look tough and capable and if Reginald were trapped in a bad place it would be exactly people like this he would want coming to rescue him. Even that monstrous dog behaves differently to any dog Reginald has ever known. Not that he has known many dogs. Filthy things always licking their own orifices and defecating in public, and they always seem to sense his fear of them too which in turn makes them suspicious of him which in turn makes him more fearful of them.

The ever running monologue of Reginald's thoughts end abruptly as, on the monitor, he watches the first of the infected run from the nearby houses. Shouts are given and shots are fired.

With a commanding view of all four corners, Reginald tracks the entry points as they appear in ones and twos running from doors, buildings, vaulting low walls, navigating tight turns and running flat out to their certain death.

Two from the left and through the maelstrom of noise Reginald matches the sounds of their voices to the image seen on the display. A man and woman both old and frail but running as though they were teenagers. A few seconds later and another two from further up come bursting out into the street. The other side of the road, two more and a few seconds later another one appears.

He leans forward staring intently at the figures as they appear and then get gunned down. There's not enough of them to even suggest a threat to Howie and the group but seemingly the noise of the firefight draws more, but...but no. Something. What? He scans the four images and for the first time the gunshots outside don't make him wince. He is absorbed with a prickling notion of some-thing...something not right. Yes! That's it. It *seems* as though the noise of the firefight is drawing them out but it looks staged. The infected always mass together either in big hordes or smaller groups. These are all separated into couples or singles and coming from all different direction but actually from the same two primary sources. There is only one main road through this village and the buildings on either side pretty much form the whole of the village. Why would they be separated and split on both sides of the road? They wouldn't be. They have been prepared and were waiting. Yes, yes that's right. The more he thinks it the more apparent and obvious it becomes.

Are they probing? If not probing then what is the purpose? An old man running from the same garden that two came from a few minutes ago. Now two more old people from two gardens up from the last entry point. All of them being gunned down and shot to bits by the staggering fire rate of the assault rifles outside. Voices shouting *magazine* and orders given to watch this side, look up to the top, two more coming from that direction.

Then it's over and the last one falls as Meredith is released to hunt through the bodies for any that still live or make noise.

What does it mean? What is the reason? Maybe this was the organic positions of the infected persons at the point of arrival by the two vehicles but that goes against everything they have encountered so far. Reginald was never turned in the true sense of the meaning but he was present enough to know they have an instinct to gather and mass collectively so that reason can be instantly discounted. What else? Probing? No. That does not seem right. The infection knows how many they have and what weapons they use. There would be no reason or objective gained by doing that. The infection will know the inside leg measurement of every person within this group by now, including that bloody dog.

No. There must be another reason. *Think Reginald think, use the intelligence you were gifted with and think.* Perhaps it was staged solely for the appearance of the event. Would it do that? It certainly looked staged. Almost as though Howie was turning up and the infection *had* to provide some baddies to kill so it threw them out in little groups to give Howie something to shoot at. A ridiculous notion and it makes Reginald snort quietly with a minute shake of his head as the idea is disregarded as quickly as it was formed.

No. There was a reason but...or maybe there wasn't. Maybe they were just chasing some other survivor and they ended up all over the place just as the two vans arrived. No conspiracy, no reason, just a natural order of events based on a myriad of variables too vast to calculate, and anyway, what would he gain from even thinking it was staged? He's not part of this group but tagging along, an observer, a coward hiding in the back of an armoured van and letting those more capable defend his life and liberty.

Oh come on, Reginald. You know it was staged. You had a completely different view to those engaged in the combat. Listen to them now cheering and guessing at how many bodies they culled. Lighting cigarettes and talking about finding more blasted coffee. They were doing the actual killing and the reason you want to see something strange is so you can be a part of the group to self-justify the reason for your presence. He leans back and tries to adjust the tie knot that isn't there before huffing with frustration. Hot again with the air conditioning off. Should he have some water? If he drinks more water he will need a toilet break before too long and the last thing he wants to do is ask for a toilet break and be subjected to urinating in front of the other men.

It was staged. He leans forward and stares at the monitor again while that idea, that silly notion of the infection sending them out so Howie would have something to shoot at refuses to go away. Perhaps that exact idea is silly but still, it certainly did appear like that. In the town where they found this armoured van Howie was shouting at the infected person that they were going to the next town and when they arrived the infected persons were all lying down. Then they skipped a town to hit the next one along, in this case the chintzy *homemade sickeningly sweet bogey filled jam jar* awful thatched tea garden village.

'Next?' The unmistakable tones of Clarence from outside and

this time, instead of fretting into his hands, Reginald pays attention and stares at the sealed rear door.

'Dunno,' Howie says, 'where you reckon? Did anyone bring that map? Paula? You're in charge of shit like that.'

'Me? I'm the personnel manager. One of the army blokes should have brought the map.'

'Ah well, sod it. We'd only look at the green and grey splodges anyway. Well, we can go back to that one we went through or...'

'It was very flooded,' Roy interrupts, 'the one we went through I mean.'

'Yeah that's true,' Howie says wistfully and no doubt drawing on his cigarette. Reginald checks the monitor and nods in satisfaction at seeing Howie inhaling, 'so...er...miss one again? Everyone up for that?'

God no. That's the worst thing to do. That is not a plan but leap-frogging and something a child could work out.

'Yeah why not,' one of the lads says, Blowers maybe?

'Isn't that a bit samey?' Paula asks as Reginald breathes a sigh of relief.

'Only because we know we're doing it,' Marcy says as Reginald goes back into panic mode, 'samey to us but will it work out the plan that quickly?'

Yes. Yes it will. God yes it will. Somebody say something.

'Yeah fine,' Paula says, 'I'm not bothered...can we stop for a break after the next one though. This heat is so draining.'

'Isn't it,' Charlie says in reply, 'I can't stop sweating.'

'My knickers keep going up my arse crack,' Blinky informs the group.

He should say something. Interrupt them before they make the decision and move out. They are pumped up from the fight and not thinking clearly but, but he can't say anything. It was yesterday that did it. In that blasted village of Finkton and having to run for miles and miles then cower on the stairs while everyone else did the fighting. Completely out of his depth and therefore the exclusion of capability extends to the self-imposed social exclusion also and the firm belief that he is not one of them, therefore he has no right to say anything and his already depleting pride does not wish to be damaged any further. Oh they would listen, he knows they would, but they would do it with overly earnest expressions and soft patronising voices before choosing to do what they want anyway.

Maybe he could stay here? This village has just been cleansed of the infected. He could find a nice pretty thatched cottage and use the fossil fuel burners to stay warm while eating the bogey infested jams and spreads. An absurd idea and Reginald knows full well that he would perish from fright during the first period of darkness. He is not a man to be alone, but then staying with this group means certain death. What to do? The turmoil of the situation frays the edges of his already frayed nerves and he sinks once again into a state of twitches, trembles and trying to adjust the tie knot that isn't there.

The chatter outside ends as the group disperse back to their chosen vehicles with the promise of a coffee break after the next attack. Listening to the cheery calls and confidence only serves to magnify the conflict within him and give water to the seed of doubt that he is wrong. Except he isn't wrong. He can't be wrong. Maybe he is wrong. Is he wrong? *Am I wrong? I mean they've fought battles ever since this began and they've only got stronger and faster. Maybe this is the right thing to do and the fears I am feeling are justified but not necessary. Howie is no fool. Clarence is highly experienced and Dave is an exceptional human being, they are all exceptional human beings so yes, I am being fretful for the sake of it.*

For a few minutes he works hard to settle the anxiety and closing his eyes he draws a long breath in through his nose before slowly exhaling from his mouth. Breathe in. Breathe out. *Everything is fine.* Breathe in. Breathe out. *Howie knows what he is doing.* Inhale. Exhale. *I am always anxious and my current anxious state is a by-product of the extreme events we are experiencing.*

These people are protecting my life and for that I should be thankful and do what little I can. I will watch the monitors and try my hardest not to be so cowardly.

His heart rate eases. The immediacy of the panic abates just enough for him to open his eyes and look to the monitor. Roy and Paula in the front chatting animatedly and the air temperature starts to reduce with the beautiful cooling air blowing into the back. *Everything is fine. Everything is fine. They know what they are doing and the derring-do attitude they display is what has kept them alive for so long. That daring confrontational aggression and fortune favours the brave, but then fools rush in where angels fear to tread. Ah but if there were no fools there would be no wise men. Yes that is true but they have the courage of their convictions and the only thing to fear is fear itself and these people really know what they are doing but then a little knowledge is a dangerous thing and you don't know what you don't know. They think they are being random but the predictability is clear within the path they have chosen.*

'Reginald, are you okay?'

The question snaps his head up as he twists round to face Paula leaning through the doorway.

'Reginald?' She asks again with that concern dripping from her voice.

'Fine,' he says curtly, 'I am fine. Thank you.'

'Well okay,' she says as though clearly not believing he is okay, 'one more then we're stopping for a break.'

'Great, yes that will be great.'

One more? There won't be a one more. This could be it. The last one. Howie told the infected in the first town they were going to the next town and that gave direction and intent to the infection. Then they only killed what they could see immediately in front of them so one left alive somewhere would also give direction and intent. They skipped one and hit the last place giving not only the direction and intent but the pattern of application too. If Reginald were the infection he would be working out the pattern and making ready.

What would I do if I was the infection? I would wait and see which town they hit next and let the kills happen naturally. I'd cement the confidence within the group and let them think that they are achieving what they set out to achieve. I would perhaps show some elements of desperation to make it look normal but behind that façade I would be planning to meet the next attack by using my collective knowledge of the vicinity, geographical knowledge and awareness of physical features given to me by that same collective knowledge. What exactly I would do is wholly dependent on the landscape of the vicinity to be used. Alas though, I am not the infection but instead a frightened small man wearing ridiculously ill-fitting clothing designed for people that have broad shoulders and muscles. My body is soft and not designed for such things. It is my brain that has always been my most powerful muscle.

A housing estate appears on the monitor complete with an enormous sign board displaying an image of executive style two, three and four bedroom detached houses built to the highest standard to suit your growing family needs. Ubiquitous red brick with stylised windows and slate roofs and an invitation to view the show home now before it's too late. *It is too late. It is too late for everything.*

With the housing estate counting as the next centre of habitation they barrel on in the mini convoy of armoured personnel carrier and armoured cash in transit van through the rapidly receding and evaporating floods on the roads. Past fields resplendent with sheets of glistening water lying tranquil and serene. Past forests of trees looking gorgeously green from the deluge of life giving water and now standing tall to reach the golden rays of the sun. Birds swoop through the air catching flying insects, calling out with birdsong. Seagulls cry and land in the deeper floods so happy in this new landscape. Life outside the vehicles goes on and already the air is clearer as the pollution levels reduce.

Life inside the Saxon is confident with Howie laughing and sharing jokes with Marcy and the others. Weapons being checked. Conversations going on with faces glowing from the heat of the day. In the front of the second van Paula and Roy talk quietly, sharing observations and enjoying the company of the other.

Life in the back of the second vehicle in the mini convoy is fraught and tense with Reginald furiously thinking if getting to this next town would give the infection enough time to arrange a nasty surprise. Surely not. Surely it has only been a few minutes since the thatched village.

'*Ladies and gentleman this is your tour guide speaking, up ahead we have the town of Foxwood...Foxwood...the town of Foxwood lies just ahead...this was the scene of a famous battle fought by the glorious leader Howie and his intrepid group of survivors...*' Marcy's voice strong and proud and amplified through the speakers, '*...an interesting fact of the history of Howie and his intrepid group, and one that is not recorded in the history books, is that although Mr Howie was known to be the leader it was in fact the women of the group that were in charge as the men were completely incompetent and...*' Howie's voice in the background protesting. The deep voice of Clarence also calling out while Charlie, Blinky and Paula all cheer noisily. '*Anyway, Foxwood is ahead... Roy and Paula would you care to follow us in so we can get this done and stop somewhere for a nice coffee?*'

'*Sounds lovely,*' Paula replies through the radio, 'oh hello,' she says in surprise at Reginald hovering by the open door to stare out the front windscreen, 'you okay?'

'Hmm? Yes, yes fine. Just getting a better view of...of the er...of the landscape...' Reginald says staring ahead at the back of the Saxon and wishing they were in front so he could gain a better view of the town as it appears. High hedgerows on both sides and they pass a narrow junction to a road running between fields of pasture and grazing land. Through the gaps in the hedges and using the rise of the road as it lifts up he spots the roofs of the town ahead and to the right. The road they are on is a main A road and if the town is off to one side then this road will run straight across the left hand edge of the town and straight out the other side. Yes, there's the road now running straight on. Must be a Roman road built thousands of years ago by gifted engineers wishing to have a straight route from garrison to garrison. They will have to deviate from the main road *into* the town to seek whatever infected might be there.

Too many variables to factor into the thought processes. Would the infection count the housing estate as a place of habitation? Would it therefore count this township as the next one to be hit? And if the town lies off the Roman road then it will be very old and full of twisting lanes and streets built round the existing dwellings and buildings. Another crest and he catches sight of a woods on the far side. Densely packed trees in the distance and no doubt the landscape feature that gave the name to the town. With the woods in view he gains an idea of the size of the town and unless there are any smaller tracks or country roads leading through the woods then it means this A road is the only way in and therefore the only way out.

'Reginald!'

'Pardon?' Reginald blinks at his name being called so sharply.

'I said are you sure you're okay?' Paula stares hard at him with her assault rifle lifted onto her lap and her bag already on her back. When did she put that on? Was it already on?

'You were miles away,' Roy observes with a glance up back to Reginald.

'Yes, yes indeed,' Reginald blinks and swallows with nerves.

'*Paula? The main road runs past the town...junction ahead which we'll take and Howie thinks we'll be straight in the town. It doesn't look very big.*'

'*Yep got it,*' Paula says into the handset.

'There it is,' Roy says leaning to the right to see the junction ahead of the Saxon, 'Is my rifle there?'

'Got it and it's all ready too with a fresh magazine and I've put new ones in your bag and wiped the blood from your arrows...'

'I wiped them,' Roy says with a look down at his bag being made ready.

'Not very well,' Paula says as they turn into the junction after the Saxon.

Reginald moves back to his desk and the monitor with frustration at not been able to see the road ahead or the layout of the town. He needs a map or access to the internet. Maybe a camera fitted on a high pole on the roof that he can turn and gain a birds eye view. A drone. An aircraft. A helicopter but more than anything a bloody map. What's ahead? Where is the centre of the town? What roads leads from it and where do those roads go? *This is impossible. These blasted fools could be rushing into a fatal mistake. Say something. Tell them to stop and get out now while they still have a chance.*

Yet the layers of fear that run so deep to his core prevent him from speaking out. Fear at looking stupid. Concern that he will be wrong. Worry that they'll ignore him and the ever present worry that he does not belong, contributes nothing and does not have the right to intervene. The same thoughts swim in the emotional responses as his brain yearns for more information and seeks to counter what moves will be made by the other player.

The other player? He sits bolt upright aghast at the thought. This is life and death not a gentle game of chess being played at the local club, although he was always really very good at chess. A good mathematician and able to not only predict the moves made by the opponent in accordance with that character and mannerisms of that person but also a thorough understanding of strategy. It was the same when he played Dungeons and Dragons years ago. Read the opponent, read their predictability and know what they will do.

The vans stop. Doors open and no speaking now as the tension of the situation mounts and Reginald stares hard at the monitor cursing Roy for the poor parking position. Too close to the Saxon and at an angle so only the driver side rear camera shows any view and that's just a glimpse of a building line. How can he possibly be expected to counter the moves of the other player if he can't see the board?

Turning slowly he stares at the hatch leading to the front cabin. There's no firing yet so they haven't seen anything awful. If he stays close he can pop out, have a look then run back into the safety of the vehicle. Yes. A quick look to get an idea of the layout and then back inside. Damn it! If only he had some paper to sketch a quick street map, but no, that wouldn't help as he'd only be able to sketch what he could see in the immediate vicinity and he knows his memory is absurdly good at recalling things like that.

He scuttles across to the cabin, climbs through and out the driver's door into a wall of heat that makes him sway on the spot with eyes squinting at the harsh glare of the sun. My god this is like jungle heat, so humid. Thank goodness he isn't carrying a heavy rifle and a bag full of heavy magazines and equipment.

With his hands shielding his eyes he lets his vision adjust to the glare with the closer features coming into focus first. In the middle of an old High Street with an array of shops and stores stretching off on the right into the near distance. Junctions everywhere. Alleys and paths leading between the buildings. Down and to the left a grassy area complete with a gravel circle surrounding a large pond bulging from the excess water of the last day or so. The ground has mostly dried out. Some puddles here and there but rapidly shrinking. Some signs of looting and a rotting corpse lying on the pavement outside the broken window of a mini-supermarket.

'Have you seen them?' He asks walking towards the group ranged round in a rough circle with rifles raised and ready. So intent on scouring the view around him and he doesn't spot the heart bumping jolt the group display at the sudden voice so unexpectedly calling out.

'Fuck me,' Cookey mutters turning back to his assigned section.

'Reginald?' Marcy asks in surprise, 'what the...'

'Have you seen them?' Reginald asks again.

'No but why are you out of the...'

'What about that dog,' Reginald asks peering through the group to spot Meredith sniffing the ground, 'has she shown a reaction?'

'No, mate,' Howie says, 'not yet anyway...what's up?'

'Up?' Reginald asks with a plummeting sensation at every head turning to look at him, 'I er...I wanted to er...' he looks round more gingerly now. The pond has two paths leading into it from the other side and what looks like a playing fields further away. Further down the road are more shops, buildings and houses. Some cars parked up. On the right side are two narrower side streets leading into this road but the buildings are high which reduce the view down them from this angle. 'Has anyone checked down there?' He asks motioning towards the closest side street opening, 'what about that one?' He points further up the road, 'and over there...where do those paths go? The ones behind the pond?'

'Er, we just got here, Reggie,' Howie says.

'Reginald,' Reginald says automatically.

'Reggie, what are you doing?' Marcy demands.

'Do you need the toilet?' Paula asks, 'do you want someone to go with you?'

'No I bloody do not want anyone to go with me for the toilet. I am an adult not a child!'

'Reginald!'

'What, Marcy? I am more than capable of expressing a desire to urinate should the need arise.'

'Sorry, Reginald. I was only asking...'

Reginald turns slowly in a circle staring back up the road they came down and up at the windows of the buildings. Nothing here. There's nothing here. What does that mean? Maybe it did not count the housing estate as a town so therefore this is not the natural next target as this would be the one that should be missed out. Yes, that's possible.

'Reginald?' Marcy snaps, 'what the hell are you doing?'

'Shush,' Reginald waves a hand at her while still slowly turning. Or time? Perhaps there wasn't enough time for the infection to draw host bodies into this place. They are off the main road and maybe the infection has already taken everyone from this town to be used somewhere else…That's it.

He spins back to the group and Marcy glaring at him.

'Reggie,' Clarence says in his low rumbling voice, 'you okay, mate?'

Which way? If they were here and the infection discounted this town then it could have already drawn them to the next town but which way would they go? The road they came in on is here and that leads up to the main road that runs left to right. They came from the left and when they leave they will be heading towards the right which is in that direction…

'You're worrying me now? Are you sick?' Marcy walks towards him with genuine care in her voice.

He waves a hand with irritation on his face, 'please!' He barks, 'just be quiet.' Yes. Yes that's right. The woods are behind the town and open farmland on the side they came in on. So they would head to the side where the duck pond is.

'I need that dog,' he turns abruptly and strides past a dumbfounded Marcy and into the centre of the gun wielding circle, 'come with me,' he says to Meredith and steps away towards the duck pond then stops and looks back, 'come with me,' he says again, 'dog…come with me…'

'Reginald?' Marcy asks again as everyone else just stares at him.

'Can someone make that dog please come with me.'

'For what?' Howie asks.

'To sniff,' Reginald says as though the answer is obvious, 'she can smell them...I think they went that way,' he adds pointing to the duck pond.

'You what?' Howie asks lowering his rifle and taking a step closer.

'They went that way...I think they went that way...I'm not sure if they went that way and I need the dog to tell me or show me or... or do whatever it is she does to see if they went that way...'

'You had enough water today, Reggie?'

'Yes! I have had water,' Reginald snaps not looking at Cookey, 'and I do not need a toilet break and...how do I make the dog work?'

'Reggie,' Howie says patiently, 'what makes you think they went that way?'

'Please!' Reginald groans with exasperation, 'I want to see if they went that way but...how can I tell if they went that way?'

'Dave, Clarence and Nick with me...everyone else stay here and keep your eyes up...go on then, mate,' Howie says with a nod towards the pond, 'Nick, get Meredith to come with you.'

'Come on,' Nick says clicking his tongue as Meredith rushes instantly ahead of the small group breaking away.

Reginald strides ahead swamped in the ill-fitting black clothes with his glasses sliding down his sweaty nose. He turns back and steps quickly aside as Meredith bounds past him and turns to follow her, 'how do you make her sniff the ground?'

Howie glances at Clarence who shrugs and shakes his head. Nick shows the same confused expression.

'She is sniffing,' Nick calls out.

'Her nose isn't down on the ground,' Reginald shouts back.

'Yeah mate, she er...what...it doesn't work like that.'

'Work like what? She doesn't work? Can you make her work?'

'No, I mean,' Nick looks to Howie for help.

'He means,' Howie says, 'that Meredith will smell everything on the ground as she passes...if she gets a scent she's interested in she'll drop her nose and start...like that! See...she's got her nose down now.'

Metres from the path leading into the duck pond area and Meredith stops dead with her nose planted to a spot on the ground. She turns a half circle and works back into the street away from the duck pond.

'Wrong way...you're going the wrong way,' Reginald calls out, 'make her go that way,' he adds motioning towards the duck pond.

'Calm down,' Clarence says, 'what are you doing? Reginald? Tell us and we can help. STOP.'

The rough order brings Reginald to an abrupt halt and he turns with a scowl back to the three walking behind him.

'Tell us what you're thinking,' Clarence says again.

Out of the group, Reginald likes Clarence the most. Something about the size of the man, his relaxed and easy manner and the way he always takes time to talk to him.

'I think they went that way,' Reginald forces himself to speak slowly, 'and I want to know if they did go that way...and I thought the dog will track them or...or smell them or...I don't know...'

'Okay,' Howie says calmly, 'so you want to know if they went through this section? Is that right?'

'Yes!'

'Okay, Dave can you see anything?'

'I'll try,' Dave says dully with a hard glare at Reginald, 'wait here.'

'She's coming back,' Reginald says excitedly as Meredith sweeps past him with her nose to the ground as she follows a scent trail across the road and onto the gravel surrounding the pond, 'what can she smell?'

'No idea,' Howie says with a low laugh and another shake of his head, 'oh hang on...her hackles are up...'

'She's growling,' Nick says in a rush of words that has the three men lifting their weapons to face into the open area beyond the pond.

'You got something?' Blowers shouts from his position back in the road.

'Standby,' Howie shouts back.

Dave follows the dog into the gravel section and straight across to the grassy perimeter and down a gently sloping bank onto the playing fields. His rifle held steady while his eyes scan the ground ahead and to the sides. A few metres into the field and he stops to stare round then turns back to face the others, 'through here,' he says, 'maybe three or four abreast...grass is trampled down...'

'Recently?' Howie asks.

'Yes, Mr Howie. An hour or two at the most,' Dave replies.

'I knew it. I knew it,' Reginald mutters and turns to face Howie, Clarence and Nick, 'it didn't count the housing estate.'

'Er, what didn't count the what?' Howie asks.

'The infection,' Reginald says while nodding rapidly, 'it did not count the housing estate we passed as a centre of habitation.'

'Right. I don't know what that means,' Howie says.

'Ha,' Reginald claps his hands together, 'yes...yes you see...we have the start of a show of a hand. Yes...the defined parameters are showing...'

'Um, Reginald?' Howie asks slowly.

'I was right, or at least one of my options were right. Yes indeed. The other player has just shown us something we might be able to use.'

'Use? What other player? Where are they going, Reggie?'

'Reginald,' Reginald says, 'and they're going to the next town to wait for you,' he adds with another curt nod.

'How do you know that?'

'You wanted a coffee break then I suggest you do so here, although,' Reginald stops to hold a finger up, 'we are being watched as we speak.'

'What the fuck is going on?' Nick asks.

'I need a map,' Reginald says striding back past them towards the others, 'yes yes yes, we're being watched right now...there will be one, Mr Howie...somewhere near here...'

'Reggie...mate...' Howie calls out as they start jogging after him, 'slow down...what's going on?'

'Reggie?' Marcy calls out as he walks back towards them, 'what is...'

'He's fucking lost it,' Nick mutters, 'what the fuck is he on about?'

'Right, Reggie,' Howie says forcing some authority into his voice that at least brings Reginald to a stop in the middle of the main group, 'mate, how did you know they were going to the next town?'

'I've already said how I know,' Reginald says with a roll of his eyes, 'because you counted the...'

'Yeah I got that bit, I counted the housing estate as a centre of... whatever you said.'

'Habitation.'

'Yeah habitation.'

'What's he on about?' Paula asks.

'Okay, hang on,' Howie holds a hand up to keep everyone quiet, 'Reggie said he knew they were going that way...through that bit where the pond was...Dave went in and said a group had gone through in the last hour or two and Meredith was growling when she sniffed the ground...'

'So they did go that way?' Paula asks as though to clarify.

'Guess so,' Howie says shrugging, 'and then Reggie said it was something to do with the housing estate...'

'What housing estate?' Cookey asks.

'I came from an estate, d'you mean mine?' Mo Mo asks helpfully.

'Shush,' Reginald says with a sudden alert expression that has every rifle snapping up and everyone looking for the target, 'we can't talk here...'

'Fuck me, Reggie!' Blowers groans 'I thought you saw something...'

'They will be watching us,' Reginald says quietly and pretending not to speak by keeping his mouth as closed as possible, 'everyone act normal.'

'What the fuck?' Nick mutters again.

'Mr Howie, please...please just trust me...' Reginald says with his lips still pursed while he casually looks about the area, 'just stand everyone down as though we are moving back out and we'll find somewhere else to stop and talk.'

'Reginald, you are not making any bloody sense,' Marcy says.

'Mr Howie,' Reginald rushes the words out, 'they will be watching and listening and we've already given enough of the game away.'

The group stare round at the doors and windows, eyes scanning the intact and broken glass.

'Anyone see anything?' Howie asks quietly, 'Dave? Mo?'

'Nuffin'' Mo Mo mutters.

'Meredith is relaxed,' Nick says looking down at the dog.

'Reggie,' Howie says turning to look at the clearly very frustrated man, 'listen mate...'

'My name is Reginald and I am right! Do not say a word here...' he says locking eyes on Howie, 'they will be watching and most likely listening...what we have already said is damage enough...'

'Yeah I get that,' Howie says gently, 'but mate you're kinda not making much sense right now.'

'Right. I see,' Reginald feels the first plummet of his nerves at the awkward looks being sent his way by everyone else. Some of pity, some glaring. This is the reason he didn't speak out before. He knew they wouldn't listen. 'No, no you are right,' he says more to himself and visibly sagging on the spot, 'yes indeed, I forgot my place. Please forgive me and of course my apologies to the group for the intrusion and...'

'Pack that in,' Clarence cuts in with the sharp rebuke.

'Okay,' Howie says quietly, 'we do as Reggie says and move out. Which way are we going?'

When no one answers Reginald looks up to see every face staring at him and Howie waiting for an answer, 'you're asking me?'

'Yes. Which way?'

'Oh right. Gosh. I. Well. We need some...I would suggest we go back the way we came...'

'Okay, back the way we came it is,' Howie says glancing round at the team.

'Unless,' Reginald says holding a pointing finger up, 'I wonder...I wonder if we could find the sentry and stay here but no, no that would give the game away that we know they left one behind to watch out for us...but then...'

'Reginald,' Marcy groans.

'Shush,' Howie cuts her off with a hard look, 'let him think. Take your time, Reginald.'

'Yes yes indeed,' Reginald stares round at the immediate view, 'yes they wouldn't be expecting us to come down this road but rather to go straight past on the main road so there would be no point in placing an observer all the way down here,' he says with a look of triumph at Howie, 'we need to stop here for a refreshment break.'

Marcy clears her throat pointedly, 'Reggie, you just said we have to leave here and not say anything.'

'Yes I know but now I am considering the fact that...you see the predictability of your plan was going to be the downfall and I was right, or at least by coming here I found I was right. They will be waiting for you at the next town. Lots of them.'

'He said that a minute ago,' Howie says to the alarmed looks on the others faces, 'Reggie, I say this respectfully but you still ain't making any sense. Do you want us to stop here or move out from here?'

'Er, why are we asking Reggie that question?' Marcy asks.

'No. Yes,' Reginald says thinking furiously, 'yes we need to leave here...and continue on the same road as intended as though heading towards the next town but,' he holds that finger up again, 'we can stop for a refreshment break on the way...but not at the next town because they will be waiting for us at the next town so I suggest we stop *before* we get to the next town. A good distance from the next town and somewhere we can talk in private.'

'Fuck,' Howie says lifting his eyebrows to absorb the rush of words, 'private? What you mean me and you?'

'Pardon? No I mean us. You. All of you and me. Somewhere we can all talk in private that is not being overheard or watched.'

'Okay. So a house?' Howie asks hopefully, 'a house before we get to the next town? Is that right?'

'Yes,' Reginald nods, 'but it has to be isolated so you must check it thoroughly,' he looks to Dave, 'you must check it very thoroughly,' nervous, sweating, clearly terrified but also full of a new energy and the man obviously has something to say.

'We'll check it,' Howie says, 'everyone load up. Reggie? You staying with Roy?'

'Hmmm, yes...I need to think and get my thoughts in order. Yes. Yes I think so.'

'Right,' Howie says slowly, 'moving out then.'

A t his desk he stays quiet. Deep in thought with a hundred strands of ideas all forming to move organically through their natural cycles. Right hand resting on the surface of the desk. Left hand on his lap. Staring ahead but not seeing. Not twitching now either apart from his right foot which taps the floor in a steady rhythm that gives cadence to the speed of the thoughts, slowing when those thoughts hit walls and speeding when those walls are either beaten through or navigated round.

'I just don't like being spoken to like that,' Paula says purposefully loud enough for Reginald to hear, 'I was merely asking if he needed anything.'

'Yes I know,' Roy says trying to adopt a soothing, understanding but not patronising tone of voice which is a complex thing to do when you're tucking in tight behind a whopping great army vehicle trying to turn in the road, 'but he isn't a child, Paula.'

'Well. Just well,' Paula huffs knowing she *was* treating Reginald like a child but it was her instinct to care for the group and make sure everyone was okay and you can't fight instinct.

'Maps!' Reginald blurts, 'we need maps. Tell Mr Howie we need to get maps,' he adds rising from the chair to the hatch into the cabin, 'ordnance survey maps of the area. We need ordnance survey maps of...'

'Now?' Paula asks taking care not to speak like an adult to a child.

'Yes now,' Reginald scoffs and tuts, 'of course now, we need maps now. Tell Mr Howie to get maps. Ordnance survey maps and I will need the scales to be...

'Paula to Marcy, Reginald is saying we need to get some maps.'

'Ordnance survey maps. Tell them we need ordnance survey maps.'

'He's saying we need ordnance survey maps.'

'Okay, hang on.'

'Oh gosh no, don't tell them we need maps over the radio! What was I thinking?'

'Too late,' Paula says bluntly.

The Saxon comes to a halt in front as the rear doors burst open to reveal Dave, Blowers and the rest all leaping down and running back to the shops on the High Street. Meredith bounding to go with them.

Windows smash. Doors are forced and Reginald watches with impatience as they run into the shops one by one and then reappear empty handed before running down to the next one and finally all running back to the Saxon again empty handed.

'No maps,' Marcy reports over the radio.

'But we need maps,' Reginald points out, 'ordnance survey maps. Tell them to find some.'

'Reggie, you can't just snap your fingers like that,' Paula says turning to face him, 'they've checked the shops and they couldn't find any.'

'Reginald, it's Howie. No maps here. Are they essential?'

'Here,' Paula says handing him the handset.

'How does it work?'

'Press the button and speak into it.'

'Like this? Is this right?'

'Yep that's it, Reggie.'

'Reginald. Yes we need maps...ordnance survey maps...FOR FOOD! Yes we need the maps to make sure we know where the places are to get FOOD...er...over?'

'Why are you shouting the word food?'

'Because we need...the...maps...to...get...food...but not for any other reason...'

'Oh I get you, yep with you now, mate. Right we need maps for food...er...no maps here though...we'll find some somewhere else.'

'When?'

'I don't know but we'll find them somewhere else.'

'Where?'

'I don't know that either, Reginald.'

'Will it be soon?'

'Yes, we'll find some soon.'

'How soon?'

'As soon as possible.'

'Today?'

'Yes, today.'

'Before we stop for a refreshment break?'

'Fuck me....yes we'll find some before we stop.'

'Where from?'

'How the hell...I don't know, Reggie. We'll have to hunt round or look in the next town...'

'We cannot do that.'

'Yes I just realised as soon as I said it. Er...maybe we'll find a house with some maps? People keep maps don't they?'

'No. People use Google and satellite navigations aids. People do not use ordnance survey maps unless they have a reason for the use of an ordnance survey map such as walking, orienteering, hiking, camping and pleasure activities in the countryside at large...'

'Are you and Dave related?'

'I...pardon?'

'I mean you're the same size and...you're very similar in many *ways. Dave? Are you related to Reggie? He said he doesn't think so. And he hates being called David the way you hate being called Reggie. Maybe you are related.'*

'There is no relevancy to this issue of any form of kinship with Dave.'

'Yep, you and Dave are definitely related. Cousins maybe?'

'Really, Mr Howie. We are discussing the sourcing of ordnance survey maps which we shall need to locate as soon as possible and before we stop for a refreshment break but also without going to the next town.'

'Dave was adopted! He was. Dave you were adopted right? He was adopted. Hey maybe you're like brothers or something.'

'Can we focus on finding ordnance survey maps please?'

'Yup, will do. If we find a scientist person we'll get them to do DNA tests on you both. I bet you're related. Everyone in here thinks you must be related...apart from Dave who isn't really saying anything but then that's quite normal for Dave.'

'He's got a point,' Paula says staring at Reginald as though examining him, 'you are the same height. Dave is a lot slimmer and muscular than you but...'

'I am not fat.'

'Eh?'

'I never said fat I just said Dave was slimmer and more muscular.'

'Therefore implying I am fat. I am not fat. I am not toned I grant you that but...perhaps I carry some extra weight around my mid-section but I can assure you I am not a gluttonous slob.'

'Reggie, are you talking to Paula? You're pressing the button.'

'There really is a lot of similarities though,' Paula muses, 'Roy? Don't you think?'

'I don't care. Are we going now?'

'What's got into you?'

'Nothing, but we're wasting time and I would like a coffee.'

'Someone's getting grumpy.'

'Howie to Reginald, is it okay to go back to that village we were in? The one with the thatched roofs? They'll more than likely have maps there and we can get a coffee and have a break...plus we killed everything there...'

'Yes I think that will be fine but we must...must...be sure of the er...of the safety...of the er...we really should take great care in ensuring the chosen location for our refreshment break is a place that is er...that is not inhabited by er...'

'Don't worry, we'll check it thoroughly. We'll get your cousin to do it.'

'Dave is not my cousin but yes, if Dave could check it thoroughly then it would be er...beneficial to our er...current situation in that we can er...enjoy our refreshment break without fear of er... being attacked or disturbed...'

'Righto. Roy, we're going back to the thatched village.'

'I do feel somewhat grumpy,' Roy says as he tucks in behind the Saxon.

'You sound it,' Paula replies stretching her legs out and sighing, 'blood sugar.'

'What?'

'Your blood sugar has gone down. You need a drink or something.'

'What? Oh my God...'

'What? Oh, Roy. I didn't mean it like that...'

'I'm diabetic.'

'You are not diabetic.'

'I'm going into a glycaemic coma.'

'You're not diabetic.'

'I did a test,' he says as they reach the junction and turn back onto the main road they used earlier, 'just before I met you. I did a test.'

'Was it okay?'

'It was fine but I think I must have developed diabetes after.'

'You have not developed diabetes.'

'This heat and not eating at proper times. It can happen like that.'

'Roy, you're not diabetic.'

'I'm thirsty,' Roy whimpers, 'that's a sign of diabetes.'

'It's as hot as a bloody jungle. We're all thirsty. Here, have some water.'

'And I need to urinate,' he says swallowing as his hands grip the steering wheel, 'thirsty...needing to use the toilet....bad moods... they're all symptoms of diabetes you know.'

'Yes but you could just be thirsty, need a wee and be grumpy because it's hot and we're pissing about all over the place.'

'I've got diabetes,' he says, 'I know it. I knew it would get me. I'll need insulin and a blood testing kit...I'll need a doctor. Should we go back to the fort? Tell Howie I'm having a glycaemic attack and we should head back to the fort.'

'Roy, you are not having any attack of anything. You are just hot and thirsty and needing a wee.'

'But...but...'

'Okay, we'll stop and have a drink and if you still think the same we'll find a testing kit. Okay?'

'Okay. I'll try and hang on.'

'Yes, you hang on.'

'Be prepared to take the wheel in case I collapse.'

'I will.'

'Do you know the recovery position?'

'Yes, Roy. I know the recovery position. You just need some sugar or something to eat...but not because you're diabetic but because we're all hungry and hot and thirsty...that village will have food. All those tea gardens and jam doesn't go off. I bet they have loads of jam.'

'The jam will be full of bogeys,' Reginald shouts from his desk.

'Jam does go off,' Roy says.

'It's a preservative, it doesn't go off if it's sealed properly.'

'It's full of bogeys.'

'I don't want to get poisoned. You have to be careful of things like that when you're diabetic.'

'You are not diabetic, Roy.'

'I feel shaky.'

'You're shaky because you've got yourself all worked up.'

'My heart is beating faster.'

'Because you've got yourself worked up.'

'I think I'm having the glycaemic attack now.'

'You're not.'

'Be ready to take the wheel.'

'I'm ready.'

'Oh god...I've got diabetes. What if it's type one? I bet it's type one. Oh shit I've got type one diabetes.'

'You...it's not...okay let's just get to the village and have a drink.'

'I might not last that long.'

'You will.'

'The jam will have bogeys in it.'

'Paula to Marcy, you got any spare seats in there?'

CHAPTER TEN

D*ay Eighteen*

BRIEF UPDATE No 2

I HAVE SPENT the morning moving swiftly through towns and villages and it is really quite incredible the distances that can be covered by a horse on empty roads.

MOST OF THE places were non-entities. Small hamlets of cottages with barely two or three streets and other than the now usual signs of damage either from the event or the storm there was nothing to indicate the passage of a group of soldiers.

ONE CHANCE DISCOVERY however has led me on what now

has proven to be the correct route and I think I am only a short time behind them.

A TOWN WE PASSED THROUGH, *larger than many others and very flooded with much debris and flotsam floating about. There was something about it that made me circumspect and wary and Jess started showing signs of being unsettled too. She became somewhat fractious as though she could smell something in the air and the very place had a foreboding feeling that I did not like.*

IT WAS A BODY. *Just a single body amongst many others floating in the deep waters bordering a hastily vacated poorly made scaffold board band stand. I gather there was some festival taking place when the outbreak first hit. It was a mere glance at the body, just a trifling glance and no more than a flicker of my eyes to the side and I happened to see, in that snatched glance, a bullet hole in the forehead of the corpse of the infected male.*

That immediately drew my attention as the entry point was exactly mid centre of the forehead which is the same thing I had seen on some of the corpses in Finkton. It may be nothing. It may be entirely coincidental but I think not. To shoot a moving being through the forehead speaks to me of Special Forces training.

THIS FIND MADE *me search harder until I discovered what appeared to be a recently damaged wall and two large metal gates that had been rammed aside in order to gain access to the secure yard of bank within which were several armoured vehicles. I also noted, and I am proud of myself for my detective work, that the rear of the bank had been entered and a dry spot on the ground made me realise one of the armoured vehicles had been taken.*

. . .

IT IS hot but at least it has stopped raining. Jess is faring well and seems to be enjoying the exercise but I for one will be glad to put this town to our backs and continue our search.

NB

CHAPTER ELEVEN

'We'll use that one,' I point ahead over a low wall to a building set back from the road with a pretty red and white striped awning stretching out over a range of seats and tables. We're further up from the brief firefight we had a little while ago and the bodies are still slumped in the road. Everything here is thatched. The shops. The houses. Even the bus stop shelter has a thatch on it. I bring the Saxon to a stop and step out into that wall of heat that sucks the air from my lungs. I've never known heat like it. Energy sapping and too close for comfort. Sweat pours off all our faces and we keep drinking water to replenish the loss of fluids which just makes everyone need a piss.

Meredith is suffering the most with her thick coat that is shedding by the handful. She's panting non-stop and so desperate for air that the lads opened the back doors to try and get some breeze through the vehicle.

Everyone gets out but slowly and I see the wince from face to face as they walk into jungle humidity.

'Maps?' Marcy asks walking round to meet me with a glistening face that only makes her look even more attractive.

'Yeah, you got any idea what's got into him?'

'Reggie?'

'No the fucking Pope...'

'Funny,' she grimaces at me, 'and no I don't. He's never been like that before.'

'Is he intelligent?'

'Oh god yes,' she says emphatically, 'but with that intellectual intelligence. You know, like chess and crosswords and things like that but no common sense.'

'Okay, we'll search these shops...'

'You don't have to humour him you know.'

'Yeah I know and you don't have to feel responsible for him either.'

'It's because of me he's here,' she says, 'so I will feel responsible for him and his actions.'

'We'll see what he wants to say, if that is, he can get the bloody words out in a way we understand.'

'Let me handle him.'

'All yours,' I say with relief, 'your eyes are better again today,' I add when she looks straight at me.

'Yeah?' She steps closer and widens her eyes while staring at me, 'are they still red?'

'Little bit but you wouldn't notice now, not unless you were looking really closely,' I stare back and feel an overwhelming urge to lean forward and kiss her, which must be displayed on my face judging by the smug smile she gives.

'Sod off,' I step away and force myself to look away.

'You wanted to.'

'Did not.'

'So did, I'm so hot...so bloody hot,' she pulls the bottom of her top away from her body, shoves a hand up between her boobs and pulls it out to show me the sweat, 'got sweaty boobs.'

'Oh for fuck's sake,' I groan and walk off.

'What?' She laughs, 'I'm only saying.'

'And showing.'

'You wish,' she quips.

'Maybe I do,' I turn back with a grin and claim the victory of seeing surprise on her face.

'What did you say?'

'Right everyone, we're looking for...'

'Maps,' I get a chorus of voices calling back at me.

'Ordnance survey maps,' Cookey says exhaling heavily, 'and he wants scales of one in fifty and one in twenty five and whatever else we can find and as many as possible and they have to be ordnance survey and...yeah shit like that.'

Reginald appears behind Clarence, 'the scale is vitally important,' he says quickly, 'and yes, find as many as you can.'

'Yes, Reggie,' Cookey says heavily.

'Roy, you stay out here with Paula, Reginald and Marcy keeping watch. Blinky and Charlie with me searching that first thatched souvenir shop, Blowers and the lads take the next thatched shop up and Clarence and Dave the thatched one further up...then we'll check the thatched bus stop then the thatched toilets and finally get to that thatched café for a thatched drink and when we've finished we'll get back into the thatched Saxon and get the fuck out of here before someone starts thatching those dead bodies on the ground.'

'Huh,' Blinky snorts laughter, 'I like thatch.'

'Blinky!' Charlie groans. We all look to Cookey for a return comment but he shrugs and waves a dismissive hand.

'Too hot, sorry,' he says.

'Come on then, let's get it done,' Charlie and Blinky move towards me as the rest filter off, 'you two okay?'

'Hot,' Charlie says with a roll of her eyes.

'Fucking hot, Mr Howie,' Blinky blurts, 'like really fucking hot but I'm not bothered or anything.'

We walk towards the front of the store and I turn, as always, to check behind and catch a look from Marcy with her head cocked to one side and a questioning look on her face that makes me stop in confusion, 'what's up?'

'Nothing,' she turns away quickly.

'People are weird, so...Blinky, have a look through the window and see if you can spot movement while Charlie and I check the back...do not enter until we're back with you.'

'Sir, yes Sir,' Blinky snaps.

'Howie is fine,' I say.

'Mr Howie,' Blinky says.

'Okay, so...Charlie, we'll head down that alley and see if we can see through the windows or get to the rear,' I go first with my rifle raised and her following a few feet behind, 'window there,' I point out to the first barred window clearly sealed shut from years of overpainting. 'Have a look,' I keep watch while she presses close and peers through the grimy glass.

'Nothing, store room by the looks of it.'

We head down the alley to the rear wall and through a gate into the enclosed yard, 'back door and a window either side of the door... we're looking for any signs that someone has been through here, if the door has been opened recently...that sort of thing...we're listening too, for any sounds from inside...and if we can smell anything too...' I speak low and turn constantly to scan the sides, rear then back to the line of the building. She does the same but moves in a crouch to the side of the closest window and eases up to peer through the glass.

'...you'd better check this, Mr Howie.'

The tone of her voice has me moving to her side to look through into a room with a large table overturned on its side.

'Nothing else is disturbed,' I whisper, 'all the pots and pans are hanging up, the cupboards are closed...no signs of blood anywhere...we'll check the other window.'

We move in a crouch past the door to the other window but it only offers the same view from a different angle. A sealed room with the single exit door closed and a table overturned.

'Looks like a staff room,' Charlie says, 'see the notice board on that wall, it's got one of those health and safety posters on it.'

'Where? Yep got it. Good spot, well done,' I offer her a quick smile, 'try the back door handle, see if it's open.'

She nods and steps away to gingerly push on the handle and slowly exerts more force before giving up, 'locked,' she says quietly.

'Back round to Blinky then.'

'Will we still go inside?'

'Yeah but we'll let Roy know to watch this alley while we go in...in case anything comes out the back while we're going in the front. Blinky, the back is closed up but a table inside the back room has been turned over.'

She nods eagerly and grips her weapon at the prospect of having something to shoot at.

'You try that main door, see if it's open. If it is open then push it and step aside so Charlie and I can get a clear shot at anything coming out, got it?'

'Yes, Sir,' she nods and rushes to the door, checking over her shoulder as Charlie and I get in position, 'ready?'

'Yep,' I nod and she yanks hard on the handle, pushes the door open and steps quickly to one side as I suddenly realise I didn't ask Roy to watch the alley to our side.

'Roy,' I call out.

'Already on it,' he says quietly from a few feet to my side.

I go forward with the rifle raised and aiming. Into the main shop floor and a confusing array of shelving all filled with more thatched objects ready to be sold and no doubt imported from China where they had child slaves weaving the thatch on the bird boxes. Jars of jam, marmalades and preserves adorn one side. Every one of them fitted with those frilly checked cloth lids held in place by a rubber band. The air is stale and hot, filled with the scents of fruit and merchandise and the fetid stench of a decaying body that has now become so familiar.

'Smell that?' I ask the girls behind me.

'Body?' Charlie asks.

'Yep, normal dead by the smell of it...it's a different smell to the other things.'

'So that means there are no infected in here?' She asks.

'How do you figure that?'

'If there's a dead body doesn't it mean it died and didn't come back so therefore...I mean if one was in here it would have turned the one that is dead?'

'Good thinking but it could have been a suicide, someone bitten too deeply to come back...it could even be an infected person that got killed so until we know we don't make any assumptions. Check behind the counter but keep your weapon trained on that curtain,' I say motioning towards the drawn curtain separating the shop floor from the rear private area. Charlie goes forward, taking each step carefully and I glance over to see the rifle is held steady and Blinky working closely behind her.

'Not too close, Blinky,' I say softly, 'if Charlie jumps back she needs space to move.'

'Got it,' Blinky says taking a small side step, 'that better?'

'I know where she is, Mr Howie,' Charlie says, 'it's the same on the pitch...knowing what space you have to move into.'

'Of course, my apologies. I didn't mean to patronise you.'

'No no,' she says quickly, 'we're both glad of the lesson, oh... yes...the body is halfway under the curtain.'

'Can you see the head?'

'No, just the legs.'

I edge to the counter and peer over to see a pair of legs poking out through the curtain. An old lady with wrinkled tights and this close I can smell the stench of shit and piss from her bowels and bladder voiding when she died.

'Tricky one,' I say, 'is she dead or pretending?' She is dead but it's a good lesson for these two to consider, especially after the ones in that plaza all lying down.

'She stinks of shit,' Blinky says, 'and piss...and jam...and everything is fucking thatched...can I shoot her?'

'You want to shoot her?' I ask.

'To see if she's dead. She'll soon fucking move with a bullet in her fanny.'

'Blinky!'

'What? She will.'

'What if she's not dead?' Charlie asks, 'you'd kill her.'

'Not dead? What you mean like properly alive?'

'Yes, excuse me? Are you alive?' Charlie calls out politely.

'She's dead as fuck,' Blinky says, 'she's shit herself and pissed all over the floor.'

'Sick people do that too.'

'What and then lie in it for seventeen days?'

'She might have fallen yesterday, I say hello? Can you hear me?'

'No she can't bloody hear you cos she's fucking dead.'

'You don't know that,' Charlie says tightly, 'Mr Howie? Could she still be alive?'

Funny thing is that I was convinced she was normal dead but now she's mentioned it and planted that seed in my head.

'Er...I guess so...tap her foot and see if she responds.'

'I'll kick her bloody foot.'

'Blinky you're so blood thirsty.'

'Yes and normal thirsty too so kick that granny so we can get to the café and have a drink.'

'I'm not going to kick her. I shall tap her foot with the rifle and see if that forces a reaction.'

'You alright?' Clarence asks coming through the doorway, 'we found a load of maps.'

'Oh nice one, well done. Who found them?'

'Cookey and Mo,' he says staring at Charlie bending over and poking something behind the counter.

'Hello?' Charlie calls out politely, 'can you hear me?'

'Er, what's she doing?' Clarence asks as the lads push in behind him.

'Found a body,' Blinky says, 'dead old granny that shit and pissed herself and stinks of jam but Charlie won't give her a kicking so she's tapping her foot to see if she's alive.'

'Oh,' Clarence says as though it makes perfect sense.

The lads squeeze through the shelves knocking thatched bird boxes and thatched pencil cases onto the floor in a rush to see Charlie poking the end of her rifle into a dead ladies foot.

'Ooh you can't see her head,' Cookey says, 'so you think she's alive then?'

'Well we really don't know,' Charlie says pushing the barrel into the foot again while making ready to flee in case it jolts up.

'You're so posh,' Cookey says, 'Blowers, go round and give her the kiss of life.'

'Who? Charlie or the dead one?' Blowers asks.

'Ha! You fucking wish.'

'She might not be dead,' Charlie says, 'hello? Are you alive?'

'She'll be dead from old age by the time we've done anything,' Blinky says, 'just shoot her in the foot and see if she screams.'

'I am not shooting an old lady in the foot.'

'You did earlier,' Nick says, 'and in the head...and the stomach...'

'Yes well that was different,' Charlie says standing up, 'she's not responding,' she adds in a serious tone that has the lads cracking up.

'Nick, call an ambulance,' Cookey says.

'AMBULANCE,' Nick shouts.

'What's going on?' Roy asks from the doorway, 'who needs an ambulance?'

'The dead lady,' Cookey laughs, 'or not dead lady...we're not sure yet.'

'Charlie,' Blowers says trying to suppress the giggles, 'you'll have to pull the curtain back and see.'

'Oh gosh, will I? Yes I shall have to shan't I. What? What is so funny? Oh stop it and piss off the lot of you.'

'She swore!' Cookey exclaims, 'she actually swore with a proper swear word.'

'I swear all the time actually,' Charlie says pointedly, 'when I need to that is.'

'Can we please just shoot the old granny and get a drink...hang on a fucking minute,' Blinky says looking round, 'Clarence said you found the maps...then we can go get a drink instead of playing with pissy pants down there.'

'We can't leave her,' Charlie says edging towards the curtain.

'Ooh go on,' Nick urges softly but I notice his rifle raises an inch to be ready just in case.

'Want me to do it for you, Charlie?' Mo Mo asks.

'Oh thank you, Mo Mo,' Charlie beams at him, 'that is very gallant but I shall do it now I am here.'

'You're gallant you are,' Cookey says to Mo with a snigger.

'What's gallant mean?' Mo Mo asks, 'is that like a bad thing?'

'Bad as fuck mate,' Nick says, 'Charlie effectively said you're a wanker.'

'I did no such thing,' Charlie says leaning over the body and trying to grasp the curtain folds, 'it means you were very polite and nice...knights of old times were said to be gallant. It is a very manly trait.'

Mo Mo's eyebrows lift at the realisation of the compliment and I swear he floats up off the floor again.

'Oh dear, oh dear...it appears she has no head,' Charlie says sadly peeking through the curtains and the room erupts in an explosion of laughter.

'She still alive though?' Blinky asks with delight, 'kick her foot again.'

'I didn't know she had no head,' Charlie sighs, 'poor love...I wonder where her head is?'

'Let's see,' Cookey asks craning forward as Charlie yanks the curtain back, 'oooh,' he recoils with a grimace, 'she been chomped to fuck...'

'Chomped?' Charlie asks with a puzzled shake of her head.

'Eaten,' Blowers says, 'they ate her neck and made her head come off...it's probably rolled down the other way.'

'Oh,' Charlie tuts sadly, 'you poor love,' she adds.

'Can we get a fucking drink now?' Blinky asks, 'I'm so thirsty I'll be drinking my own piss in a minute.'

'Urgh that's so gross,' Cookey wails.

'Not as gross as drinking someone else's piss,' she says as they start to file out, 'if you were on a desert island with another person and had nothing to drink...would you drink your own or the other persons piss?'

'Who is the other person?' Nick asks.

'Why? Does it matter?' Blinky asks.

'Well yeah,' Blowers says, 'like...I wouldn't drink Cookey's piss but someone clean and nice and...'

'Like Charlie?' Cookey asks.

'Yeah like Charlie.'

'You'd drink Charlie's piss because she's pretty?' Blinky asks stopping in the doorway and glaring back at the lads before shrugging, 'yeah I would too, Charlie we're all drinking your piss if we get stuck on a desert island.'

'Okay then,' Charlie says brightly with a roll of her eyes, 'well that was an education,' she adds quietly to me, 'I am so sorry for the delay I caused.'

'No don't be silly, you did the right thing.'

'Right thing? What by causing everyone to wait?'

'No by being a human being and taking the time to check first, she might have been alive. None of this is worth it if we don't do the right thing.'

'You two coming?' Marcy asks from the door.

'Yep, the lads found the maps,' I say walking towards her, 'bet Reggie will be pleased.'

'I'm sure he will,' she says as Charlie passes on to join the others, 'you were having a nice chat just then.'

'Eh? Oh. There was an old lady behind the counter and we couldn't tell if she was dead or not because of the curtain but then Charlie pulled it back and her head wasn't...why are you looking at me like that?'

'Like what?'

'All weird, like angry. What's up?'

'Nothing,' she says turning away.

'Roy, you do not have diabetes. It's the heat!' Paula exclaims with her own angry flushed red face.

'Mr Howie, I have the maps and I really need to explain the folly of your plans.'

'I am thirsty. I am grumpy and I need the toilet. They are all symptoms of diabetes which is a life threatening illness which can be fatal if not treated...'

'The maps, Mr Howie...'

'Clarence, can you get the door to that café open please.'

I follow in his wake as he strides to the door, adjusts his step once and slams his right foot into the door just below the lock causing it to implode off the hinges and crash into the counter a few feet away. I walk straight in with the rifle half raised. A quick look round and everything looks normal. The air smells stale but normal, apart from the smell of foul milk and foodstuffs that is. The dust on the floor is undisturbed.

'That'll do me,' I announce to no one in particular and head to the double sized Coca Cola fridge, open one side and select a can of Orange Tango. It's too hot. Everything is too hot. I pop the lid, listen to the fizz of the bubbles rushing to the opening and then guzzle the sugary goodness into my mouth. The taste is incredible and almost overpowering. After days of water, tuna, pasta, coffee and baked beans this is divine. Glucose rushing into my blood-stream and an instant surge of energy. My belly reacts too at the carbonated liquid as I gulp the whole thing greedily in one go and release an almighty belch.

'Now that,' I sigh and discard the empty can to one side, 'was fucking lovely.'

'Yeah?' Clarence asks reaching past me to take the same flavour from the display.

'Definitely,' I reply taking another one.

'Clear?' Dave asks coming through the broken door.

'Clear enough,' I reply and watch him disappearing through the door to the kitchen as everyone else piles in, 'shush now,' I hold my hand up at the clamouring voices, 'not a word or I'll tell Dave you called him a twat.'

Silence falls. Glorious silence broken only by the shuffle of feet as cans of pop are handed round. Silence broken by ring pulls being opened and the fizz of bubbles. Silence broken by thirsty people lifting cans to gulp the contents and swallow the beautiful stuff down and silence broken by a chorus of belches.

'Clear,' Dave says with a reproachful look at me.

'Tango?' I ask him, 'Orange or Apple?'

'I don't mind.'

'Apple it is,' I hand one over to him and quickly raise my finger as Cookey goes to say something, 'still in quiet time.'

He nods and finishes his can. A clunk as his hits the floor to join the other ones already discarded.

Nick heads into the kitchen and I listen as he runs a tap and comes back carrying one bowl for Meredith and another larger bucket half filled with water which he carries to the fridge and starts taking the warm cans to place inside.

'Nice,' I say and take another drink, 'and still in quiet time,' I add before Cookey or Blinky can say anything.

After finishing the second can I plonk the empty receptacle down on the new bin, that being the floor, and start patting my pockets down as the non-verbalisation of a signal to Nick that I need a cigarette. One appears magically in front of my face which I take and head outside with the other dirty smokers, light the cigarette and poke my head back inside the door, 'you can talk now.'

Paula lights up. Blowers and Cookey both light up and join Nick and I as we exhale plumes of tobacco smoke into the air.

'Would anyone like a Tracker bar?' Charlie asks poking her head out of the door, 'there's a basket of them on the counter.'

'Is it thatched?' Cookey asks.

'Er no,' Charlie says glancing back into the café, 'shall I bring them outside? Mr Howie? Are we sitting outside?'

'Yep,' I reply and drink my can and smoke my cigarette and feel the rush of sugar buzzing through my body.

'Biscuits too?' Charlie calls from inside, 'the chocolate bars have melted though.'

'Bring them all out,' Paula says, 'lads, do you want to pull those tables together?'

Three tables are pulled together and chairs arranged round the sides as snack bars and biscuits are brought out with the bucket of cans bobbing in the cold water. Slowly the chairs fill up and I spot the almost hazed look in their eyes from the sugar hit as the thirst abates and we start to cool down. Everyone apart from Dave is red faced and sweating. The toilet inside flushes and a few seconds later Roy appears smiling wryly at Paula.

'Better?' She asks smiling warmly at him.

'Yes,' he says, 'thank you and sorry.'

'Nay bother,' she says patting the seat next to her, 'have another can and rot your teeth...I was joking!' She adds at the look on his face.

'Everyone here?' I ask.

'Blinky is using the toilet,' Charlie says.

'In that case, I shall eat a Tracker bar full of fruit and nut goodness to increase my sugar levels even more than the spike they have just experienced, awesome. Anyone want one?'

'Got one,' Nick says with a mouthful.

'No surprise there,' Blowers says, 'gutsy fucker, why aren't you fat? You should be fat the amount you stuff in your mouth.'

'Good genes.'

'Levi's?' Cookey asks, 'oh that was such a shit joke.'

'All your jokes are shit,' Blowers says.

'Your willy is covered in shit.'

'Alex!'

'Sorry, Dave.'

'Willy?' Blowers asks after a few seconds pause.

'Being polite,' Cookey mutters, 'hey she's back,' he says as Blinky walks out from the café.

'Don't go in the bog,' she says, 'I had a dump and it stinks.'

'Thanks for that, Blinky,' Paula says.

'Can I ask a serious question?' Cookey asks.

'No because it won't be serious,' Paula replies.

'No, proper serious...like not pissing about.'

'Go on then,' she sighs.

'You know women,' he starts.

'Er yeah, I am one,' she says.

'No no, I mean when women are all together is it true that their periods all come at the same time?'

'What?' Blowers spits his drink to the side, 'where did you hear that?'

'Dunno, can't remember,' Cookey says.

'Yes it's true,' Paula says, 'not immediately but eventually yes.'

'Whoa, so cool,' Cookey says, 'and see, told you it was a serious question.'

'So,' Nick says swallowing his mouthful,' how long does it take?'

'It depends,' Paula says, 'the cycles could all be at different stages but eventually we'll all sort of happen together.'

'Why?' He asks.

'I don't know,' Paula laughs.

'It's called menstrual synchrony,' Charlie says, 'or the McClintock effect,' she adds in her cultured voice, 'Martha McClintock did a study that showed that the start of the menstrual cycle of a group of women living in close proximity will eventually find they coincide. However, the study was later replicated and did not show the same results. Various suggestions and hypothesis have been put forward, one of them is the lunar cycle believe it or not, and pheromones too.'

'Don't mention pheromones,' Cookey says coughing into his hand.

'Pheromones? Why?'

'Leg humper,' Marcy mutters at me with a smile.

'Don't start,' I groan, 'it's too hot.'

'So you're all going to be moody together then?' Nick asks to a low chorus of groans from the women at the table, 'ha,' he grins at the glares, 'sorry,' he adds when they don't smile back.

'Business,' I say after swallowing the last mouthful of Tracker, 'Reggie? I mean Reginald, the floor is yours, Sir.'

'Hm?' He looks up from studying the map spread out on the table in front of him, 'I'm sorry, did you say something?'

'All yours,' I say to him, 'what do you want to tell us?'

'Your plan is flawed and you'll get everyone killed,' he says bluntly.

'Reggie!' Marcy snaps.

'No no, hear him out,' I say with the humour all gone now.

'I don't mean your plan, Mr Howie. I mean the plan you all suggested this morning. That plan. That plan will get you all killed before this day is done.'

'How so? We've only been two places...here and that plaza.'

'Three,' Reginald says, 'the plaza, this village and the town with the duck pond and by that process I was able to deduce exactly where you would go next and if I can deduce that then so can the infection. In fact the infection already has and is planning to meet you at the next place.'

Looks are exchanged round the table. Clarence leans forward

to listen intently. Paula interlocks her fingers and rests her hands on the table. Roy watches Reginald closely.

'Keep going,' I say when he doesn't continue.

He looks round nervously and takes his glasses off to wipe the lenses, pushing them back on and I notice his hands move to adjust something at the base of his neck.

'You see,' he says in a quieter voice, 'the town where we found Roy's new vehicle, you told that infected person you were going to the next town. That gave everyone a starting point and the fact the infected were all laying on the ground when we arrived suggests they knew you were coming which therefore shows your words to the infected person had been heard *and* understood.'

'Okay,' I say.

He rushes on before anyone else can say anything, 'from the plaza we came here and I, because I was not directly involved in the fighting, I was able to watch where they came from and I'm afraid to say it was staged...'

'Staged?' Paula looks up sharply.

'Exactly that. Staged. It was almost as if the infection was sending them out in ones and twos to give you a false sense of security. A degree of perhaps having an opponent you could defeat easily and all the time it was testing you, probing, seeing where the weak spots are, detecting the chinks in the armour. From there the other player predicted you would not consider the housing estate as a centre of habitation and would consider the duck pond town as the next geographical town to be missed and therefore the town *after that* would be the next target. Which is how I concluded the other player would have diverted resources from the duck pond town towards the next one.'

'Why the duck pond? The direction?' Clarence asks, 'how did you know that?'

'The town was bordered on one side by a wood. Indeed the town is called *Foxwood*. On the side we came in on was open pasture land and the main road we were on also went in the same direction as they passed while heading through the duck pond. You see, that was the logical direction of the next town. Now, please don't think I am underestimating your ability to do battle and I have no doubt that you would have succeeded at the next town which brings us to the next issue which is time. The opponent would not have had enough time to draw ample hosts to throw against you and my suggestion is that you would have been once again probed and tested to confirm the pattern and direction of your intended route. By the fifth or sixth you would have come unstuck with a trap lured to pull you in with overwhelming adversaries.'

'And you know this how?' Paula asks.

'Because it is precisely what I would do. If I was the opponent I would play to my advantage which is having an almost limitless supply of host bodies to sacrifice in luring you towards a final confrontation whereby I would ensure you did not survive.'

'Fuck me,' I sit back in the chair and look round at the rapt and shocked faces, 'so...I...fuck me...'

'You said you were going to apply a random methodology to the way you attacked them whereas in fact you are simply leap-frogging from town to town. That is not random. That is the exact opposite of random.'

'We might not have stuck to it,' Paula says with a hint of defensive in her tone.

'You would,' Reginald says almost disdainfully, 'because you were winning. You would have continued to achieve what you perceived to have been "great kills"' he makes quote marks while he says it which just irks Paula, 'and so you would have continued. I mean why change something that is achieving the required result.'

'Fuck me,' I say again.

'Okay,' Clarence says slowly, 'so we change the random way. We could just stick a pin in the map and attack the closest town to the pin. That's random.'

'It is not random,' Reginald says, 'it is not random at all. The thing about random is that it has to be truly random...' he stops to lay his hands on the map in front of him, 'the infection is a hive mind but it is still operating within the parameters of human intelligence and I would suggest that it is similar to a CPU...a computer processing unit. It calculates and works at a far higher pace than any normal human mind can work...but it is still restrained by the set parameters of the programme. In this case,' he looks round at the table, 'we are the programme. Our minds and the way we plan, function and the methods we use in our everyday lives. Whatever method you use will never be random.'

'Are we in the Matrix?' Cookey asks.

'Shush,' Paula waves a hand at him, 'go on,' she says to Reginald.

'A pin in a map *is* random,' Clarence asserts, 'do it blindfold then...that *has* to be random.'

'A pin in a map will be a random starting point and yes, the infection or the opponent will never be able to work out where that pin would end up. Unless of course,' he adds icily, 'it knew the height, weight and body composition of the person placing the pin and the height of the drop of the arm holding said pin and the size and layout of the map being used...'

'Do what?' Blowers asks.

'Take Clarence if you will,' Reginald says, 'if he were to stand up, take a pin and drop his arm down and thereby choose a random place we would be able to work out, in advance, the likely place the pin would fall given his height, the dropping distance of his arm and the size of the map being used...it would not be precise but it would be close. Therefore a pattern is already formed and one that is within the parameters of the programme.'

'Fuck me,' I say again.

'No. I don't believe it,' Clarence says.

'Please stand,' Reginald says to the bigger man and pulls a pen from his pocket, 'this is your pin,' he hands it over then adjust the map so it is directly in front of Clarence, 'close your eyes and choose,' he says.

Clarence does as bid and after hovering his arm he lets it drop gently on the map and draws a dot with the pen.

'Very good, now you must repeat the action as we have attacked the field you have chosen and killed the cows so now we must attack the next location.'

'Did I get a field?' Clarence asks squinting through one eye.

'Again please,' Reginald moves to his side and watches as Clarence lifts his arm and again lets it drop gently to the map where he draws another dot, 'and again,' Reginald says and watches as Clarence repeats the action, 'hold still but keep your eyes closed,' he takes the pen from Clarence's grip and quickly outlines a rough circle on the map before pushing the pen back between the huge digits of Clarence's hand, 'and again please.'

'Shit,' Cookey is the first to voice the surprise when Clarence drops his arm and draws the dot in the middle of the circle.

'What?' Clarence asks opening his eyes.

'Your *random* selection just got everyone killed,' Reginald says.

'How?' Clarence asks.

'Reggie drew that circle,' Paula leans over to trace the line of pen that Reginald drew, 'and you landed in the middle of it.'

'So fucking cool,' Nick says.

'Your height, weight, girth, length of your arm, the drop from your arm to the table and the size of the map can all be used to calculate the area within which the pin, *or pen in this case,* will drop. It is not random. Not random at all.' Taking his pen he slides it back into his trouser pocket and sits back down with an air of disquiet and worry.

'I apologise,' he says stiffly after the lengthy pause of the rest of us taking in everything he just said, 'I did not mean to undermine you but merely to highlight that whatever you *choose* to do and whatever plan you come up with the infection, with its hive mind capability, will outthink you.

'There are thirteen people in this group of varying sizes and indeed, we have various maps of various sizes so the variables of who is assigned the pin and which map is used at what height and distance all increase the statistical odds of the opponent not being able to know our destination. As Clarence almost got correct, the first would be very hard, but not impossible, to predict, but the second destination would not. The opponent knows that Mr Howie leads this team, it will also know, through gaining Lani's mind, that Paula, Clarence and to a certain extent, Simon all play active parts in the leadership and direction this group take. Therefore the opponent will know, after the first destination has been chosen, where the likely second destination, or objective, will be.'

'Holy fuck,' Cookey mutters, 'Reggie is Morpheus...'

'Okay then,' I say leaning forward, 'then we don't do the pin but just pick a town completely at random...like just choose one without any regard to where it is.'

'Please,' Reginald says sliding the map towards me, 'where are we now?'

'Fuck, I've got no idea,' I say staring down at the map, 'er... anyone got an idea?'

'Find the hotel we stayed at and work from there,' Roy suggests.

'It matters not the actuality of our location, please just choose any place on the map and we will assume, for this purpose, that we are at that place.'

'Okay, here then,' I jab my finger down onto what looks like a small town.

'Please choose where you would attack first.'

'Okay, er...' I look round at the grey smudges indicating the urban towns and places of populace, 'doesn't really matter which is the first so....this one,' I tap my finger on a grey section.

'And the next please,' he says tightly.

'Ah right, so the next is random so...er...this one,' I skip a few other grey sections and tap a bigger one to the north.

'And the next,' he says.

'Next? Er...random again so....this one,' I say with a shrug and tap a town a few miles to one side.

'And the next,' he says.

'This one,' I tap a splodge on the map.

'Excellent,' Reginald says without any trace of my choice being excellent at all, 'you have attacked four towns but by the fifth you will be trapped and decimated. Or rather,' he adds with a look round at everyone, 'you will get everyone here trapped and *they* will be decimated.'

'How?' I ask as the tension round the table increases tenfold.

'You have selected a pattern of up then to the side then back down...effectively working to the points on a compass.' He slides the map back towards him, 'North. East. South,' he taps the towns I selected in turn, 'your next choice would be West and given the preset range of your arm and the choices you have already made I would predict your next *random* choice will be this one,' he settles a finger on a grey section, 'and if I can work that out so can the infection.'

'Fuck,' I lean back from the table and blink slowly, 'I probably would have chosen that one,' I admit audibly.

'Fucking Derren Brown...' Nick says, 'fucking awesome.'

'Reginald,' Charlie says politely, 'sorry for interrupting you but are you saying that whatever we choose, or whatever method we choose it will be worked out because we're using our minds which are preset within the confines of the way we are taught to think?'

'Yes,' Reginald looks up with surprise, as do the rest of us, 'that is exactly what I am trying to explain.'

'So Mr Howie, although he thought he was choosing random towns, was sub-consciously using the points of the compass, albeit he was skipping towns on the map...but because of the length of his arm and the height of the map on the table he was moving to a pre-defined range of areas.'

'Yes!' Reginald says.

'And you say that the infection will be able to work this out?'

'Yes! Of course it will. It knows everything we know and more. It has access to every memory and fact known by every host body. The fact that we are in the infancy of the evolution is the only reason we are still alive and not yet wiped out.'

'Huh?' I ask stupidly.

'Think about it,' he says looking round the group, 'to have access to every fact, memory, experience, knowledge of every human mind and brain...to be able to use all of those facts to your advantage. Say a mathematician is a host body. The infection will have the expertise of that mathematician and the same with a soldier,' he points to Clarence and Dave, 'to military leaders,' he points to me, 'accountants, archers...hockey players...the infection *will* evolve beyond our understanding of intelligence. Think of what it has done already? It has taken host bodies from being barely functioning to Marcy. To having the ability to allow the host body to use their own minds. To experimenting with what works and what does not work and it is doing it at a rate and size we cannot fathom or comprehend. It is said that if the Roman Empire had not fallen we would have been putting men on the moon a thousand years ago. The infection will achieve what we have been striving for within a matter of weeks.

'Simply put. We are playing against an opponent that is learning faster than anything we have ever known in our entire combined history. We are pitted against a foe of unimaginable power. They were lying down!' He exclaims with his hands waving in the air, 'lying down.'

'Still killed 'em though,' Blowers mutters trying to show a level of confidence that none of us feel.

'Of course and you'll kill many more and what a clumsy, ham-fisted silly infantile thing to do. To lie down and pretend to be dead. To play dead. We have that dog who can smell them and we have eyes that can see them moving...' he stops to look round again, 'silly stupid and ridiculous...but...it shows the start of a complex thought process. To deceive. To trick. To pretend one thing while intending another. To lure. To trap. Lying down was today. What will be tomorrow or the next day? We have to think beyond what is now and work to predict not only the next move on the board but we have to predict the next ten moves on the board and consider the reaction to every move you make.'

Silence. Profound and deep and every heart sinks at the realisation of our own stupidity. At pretending to be professional soldiers and doing something great when in fact we're being played and no better than bloody children throwing stones against an invading army. I look round the table at the faces of the twelve other people and feel foolish that I ever thought we could make a difference.

'Fifty million?' I look across to Dave.

'Yes,' he says as dull as ever.

'Fuck,' I snort, 'how many bullets have we got?'

'Not fifty million that's for sure,' Clarence says.

'Why fifty million?' Charlie asks looking between the three of us.

'Something Dave has always said,' I reply, 'that there were fifty million people in this country...'

'And we've killed a hundred thousand at the very most,' Clarence says.

'Hundred thousand?' I scoff, 'probably half of that if we're lucky. Well, that's kinda sapped the motivation.'

'I am sorry,' Reginald says gravely.

'Don't be,' I say to him, 'better we know what we're up against and plan round it...fuck...what did we kill in this village? Twenty? Thirty at the most?'

'Not all fifty million will be infected,' Paula says, 'Marcy, when you were er...you know...'

'Yes I know,' she says quietly.

'When you were taking people, what was the rate? As in I don't know...for every hundred you went after how many did you actually infect and turn?'

'Probably ninety nine out of a hundred.'

'Oh,' Paula sags, 'shit. So we give up?' Paula asks the group then looks to Reginald, 'are you saying we can't win?'

'Oh good lord I am not saying anything of the sort. It is not my place to say you should stop or continue but I could not sit back and watch the folly of your endeavours any further. Indeed, I offer my upmost apologies for the manner of my intrusion into your affairs but...'

'*Our* affairs,' I interrupt, 'so what do we do?'

'I don't know,' he blurts, 'truly I don't know.'

'Reginald,' Clarence leans forward to rest his bulk on the table, 'what method of attack can we use that the infection won't be able to work out?'

'Good question,' I say with a nod at Clarence then another at Reginald who shifts uncomfortably in his seat at the attention being placed on him once again.

'I am sorry,' he says in mild panic, 'but I am not a person who can make decisions that puts the lives of others at risk. I simply cannot do that.'

'I make the decisions,' I say injecting some firmness into my voice that earns a glance from a few others, 'but I do it after taking into consideration the knowledge and experiences of everyone else...'

'Is that the Tesco School of Management again?' Marcy asks with a wry smile.

'Might be,' I smile back, 'but the thing is, Reginald. Is that it won't be you deciding the fate of everyone. It will be me.'

'But what if you form a decision based on something *I* say to you that ultimately led to the death of everyone. I truly do...'

'Then we'd all be dead,' Paula says bluntly but in a kind voice, 'the same way everything we've done so far could have led to our deaths.'

'May I?' Roy asks me.

'Carry on, mate.'

'Reginald,' Roy says turning to the other man, 'tell us about random then...how we can choose a random selection method.'

'Before we even contemplate that question you need to be sure of your goals and objectives?'

'That's simple enough. Kill as many as possible.'

'Is that realistic?' He asks, 'considering the numbers you are up against? Should you not be looking to seek the answer to the question of your immunity? Why Marcy and I were infected but are now seemingly ridding our bodies of the virus?'

'How? Where?' I throw the questions out and watch as he balks slightly at the force of my voice, 'I am asking you not confronting you, Reginald. If you have any thoughts or ideas in that direction then say so. I mean we got four doctors and a ton of equipment but...'

'They were general practitioners of medicine,' Reginald says, 'you need experts within the fields of virology, scientists...'

'Which we'll never find,' Paula says quietly, 'we got lucky with the four we found but none of us would even know where to begin looking for a virologist.'

'London,' Marcy says, 'at the big hospitals.'

'Have you seen London?' Clarence asks her, 'we have.'

'The idea was to be away from then fort and use guerrilla tactics to cull their numbers,' I say, 'but now I'm questioning if we should be doing that? Should we?' I ask the group, 'we were going to be seen away from the fort...fight back...show them we're not cowed...but now, taking into account what Reginald just said, is that the right thing to do?'

'What do you want to do?' Marcy asks me as every face waits for the answer.

'Me? I want to fuck 'em up as much as possible and irritate the shit out of it. I want that bastard thing to know we're fucking it over bit by bit and getting good at it. But after what Reginald just said... well, common sense says we should leg it and find somewhere safe to hide but they'll come and keep coming. They won't stop and if what Reginald says is true, which it is because we've all seen how clever the bloody thing is getting, then it'll work out how to get into the fort and every other safe place. So yes, while my common sense says run and hide I know we're just buying a bit of time before they find us.'

'Then we do that,' Marcy says with a firm nod.

'Oh no, no no no,' I say waving my hand at her, 'this isn't a decision for me to make. This has to be a collective decision.'

'You just said you make the decisions.'

'Yeah but...'

'You did say that,' Paula says.

'Yes but...but what I mean is...I mean, fuck it. Yes I want to keep going and attack but only if it's the right thing to do.'

'You sound like a politician now,' Marcy says, 'who cares if it's the right thing or not...we'll never know if it's the right thing as there is no precedent for this ever happening before. Whatever you decide *is* the right thing to do and if it leads to all us all getting killed then so be it, we're on borrowed time anyway. What? Don't look at me like that? We *are* on borrowed time. I died. I was killed. Murdered. So was Reggie. Paula was coping on her own and surviving but how long would that have lasted for? Charlie and Blinky might have lasted another couple of weeks in that house before it found them or god forbid some other men found a house full of young women.'

She stops and shakes her head sadly while looking round the table, 'the sun is shining, the weather is warm and we're in good company...anything else is a bonus. Paula said something to me this morning that made me think.'

'What did I say?' Paula asks with a worried look.

'You said about taking comfort when you can.'

'Er yes but that was a very specific conversation.'

'The principle is the same. This is our comfort. This right now. Sitting in a café drinking free soft drinks and having the ability to hold a conversation. Who else can do this right now? Who else has the wherewithal to have made this happen? We did. We made this comfort in spite of the infection so we are already winning and like I just said, anything after this is a bonus.'

'So what do you want to do?' I ask her softly, mesmerised by the passion of the way she was speaking.

'Kill the lot of them,' she says bluntly and grins round at the shocked expressions, 'you weren't expecting that answer were you?' She laughs, 'what they did to me...and Reggie...and what it *made* us do cannot be forgiven. Kill them. Kill them all and even if we only kill one more before we all die then it's one less to ruin someone else's life completely.'

'Fair enough, Clarence?'

'Same,' he replies, 'keep going.'

'Dave?'

'Your decision, Mr Howie.'

'Paula?'

'Keep going.'

One by one I ask the question and get the same answer *keep going. Keep going Mr Howie.*

The last one is Reginald and I left him until the last on purpose, 'Reginald?'

'I cannot...'

'Wasn't going to ask you that,' I cut him off, 'I was going to ask you how we do it?'

'How?'

'Yeah, how? This next town you were saying about. We should go there,' I say with an eager nod, 'can't we somehow make them think we're still doing the same thing but get them trapped instead?'

'Ooh you dirty bastard,' Paula laughs.

'Yeah, why not?' I grin at her, 'fuck 'em. Reggie? Sorry, I mean Reginald...what do you think?'

'Really, Mr Howie. I am not a military strategist. This is not something I can even begin to...'

'You just bloody did,' Clarence sputters, 'Christ, Reggie. I've met officers with less military strategy than what you just said and if Chris was here he'd be creaming his pants. Man up and spit it out.'

'I don't know. I cannot even know where to start to...'

'Yes you bloody can,' Clarence booms, 'it's written all over your face and that little glimmer in your eyes is telling me you're itching to have a go.'

'A go? Have a go? What on earth do you mean?'

'You play chess, right? This is a game of chess. You even called it the other player.'

'I did no such thing.'

'You so did,' Cookey laughs, 'we all heard it.'

'Okay, just this next town,' I say, 'do we go barrelling in like before or sneak in like sneaky mother fuckers?'

'Again it depends on the end objective,' Reginald replies immediately, 'if you want the other...I mean...'

'Ah you were gonna say other player,' Nick says.

'Yes I was but nevertheless, if you want the...opponent...to know you know what they know then yes, use stealth and surprise them but my guess is you'll be able to withstand the opposition with relative ease simply because the opponent does not have the time to draw such numbers as needed to complete his... its...objective.'

'The infection isn't a man,' Paula says, 'you said it was intelligent.'

'Ooh, harsh,' I say as the men all draw breath and make low noises.

'So we go in like before and let it think we're still on track... what about after that?'

'I need to know where we are,' Reginald says staring at the map in front of him.

'Foxwood,' Nick says, 'that was the place with the duck pond, is that on there?'

'Foxwood,' Reginald mutters staring down, 'can you see it?'

'Me? I can't bloody read,' Nick says, 'how do you spell it? Charlie, you have a look.' He swaps seats with Charlie and draws his packet of cigarettes out to hand round.

'Foxwood,' Charlie says holding her finger on the map, 'right here.'

'Ah yes, yes so it is. Indeed. Yes. Yes indeed. Foxwood. Indeed,' Reginald mutters as he examines the map closely.

'What scale is that?' Charlie asks, 'is that a one in fifty?'

'Indeed it is. One in fifty.'

'Have you got a one in twenty five?' Charlie asks leafing through the pile of maps brought back by the lads, 'it will have greater detail on the layout.'

'Indeed it will but we'd need a one in twelve or ten for the exact street layout.'

'We'll never find a one in twelve,' Charlie says, 'unless we can find a surveyors office. Here,' she says opening a map, 'oh sorry, Paula,' she adds as she tries to open the map and knocks Paula's empty can over.

'You carry on,' Paula says with a look at me. I shrug my shoulders as we all stare at Charlie and Reginald.

'Foxwood,' Charlie says running her right hand gently over the surface of the map, 'Foxwood...nearby features?'

'Er...lake to the south,' Reginald says without looking up, 'got it?'

'Lake?'

'Yes. Lake. Let me see,' Reginald stands to lean over the table at the second map, his left hand on the first and his right on the second. He looks between the two tracing features until a look of recognition crosses his face, 'yes here, Foxwood.'

'Gosh it's tiny,' Charlie says peering down.

'That's what Blinky said about Cookey's knob,' Blowers says.

'No she said it was sharp and pointy.'

'And small,' Blinky says with a grin.

'Is that helping?' Paula asks them, 'is it? Is it helping them work?'

'Er, no,' Blinky says looking down.

'It isn't is it? It's not helping.'

'Sorry, Paula,' Blowers says.

'You sound like a teacher,' Roy chuckles.

'Do I? Good,' Paula says with a nod and a wry grin.

'So you er...you know how to read a map then, Charlie?' Clarence asks casually.

'Yes,' she says politely with a glance up.

'Right. That's good then,' he says as she looks back down to examine the map.

'Don't you?' I ask him.

'Oh god,' he says with a look of horror, 'we did learn but we used satellite navigation all the time...I could find a route but...'

'Dave?'

'Yes, Mr Howie.'

'Can you read a map?'

'Yes, Mr Howie.'

'Dave can,' I smile at Clarence.

'I said I can too,' he blusters.

'So what's the difference between them?' I ask the two figures bent over the table, 'er...right...busy then?'

'Hmm, what? Sorry,' Charlie looks back up again, 'sorry was that question directed at us?'

'What's the difference?'

'The difference in the scale?' She asks.

'One in fifty,' Reginald says without looking up, 'means one centimetre on the map represents fifty thousand centimetres in real life or five hundred metres...'

'And that's which one?'

'This one,' Reginald taps his map, 'the size of the geographical area is larger,' he says sweeping his hand over the map, 'and we have some detail such as topography, dense urbanised areas, forests, open land and larger features.'

'Oh right,' I reply, 'and the other one does what?'

He looks up at me for a second and blinks.

'What?' I ask him and look round, 'what? Don't tell me I'm the only one that doesn't know the difference...'

'One in twenty five means one centimetre to two hundred and fifty metres,' Charlie says without any trace of condescension, 'most leisure maps will be one in twenty five. The one in fifty shows the whole of the area in less detail whereas the one in twenty five shows a smaller area but greater details. For instance, it shows the main road going through Foxwood and most of the smaller roads but not the shape of the buildings or junctions.'

'Unless they are buildings of significance,' Reginald says.

'To get a real close up of a town and exact road layout we'd need a one in ten thousand scale but they're not so common unless we use road atlases but with the onset of satellite navigation they have become somewhat rare. I would hazard a guess however that most service stations, especially motorway service stations would stock them...some older drivers still use them,' Charlie says, smiles and looks back down as we all stare in silence.

'You'll catch flies, Cookey,' Marcy says.

'Yeah,' he says with hearts in his eyes, 'that was so fucking cool. Charlie and Reggie are like...like...fucking clever as fuck.'

'Foxwood is here,' Reginald says tapping the spot on Charlie's one in twenty five map and looking over at me, 'and Foxwood should have been missed out because of the housing estate which makes the next target Hydehill,' he says tapping the map again, 'then we miss the next one, presuming that is we are staying on the main road and the next target after Hydehill is Brookley.'

'How big is Hydehill?' Clarence asks.

Charlie leans over to stare for a second, 'approximately the same size as Foxwood, perhaps just a smidgen larger.'

'A smidgen?' Cookey asks, 'cool word.'

'Thank you,' Charlie beams, 'I would say most of the towns and villages in this area and on the road we are following are between the size of this village and Foxwood.'

'Small villages really then,' Clarence says looking at me, 'where's the next biggest one that we'd hit if we were staying on the leap-frog pattern.'

'Brookley is here,' Reginald says, 'which is just a village, then miss one...Flitcombe we would attack but that looks the same size as Foxwood?' He says looking at Charlie.

'Oh gosh yes, really not a big place at all. However the next target place after that must be here?'

'Stenbury,' Reginald says in answer to Clarence.

'Is it big?' Clarence asks.

'You can see,' Charlie says lifting the map up and stepping back to show everyone, 'this is Foxwood where the duck pond is... oh I can't hold it and show you at the same time.'

'Foxwood,' Reginald says moving over to point at the small town on the map then traces his finger along a thick red line, 'Hydehill...Brookley....Flitcombe and then Stenbury,' he stops moving his finger and taps lightly on the map. The others are all small in comparison to Stenbury which sprawls with a much bigger grey splodge and with several main roads running through it.

'Is that where you would plan to get us?' I ask.

'Stenbury? Yes. I would draw you through these smaller towns by giving you some opposition. Enough to build your confidence and give you a sense of security before getting you into Stenbury.'

'How would you do it?' Marcy asks.

'I don't know,' Reginald says with a look of alarm, 'I'm not a military person.'

'But you'd know how to get us there,' I say, 'so what would you do once we were there?'

'I don't know,' he says again, 'I can plan strategy but not combat. I am not a combat expert and nor would I know how to use topography to aid such a thing. For a start I would need a map that has a far higher level of detail than a one on twenty five. I'm not even sure a one in ten would suffice. The opponent however, will know every street, corner, junction and building there.'

'Yeah but it's still thick as fuck,' I say, 'so we've got that on our side.'

'We hope,' Paula says with a look at me.

'Okay,' I nod slowly and look down for a few seconds while thinking, 'I'd say we keep going and hit those towns you said then stop and re-assess before we get to Stenbury. That gives Reginald and Charlie some time to examine the maps and maybe work out a way of getting us into that town without being seen...so we can fuck 'em over.'

'Sounds good,' Clarence says clapping his hands together.

'We have a cunning plan,' Roy says.

'I'm so sorry, what did you just say?' Reginald says with a step towards me.

'I was just holding the map,' Charlie says quickly to me.

'One thing I've learnt,' I say standing up, 'is that we have the right people doing the right jobs. Dave kills everything. Paula plans everything. Cookey takes the piss out of everything. Roy catches everything. Nick sets fire to everything...'

'I do not...'

'Can you two work together?'

'Er, what do you mean by work?' Reginald sputters, 'work at what? With what do you want us to work? To what aim? Oh gosh I wish I had never said anything now, really I do...'

'I was just holding the map,' Charlie says again.

'Can you work together? Reginald, will it help if Charlie works with you?'

'Oh gosh.'

'Was that gosh directed at me?' Charlie asks.

'Gosh no, I mean gosh to the suggestion posed by Mr Howie.'

'But I can now fire a weapon, Mr Howie.'

'Yes you can,' I say to Charlie, 'but one less weapon being fired won't hurt us as much as having the ability to strategize.'

'Good word,' Paula says with an affirming look.

'Strategize? Yeah I thought so too. Everyone ready?'

'Ready? Oh my lord no I am not ready. Not ready by a long... distinctly not ready...we have to examine the maps and plan ahead and...'

'Yeah you can do that while we're kicking the shit out of that first place...what was it?'

'Hydehill,' Charlie says.

'But there is only one seat at the desk in Roy's van,' Reginald says standing up and panicking.

'Chair,' I pick one up to show him, 'loads of them about.'

'Perhaps Reginald would care to work alone?' Charlie asks, 'I assisted here but...'

'No no, I would be delighted to share the burden of this awful task set to us. Indeed if I had known this would happen I would have stayed silent and truly I am not capable of doing the task set to me by Mr Howie and I fear greatly it will end in a terrible way and I will to be to blame so yes, sharing the burden of responsibility for so many lives will of course be a good thing and...' he pauses, blinks and stares round at everyone with a look of intense terror, 'I wish I had not said anything at all.'

'And let us all get killed?' Marcy asks him sharply.

'Oh gosh no, no I would not do that.'

'Reggie,' Marcy fixes him with a stern look, 'you've always told me how much of an intellectual you are. Now prove it.'

'Gosh yes I have said that haven't I. Yes. Yes indeed. This is my own fault. I am my own undoing.'

I push on before he can talk or think his way out of it, 'grab a chair then, or you might find a comfortable office chair in one of these buildings...lads, who fancies finding a nice office chair for Charlie?' I ask and watch the five of them burst up and into the café digging elbows into each other.

'Popular then,' Marcy says with a grin that harbours on being slightly too forced for my liking.

'I couldn't say,' Charlie replies folding the maps up.

'We'll need radios, Boss,' Clarence says still sat back in his chair holding one huge hand round a can of Tango.

'We've got radios.'

'Not when we're on the ground we haven't. How will Reginald and Charlie communicate with us?'

'Communicate? What for?' Reginald blusters with a fresh wave of panic.

'So we can talk,' I say with a casual shrug, 'you know, in case we're separated and you get surrounded or something.'

'Surrounded?!'

'Oh god, no not *surrounded* like actually surrounded,' I say with an imploring look to Paula.

'Just stay inside if they attack the van,' Roy says in a confident tone, 'they won't get in that...'

'Get in? Attacked? Surrounded?'

'You said they're going to be waiting for us,' Roy says, 'especially the closer we get to Stenbury.'

'Oh gosh...'

'Yeah not helping, Roy,' I say with a groan, 'you won't get attacked or surrounded, but just in case of anything we'll get radios from somewhere...anything else? Reginald, Charlie? What else do you need?'

'A lie down in a dark room,' Reginald whimpers.

'Whiteboard markers, clipboards, paper, pens,' Charlie says picking the now folded maps up, 'oh and a magnifying glass if you can find one.'

'A magnifying glass?'

'The maps,' Reginald says in a weak voice. He looks as though he's about to faint actually, 'the details can be very small.'

'Am I keeping my rifle?' Charlie asks.

'Yes,' Dave says, 'at all times with a fresh magazine loaded and ready.'

'You're going to be Reginald's bodyguard,' Paula says standing up and stretching with a slow grin.

'There's no office chair,' Cookey says coming out the door, 'I'll check over the road.'

'It's no bother,' Charlie says, 'I can use one of these...oh they've already gone.'

'Cookey would offer himself as a chair if he could,' Paula says watching them run across the road, 'actually I think they probably all would.'

'Load up then, we taking those cans?'

We do take the cans, and pilfer a load more from the café and the Tracker bars and biscuits too while the lads and Blinky push, carry, pull and argue over a worn out old office chair on wheels that gets pushed, lifted, pulled and argued over into the back of Roy's van.

'Got these,' Mo Mo presents an array of pens in his hands to Charlie with a sheepish smile.

'Thank you, Mo,' Charlie says taking them.

'Got paper,' Cookey says shoving a pack of printer paper into her hands.

'Thank you, Cookey.'

'Clipboards,' Blowers says, 'could only find two, is that enough?'

'You've all done very well, thank you.'

'I got you this,' Blinky says holding her middle finger up, 'seeing as I know you and have already seen you naked in the showers and don't feel the need to get in your knickers.'

'And thank you, Blinky,' Charlie says rolling her eyes.

'Fucking hang on,' Cookey says, 'you've seen...I mean...'

'Shut up, Cookey,' Blowers hisses.

'Shutting up,' Cookey nods.

'And I think I just made four new best friends,' Blinky says with a laugh, 'do I tell them about your tattoos?'

'I do not have any tattoos,' Charlie says brusquely.

'Have you got a tattoo?' Cookey asks.

'No I do not.'

'Does she?' Cookey asks Blinky.

'Nooo,' Blinky says mock seriously, 'Charlie? Tattoo? Like fuck she'd have a tattoo.'

'Argh, I can't tell if you're pissing about or not,' Cookey wails.

'Charlie? Are you ready?' I ask cutting through the conversation.

'Yes, of course. Reginald? Oh he's inside. Right I will see you all later.'

'Mr Howie?'

'Yes, Cookey and if you're going to ask me if you can go in Roy's van the answer is no.'

'Paula?'

'Same, Cookey.'

'Clarence?'

'Get in the Saxon.'

'Dave?'

'Now, Alex.'

'Yes, Dave. Sorry, Dave.'

CHAPTER TWELVE

D *ay Eighteen*

UPDATE No 3

THEY ARE SPECIAL FORCES. It is without doubt now. The skill of this group tells me they are a professionally trained and professionally organised cohesive combat unit operating to an incredible standard.

MY MIND IS FILLING with images of soldiers in combat uniforms working with discipline and structure where every move is thought in advance and every strategy is implemented with the greatest of judgement and taking into account every factor.

IN FACT. I would confidently wager this group were trained for this specific purpose.

THE TOWN I am in now is another middle sized market town with a highly confusing one way system that appears to have been developed by monkeys in a zoo using crayons. It is more open plan than the previous where I discovered the armoured vans therefore it did not give me the sense of foreboding.

JESS DID REACT THOUGH and again she commenced snorting and throwing her head about as whatever smells and scents reached her nose.

WHAT WE DISCOVERED IS akin to the findings in Finkton. Hundreds of infected corpses all killed within the main plaza of the town. It appears they were running or moving towards the road bordering the northern edge and from that position I found many shell casings of military grade ammunition. The same size and type that fits my M4 assault rifle.

I am very excited. Really very excited and I am writing these notes in haste to continue but one thing, no two things I must record before I move on.

THE REASON I consider they were trained for this specific purpose is the use of arrows to kill the infected hosts. Arrows from a bow embedded in eye sockets, necks and throats and a large built male was stuck like a pin cushion so I can only imagine the reasons why the soldiers fired so many into him. Could he have been something different? Could that single undead have been mutated so that he kept on charging despite the many arrows in his arms, legs and torso?

OF COURSE THE ammunition will eventually run out so the use of bows and arrows is an obvious choice and I can only surmise that the officers in charge of this unit decreed for some of the soldiers to practise the use of the bow during this skirmish.

THE SECOND REASON for my hurried note and something I wish to note are that I found several detached arms littering the ground all of which had teeth marks. Not human teeth marks but those from a large predatory animal.

AGAIN I CAN SURMISE they have trained attack dogs and the use of the detached arms were for training purposes. Why else would they rip the arms from the corpses?

I NEED to find this group and join forces with their officers. With their protection and working in tandem with such a disciplined army we should progress seeking those on my list, and of course I need to also inform the officers that a certain dark haired soldier appears to be immune.

IT IS STILL NOT RAINING. But it is now very bloody hot.

NB

CHAPTER THIRTEEN

'Right. So the way I see it is that we've let the infection think we're doing a particular thing to the extent its planning something cunning and horrible for us but now we've realised it knows what we're doing and we're still going to do it so it thinks we're still doing it and that way we can screw it over...while it thinks we're still doing the thing we're doing even though we know what we're doing and the infection *thinks* we're still doing the same thing even though we're actually not doing it but pretending to do it...Is that right?' I look across to the passenger seat and get a blank stare in response.

'Dave?'

'Yes, Mr Howie.'

'Why aren't you at the back?'

'Marcy said she wanted some air.'

'Oh...right...so much for giving orders then. Anyway, did you hear what I said?'

'Yes, Mr Howie.'

'Did it make sense?'

'Yes, Mr Howie.'

'So we're going to keep doing it and the infection is thinking we're still doing it so we can let the infection think we're doing it and then we can screw it over. Is that a good plan?'

'It is a plan.'

'Is it a good plan?'

'A plan is only good if it works.'

'Okay. But in the world of planning, is this a good one?'

'If it works the yes, it is a good plan.'

'What if it doesn't work?'

'Then it is not a good plan.'

'Figures. But...do you think the plan will work?'

He stares at me then looks ahead without a flicker of expression adorning his face, 'the enemy is predicting a course of action and one that we are going to adhere to in the pretence of maintaining that course of action so the enemy continues to believe in the accuracy of the prediction.'

'Yes! That's what I said.'

'Yes.'

'Yes. That's the plan. Is it a good one?'

'It is a plan.'

'A good plan. Is it a good plan?'

'It is a...'

'Right. Stop it. Do you think the plan we have is a good plan and you are not allowed to say it is a plan.'

'But it is a plan.'

'Yes I know it is a plan. We've established it's a bloody plan. Is it a good plan?'

'A plan is only good if...'

'Fuck's sake. Do you think the plan will work?'

'There are considerations.'

'What like?'

'We have to act as though we know nothing of the plan.'

'But we're doing that by still doing er...that...er...still doing it.'

'Yes.'

'Eh?'

'Yes, Mr Howie. We are still doing the thing the enemy has predicted we will do but we must be sure that we do not subconsciously alert the enemy to our knowledge of the fact we are aware of their prediction and are working towards a bluff.'

'Double bluff,' Clarence says from behind.

'Bluff,' Dave says.

'Double bluff.'

'Bluff.'

'Classic double bluff you've got right there.'

'Bluff.'

'It's a double bluff. The infection thinks we're doing one thing...which is what we're doing...'

'Bluff.'

'But we're only doing it to bluff it, I mean bluff the enemy so that's a double bluff.'

'One bluff. We are bluffing the enemy.'

'No. Dave. We are double bluffing. The first bluff is by knowing the enemy knows what we know. The second is by doing it anyway. That is a double bluff.'

'It is a bluff.'

'It's a sodding double bluff.'

'It is a bluff.'

'Boss, it is a double bluff.'

'You telling me or asking?'

'Asking.'

'Christ I don't know. Er...so we're doing what the enemy...fuck it...the infection thinks we're going to do while knowing it's thinking we're going to do it...is that a bluff?'

'Yes,' Dave and Clarence both answer.

'Is it?' Marcy calls out, 'aren't we just tricking it?'

'That's what a bluff is,' Clarence says.

'Why is it called bluff then? Why not just call it a trick?'

'A trick is something else,' Clarence says, 'but this is a double bluff.'

'What's a trick then?'

'We're talking about bluffs right now.'

'But a bluff is a trick.'

'No. A trick is a trick. This is a bluff and because we're doing it twice it is a double bluff.'

'I'm with Clarence,' Nick says, 'we know the infection has worked out what we were going to do but we're doing it anyway to trick...'

'Ha!'

'Still a bluff,' Clarence says.

'Nick said Trick.'

'Yeah,' Nick says, 'but the trick is part of the bluff.'

'So the bluff *is* the trick,' Marcy says.

'No the trick is the bluff,' Nick says, 'we're *bluffing* the infection by *tricking* it into thinking we're doing the thing we were going to do even though we know it was going to end badly but now we know that we're doing something else...'

'Are we?' Cookey asks, 'I thought we were still doing the same thing.'

'We are, but we're tricking...bluffing the infection into thinking we're still doing it,' Nick says.

'So,' Cookey says then pauses, 'so we are doing what it thinks we were going to do.'

'Yes and that's the tr...bluff.'

'But, how the fuck is that a bluff or a trick if we're doing what the infection thinks we were going to do anyway?'

'Only until Stenbury you thick twat,' Blowers says, 'weren't you listening?'

'Yeah but...fuck I'm confused. What's happening in Stenbury?'

'Fucking hell, Cookey,' Blowers groans, 'what were you doing?'

'When?'

'Fucking hell! At the table we were all sat at?'

'Oh. Yeah I was miles away. I lost it when Charlie stood up.'

'What?' Nick asks.

'She was right in front of me,' Cookey says, 'like right there. Holding the map...like right there...'

'You were watching her arse instead of listening to the plan,' Blowers says.

'Yeah pretty much,' Cookey says, 'why? What's happening in that place you said?'

'Stenbury.'

'Yeah there. What's happening?'

'The infection is getting a shit load of zombies ready to kill us.'

'Oh. Oh right. Yeah. That's bad. She has a lovely arse.'

'Oh my god,' Blowers groans, 'Mo, were you listening?'

'Yep.'

'So you heard it all?'

'Yep.'

'Bluff or double bluff, Mo?' Nick asks.

'Er...'

'Is it a single bluff by tricking the infection by doing what it expects or a double bluff by doing it *because* it knows we're going to do it?'

'Er...'

'Mo was sat next to me,' Cookey says.

'Really?' Blowers asks, 'Mo?'

'Er...'

'Fuck's sake, Mo. Blinky, were you listening?'

'No I zoned out.'

'When?'

'When it got boring.'

'Humanity is fucked,' Blowers says plaintively.

'What's the first place we're going to again?' I ask.

'Foxwood,' Cookey says, 'see I was listening.'

'We've been to Foxwood you dumb twat,' Blowers says, 'we're going past Foxwood to Hydehill.'

'We're going past Foxwood?'

'Yes.'

'So in effect we *are* actually going to Foxwood, but just not stopping.'

'I'm going to shoot you.'

'We're going to Foxwood and then to Hydehill.'

'Dave, can I shoot Cookey please?'

'I bet you want to shoot me...'

'Oh god noooo.'

'Shoot all over me more like.'

'Fuck...'

'I'm not bending over for the soap in the showers I tell you that for free.'

'What? Where did that come from?'

'You big dirty brute.'

'What the fuck? You've lost it, mate.'

'Yeah, you *want* me to lose it don't you...eh? Don't you? Yeah got your number.'

'You're such a dick.'

'You like dick.'

'Fuck off!'

'You like...er....fucking off.'

'Cookey...stop...'

'You like stopping...especially after starting when someone has dropped the soap in the showers...'

'Co...'

'You love cock.'

'I give up.'

'Yeah you like giving up and being submissive.'

'...'

'Your mum,' Cookey adds with a finale of a nod and grin while sitting back to interlock his hands behind his head, 'Cookey one,

Blowers nil. So anyway, stop fucking about. What's going on in Stenburyshireville or whatever it's called? I think Charlie and Reginald need some help. I could hold the maps for them or like... just stand there and fan them or something.'

'You need to know what we're doing,' Clarence says, 'we are going to Hydehill first...'

'Oh I got that bit,' Cookey says, 'we're doing every other town until we get to Stenbury...I just didn't listen after that.'

'Cookey. Quiet now,' Clarence says.

'Roger, being quiet.'

'Hydehill first, then er...'

'Brookley,' Marcy says.

'Then Brookley then...was that it?'

'We're you listening?' Cookey asks cheekily which draws a sharp intake of breath from everyone else.

'You are a cheeky sod today,' Clarence says, 'and we're going to fall out if this carries on.'

'Sorry.'

'Switch on, shut up and listen.'

'Sorry.'

'Marcy,' Clarence says, 'do you remember the town names?'

'Hydehill first, then Brookley, then Flitcombe and Stenbury is after that but we are stopping before we get to Stenbury to reassess.'

'But,' Clarence says and even though I'm facing the other way I would bet a million he is glaring at the lads to make sure they're listening, 'the infection knows we are coming. Reginald, however, is confident that we will be allowed to win each fight until we get to Stenbury.'

'Allowed?' Blowers asks, 'I don't like that.'

'What?' I call back.

'Being allowed to kill them. We'd kill them anyway.'

'We're going along with it,' I say, 'and we'll act normal and not give anything away that we know that they know what we're doing.'

'Fucking confusing,' Blinky mutters.

'We're going places to kill things,' Marcy says.

'Got it, fucking awesome,' Blinky says.

I glance across to Dave staring out the front windscreen, 'so mate, good plan then?'

CHAPTER FOURTEEN

'I really don't know what they want us to do. Really I don't. What are we meant to do? How? I don't know. Really I don't know. It's too much. Too much I say.'

Charlie listens patiently, waiting for the nerves to ease while she sits to one side of the desk and glances from Reginald to the monitor and the quadrant of images on display. She looks round at the interior and notes the rail running along the walls that will be perfect to hook or pin the maps up on. The desk is big enough for one map to be opened out if it's folded a bit to show the relevant area. Actually, if they fold them correctly they can have two maps on the desk and the rest pinned to the rail.

'The pressure is just terrible. We are holding the lives of others in our hands...'

His feet tap on the floor causing his knees to bounce and with his legs closed tightly together it gives him an almost comical appearance, if you don't look at the angst so evidently etched into his face that is. His hands keep moving to do something at the base of his neck and only after the fourth of fifth time does she realise he is trying to adjust a tie knot. They tremble too, his hands. Tremble and shake as he drums his fingers nervously on the desk and fidgets.

'What you said was amazing.'

'One wrong decision and everyone dies. How can someone work under that pressure? I mean...what? Sorry, what did you say?'

'I said that your ideas are amazing, what you said back there.'

'Oh, oh gosh that was a simple logical thought process but the...'

'I am sorry to interrupt you, Reginald. But it was more than a simple logical thought process. None of the others had the same thoughts or followed them through to the conclusion that you did.'

'Ah yes but you see they are ensconced within the action as it were so they lack the perspective of someone watching in from the outside. Should any of them have been in my position then I am sure, given time, they would have reached that same conclusion.'

'They would have been dead by then.'

'Well yes, a valid point and I will concede to that fact.'

'But now they will not be dead because you were brave enough to speak out and therefore you have saved them, us...you have saved all of us.'

'Indeed yes, for now perhaps I have taken action that has altered the proposed course which may well prevent such an immediate loss of life. However, because I presented my thesis it is then not fair to impose such a burden of responsibility by assuming I, or indeed we, have the capability to plan for them.'

'Yes I see that point but may I say, respectfully, that I do not believe they are imposing the burden. If you, or we, were to present back to Mr Howie that, after careful consideration, we are not able to provide any assistance in planning then I am sure he would accept that decision without prejudice or judgement.'

'Ah but then herein lies the rub that if left to act alone without the guidance of planning that yes, he may well make decisions based on what is known at this time, but what if it changes? What if the other player works out they we have mitigated their plan and then plans something else?'

'In which case we will have to continue to monitor, albeit, we, or you, may not play an active role in the planning, execution or direct combat but more work in a passive overseer, almost consultant role of monitoring and reporting when the need arises.'

'Ah yes, yes I see. So perhaps I, or we, shall not be able to present a military plan in the format that Mr Howie requires but rather we observe, such as I have done already, and verbalise our concerns or opinions as and when the need arises.'

'I think so, however, we do not know that you, or we in this case, cannot do what is requested without first trying. Surely intelligence is not based on what you know now but rather the ability to continue to learn and advance your understanding and knowledge.'

Reginald pauses, thinking, nodding slowly, 'indeed, intelligence does come from the continual use of cognitive function to enhance one's own understanding and knowledge. He who ceases to learn may well cease to know.'

'Who said that?'

'I said that.'

'Your quote?'

'Indeed.'

She pauses, thinking, nodding slowly and noticing without looking that his feet have stopped tapping and his hands are now interlocked across his stomach without tremble or shake and the expression on his face is changing from fear riddled to contemplation.

'Perhaps, as an exercise,' she suggests casually, 'we could follow the teams advancement through the next...say we call it the next target location? What was the name?'

'Hydehill I believe, yes, yes it was Hydehill,' he leans forward and taking one of the maps he starts to unfold it on the desk.

Taking her cue she reaches for the map underneath and she too starts to unfold it.

'The desk is only big enough for one map,' she says as though somewhat disappointed.

'Not if we fold them to show the section required, here,' Reginald finds the area he needs and refolds the map to half size and lays the map flat'

'Oh I see,' Charlie copies his actions and grasping the lip of the desk she pulls herself in closer as she lays her map down next to his.

'One in twenty five,' Reginald says tapping the map on the right in front of him, 'and yours is one in fifty?'

'Yes, one in fifty,' Charlie says, 'have we two one in twenty fives?'

'I believe we do,' Reginald replies leafing through the stack, 'yes we have another one here.'

Instead of taking it from him she tentatively holds her hand out, 'may I?'

'Of course,' Reginald hands it over and waits as she opens it out to the same folds as his one in twenty five scale map before laying it on the desk.

'There,' she says, 'we're both looking at the same thing.'

'Indeed. A duplication,' Reginald says glancing between the two, 'and a pity the scale is so vast.'

'Mr Howie will have to accept that,' Charlie says politely, 'that we can only work with what we are given.'

'Indeed,' Reginald says righteously, 'indeed he shall have to be accepting of that.'

Leaning forward she pulls the chair in tighter to the desk taking care not to bump Reginald's chair in the process while being mindful that he retains the central position to the desk and she off to the side, 'Foxwood is here,' she says placing a finger on the small village indicated on the map, 'I wonder,' she muses gently, 'what we can match from the map to what we witnessed as physical objects. Is that the pond?' She asks knowing full well that the blue section on the map is the pond in Foxwood.

'Er, yes. Yes that must be the pond as it is the only expanse of water shown within that vicinity.'

'Okay, duck pond...so that cross symbol represents a church? Is that right?'

'Yes yes, a bold black cross is the sign of a religious building. See here, they are within nearly every village and town,' he says motioning to the various bold black crosses on his own map.

'Interesting, do they use different symbols for differing places of worship in relation to the differing religions?'

'An interesting question. I know of three different symbols used. There is a blue cross for a cathedral, the black cross with a square underneath represents a place of worship with a tower whereas a black cross with a circle underneath represents a place of worship with a spire or a minaret or dome. So in effect, the black cross with a circle can be used to identify a place which may not be a Christian place of worship.'

'I did not know that,' she says softly, 'here in Stenbury,' she says holding her finger on the map, 'there is a cross over a black circle, so that could be a mosque or other religious place of worship?'

'Yes, or it could also be a church with a spire.'

'You'd think with the onset of greater religious sensitivities that they would denote a wider range of symbols.'

'Indeed but then the argument could be brought forward that map makers are independent of all cultural values and therefore they merely observe and record what is in place at that time without deference to the religious or cultural meaning.'

'Yes but they are using a cross which is a symbol of Christianity and that same cross could be used to represent a religion that is *not* Christian in origin.'

'Again a valid point and should civilisation start again perhaps we could bring it their attention.'

She smiles at the gentle joke, 'I think we should. This is the woods behind Foxwood,' she says indicating the green section on the map, 'this orange coloured line represents the road running through the village...'

'Yes and the red line here is the road we are on now but do note that red lines are used both for dual carriageways and for main roads, the key is the thickness of the line.'

'Blue is motorways?'

'Yes, orange is secondary roads and the red and white striped are narrow roads with places to pass.'

'Ah yes I see one here.'

'Do you understand the gradients?'

'Yes, a series of concentric in appearance circles that, when seen closer together, show a steeper incline and I think I am right in saying the l.eight above mean sea level is shown with a numerical value, is that correct?'

'You are correct but they are not concentric circles.'

She doesn't point out she said they were concentric in appearance but stares down with a finger that traces lightly over the thick paper. Manipulation is never nice but gentle manipulation is done with every human encounter and she does notice his hands are now entirely steady and his tone is neutral with that comforting level of condescension reserved for the true academic at work.

'Howie to Paula, we're just about to pass Foxwood.'

*'Hi, Howie, thanks for that...*did you hear that in the back?'

'We did, thank you, Paula,' Charlie calls out as Reginald winces.

'They should not be using names and places on the radio,' he says quietly, 'it is not beyond the capability of the opponent to listen to our transmissions.'

'I do agree, however, we are only doing what is expected and at this stage, the opponent will only be hearing that we are maintaining the same course. Perhaps we can advise Mr Howie that after Flitcombe we should desist from using names and locations?'

'Yes, yes we'll do that.'

'Or, perhaps given the circumstances we could consider making fake transmissions to enforce the subterfuge should the opponent by listening.'

'Ah yes, a suggestion that can be given consideration at the appropriate time.'

'Should we maintain a record of our suggestions or advice to be given? So we don't forget? That is something I can do.'

'If you wish yes, a record will perhaps be appropriate.'

The clipboard is within arms-reach with fresh paper ready to go and a pen wedged into the spring mechanism at the top. Neat handwriting and the first suggestion is logged, ***advice ref. use of names on radio / maintain subterfuge.***

A natural break in the flow of conversation and she takes advantage to subtly progress matters.

'So we're here,' she says at the point on the map where the orange line of the road through Foxwood runs from the red line of the road they are on, 'and we go along here until we reach Hydehill which, by all appearances, is not a big place at all.'

'No, not a big centre of habitation.'

'What could we assume?'

'Assume?' He asks with a slightly sharper tone but she carries on as though unaware.

'Of Hydehill. Could we assume the shops and stores will be on the main road running through?'

'Oh I see. Well yes, yes I think we could. There are very limited side streets shown on here, of course there will be more than shown but if you were planning a commercial endeavour you would wish to capture the best location for both residential and transient custom. Therefore the main road would be the best location.'

'Yes, and they would need parking in order for your customers to stop. So we can expect a main road with shops and stores with either on road parking or a nearby car park.'

'Of course and this being England there will be a public house and a post office.'

'P.O. Is that post office?'

'P.O? Yes, ah yes there it is on the main road as we correctly predicted.'

'Church is here, or rather a place of worship and the shape is square so we have a place of worship with a tower. Actually, that could be important if we...if one were to be looking for places of height say for observation.'

'Yes and taking that one step further we could also suggest that a post office has a secure inner area used for the storage of money...'

'Which could be used as a safe fall back point should the need arise.'

'Yes,' Reginald says nodding, 'in the same way we could assume a public house will hold ample supplies of refreshments. You should note that suggestion down.'

'But public houses are not denoted on the maps,' she says adding to the list.

'You are correct, they are not on ordnance survey maps of this scale.'

'It was a good suggestion though. Hydehill has one church with a tower, a post office on the main road and look here, there is an orange coloured road feeding into the red coloured main road running through and that orange secondary road joins another main road a short distance away.'

'Where does that second main road go?'

'It runs through another series of villages, farms and what looks like open heath land.'

'A viable route for the opponent to use to move host bodies into Hydehill or even through Hydehill towards Stenbury.'

She stares down, tracing along the second main road as it runs through the towns and villages marked on the map visualising the infected moving along the road with a predefined number peeling off to stay in Hydehill while the rest move on.

'Placing myself in the position of the other player,' Reginald mutters more to himself but wishing to show his intelligence, 'I would try and hold them at the junction.'

'Junction?'

'Where the secondary road meets the main road through Hydehill,' he says without looking at her, 'yes, yes indeed I would use this location to buy time to enable me to position my pieces to a more advantageous...er...position.' Damn it, why did he say position twice? He should have thought of a different word.

'And there are quite a few side roads around that area of the junction,' Charlie says not mentioning the fact he said position twice when he could have used any number of other words, 'actually there is one that runs from before the junction and appears to go round the back of the buildings fronting onto that main road and connects with the er...main road before the junction.'

'Yes I see it, I would leave the junction of the side road clear until they were past and committed at the crossroads and hold a reserve force behind the buildings to come round and attack them from behind,' Reginald says glancing up at her.

'That is supposing you wished to win the fight when in this case the infection *does not* wish to win the fight,' she says.

'No that is true but it will need to gain time and still give the sense of victory which can be done by allowing Mr Howie to deal with those at the crossroads and then bring in some more to attack from behind and therefore prolong the battle and still give a greater sense of achievement.'

'Good morning, this is your captain speaking. Please fasten seatbelts in preparation of the landing as we will soon be coming into Foxwood...fuck it, we've done Foxwood, I meant Hydehill... bollocksed that one up didn't I? Anyway, Hydehill is just ahead.'

'Thanks, Howie. We're ready.'

'Paula,' Charlie calls out, 'we think they'll meet you at the crossroads on the main road where the shops are.'

'Oh right,' Paula says twisting round to lean through the open door, 'how did you work that out?'

'Reginald was examining the maps and...'

'There will be a smaller junction to the left going into a side road,' Reginald says quickly, 'we think they will use that to send reinforcements down to attack you from behind.'

'I thought they wanted us to win?' Roy asks.

'We have predicted the opponent will be trying to gain more time so perhaps it will send the second force down that road towards the end...that is if we are correct which, of course, we may not be, in fact you should not rely on anything we have said to any degree of reliability.'

'Don't worry,' Paula says with an earnest look, 'we'll keep it in mind.'

'If you park near to the junction we'll be able to see from the cameras,' Charlie says.

'Which junction?' Roy asks, 'the main one or the other one you said about?'

'The one for the side road, Roy,' Charlie says.

'*Paula to Howie...*'

'Good God don't transmit that!' Reginald yells.

Paula presses the button to speak into the handset with a glare at Reginald, 'Paula to Howie, *ask Nick what the chances of our transmissions being heard are.*'

'*Hang on, he heard you...I'll put him on.*'

'*Paula, it's Nick, you there?*'

'*Yep it's me. We couldn't get Roy's radio to talk to the Saxon radio so we used a radio from another cash van to put in here and I'm guessing they're probably encrypted.*'

'So they can't be hacked?'

'*Hacking is something different but the chances of someone else having a radio with the same encryption software are low but not impossible.*'

'*Okay, understood. Ask Marcy if it's likely the infection would do that?*'

'*Er...she says how the hell would she know.*'

'*She was...never mind...*Christ, I'm offending everyone today,' she mutters darkly to herself:

'It's very hot,' Charlie says tactfully, 'and so humid and sticky.'

'Yes,' Paula says sharply then seems to realise the tone of her own voice so turns and offers a smile, 'sorry, yes it is. Don't worry we'll tell the others what you said.'

'Quietly, you must tell them quietly and give nothing away.'

'Yes, Reginald. We'll do it quietly.'

'The opponent must not be alerted that we know what...'

'Yes, Reggie! I heard you.'

'Reginald,' Reginald mutters at the harsh rebuke while Roy stares diplomatically ahead and Charlie examines her fingernails.

CHAPTER FIFTEEN

The battle for Hydehill

The main road through is wide and straight. Shops and stores on both sides with parking spaces out the front and on the way into the town we pass the obligatory post office and a church set back amidst a rapidly overgrowing garden and thick weeds sprouting at the base of the gravestones.

A junction on the left leading to what looks like an access road running behind the main shops. Cars still parked up in the spaces on the road and no doubt left by the people who lived in the flats above the shops. Windows broken and the puddles on the road are fighting valiantly but losing badly against being evaporated. No jokes now and the sounds of weapons being checked come from behind me. Magazines taken out. Magazines rammed back in. Bolts racked. Straps adjusted. Bags pulled on. The gentle dink of hand weapons being lifted. Dave, next to me in the front checks his rifle first then draws and checks his pistol before running his hands along his beltline checking the hilts of the knives are in place. Clarence clearing his throat, Marcy taking a deep breath.

'I'll puke soon as we get out,' Blinky says hoarsely.

'Okay,' Blowers replies in a dull tone, 'we're down one with Charlie so stay together and stay alert. Nick, keep Meredith with you until we go to hand weapons.'

'Got it.'

'Will we go to hand weapons?' Blinky asks in that rush of words.

'Dunno, see how it goes,' Blowers says gruff with the expectancy of the fight.

'I've only got a knife.'

'It'll do for now,' Clarence says, 'if it goes to that then stay close to me or the lads, same goes for you, Marcy.'

'I'll stay with Howie,' Marcy says.

It starts. The pulse of my heart rate increasing. The gentle pounding of blood starting to rush past my ears.

'They're here,' Mo says abruptly at the same second Meredith gives voice with a low growl.

'Uncanny,' Clarence mutters, 'you're a human German Shepherd, Mo. See anything?' He adds standing up to lean over the seats and stare through the front.

'Not yet.'

'You stopping at that big junction?'

'Yep, everyone ready?' I get a low murmur of voices in response as I slow the speed down to a crawl over the last few hundred metres while we scan the sides, doorways, windows, recesses, mouths of alleys, 'remember,' I say as I bring the vehicle to a halt, 'don't give anything away. Everyone out.'

Weapons up and the doors open as we vault the drop into the wall of incessant heat that instantly brings the sweat to bead on our foreheads.

'Blowers, junction,' I motion to the mouth of the wide junction to the left side.

'On it, Blinky, stay close to...you alright, Blinky?'

We all turn to see her bent double retching to spew on the ground, 'told you,' she says with a belch as she stands upright wiping her mouth.

'Stay between Nick and Mo, spread across the junction.'

'Howie,' Paula calls my name jogging easily from Roy's van. I stop and wait expecting her to say something but she waits until she gets in close and drops her head as though to talk to the ground, 'Reggie and Charlie said they'll be sending more down from that side road back there,' she says with a gentle motion of her head back to the road we came along, 'but probably not until we've almost finished.'

'Okay, tell Blowers and the others,' I nod and look round as casually as possible.

'They also said this is the place they'd meet us but,' she looks up and round, 'but...'

'Meredith was growling,' Clarence says quietly, 'and Mo said they were here.'

'How does he do that?' She asks glancing over to the young man standing by the junction with the others.

'No idea, Roy...you alright keeping an eye behind us?'

'Yep, Charlie and Reggie have a view from the cameras at the back too.'

'Good,' I move round in a slow circle, 'we're ready then...'

'WE WE'RE MOSTLY RIGHT,' Charlie says speaking in a hushed whisper now.

'Mostly? I would say we were wholly right,' Reginald replies with his eyes glued on the monitor watching the rear view and the junction to the side road back in the distance.

She rises from the chair and moves to the thick riveted Perspex window on the driver's side to look out at the shops and buildings.

No movement. No motion. She moves to the other side and scans the view, 'nothing,' she mutters and glances down to the monitor and the image of the others all spread out near the main junction, 'do you think we were wrong?'

'Good god no,' Reginald snorts, 'were you expecting them to be waiting here? No no no, that would tell us they were expecting us. No, they'll be stacked up in those buildings at the sides waiting to come out in dribs and drabs.'

'Is that what you would do?'

'It is exactly what I would do. A few minutes to let them wonder if this town has any infected left and then send them out to the slaughter.'

She watches his right foot tapping and the his hands constantly going to the base of his neck as his reaction to the tension of the situation starts to show, 'but they will come from behind us and our group,' he taps lightly on the screen at the figures, 'are all in front of us which has left us isolated and alone...' he looks round to the back doors, 'are they locked?'

'They are self-locking,' Charlie says.

'And the front? Is that locked?'

'Same,' she says politely, 'we are safe in here.'

'Safe,' Reginald snorts again, 'no such thing anymore.'

'I've got the rifle if anything does happen,' she says as reassuringly as possible while taking care not to sound patronising.

'Yes. Yes indeed you have,' he says almost absent mindedly from watching the monitor as his hands once again move to adjust the tie knot that isn't there. He picks up a bottle of water from the desk and takes a sip with a look of distaste, 'I need tea not water,' he mutters.

'Tea? What kind do you like?'

'Camomile or Darjeeling,' he whispers, 'I always have tea when I am thinking. I cannot think without tea.'

'You've done very well so far.'

'Under pressure and under duress but to maintain cognitive functionality I require tea to drink and...there! See?'

'Where?' Charlie moves quickly to sit down and pull her chair in as Reginald leans closer to the monitor, 'right where I said. The first one cometh,' he says with an air of satisfaction.

A single undead staggering from an open doorway to a betting shop. Elderly with straggly grey hair and wearing a pair of filthy stained pyjama bottoms.

'Oh now,' Reginald groans shaking his head, 'ham acting, awful ham acting...look at him pretending not to know they are there...oh look now he's seen them. Did you see that double take?'

'I did,' Charlie chuckles at the old man staring left and right then showing a start as he locks eyes on the group a short distance up the road.

'Now he'll have to *alert* the others in the area,' Reginald says making quote marks.

The howl reaches them, albeit dulled and dampened by the thick walls of the sealed van and then he's off. A loping jerky run into the road and towards the weapons being held ready.

'Gunshot,' Reginald says pre-empting the events, 'they will shoot him and a minute later we will see more coming as though drawn by the noise and the gunshot.'

'We shall see,' Charlie says watching the monitor as the elderly man runs up the road.

'YOU OKAY?' I ask Marcy as we wait for something to happen.

'Hot,' she says bluntly, 'and pissed wet through with sweat,' she adds, 'and it's making my hair greasy,' she adds again, 'and my knickers are sticking to my backside,' she adds again with an uncomfortable shift on the spot, 'wish I was naked,' she finished with a huff.

'You'd distract everyone if you were naked.'

'Pervert,' she says but smiles as she speaks, 'are they coming or what?'

'Hope so. Reginald might be wrong though.'

'No he won't be,' she says with a groan either at the heat or at Reggie, 'he's too clever for that. Oh god I just want to lie down in a cold bath of water.'

'Sounds nice.'

'Can we find somewhere so I can have a bath tonight?'

'We can try.'

'I'll bet Paula would love one too. Why did she ask me that?'

'What?'

'On the radio, when Nick was talking to her, she said to ask Marcy what the infection would do.'

'I dunno.'

'Just because I was one once doesn't mean I know everything about them.'

'Yeah but...'

'I mean is that what everything thinks if they have a question about the infection? Just ask Marcy?'

'Er, yeah?'

'It's not on.'

'Is it not?'

'I'm being serious!'

'Okay,' I say quickly at the look of anger on her flushed face, 'I'm only playing.'

'It's too hot for playing,' she huffs again, 'scratch my back for me,' she says turning round to face away.

'Where?'

'Under my bra strap.'

I reach up to feel for the bra strap and start rubbing above it.

'No under it, no actually under it...put your hand up and get underneath the strap.'

'Oh, see what you mean,' I reach down and get my hand under her top and push up towards the strap, 'fuck me you're sweating.'

'Sorry, is it gross?'

It isn't gross. It isn't gross at all. In fact it is the opposite of gross.

'Howie? Is it gross?'

'Huh? Er...no, no it's fine,' I find the strap and get my fingertips underneath and start running them side to side across her skin making her curl her shoulders forward to round her back out.

'Oh that's good,' she groans, 'so nice.'

'Contact,' Clarence says and turning to look before facing away with a shake of his head, 'when you're ready.'

'My back was itching,' Marcy says.

I draw my hand out and look round, 'where?'

'Down there, old bloke pretending not to see us...oh he has now bless him, here he goes...see him?'

'Yeah,' I take a step forward and shield the sun from my eyes to watch an old man in filthy pyjama bottoms running into the street giving a strangled howl, 'just him?'

'Looks that way,' Paula says, 'for now,' she adds in a low mutter.

'Movement,' Dave says as quiet as Paula, 'in the Spar.'

'Spar? Where's that?' Marcy asks quickly.

'Next to the bakery,' Paula says turning round to grin.

'Don't fucking start, do you think every town has a Spar?' I ask with a sudden thought.

'Seems that way,' Marcy says staring at the red strip over the front window of the shop.

'Got them on army bases too,' Clarence says.

'No way, really?'

'All over the place,' he says casually, 'unlike Tesco which just rip people off.'

'Oi,' I say warningly, 'every little helps.'

'Is someone shooting him?' Paula asks, 'you know...just wondering seeing as he's getting quite close.'

'Poor old bugger is wheezing like a train,' Clarence says with a wince, 'can hear him from here.'

'Trains don't wheeze,' I say.

'It's a saying,' he says.

'Is it fuck. Dave would you...righto that's him dead then...you know, I might have been about to ask something else,' I say as he re-holsters the pistol.

'Were you?'

'No, But I might.'

'Oh. Okay.'

'Well,' I announce loudly, 'that was a fucking thrilling battle.'

'Don't goad them,' Paula says with a soft chuckle.

'One old codger? Is that it for this town?' I ask the group, 'Blowers? You see anyone?'

'Nothing, Mr Howie,' he shouts back, 'you think that was it?'

'Must be.'

'We moving out then?'

'Yeah,' I turn round in another slow circle wondering when they're going to make a move, 'guess so...'

'CONTACT,' Dave's voice recoils round the street as the sounds of people moving fast come from the building line.

'CONTACT,' Nick shouts facing towards the building on the corner of the junction.

'CONTACT,' Mo shouts from the other corner.

'Bout fucking time,' I mumble into my hand.

'That side,' Paula shouts aiming down the street to the shops adorning the side past the junction as Clarence steps back to fall in beside me.

'More than I was expecting,' he says.

I nod back as my heart starts racing at the sight of the hordes charging towards us from nearly every side. Only the junction itself is clear but they come from the shops either side and opposite. From doors they pour out howling into the air.

'FIRE,' I yell and the air fills with the sound of assault rifles spewing bullets in every direction.

'REGINALD,' Charlie says with alarm, 'there's too many and they're coming too fast...'

'No no,' the small man says shaking his head, 'this is what was expected.'

'I think you're wrong,' she says lifting her assault rifle and checking the magazine, 'why are they pouring out like that then? It's so obvious they were waiting now.'

'It is only obvious because we were aware of it...'

'I thought they would come out slowly, like they did in the thatched village.'

'That was too staged. The opponent has realised it was too staged so now it is countering that by sending them out too fast. It is still learning. Remember that.'

'Are you saying this is a mistake then? A miscalculation?'

'I am saying precisely that. Which in itself gives some alarm as the ability to assess and adapt to the perception of mistakes is perhaps more evolved than even I anticipated but, but having said that I would maintain that this is still what was expected.'

'Are you sure?' She asks moving back to the desk clutching the assault rifle, 'if you're not sure then say so and I'll go out to help them.'

'Mr Howie and his cohorts have faced adversaries many size this number and walked away unscathed. In fact I would wager Mr Howie and Dave could see off this attack on their own armed only with a pair of spoons.'

She sits down, her heart racing at the sight of the battle and the guns booming into the air. She fought yesterday in the house and again today but they were different. It was hand to hand in the house and the villages this morning were easy so the sight of the hordes charging across the ground fill her with a pulsing sense of fear and an urge to be doing something, to be fighting instead of watching from a comfy chair in the back of an armoured van. Four feet tap on the ground now and while Reginald's hands tremble at the inner voice telling him he may have been wrong so hers turn white at the knuckles from the pressure applied from her grip on the weapon.

Bodies slump and are blown back. Heads bursting apart from the perfect hits given by Dave. Shouts of magazine sound out amidst the firefight and the howls of the infected coursing across the street and still pouring from the building line.

'Reginald,' she says with a heavy breath, 'if they are putting this many here how many will they have for Stenbury?'

'I was considering that very same thing,' he says with another attempt to fiddle with the tie knot that isn't there.

'There has to be hundreds here,' she whispers, 'hundreds to be sacrificed...if that is, you are right.'

'Indeed,' he says weakly.

'Hundreds sent to be killed to buy time?'

'They have millions,' he says turning to stare at her, 'I was with Marcy when she was...well, when she was terrible. Most terrible,' his voice trails off at the memory, 'the numbers she...we...took were staggering but still nothing compared to the potential reach of the infection.'

'Hundreds here could mean thousands at Stenbury,' she looks away from the hurt in his face and watches the battle on the monitor.

The noise is incredible and every sound can be matched to an image but there are too many sounds and too many images. She recognises burst fire, single shots and the voices shouting and somewhere in amongst that wall of noise is Meredith barking. She leans closer to watch Blinky standing with her feet planted apart and the way she aims, fires, aims, fires. Small movements but done perfectly. She screams magazine into the air and slams a fresh one home, takes a step forward and continues to fire. Cookey dropping down to kneel. Nick taking two steps out to gain a better aim. Mo rock solid and the weapon hardly seems to move when he fires. Clarence and the size of him makes the rifle look tiny. Dave, as small as Reginald and firing single shots but every shot is a kill.

Marcy and Paula firing bursts into the mass heading towards them. Everyone working together, covering each other and now she thinks it she looks closer at the way they're spread out. Seemingly random but no flank has been left uncovered as they form a rough wide circle with the beast of the dog in the middle waiting for any that may break through.

It changes her perspective. These people are experienced, functioning, hardened and deft. Paula shouts magazine and instantly Roy and Howie both adjust their aim to make sure the gap left by Paula is covered. As she rises so they re-adjust and on it goes. Hundreds is now not enough, not against these people and now she can see how they've survived. The silly jokes, the banter, the mocking, piss-taking and flirting all mask a raging desire to kill and hurt those that took everything from them. Without thinking and without asking she presses a button on the monitor to make one image full screen and almost gasps at the look of intense focus mingled with abject fury on the face of Mo Mo. He is raging inside. Teeth barred. Eyes wide. Feet planted. Nick just to one side and she can see what looks like a wry smile on his face, that he knows something they don't know, that they can't be beaten. The biggest shock is Cookey. The smiling laughing joker now a man with broad shoulders and a snarl that transforms him completely. His blond hair as wet and as clinging to his scalp as the black top does to his body. She leans just that smidgen closer with her eyes travelling over his shoulders and arms, down his long legs and back to his face that is puckering up with a mock kiss as he stares cross eyed. She bursts out laughing, a sudden noise that makes Reginald jump and instantly press a button on the monitor.

'We need to watch behind us,' Reginald says with a sigh.

'Of course, sorry,' she says quickly but her eyes linger for longer than she would have realised.

'MAGAZINE,' Cookey shouts dropping down to one knee.

'Why are you kneeling to change?' Blowers shouts at him.

'Just am, fuck off.'

'You're such a dick,' Blowers shakes his head and fires into the horde, 'you think she's watching you?'

'Get fucked,' Cookey shouts as he stands up, plants his feet wide and fires in what he hopes is a manly looking pose.

'What the fuck are you doing?' Nick says glancing back.

'Fuck off,' Cookey says again.

'Are you snarling?' Nick asks, 'Blowers, what's he doing?'

'The fucking idiot thinks Charlie might be watching him.'

'Twat,' Nick chuckles and fires a burst into the human bodies running towards them.

I glance back to see Cookey is giving it a good snarl but with his hair soaking wet and his top tight against his frame he does actually look quite good and I can't help but laugh when he puckers up and pulls a quick silly cross-eyed face. I could tell him off but we're not in danger. They're falling in droves and we've almost won already.

'Single shots,' Dave orders, 'preserve ammunition.'

For a second there is a weird silence as every gun falls quiet and the air fills with a series of dull clicks as we change the fire selection. A second or so later and we're back to plucking shots with careful aiming.

'I guess we'll see if Reggie was right,' Clarence says to me.

'Guess so,' I say looking down the main road past our two parked vehicles.

'YOU WERE RIGHT,' she says with an explosive sigh. Sitting back in the chair she eases the rifle stock down to the floor to prop against her legs and smiles over the desk, 'that was intense.'

'Intense?' Reginald asks with a slow blink of his eyes and suddenly he looks old, drawn, tired and the horror is there to see, 'that was not intense. Intense is still to come and the things we shall see will stay in your eyes when you try and sleep.'

She holds his gaze for a second before dropping her eyes, 'the others seem to sleep well enough.'

'Indeed,' he whispers, 'indeed they do and I wonder how they have built those walls within their minds.'

'Exhaustion probably,' she says, 'what was it like?'

'To what do you refer?' He asks knowing fully well what she is asking.

'Being one of them.'

He inhales and thinks, 'it was, it is...imagine if you will, or think of something that has happened in your life that you placed great emotional attachment to but as time passes so that emotional attachment eases. Perhaps it is like that. My mind was not truly my own and although I possessed the essence of my character it was not the individual that was in control of it.'

'And the things you did?'

'I was as much a coward then as I am now,' he says with a tight smile, 'I think *that* part of my character can never be suppressed.'

'But you were there when they happened?'

'Yes, yes I was and for that I was as complicit and as guilty as a witness as Marcy was for the level of destruction and death she wrought and make no mistake about it, the things she did were abhorrent and beyond anything you could imagine. Our sins for that are unforgivable but the mitigation we present is that we were controlled and not functioning under our own mindful state. I can see on your face you are wondering how such acts can be perpetrated without any ability to prevent it...'

'No no...'

'And my answer is that it was entirely and completely organic. It was not an audible voice giving orders but an intrinsic part of our minds like it had always been there. Do you know we did not feel pain? We did not need to sleep or rest and the host bodies that Marcy infected were able to cure their forms of disease and illness...' The story of how they all came together was told yesterday in the shopping centre but these minute details were not shared and she listens now with rapt attention as his mind meanders into the recent past, 'diabetes for instance. There were host bodies that by rights should have died within hours of being infected but whatever abilities the virus has, it appears one of them is to fix such afflictions. There was a boy,' he says quietly, 'in a house, a grand house that was once the residence of Queen Victoria...'

'Osborne House?'

'The same,' he says, 'you know your history. Yes a boy that had suffered a serious assault, he was dying,' he speaks quietly his voice lilting with emotion, 'Marcy convinced his family to let her turn him and thereby save him, and she did it too. She took what was inside of her and placed it in him, the tiniest drop mind and he died but came back and he felt no pain from the injury he had sustained. That, that was turning point for her I think, that she realised this virus was meant to heal not to harm.'

'What?'

'Yes, it is obvious. This thing prevents death, pain, suffering, disease, hunger, thirst...'

'It makes them kill everything in sight.'

'It does now but is that what was originally intended? Is it a tweak in a DNA chain or the genealogy? I have a fundamental belief that what one can do all can do...'

'I know of this,' she says intently, 'we are all capable of what the most intelligent can do.'

'Yes but we do not know how. It is the same. Marcy, through the course of her infection, went from a thirst for death and destruction to a belief in finding a way to take what she had to... well, to make things better if I may be so blunt, and her belief is that it is only through Howie that she can achieve that.'

'I see but...' movement on the monitor but not from the cameras mounted to the front but from those behind, of a horde pouring from the junction into the road, 'they're coming,' she says quickly.

'From the side road? Ah yes, yes...so they are...'

'I can fire from the back doors,' she says rising from the chair.

'No you mustn't,' he snaps, 'that would give away our position and the fact we are in here...'

She stops dead cursing inwardly at her own lack of thought, 'of course, sorry. I...I didn't think.'

'Mr Howie has seen them,' Reginald says commentating from his observation on the monitor and a second later the first shots are fired as the second part of the fight gets underway, 'we are in the firing line,' he says fretfully and the nervous manner sweeps back as his hands move instinctively to his neck, 'I do hope this vehicle is bullet proof.'

A dull ping from the back makes them both duck followed instantly by Roy shouting *don't shoot my bloody van you idiots.*

Five minutes later and it's done. The few sent from the road are dispatched with the same brutal efficiency and Meredith is released to finish off the crawlers.

'All done,' Howie calls banging on the back door. Charlie opens up, swinging the door in to reveal them all checking weapons and Cookey grinning widely.

'Did you see me?' He can't help himself but ask outright.

'Yes I did,' she laughs, 'very funny.'

'Did you laugh?'

'Yes and I almost got told off by Reginald for watching you.'

'Watching me?' He asks with a broad wink, 'eh? Watching me were you?'

'You wish,' Blowers mutters.

'You both alright?' Howie asks peeking through the door to Reginald at the desk, 'that went exactly as you said, Reggie.'

'Reginald, yes, yes we observed it from here.'

'Spot on, mate. Totally spot on. Anything for us? Any feedback?'

'Yes, can you not shoot the van next time please?'

'I said that,' Roy shouts from somewhere, 'I can't see any damage though.'

'Perhaps we could be parked within the circle?' Charlie asks, 'it would make sense for both vehicles to be in the centre.'

'Why didn't you two think of that?' Howie asks looking at Clarence and Dave.

Clarence shrugs nonchalant and smiles, 'why didn't you?'

'Fair point, yeah we'll do that next time. Anything else?'

'Radios to communicate,' Charlie says, 'we saw them coming from the road before you became aware of them...we could have alerted you.'

'Yep, actually,' Howie says ducking out of sight for a second then reappearing, 'once Meredith has finished doing her rounds we'll have a look.'

'There may well be some left to observe,' Reginald says.

'So? We're just looking for radios and supplies. That won't give anything away. Will it?'

Reginald thinks before answering, 'no...no but we must be sure not to verbalise anything in relation to...'

'We won't,' Howie says abruptly still with the flush of battle in his face, 'fuck me this heat is unbearable, you both drinking plenty in there?'

'We are,' Reginald replies.

'Can I come to look for supplies?' Charlie asks.

'Yeah sure, we'll be a few minutes yet. Nick you got a...ah well done, he's got one waiting like a mind reader, you got a light? Ah cheers, everyone get fluids and watch out for crawlers in case Meredith misses one.'

I TURN AWAY from the back of Roy's van and walk a few steps into the street as Charlie vaults down onto the hot tarmac. The humidity is through the roof, like an invisible invasive force working to sap our energy.

'Water,' Dave at my side handing me a bottle while drinking from his own.

'Ta,' I prop my rifle against my legs, unscrew the lid and chug it down in one go, 'went well.'

'Yes.'

'We need radios.'

'Yes.'

'Maplins down there,' I say using my water bottle to point down the street, 'bit fucking fortuitous don't you think?'

'What is?'

'Maplins being here.'

'They are a chain store,' he says after a pause.

I start towards it while drinking from the bottle. He falls in beside me and I hear everyone else moving behind us.

'Maplins?' Clarence calls.

'Yeah,' I call back without turning round and pour the last bit of water over my face to rid the sweat stinging my eyes, 'Nick, we need anything else?'

'Don't think so,' he says, 'batteries while we're here.'

I keep my eyes fixed on the front door and the car backed up to the front plate glass window at a weird angle. Getting closer and I can see a rope running from the back of the car through the smashed glass and hooked onto the protective shutters on the inside as though someone parked up, got the hook attached but failed to make it safely back the car.

Every decision we make and every action we take can make the difference between living and dying. Maybe the person was trying to get batteries or torches, wiring, or something else that could have helped them survive and in taking the risk they put themselves in danger, and quite possibly fell to that same danger. Then the idea pops in my head that this could have been done as the world was starting to fall, maybe someone tried to take advantage of the chaos to bag some goodies. Either way they ain't here now and they didn't get inside either.

'Handy,' Nick says walking towards the car, 'think it'll still run?'

'Give it a go,' I say wishing I had more water and thinking about changing into a dry top, and pants, and socks, and trousers.

'Better than me smashing the door in,' Clarence says with a heavy sigh wiping a big hand across his forehead to remove the sweat trickling down.

Nick walks round the back of the car stepping over the rope while Clarence and I move to check the hook is already fastened through the grille on the thick mesh shutter.

'Can you get me another bottle of water out please,' Cookey asks presenting his back to Blinky who slings her own rifle and starts opening his bag.

'Get one for me after,' she says.

'Yeah course.'

Paula and Roy doing the same. Blowers lighting a cigarette and Meredith streaking across the street to catch up with us and Mo Mo screaming no as Nick opens the driver's door. The dog speeding up. Dave spinning round. Roy dropping the bottle of water from his hand. Blinky stepping back from Cookey's bag. Blowers spitting his unlit cigarette out as the undead male smashes his frame into the door on the inside which rams it into Nick's chest that sends him staggering back and the thing is out driving into Nick as he falls down in a flail of limbs. Dave, his pistol out and trying to aim but within that split second the bodies are together with no clear shot. We all react, surging forward with yells but not one of us can react as fast as Meredith who slams into the side of the male with a vicious snarl.

She rips him to the side but the beast is clinging onto Nick who rolls with the male across the ground. She whips about, spinning on the spot and with a deft movement she sinks her teeth into the back of his head and starts ragging to prevent the male from biting

Nick but still it clings on until Dave is in there, slicing like a demon with his blades cutting through tendons in the arms to make the fingers unlock. Clarence stamping on the legs breaking bones in the knee joints and Blowers launching himself into the middle to punch into the male's throat with fists that slam down again and again.

It finally releases and is pulled away by Meredith with a raging Blowers going after it as Cookey, Blinky and Mo start kicking it in the stomach and ribs. Everyone having a go and a few seconds later there is a lump of broken meat without a head and Meredith still attacking it for the sheer audacity of daring to touch her beloved Nick who lies bleeding on the ground with his eyes wide and his mouth hanging open.

'No...no....FUCKING NO,' he roars into the sky at the lacerations on his bare arms from the filthy nails of the male that raked him open, 'Mr Howie...' he stares at me, his chest heaving as he goes into terror stricken shock, 'Mr Howie...'

'Easy,' I'm at his side grabbing his arms to look. The skin is broken, opened in several places with ragged shallow cuts, 'cut me,' my hand in front of Dave and he slices to open the skin on my palm.

'What are you doing?' Roy moves towards us with shock in his voice.

'Back off,' Blowers snaps at him moving to drop to Nick's side with Cookey next to him, 'me too,' he offers his hand to Dave.

'And mine,' Cookey the same, three hands cut and bleeding.

'What are you bloody doing?' Roy demands.

'Oh my god...no...' Nick cries with tears pouring down his face, 'fucking no...I was just checking THE FUCKING CAR...'

'On the wounds,' I clamp my bleeding hand round a long cut on Nick's right wrist and rub to work my blood into his. Fuck knows if this works or does any good but we have seconds to do something and doing something is better than doing nothing.

'You'll make it,' Blowers gripping his blood soaked hand on Nick's left arm, 'you'll make it...'

Cookey pushing his own dripping hand onto Nick's arm above Blowers and Marcy is at my side pushing her open hand towards Dave. No words are needed and her skin is opened with a flick from the knife and her hand pushes against mine as she too grips hold of the lacerated skin to work her own blood into his.

'You'll make it,' Blowers says fiercely, 'you fucking will...I promise you, Nick.'

'Oh fuck,' Nick swallows and grits his teeth, 'fuck 'em yeah,' he says as the tears pour down his face, 'fuck 'em...we'll win yeah?'

'We will, we fucking will,' Cookey bites his own sobs down.

'Yeah,' Nick gasps, 'fuck yeah...we'll win...oh fuck...Mr Howie...'

'I'm here,' I lean past Marcy and grip the back of Nick's neck with my free hand and look into his terrified eyes, 'you'll make it.'

'What if...'

'You'll make it,' I cut through his words as the first tear falls from my own eyes and Clarence is there behind Nick lifting his upper body off the floor to hold the lad still.

'You'll make it,' the deep voice is soft but powerful.

'How long?' Nick glances past me to Dave.

'One minute ten seconds.'

'Two minutes yeah?' Nick locks eyes on me, 'two minutes so... fifty seconds...'

'You will not die,' I say with a power resonating through my body, 'not here, not today...'

'Mr Howie,' he whispers unblinking and his body shaking like a leaf. Meredith pushes her nose through still dripping blood from her jaws, 'oh god...can she smell it?' Nick looks down at her, 'she can smell it inside me...'

Meredith whines, her ears flattened against her head that she pushes down to rest on his stomach.

'Oh fuck...fuck....' His breathing gets faster, shallower as the seconds tick by, 'Dave?'

'One minute thirty.'

'Fuck,' he seems shocked by the answer and blinks, 'okay... yeah...yeah okay,' he steels himself with a hard look passing through his eyes, 'fuck it...'

Paula in amongst us holding Nick, her face a mask of love, worry, hope and utter despair. Roy right there staring down and Charlie holding her hand to her mouth with tears pouring down her face. Blinky staring without expression and Mo Mo glaring angrily.

'Fuck...oh fuck...if I go...Mr Howie...if I go...'

'You ain't,' I say to him with utter belief in my voice, 'I won't let it happen. Do you hear me...it will not happen.'

'You'll make it,' Blowers says it over and over as though saying it will make it true.

'FUCK,' Nick shouts again flashing through emotions as the fear builds and the seconds tick by.

'Steady, son,' Clarence soothing and deep.

'One minute forty five.'

'Fucking already?' Nick shouts, 'I want a recount...' he tries to joke but it bites off on the last word, 'Dave...shoot me in the head,' he says quickly, 'if I go shoot me through the head...promise me...'

'I promise,' Dave says and a chill runs down my spine at the way he says it so accepting of the fact. Fear courses through me, pure fear at the thought of losing Nick and that fear mingles with anger and a feeling of betrayal that we're doing everything we can so why keep doing this to us? Why? Haven't we done enough for you? Don't take Nick. Not Nick. Don't take Nick. Please. I beg you. Take me. I will give my life for his. You can have it. I will die for him to live. Please I am begging you with everything I have. Do not take Nick. Take me.

'No,' Nick whispers at me in shock.

Me. Take me not Nick.

'NO.'

Do not take him. He deserves life. He is young. Take mine. I will go with you.

'NO,' Nick screams at me, 'STOP IT...'

If you want one of us take me. Take my life but please, I beg you, leave him alone.

'FUCKING STOP IT!'

'I'll go,' a deep voice says, 'take mine.'

'One minute fifty five...'

'I have sinned more than any,' a female voice now so close to me, 'I will go...if you must take then take mine...'

'Fifty six...'

Lord. These boys have given you everything. They have done everything asked of them without question.

'MR HOWIE STOP IT...STOP IT...'

I am yours to take.

'NO!'

'I will go,' Clarence whispers into the air, 'I am old and have served...'

'Please,' Nick gasps, 'please stop it...'

'My sins are the worst and I will come with you. Leave him alone.'

'Fifty eight...'

'It's my fucking life,' Nick cries, 'not yours...not Mr Howie...I'll go...I will go but don't take them...'

Do not take Nick. I give you myself and my love and all that I am but leave Nick here. Let him live and love.

'I am an old soldier and I accept death. I am not scared of you so take me and leave the boy.'

'I am scared of you for the things I did but I go with you because of those things I did. Do not take Nick. He is clean. I am tainted. Take me.'

'I'll go,' Blowers growls the words out.

'No,' Cookey says with his cheeks glistening, 'I'll go.'

'Two minutes...'

'You cunts,' Nick gasps, 'it's my fucking life...'

Take me.

'My life and my right...'

'Take me.'

'Don't you fucking dare...none of you...'

'I'll go.'

'Leave him, I am tainted and filthy.'

'Take me. A soldier accepts death.'

'I am Dave...'

'No,' I gasp at the words as every head snaps to the small man staring down at us.

'I am Dave...'

'Dave no,' Nick whispers at an implication too profound to even contemplate for none of this can be done without Dave.

'Dave...' Clarence growls in warning.

'Dave...' I shake my head in disbelief.

'Not you,' Nick pleads in a ragged voice.

A pulsing energy moves through us making my hair stand on end. The air is thick, clogged with emotion and static and Dave stares down in all his terrible glory of never suffering pain, of never knowing the hurt inside and what it's like to love and and this, now, for Dave to join in is beyond anything I could ever think.

'I...am...Dave,' the power in his voice rattles through my bones and seems a challenge to the heavens for that man glares with a defiance that cowers us all. Then he does that rarest of things and smiles as he checks his watch.

'It's been three minutes. Now get up and get back to work. You're fine,' and walks off to inspect the front of the store.

'Oh fuck,' Nick gasps air from his mouth, 'oh my god...holy fucking fuck...'

An explosive exhalation of breath ripples around the circle. Fat tears rolling down Nick's face. Clarence closing his eyes and bowing his head. Blowers stock still. Cookey staring wide eyed.

Marcy crying and stroking Nick's face. Paula sobbing with relief. Roy wiping his eyes. We stay together. None of us wanting to move away from the pulsing energy flowing through our bodies.

'What the fuck was that?' Blowers says more to himself.

'Nick being immune is what that was,' Cookey replies softly

'Shit,' Marcy says sagging down on the spot as she gently releases the grip on Nick's wrist, 'I heard you,' she mutters and wipes her face with the same bloodied hand, 'I heard you,' she looks up at me.

'You had no right,' Nick says and swallows as his eyes widen, 'you had no right, Mr Howie…'

'Nick…'

'You had no right,' he says firmly, 'you had no right to do that.'

'Nick…'

'NO. You had no fucking right.'

'Easy, Nick,' Clarence says.

'None of you…get off me…get the fuck off me,' he scrabbles free, pushing himself past Clarence with legs that tremble and hands shaking as he tries to rise up onto his feet, 'GET OFF ME,' he screams at Clarence yanking his arm free, 'none of you had that right…' On his feet he backs away with his hands pushing through his hair smearing blood over his cheeks and forehead, 'my life…it's my life…MY LIFE,' he screams at us, 'YOU HAD NO RIGHT TO DO THAT.'

'You fucking dick,' Blowers on his feet with his fists clenched.

'Fuck you,' Nick rages at him, 'none of you had the right to do that,' he points a shaking hand at Blowers.

'Get fucked you twat,' Blowers snaps, 'we got every fucking right…'

'Like fuck you do,' Nick rages with spittle flying from his mouth and his arms smeared with blood, 'you had no right…Mr Howie had no fucking right…'

'Mr Howie has every fucking right…'

'NOBODY HAS THAT RIGHT. Nobody has the right to do

that...not Mr Howie...not Clarence...not Marcy or you or Cookey or nobody...'

'Oh we fucking do,' Blowers growls the words out.

'You ain't gods...you ain't in charge of my life and and...Mr Howie can't fucking do that...'

'Don't you fucking say that!'

'I AM SAYING IT...MR HOWIE DIDN'T HAVE THE FUCKING RIGHT...'

'Mr Howie has got every right you fucking twat...'

'NO,' Nick screams as I start to rise but find a soft hand squeezing my arm and pulling me back down and Marcy shaking her head softly.

'He does and we do,' Blowers says, 'we do cos we been with you since this fucking started and if we have earned that fucking right...'

'No...'

'Shut the fuck up,' Blowers shouts him down with a rare passion, 'you've saved me, Nick, and Cookey and Lani and Paula and everyone else...none of us would fucking be here if not for you and you wouldn't be here if not for us...we've all dug each other out the shit hundreds of times...and Clarence, Dave and Mr Howie have done it more than all the rest of us together so that does give them the fucking right...it gives all of us the right...if one of them things was about to get me you'd stop 'em and if that meant you getting bit instead of me then you'd still do it and that's the same thing...and you know, you fucking know that every one of us would do it for you which is why we're still here and doing this so yeah, fucking yeah...it's your life but your life is in our fucking hands the same as mine is in yours...that's what family do,' he stops to draw a breath and spits to the side, 'that's what family do, Nick. See,' he holds his blood soaked hands up, 'we put our fucking blood in you...and when the next one gets cut or bit you'll be doing it...'

Nick stares at the hands then across to Cookey holding his out and Marcy showing hers and finally me with my own still bleeding.

'We're all connected and fuck knows why,' Blowers goes on with words that have clearly built up and explode out with his own release of tension and fear, 'you're immune...I'm immune....Cookey and Mr Howie...Why? Why the fuck are we special? I ain't special? I'm a dumb fucking twat and I know for fact that Cookey is a dumb fucking twat and sure as shit you are so why us? Why?'

'I dunno,' Nick says, quieter now and listening as do the rest of us.

'No you don't fucking know, and there's only two fucking people that can figure that shit out and they're sat right there with cut hands from trying to save you,' he points back at me and Marcy, 'you heard him? Did you? Did you hear him in your head?'

'Yeah.'

'We all did. We all heard it in here,' he taps the front of his forehead, 'but even Mr Howie, even with him being able to do that he can't make this shit better out without Dave and Clarence and without us...all of us...Paula and Roy, Mo Mo, Charlie...Blinky... Meredith...you think this is some random shit going on? This is not random. There is a reason except we don't know what it is...'

The anger abates, the fear at facing his own death that brought the righteous shock and the explosion of rage that made Nick stagger back and away with an instinctive but flawed repulsion of the love we have for him. The hardened expression eases, his hands shaking from the adrenalin wearing off and suddenly he looks young, lost, frightened and isolated by the short distance he has moved away.

Paula on her feet running towards him and she takes him into her arms pulling him tight as his head sinks down onto her shoulder sobbing and his bloodied arms cling hard.

'It's okay,' she whispers stroking the back of his head, 'it's okay, I'm here...'

The raw emotion makes me look away and as I turn I see Roy staring hard with the knowledge on his face that Paula will never leave this group. She's tied into us and as integral as Dave and what's more, if I felt like Nick it would be Paula I'd want giving me that comfort too.

I stay kneeling on the ground staring at the glistening drops of blood and then over at the mangled corpse that dared touch one of us. I will kill them. All of them. I get to my feet and stare round at the hundreds of windows overlooking this spot and knowing it will be watching us, watching me. I hope it watches me. See me. I'll come for you. All of you.

CHAPTER SIXTEEN

'Fuck me,' Nick says coming back into the group as he tugs a crumpled pack of cigarettes from his pocket, he goes to say something but just shrugs and lights the smoke before chucking the packet over to me.

'Cheers,' I take one out with bloodied fingers and light the end as the packet gets handed round and finally passed to Blowers who takes one and holds the pack out to Nick.

'Such a dick,' Blowers mutters blowing the smoke to the side.

'Yeah, fuck you,' Nick replies gently, 'I'm immune,' he says to himself then looks round with the hint of a smile forming at the corners of his mouth, 'I'm immune.'

'You're a cock,' Cookey says standing up.

'You like cock,' Nick says.

'Oh he's back,' Cookey laughs, 'had your tantrum yeah? Feeling better now?'

'Much better,' Nick grins, 'ta.'

'Er, sorry to point something out,' Cookey says turning to face Blowers, 'but where the fuck did that come from?'

'What?'

'That speech?'

'What? It needed to be said...'

'You wrote that.'

'What?'

'You fucking did, you wrote that and been practising it every night and waiting so you could say it and make everyone think you're all deep and serious.'

'Yeah, yeah I did that,' Blowers says not bothering to rise to the bait.

'Yep, doesn't even deny it,' Cookey announces it, 'good speech though fucktard.'

'Cheers wankstain.'

'Welcome buttmuncher.'

And the world moves on, or our world does anyway. We get up with sore knees and wash the blood from our hands, wincing as the water gets into the fresh cuts. Bottles are pulled from bags and drank down thirstily and more are used to pour over our faces and heads in a pathetic attempt to cool down for a few seconds.

Me, Clarence, Blowers and Cookey show no reaction to Nick's outburst. Dave is just Dave and waits off to one side devoid of expression as ever. We've been together through so much now that nothing can damage our bond and anything said by Nick needed to be said, same with Blowers. No harm and no foul. Marcy is easy but then she's seen and done so much now that I doubt anything will shock her. The others I notice are a bit awkward for a few minutes. Like they don't know what to say or do and sometimes doing nothing is the best course of action to take.

The lads abuse each other and that humour soon spreads out until Blinky is throwing a few insults in and Cookey is telling everyone about pulling a face at Charlie who then tells everyone that she burst out laughing which made Reginald change the monitor view. Surprisingly, Roy is the first to congratulate Nick and offers his hand, one by one we all do it, apart from Paula and Marcy who give him a big hug.

Everything though, has an end and it doesn't take long before the sense of urgency to be moving and doing something starts tugging at me. Like a heroin addict needs a fix and I can't ignore it.

'Everyone okay?' I ask at a natural break in the conversation which is just a polite way of asking if we can get on with doing what we came to do, 'did you find out if the car was working?'

'Er no,' Nick says with a laugh, 'got side-tracked, sorry about that.'

'Paula, make a note please for Nick's annual assessment.'

'Noted,' she says mock serious.

'I tell you one thing,' Clarence says, 'that bloody dog adores you...I've never seen her go for anyone like that.'

'Yeah?' Nick asks, 'I didn't see...'

'Fuck yeah,' Cookey says, 'she ripped it apart in like seconds... like *shredded* it...it's over there.'

'Fuck,' Nick says turning round to look down at the body, 'where's its head?'

'I just said, she shredded it apart,' Cookey replies.

'No way? She shredded the head?'

'Yes! Like tearing it up and spitting the bits out...mind you, Clarence was breaking his legs at the time and Blowers was throat punching it and everyone else was kicking it in the ribs...oh and Dave sliced it up.'

'Shit,' Nick says with a wince, 'cheers though.'

'*You got no right,*' Cookey mimics in a high pitched voice.

'Fuck. Off. You. Twat,' Nick says moving back to the now open door of the car and pausing to check through the windows before reaching in, 'key in the ignition,' he says, 'but it's flat,' he adds standing back up, 'so all of that for fuck all.'

'Yeah fuck all,' I say with a roll of my eyes, 'apart from finding out you're immune and Mo has some innate ability to predict where they're going to be...oh and that all of you can now hear my thoughts which isn't worrying at all considering some of the things I think about,' I look at Marcy with a raised eyebrow which makes them all burst out laughing.

'Pervert,' she says.

'Probably,' I say nonchalantly, 'fuck me, Nick. You're immune!'

'Yeah, looks that way,' he says with a smile.

'Or a carrier.'

'Bring the fucking mood down, Roy,' Blowers responds quickly to the blunt comment.

'Fact is fact,' Roy says, 'do you think that does anything? Cutting your hands like that?'

'No idea,' I admit.

'Maybe it does,' Clarence says, 'the infection works in two minutes so whatever is in Mr Howie's and the lads blood could work the same way.'

'What? It doesn't work like that,' Roy scoffs, 'you don't just bleed into someone and make them better. Anti-bodies don't just transfer like that.'

'How do you know?' Clarence asks.

'I've spent more time in the doctor's surgery than all of you and I've probably had every test known to mankind and although I'm not a doctor I think I can confidently say that sticking your bleeding hand on someone doesn't cure them of the bloody zombie virus.'

'Oh,' Clarence says casually, 'maybe it does.'

'I think you are all immune,' Charlie says in that polite clipped way that gets everyone's attention instantly.

'Do what?' I ask as she shifts position uncomfortably at the sudden attention.

'You said yesterday that you had been involved in many fights and today when you were being attacked I said to Reginald I wanted to go and help and he informed me of the numbers you had previously fought and how this group attacking you were really quite small in comparison and now, as you were talking, I recalled the *way* you fought yesterday...which is really very close.'

'Right,' I say prompting her on.

She stares back at us all for a second as though deciding

whether to continue or not, 'we wore masks,' she says in a blunt way that doesn't sound blunt because she's so well-spoken, 'you do not wear masks.'

A stunned silence follows as we all follow the train of thought to the end conclusion. Staggering. Completely and utterly staggering in the realisation of the simplest suggestion of an idea.

'Oh,' I say stupidly.

'What?' Cookey asks looking round, 'I don't get it.'

'So our faces wouldn't get bitten,' Blinky says to him rolling her eyes.

'Er no,' Charlie says diplomatically, 'that is not my point.'

'What is the point then?' Cookey asks.

'My god you are so thick,' Blowers mutters.

'Even I worked that one out,' Nick says.

'Worked what one out? That we've got to wear masks so we don't get our faces bitten? For a start none of us have had our faces bitten yet and they don't really go for faces but like arms and hands and necks and shit...'

'Cookey,' Paula says quietly, 'listen to Charlie.'

'All day long,' Cookey says with a grin as Blowers and Nick both groan.

'I think the average human male body contains something like five litres of blood, at least I think that's right,' Charlie says.

'It is,' Dave says.

'And they do bleed rather a lot when Dave cuts them.'

'Arterial bleeds,' Dave says.

'And of course you all cut them rather a lot and they bleed rather a lot and of course that blood flies about into the air and on your hands and arms and faces...' she lets the words hang.

'Oh yeah,' Cookey says seriously, 'we always get covered in shit but like, they haven't bitten our faces.'

'Forget the face biting,' Paula says.

'I thought we had to wear masks now?' Cookey asks.

'Fuck's sake,' Blowers snaps, 'transference you dick, blood transference...'

Cookey nods slowly but the light of recognition still doesn't show, 'oh my fucking god,' Blowers wails, 'really? Really, Cookey?'

'Alex,' Paula says, 'Charlie is suggesting that with all the close quarters fights you've been in that some of the blood, at some point, would have gone either into your mouth or into a cut...'

'Urgh that's fucking gross,' Cookey recoils, 'and we don't fight with our gobs open.'

'Your gob is always open,' Blowers says, 'it never closes...ever...'

'So...so we've probably always been immune then?' Nick asks.

'Always open,' Blowers mutters, 'it just never closes...not ever...'

'I could be immune then?' Mo asks.

'Do you even know how to close it?'

'Fucking hang on,' I ask suddenly, 'how the hell has no one thought of this before?' I stare round at the guilty faces, 'seventeen...no eighteen bloody days of this and not one of us ever thought of that? A fucking mask? A face mask?'

'Well,' Clarence says shuffling on the spot, 'not something you think about.'

'You were both in the bloody army,' I say to Clarence and Dave, 'and you,' I add with a look at Blowers.

'Oh shit,' Cookey moans, 'do we have to wear masks?'

'You are immune you idiot,' Clarence groans, 'you do not need a mask now. You are immune.'

'Oh cool,' Cookey sighs with relief, 'thank fuck for that.'

'How the hell *are* we still alive?' I ask with a groan, 'we are so completely incompetent.'

'We're not that bad,' Clarence says.

'We should have put masks and goggles on,' I shout back, 'I didn't think of it...you never said anything, Dave didn't mention it...Paula?'

'What?'

'You never said anything either.'

'Can't think of everything and anyway, you were already well into it by the time I joined the group.'

'Roy?'

'Er,' he flounders on the spot.

'You're medically aware.'

'Er...'

'We're all shit,' I announce, 'all of us. Incompetent. Charlie, you are now in charge of everything.'

'Pardon?'

'Yay,' Cookey says, 'can I carry your bags?'

'Pardon?'

'What else haven't we done?' I ask her.

'Pardon?'

'Seriously, I'm not saying it like having a go for pointing the stupid things we haven't done out but like genuinely asking what else we should be doing.'

'I er...gosh I don't know. I don't want to be in charge.'

'It was organic,' Clarence says.

'What was?' I ask him when he doesn't continue.

'We had a few fights and it just went from there...it was an organic transition of events that allowed the present situation to develop to its current system.'

'Holy fuck that was good,' I say with admiration.

'It's what Chris used to say to the bosses when they asked why we did things,' Clarence admits.

'Yeah,' I look at Charlie, 'it was an organic transition of...er...'

'Events,' Clarence prompts.'

'Of events that allowed the present...er...'

'Situation to develop to its current system.'

'What he said,' I point to Clarence.

'Oh,' Charlie says politely, 'I was not being accusatory in any capacity and I apologise if it appears I was.'

'It was organic,' I say, 'transition of something that did something to the system.'

'Indeed,' she says, 'I fully accept that but I there is no need to justify anything to me.'

'So,' I say happily to the group, 'we may or may not be all immune and if anyone wants to test it they can go lick that dead body and Dave will wait to shoot you through the face if you turn...anyone?'

'Nah,' Clarence says after a few seconds of silence, 'I'll pass.'

'Paula? Want to lick a headless dead body?'

'Got water,' she says, 'thanks anyway.'

'Mo?'

'If I say no do I have to wear a mask and goggles?'

'We don't have any masks or goggles.'

'No then,' he says.

'Wimp,' Cookey mutters.

'You lick it then,' Mo says.

'I don't have to,' Cookey says, 'I am immune.'

'Lick the body, Mo,' Nick says, 'go on...lick it...lick the dead body.'

'You's nuts,' he says, 'but yeah okay,' he walks towards it with such a determined expression we all jump after him, 'was joking,' he laughs, 'I ain't licking a dead body. I ain't Blowers.'

'Cheeky fucker!'

'Blinky? Charlie? Roy? Anyone else?'

'What?' Blinky asks, 'Mr Howie,' she adds.

'Do you want to lick the dead body,' I ask her.

'What for?' She asks with a confused look.

'We're you listening?' Charlie asks.

'Was I fuck you were all like blah blah blah and saying boring stuff...I need a piss. Do you want me to lick it?'

'No, no don't do that,' I say quickly with a sudden fear she'll actually do it.

'Marcy?' I ask.

'What? I was already infected,' she says staring at me like I'm an idiot.

'Fair enough, didn't want to leave you out.'

'Gee thanks.'

'Anytime, doesn't change anything then. We might be immune or we might not and cutting our hands open may or may not help and we still don't know fuck all apart from Nick is immune and you all heard me thinking. Awesome. I'm glad we make progress like this.'

'Sarcasm suits you,' Marcy says.

'Yeah? I like it.'

'But,' I say to the group, 'we have learnt an important lesson. If anyone gets back in charge and questions us then we say what Clarence said so we don't get in the shit for anything.'

'Why would we get in the shit?' Paula asks.

'I dunno,' I say, 'stuff like blowing up that refinery and burning down the ferry and that town on the Isle of Wight...'

'And the housing estate Dave blew up,' Blowers says.

'Yeah and that.'

'And the munitions factory we broke into,' Nick says.

'Good one,' I say to him.

'Actually,' Paula says wistfully, 'I rather destroyed a town before I met up with you so yes, I'll keep that one in mind.'

'It's very handy,' Clarence says, 'got Chris out of the shit all the time.'

'What was it again?' Nick asks.

'It was an organic transition of events that allowed the present situation to develop to its current system,' Clarence says.

'Everyone got it? That's what we say if anyone asks us.'

'Can I use it?' Marcy asks.

'What for mass murder and genocide?'

'And we're back to that,' she says beaming at me.

'Sorry, couldn't help it. Yeah use Clarence's thing.'

'Chris's thing,' Clarence says.

'Chris's thing,' I add, 'Maplins then.'

'Maplin,' Marcy says, 'no s.'

'Eh? Oh,' I look up at the sign and the distinct lack of an s at the end, 'I always thought it was Maplins.'

'No, just Maplin,' she says.

'Oh god,' Clarence groans sizing the door up, 'it's too hot for this shit...'

'Use the Saxon, mate. Mo, can you drive?'

He looks at as though he didn't hear what I said, 'yeah, fuck yeah I can drive...you want me to get it?'

'Go for it, bring it down here and push this car out the way then back it up so we can use the rope.'

He sprints off like he's worried I'll change my mind, 'and tell Reggie we'll be here for a few minutes if he wants to come out.'

'WILL DO,' he shouts and runs to the back of Roy's van before darting over and climbing into the Saxon. A few seconds later and the engine sputters to life, a few more seconds and it pulls away to move round in a wide circle as he gains the approach to the car. We stand back and watch the grin on his face as he gets the aim right, drops the speed and pushes the front into the passenger side of the car. The engine bites as he powers on and I can see him laughing with real pleasure at the car being pushed aside like it weighs nothing. With the space cleared he manoeuvres round and backs up with Clarence guiding him in.

'Stay in there,' Clarence shouts waiting for Nick and Roy to attach the hook on the rope to the rear bar of the Saxon. They give a thumbs up to Clarence who gives his own to Mo, 'gently now,' he shouts, 'forward...get the tension...now go!'

We clear off as the rope pings to tension and the shutters resist with a loud groan before realising that resistance is futility and cooperation will be gained with or without their assistance. A wrench with the remains of the plate glass window cascading out. The shutters smash down onto the ground and get dragged clear leaving a nice big hole ready for a very excited Nick and an equally excited Roy already clambering through.

'YES! Roy look at this.' I hear Nick shouting for joy as I get to the window and peer through to see him and Roy striding towards a display plinth with some toy helicopter on the top of it.

I get through and turn to offer a hand to Marcy who sticks a middle finger up and jumps through to land deftly inside, 'that's for the genocide comment,' she says.

'Sorry,' I say.

'And any further such comments will mean you don't get to see my bum tonight.'

'Marcy!'

'What?'

'Bit loud,' I groan but Nick and Roy are too focussed on the toy helicopter.

The rest come through with Dave waiting outside to keep watch and showing as much interest in things like this as ever before.

'Where are they?' Clarence asks and getting no response he clears his throat, 'Nick, Roy...radios? Where are they?'

Neither of them turn round but stare in wonder with Roy pointing at something and Nick nodding reverentially and whispering something back.

'NICK!'

'Eh? What?' He turns round guiltily, 'what's up?'

'Radios?' Clarence says stiffly, 'where are they?'

'Er,' the lad turns slowly staring at the aisles and display cabinets fixed to the wall, 'probably er...'

'What's that?' Blinky asks walking towards the plinth with a look in her eye which suggests she'll be picking the toy helicopter up within the next five seconds. Nick and Roy move to intercept, she goes to flank but they opt for a subtly defensive position as Blinky finds the path suddenly blocked, 'what is it?' She asks again trying to peer round them.

'Is that a drone?' Cookey asks from behind them having sneaked round the back and now reaching his hand out.

'Don't touch it!' Roy shouts as Nick darts in to slap his hand away.

'What the fuck?' Cookey asks glaring at them both.

'It's worth two and a half grand,' Nick blurts, 'it's like the best you can get...'

'What is?' Blinky asks trying to step round Nick.

'Just leave it,' Nick says waving his arms in front of her.

'What this?' Cookey asks resting his finger on the top.

'What is it?' Blowers asks.

'A drone,' Cookey says.

'What's a drone?' Marcy asks.

'This is,' Cookey says.

'Helpful,' Marcy says, 'what does it do?'

'Ah you know, drones on a bit,' Cookey says and looks round waiting for the laughs and tutting when they don't come, 'drone... drones on a bit...fuck's sake.'

'This,' Roy says loudly to get their attention, 'is a carbon fibre DJI Inspire one drone with over a mile radio range and four k video live streaming and a three axis Gimbal stabilizing camera.'

We all nod and make appreciative noises, apart from Dave and Clarence who have switched on and are both staring intently, 'over a mile?' Clarence asks walking towards it.

'Yep,' Nick says, 'probably more now.'

'Why now?' Clarence asks seriously.

'Nothing to interfere with the signal,' Nick says, 'everything else is gone, no mobiles...satnavs...airplanes...taxis...clear skies.'

'Yes of course,' Clarence says, 'and a live feed?'

'High definition,' Roy nods.

We all converge to stare at the plinth. The drone is futuristic looking but strangely insect-like but like what you'd think an alien insect would look like. The main body is narrow and high but stream-lined and looks like the outer-shell the storm-troopers wore on Star Wars in a high shine white plastic. Two thin black carbon fibre arms jut out from the main body and each arm has another carbon fibre pole with rubberised landing feet bolted on. Four sets of helicopter style blades rest above each of the rubberised feet. It's sleek, modern and also a bit evil looking, like it could come alive at any minute.

'So what does it do?' Marcy asks as we all stare.

'Drone,' Nick says as though that single word explains everything.

'Yeah I heard that, what does a drone do?'

'Oh...oh right,' Nick says, 'you fly it, on a remote control and that camera,' he points to the lens poking out the bottom, 'captures a live feed and sends it back to the monitor.'

'Or you can USB from the handset to an iPad,' Roy says, 'and use the iPad as the monitor.'

'Or other tablet device,' Nick says to Roy, 'doesn't have to be an iPad.'

'Well no, but I do know for certain that you can use the iPad.'

'Yeah but iPad's aren't that great.'

'They are.'

'They ain't.'

'They really are,' Roy says, 'are you android then?'

'Me?' Nick shrugs, 'not android but not Apple either...I like to mix it up when I can.'

'Yes,' Roy says as though not wanting to be outdone, 'me too.'

'Techie fucking geeky stuff boring,' Blinky says walking off.

'I loved my iPad,' Paula says.

'Couldn't afford one,' Marcy says, 'no, that's not strictly true. I could have afforded it if I hadn't spent so much on clothes and bags.'

'That just perpetuates the stereotypical view of women,' Roy says.

'Couldn't give a toss,' Marcy says, 'I liked clothes and bags... and shoes...and perfume...'

'We can use this,' Clarence says quietly nodding at the drone, 'we used them in the field but the early ones were shit and when I say we used them I didn't mean we as in me or Chris or Malcolm because we would have crashed it within five seconds and then legged it but they sent out some kids like Nick to do it.'

'Over a mile range is good,' Nick says, 'we could get a view on Stenbury before we get there, or that next place.'

'Brookley,' Charlie says.

'That would be helpful,' I say, 'does it make much noise?'

'Not really and if we get it high enough they won't hear it...the motor is electric so it just hums instead of chugging.'

'Humming instead of chugging,' Cookey says clearly trying to find a joke but failing dismally.

'I saw a review on these,' Roy says, 'only downside is the battery is only twenty minutes at the most.'

'But if we're within a mile it shouldn't take long to get a view should it?' I ask.

'Couple of minutes at the most, Mr Howie,' Nick says, 'and,' he says turning to Roy, 'I bet that monitor in the back of your van has a HDMI connection.'

'Bloody good idea,' Roy says quickly with a grin.

'So we'll get the feed on that monitor?' Charlie asks, 'can one person operate it?'

'Two handsets,' Nick says, 'one person can do it or one can fly and the other operates the camera.'

'So we can park up a mile out from the next town, get that drone up and see what the ground looks like before we get there, bloody brilliant,' I say, 'really bloody brilliant. You two sort that out, Mo, can you bring Roy's van down here next to the Saxon and we'll get some radios sorted...how are we going to make the new radios talk to the one in the Saxon and in Roy's van?'

'We don't have to,' Nick says, 'we just put one in Roy's van with Reggie and Charlie.'

'Fucking switched on you are, mate,' I say with a grin, 'that's why we all bloody offered ourselves. We'd be stuffed without you. And Roy,' I add quickly as Marcy winces and looks away, 'I mean

both of you,' I add again, 'like both of you are switched on...and...
that's what I meant...'

'Stop digging,' Marcy mutters.

'Yeah radios,' I say with a look to Clarence then round at
everyone else also wincing, 'yeah piss off, it wasn't that bad.'

Naturally, and seeing as this is the end of the world and all that
we go straight for the most expensive radio systems on display,
which is a Motorola with each one priced at over one hundred and
fifty quid. Three on display so Clarence talks kindly to the rear
door to the stock room and persuades it to move out of the way
with his foot and we start rummaging around to find boxes, ear
pieces and all manner of accessories. A few minutes later and we're
all gathered at the back of Roy's van with Reginald still inside
watching as we open the boxes and assemble the radios and equipment while Nick and Roy mess about with the drone handsets and
the CCTV monitor on Reginald's desk.

Each radio has a long wire connecting to an earpiece and a
small clip on tube used as the press-to-talk button and we flaff
about making a pig's ear of everything until Dave steps in.

'Radio on the belt,' he says bluntly, 'wire under your top so it
doesn't snag. The chord to the earpiece loops over the ear so it can
be pulled out without risk of falling away,' he shows us his own ear
and the way he has pulled the wire over the top, 'ptt tube clips on
here on the inside of your shirt,' he says cinching his own top to
show the small plastic tube underneath the thin wicking material.

Even with him showing us exactly what to do we still end up
poking wires down sleeves and shoving earpieces up our noses.

'Channel one,' Dave says turning his radio on and showing
everyone the numerically marked turn dial, 'eight channels but we
use one as the main and if anyone wants a private conversation
they go to channel five.'

'Why five?' Marcy asks.

'Because I said so,' Dave says without hesitation, 'channel five
will be used for private conversation...'

'Private conversation?' Marcy asks.

'Yes. Private conversation.'

'What private conversation?'

'Any such conversation as deemed private.'

'I think he means if everyone is talking on channel one and say you and the boss want to talk then you two can go to channel five for a private chat while everyone else stays on channel one,' Clarence says.

'Yes,' Dave says.

'Got it,' Marcy says, 'why five?'

'Er,' Clarence says again, 'I think so we have one to four to use for the main channel, in case one is being monitored...'

'Oh. Why...I mean how would we know one is being monitored?' She asks.

'I don't know,' Clarence says.

'I see,' she says, 'whatever.'

'Test transmissions,' Dave says and strides off a few metres, 'Mr Howie, are we using names?'

'Yes,' I say.

'Is that wise?' Reginald asks from inside the van.

'Probably not but it beats having to come up with any codenames that we'll argue over for the next hour and then forget as soon as we start doing anything exciting.'

'Dave to Mr Howie.'

'Clear,' I say into my chest while pressing the button under my shirt.

'You need to turn your radio on, Mr Howie.'

'Roger. Turning on. *Is that it?'*

'Loud and clear. Dave to Clarence.'

'Loud and clear.'

'Dave to Paula.'

'Loud and clear, Dave.'

'Dave to Simon.'

'Loud and clear, Dave.'

'Dave to Marcy.'

'Loud and clear, Dave.'

'Dave to Alex.'

'Roger roger rubber duckey receiving loud and clear over.'

'That is not appropriate radio speak, Alex.'

'Sorry, Dave.'

'Do it again. Dave to Alex.'

'Yep, go ahead.'

'Alex...'

'Sorry, Dave.'

'Dave to Alex.'

'Hello?'

'Keep doing it and see what happens, Alex.'

'Loud and clear, Dave!'

'Ha, you got told off.'

'Nicholas...'

'Sorry, Dave. Loud and clear though.'

'It was not your turn. Dave to Charlotte.'

'Loud and clear, Dave.'

'So posh.'

'Alex!'

'Sorry, Dave.'

'Dave to Patricia.'

'Can you call me, Blinky please, Dave?'

'No. Dave to Patricia.'

'Um...but I hate being called Patricia.'

'No. Dave to Patricia.'

'But why...'

'Blinky, just answer him. He calls me Charlotte.'

'Fine. This is Blinky. Loud and clear.'

'Dave to Mohammed.'

'You's loud and clear, you get me?'

'That is not appropriate. Do it again. Dave to Mohammed.'

'Loud and clear.'

'Dave to Reginald.'

'He doesn't have a radio.'

'Who said that?'

'I said it,' Charlie says, 'I'm right here...you can see me.'

'Use the correct radio discipline.'

'Charlie to Dave.'

'Go ahead, Charlotte.'

'Reginald does not have a radio.'

'Why not?'

'We don't have enough. He can share mine.'

'You are wearing an earpiece. How will he hear the transmissions?'

'Er, I can put it on loudspeaker?'

'Understood. Dave to Roy.'

'Loud and clear.'

'Dave to Nicholas.'

'Loud and clear.'

'Dave to Mr Howie.'

'You did me.'

'I am calling you. Dave to Mr Howie.'

'Go ahead.'

'Radio check has been completed. All radios are working.'

'Nick, Roy, is that drone ready?' I ask.

'We need a test flight,' Roy says.

'Here? Now?' I ask.

'If that's okay?' Nick asks.

'Will it take long?'

'Er no, just a few minutes but like, we need to know how to fly it,' he explains.

'Yeah course, no worries. Did you explain to Reginald about using it?'

'Indeed they did, Mr Howie. Arial reconnaissance will greatly increase our ability to plan ahead.'

'Brookley is next, what do we know about it?' I ask while Nick and Roy dither about getting the drone ready.

'The ancient village of Brookley,' he begins, 'is named after the family of the same name. The Brookleys were famed for royal connections in the Elizabethan period and still retain their family home at the Brookley stately home which is open to the public at certain periods of the year.'

'You been reading a guide book?' Clarence asks stepping in beside me as we all slowly gather at the back to watch Reginald and Charlie at the desk inside.

'Indeed I have,' Reginald says, 'it passed the time while you were dealing with your unfortunate incident with young Nicholas to whom I believe some congratulations are in order.'

'Cheers, Reggie,' Nick shouts from a few feet away.

'Reginald,' he says automatically, 'and yes, I have been scouring the map and have concluded that Brookley is a small village roughly the same size as Foxwood.'

'Which one was Foxwood?' Cookey asks, 'was that the one with the pond?'

'Yes it was,' I snap, 'not big then?'

'No, not big at all,' Reginald says, 'however there is a large village green dominating the centre of the village which, from the tourist guide, has led me to believe is solely retained for community use so it will include a cricket pitch, benches and most likely be without a bordering fence. The green is a large diamond shape and the main road splits to run on the northern and southern perimeter of the green. Both sides are fronted by what appears to be dwelling houses of private residence but it is the northern edge that contains the post office, public house, small library and no doubt a village store. Did Charlie mention the importance of the post office?'

'No,' I say with an inward groan at what could be another lengthy explanation. The man is transformed though. The nerves are gone, his feet are steady and his hands don't keep going to his neck either. His voice is different too. The nervous overly polite nuances are gone and although his voice is still cultured and BBC clipped there is an undertone of confidence in there.

'Post offices will have a secure inner area used for the storage of cash,' he says, 'this is important as it may offer a temporary secure and defensible refuge should one be required.'

'Good idea,' I say, 'did everyone hear that? Good, where can we expect the opposition?'

'Now that is a difficult question to answer given the consideration of the road splitting to run north and south along the green.'

'Does the road re-join at the far end?'

'Yes indeed it does, there are side roads feeding from the main road on both the north and south but according to the map, the northern side has the largest section of housing behind it whereas the southern side appears to be open land with some farm buildings further out. Common sense dictates that any force would be retained on the northern side where they can be hidden but we also have to factor that our opponent wishes you to succeed in your endeavour.'

'So? Which side?' I ask impatiently.

'If it were me and I were intent on attacking you properly I would create an obstacle on the southern side and force you to take the northern road. However, any obstacle will be entirely obvious and questionable, therefore I suggest we take the southern side where fewer host bodies can be hidden which in turn means any larger force secreted on the northern side will have to cross the open green to reach you.'

'Southern road then,' I ask, 'so forgive me asking a stupid question but that's the left road yes? We'll see the road split right and left and we take the left?'

'Yes,' he says without blinking and managing to convey in that one word that I am perhaps the stupidest person he has ever spoken to, 'the left.'

'Got it,' my attention is diverted to a low thrumming noise

coming from the drone and I look over to see Nick and Roy each holding an oversize handset.

'You fly and I'll get the monitor rigged up.'

'Uh huh,' Nick replies focussing on twitching the two sticks poking out the top of the handset and watching as the drone lifts up an inch off the ground then sinks back down.

'Excuse me,' Roy squeezes through us and into the back where he attaches a cable from the handset to the monitor on the desk and starts going through the preset channel feed selections. The quadrant of images blinks out to be replaced with a screen smudged with grey light, 'I think that's it,' he mutters, 'I think that's it,' he says again more loudly.

'Roy thinks he's got it,' I pass on to Nick.

'Uh huh,' he says and makes the drone lift six inches into the air then holding it in a hover. Another twitch of his thumbs and it glides a foot or so forward then stops and banks left, stops and banks right and then stops again, 'yeah you little fucker,' he chuckles, 'got you, yep ready,' he shouts back.

'Nick said he's ready,' I relay.

'Is he flying?' Roy asks focussing on the screen, 'I'm not getting an image.'

'He's about six inches off the ground.'

'Ah, tell him to go higher.'

'Roy said go higher.'

'Higher?' Nick asks, 'we can do higher,' the drone hums louder and rises with incredible speed metres into the air. Cheers from the group and I look round to see the monitor and the image of all of us gathered at the back of the van. It takes a second for perspective to kick in and my mind to process the image. Us from above and in perfect movie quality detail. We all wave at the drone and watch ourselves doing it with Roy grinning widely. The clarity is outstanding and the width of the panoramic view is excellent. As Nick takes the drone higher we start to see the tops of the roofs and the buildings beyond with the layout of back streets, alleys and rear yards.

'Watch this,' Nick says and brings the drone down to the level of the top window in the flat above Maplin. He inches closer, learning the controls and the subtle movements needed as Roy manipulates the camera to turn up so we can see through the glass into the living room of the flat, 'can you see in, Roy?'

'Perfectly,' I say, 'how long does that battery last?' I ask concerned about draining it now.

'We've got another one on charge,' Nick says, 'are Charlie and Reggie going to be operating it?' He asks with a glance at me.

'Could do, we'll be outside the village but it makes sense if they can do it.'

'Charlie,' Nick calls her over as he brings the drone down to a gentle landing on the road. He hands the control over and starts explaining the movements as Roy does the same in the van with Reginald and the seconds tick by that form minutes and the itch demands to be scratched as that feeling transmutes into a nagging irritation that has me exhaling and suppressing the urge to ask them to hurry up.

'Patience is a virtue,' a soft whisper and Marcy's hand resting gently on my arm as she gives me a warning look.

I nod back and work to alter my outward appearance and show patience instead of irritation but I don't feel it. We've been here only for a short time but already it feels too long. We need to get on, keep moving. There is an urgency that I don't understand but it's there and cannot be ignored.

Fuck's sake. I look between Roy showing Reginald the virtues of the DJI inspire drone and all the amazing things it can do while Nick and Charlie chuckle over the way she operates the sticks on the handset. Everyone chatting amiably, enjoying the respite and being able to remain still in this invasive heat.

'Just take your time,' Nick coaches Charlie as she starts making the drone rise up and I want to shout out to not fucking take your time. Push on. Get on with it. Stop fucking about. Roy and Reginald laughing at some intellectual joke. Charlie bringing the drone down with a thump and Nick telling her it's okay as the feet are designed to absorb impacts.

'Sharp and pointy,' Blinky says laughing at something Cookey said to her.

'Try it again,' Nick urges.

'You zoom in using this button and...' Roy explaining in the back of the van. Paula sitting on the back ledge talking to Clarence. Blowers leaning against the back of the van as he laughs at something said by Mo Mo. Fingers digging into my wrist and Marcy is glaring at me now.

'I need a word with you,' she says, 'in there,' she nods to Maplin and her tone doesn't leave any room for conversation so I follow her over and through the broken glass into the shade of the store.

'What?' I ask her but she walks further down the central aisle ignoring me, 'Marcy, what?'

Only at the back of the store and hidden from view at the front does she stop. 'What?' I ask her again and the impatience shows in my voice.

She folds her arms, plants her feet and fixes me with a look, 'stop rushing them.'

'Do what?'

'Stop rushing them,' she repeats, 'your impatience is pouring off you.'

'No it isn't,' I scoff with even more irritation and go to walk off.

'Howie,' she snaps grabbing my wrist again, 'you're staying here until they're ready.'

'They'll fuck about for ages if I'm not there.'

'So? Let them fuck about then.'

'We've got to get on.'

'Yes and we will but your foot was tapping, you were snorting air out your nose like a bull and glaring round with angry eyes.'

'What? Was I fuck...'

'And you rolled your eyes like five times in a minute.'

'I did not...'

'And if I saw you doing it they would have too, don't make them feel guilty for not going at your bloody pace all the time.'

'Marcy.'

'Don't Marcy me,' she says in a fierce rush of words, 'Nick just got cut and found out he was immune...everyone was bloody sobbing five minutes ago...Christ, Howie. Let them have a few minutes to settle down.'

'But...'

'And,' she cuts me off again, 'you freaked everyone out by doing that thing in our heads and God alone knows what that's all about but please, just take it easy and slow down.'

'Slow down? We don't have time to slow down...'

'Yes we do. We have as much time as it takes for Charlie to work out how to fly the drone and Reggie to learn how to operate the camera and if they need a drink after that then they can have one, and if Cookey needs to take a poo and read a bloody news-paper then he can do it!'

'What?' I burst out laughing at the image conjured in my mind.

'The point is they're all here for you *and* Charlie and Blinky only joined you yesterday *and* Paula and Roy were thinking of leaving *and* Reggie has only just found his testicles again so he needs a bit of time for that confidence to grow *and*...'

'What?'

'I ran out,' she shrugs and smiles warmly, 'but the difference will be between rushing in and getting the job done by the skin of our teeth or taking a few extra minutes and doing it well.'

I give a humph to show my general distaste for the common sense being displayed.

'Don't humph me,' she says and laughs, 'dry humphing.'

'Very funny.'

'If Reggie is right then the infection is getting ready in Sten-bury and there *will* be lots of them which means we'll be very busy and I don't know if you noticed but it's very bloody hot and we're all struggling as it is.'

'Yeah,' I say with a sigh, 'fair one.'

'Yes?'

'Yeah but...it's like a burning itch...'

'You can probably get some cream...'

'Eh? You sound like Cookey.'

'Sorry. What were you saying? You've got an itch? Where is it?'

'No, like an itch inside...'

'Haemorrhoids? Like I said, you can get some cream. Want me to check?'

'What? No!'

'Sorry, you're being serious. Go on.'

'No forget it.'

'Oh don't sulk, you said you had an itch.'

'Yeah to get going, to keep moving...like...like something bad will happen if we don't.'

'I see,' she says with narrowed eyes, 'tell me about your childhood.'

'Oh fuck off,' I turn away, 'I'm being serious,' I add as she starts laughing.

'You look serious,' she says trying to stop the chuckles then bursts out laughing when I try and glare, 'oh stop it,' she waves a hand at me so I try and glare harder with my all out killer mean look but that just sets her off even worse so I give up and shake my head at the injustice of it all.

'Oh dear,' she says once the laughing has eased, 'you're all pent up.'

I shrug but don't say anything, 'is there anything I can do?' She asks quickly.

'Er...'

'I don't mean like that,' she groans at the panicked look on my face, 'or...well we can if you want.'

'Pardon?'

'You sound like Charlie now.'

'I'm lost.'

'I said we can if you want.'

'Can what?'

'Whatever you want.'

'Eh? Hang on...did you mean...did you say...'

'I bet you were an evil manager to work for.'

'What?' I say floundering as she flits topics again.

'All pushy and motivated,' she says, 'I hated working for people like you.'

'I'm not pushy!'

'I beg your pardon?'

'No, I mean I am now but I never used to be. I was a lazy turd.'

'Well then, be more old Howie and less new Howie.'

I go to reply but nothing comes out so I shake my head instead and blink a few times in confusion.

'Where are you going?' She asks when I turn away.

'Back outside.'

'But they're not ready yet.'

'Right,' I say looking down at the ground, 'but listen, the longer we're here the more they can prepare...'

'Let them prepare, preparation is a good thing.'

'Not us. The other side. They'll prepare.'

'So what? You'll win.'

'It's not that simple.'

'Howie, if it means we camp out overnight or go back to the golf hotel and attack Stenbury tomorrow then so be it. Oh don't look at me like that. What deadline is there? Why the all-out rush? We need to slow down and think about what we're doing a bit more.'

'No. We need to get on and kill them before they get clever and kill us and everyone else.'

'Masks,' she says and stares at me.

'What about them?' I ask with a sigh.

'Maybe if you slowed down and thought a bit more you would have thought about wearing masks and eye protection.'

'Yes maybe and maybe we would all be resting cosy in a farmhouse somewhere or maybe we'd all be dead or maybe we'd...'

'Stop ranting.'

'I'm not ranting.'

'You were building up. Just bloody calm down.'

'That's the worst thing to say to someone who's not calm.'

'I don't care,' she fires back, 'actually go for it, rant in here, jump up and down and shout if you want but you're not going back out there until they're good and ready.'

'I cannot wait,' the words come out and this time the real glare is there as the darkness sweeps through me and she recoils in horror at the look in my eyes.

'Howie,' she whispers stepping back.

'I cannot fucking wait,' it's still there, a pulsing energy coursing through my system, 'do you understand?' I step to close the gap created when she recoiled away from me, 'I cannot wait. I will not wait.'

'Howie, stop it...'

'Why are you delaying me?' I growl the words out as the darkness within threatens to consume me.

'You're scaring me,' she says holding her ground but swallowing in sudden uncertainty.

'Scaring you? I'll fucking do more than that if you try and stop...' My words cut off at the ringing slap delivered across my face and I snap my head round to glare at her as she whacks me again with fear in her eyes.

'MR HOWIE...' Dave charges in with his pistol drawn at the sound of the strike.

'Stand down,' I bark the words out, 'we're fine.'

He stops at the end of the aisle glaring down at Marcy for a second before lowering the pistol and walking away.

'Don't ever threaten me,' she whispers when he's gone, 'don't you ever threaten or talk to me like that again.'

I take a breath and feel the stinging sensation across both cheeks as she draws her own steadying breath, 'I'm sorry for hitting you,' she says tightly, 'but don't ever threaten me again.'

I nod. I know I was wrong for saying it but that anger, that pure fury driving me is still there and it won't go away. I need action. To be going. To be killing and Sarah's words come flying back to me, *you're enjoying this, you're getting addicted to it.* On the top of the wall in the fort and I can feel that day now. I can feel the urge to fight and keep fighting only it's stronger now than it was back then. Am I enjoying it? Am I addicted? She tried telling me to stop, to only do what was needed and no more. What is needed? How much is enough?

'It's hot,' I mutter as the sweat glides down my forehead and again go to walk off but again she's there, gripping my wrist and credit where credit is due but Marcy is both brave and stubborn as hell.

'Not yet,' she says gently, 'calm down first.'

'I'm calm.'

'Okay, just another minute then until that flush has gone.'

'I'm flushed because it's hot.'

'Okay,' she remains calm and drops her bag onto the ground and bends down to undo the top before glancing up as though in fear I'd walk off, 'stay there.' She pulls a bottle of water out and stands up while unscrewing the top, 'lean forward.'

I do as told and close my eyes as the water pours over my face and I flinch involuntarily when her hand touches my forehead, 'relax,' she says, 'I won't hurt you.' She works her hand through my hair pushing the water through then down over my forehead and gently brushing my closed eyes, nose, cheeks and down to my jaw. 'Stay still,' she whispers and does it again from my hair down my face to my jaw, 'better?'

'Yes, thank you.'

'You're a right diva when you don't have your snickers,' she says with a smile when I open my eyes, 'now do me,' she hands me a bottle and closes her eyes, 'do you remember that advert?'

'Yeah,' I chuckle and unscrew the lid, 'ready?'

'Oh yes.'

She's stubborn, brave and something else too, she's bloody switched on. I'm not intellectual or even intelligent like Reginald, Roy, Charlie and Paula. I can't make jokes as fast as Blowers and the lads, I can't be blunt like Blinky and not worry about speaking my mind but I bloody know when a pretty girl is using her looks on me and right now, Marcy is going for the full on experience and getting me to run crystal clear water over her hair and face knowing full well I'll be completely absorbed. It's cheap but fuck it, it also works a treat and I'm gone. Staring at her skin and feeling the softness of it under my fingertips as I work to sluice the sweat off and gently bring my hand from her scalp, down her forehead to her nose and those eyebrows and down the high cheekbones to the full lips. My hand stops at the point of her chin with my forefinger under and my thumb over. I tilt her face up and close the distance with an overwhelming urge to kiss her while expecting her to open her eyes and recoil again or laugh at me. It takes forever but the anticipation has my heart booming in my chest and I pause, holding off to enjoy that sensation of wanting but not having. She opens her heavy eyelids and locks eyes on me, unmoving but daring, challenging and there the same want I feel inside is portrayed in her expression. Her lips twitch to smile but not mocking me and she moves the last few inches and sinks her lips on mine to an explosion of pure touch that makes my heart miss a few beats and my stomach flip over a few times while my legs go all rubbery and weird.

Everything can wait now. The whole world and all that is in it because it doesn't matter. Nothing matters but this second. The kiss we shared yesterday was born of peril and the fear of imminent death and it was wonderful and glorious but nothing compared to right now. Since I've met her, since the first minute on the flatlands outside the fort when time seemed to stand still and I saw the seasons of years pass in a second and the ground heaved to send me flying into the sky, since then I have wanted this and now, to have it, to share the gentlest of kisses is the most perfect of moments I have ever known. More than that. It is everything and all. We don't move but remain stock still with our lips touching, eyes closed, my hand still on her chin and my other holding the water bottle. Maybe she does it to delay me. Maybe she is only giving her lips so I won't rush the lads and push them on, maybe she wants the infection to win and is buying time, or maybe, just maybe she is kissing me because she wants to do it and as though she can read my thoughts she pushes harder into me but not driven by lust but by a consuming desire to be closer. I do the same and the feeling grows. A sense of completeness, of wholeness. I drop the bottle and snake my hand through her hair and it increases yet again. Her hands find my head and again it grows. Every movement made, every motion taken to close the gaps between us heightens the feeling of it being right but still not driven by lust or a need to fuck on the floor. Not that. Deeper and infinitely more powerful and it feels like we're being lifted from the ground and floating in a void of nothing where nothing exists except that sensation. It is right. It is correct. More than appropriate and the unmistakable perfection of the feeling legitimises the very thing we are doing. Now I don't want to go to Stenbury or Brookley or Flitcombe or anywhere but yet I have to go to those places and I know it is pre-ordained and expected but not by the infection but by something else. By this.

Her lips part and slowly the feelings of man and woman creep to infuse with the other perfect sensation of being right but we are human and again it is right. A taste is given and a want builds to have more, to take more but to only take what is given and she gives to me as I do to her. Lips opening as the warm air from our lungs exhales into the others. We breathe each other. We taste each other. We give ourselves to the other for nothing is more human and loving than to kiss. More than sex. More than making love. A kiss is the most intimate act and a kiss given with love, with consent, with need and desire to give pleasure and receive pleasure and focus that sensation is as powerful as anything ever known. Lust will taint it. Lust and the organic reaction of the body to copulate to further the species but if they can be withstood to stretch the moment of the intimacy then the reward will only be greater for it and our reward is given freely.

When we part we do so not because the desire has finished because the desire has increased to such a height that nothing short of divine intervention could satisfy it now, and to be blunt, we don't have time to start shagging on the floor of Maplin. No, we part because the perfection of the moment has been reached and to end now will hold that perfect moment forever and always.

We don't speak but remain still and close. Breathing as our hearts start to return to normal and the dilation of our pupils retract to where they should be.

'Why us?' She whispers, 'why do we have to fix this?'

'I don't know.'

'I wish....'

'I know...me too.'

'But we can't.'

'No,' I reply, 'we can't.'

'One day?'

'Yes. One day.'

'Promise?'

'I promise. You too?'

'I promise too. One day.'

'One day,' I say and gently ease away. She closes her eyes as though savouring the moment and not wanting it to end and I'd give anything to go back and just stay with her. No. I would not give anything. I look outside to the group all chatting and drinking cans of fizzy drink and past them to Reginald and Charlie pouring over the maps at the desk. No. I wouldn't give anything.

'Ready?' I ask.

'I am,' she says picking her bag up, 'you?'

'Am now,' I smile.

'Oh is that what it takes to calm you down?'

'Maybe,' I chuckle, 'in fact yes, exactly that.'

'Noted,' she says, 'I'll be your chief calmer downerer.'

'Marcy,' I say as she looks at me, 'thank you and sorry for what I said.'

'S'okay,' she shrugs the bag on, 'I slapped you twice for it.'

'Yeah,' I say rubbing my face, 'you can hit hard.'

'Yep, you learn when you're this beautiful,' she says.

'So vain.'

We head back outside to a group of people pretending not to notice that we've been gone and Dave giving Marcy a very blank stare that goes on for a few seconds longer than it needs to, but then it is Dave and she did slap me and it's lucky he didn't shoot her on the spot.

'We're all ready,' Nick says cheerfully.

'Yeah?' I ask everyone, 'sure? We can stop for a drink if anyone wants one...or if anyone needs a poo.' Blank looks come back which slowly adjust to Marcy in obvious realisation that she's said something to me, 'fair enough, load up then.'

'Mr Howie,' Reggie calls out, 'we've identified a field half a mile from the village that is screened by a wooded copse for the deployment of the drone aircraft.'

'Great stuff, mate. Give us a shout when we're close.'

We get into the baking hot oven of the Saxon and instantly wilt. Engine on. Doors closed. Air conditioning on full and we pull away from Hydehill.

CHAPTER SEVENTEEN

D^{ay Eighteen}

UPDATE No 4

I AM DEFINITELY on the correct route. A small village full of thatched cottages and in the main road are a few dozen corpses and with more of the same military grade shell casings glinting in the sun.

On inspection of the bodies I can see they have been shot with clear precision and many of them with that tell-tale signature of a bullet hole in the precise mid centre of the forehead.

Next to the main road is a café and it is there the officers must have stopped for a planning meeting. Empty cans of soft drinks, water bottles and chocolate bar wrappers left in situ and a large bucket of water brought out for the attack dogs.

I am now even more excited. The fact they fought a battle then calmly stopped for a tea break is a sight that warms my heart for it tells me they have retained order and structure and an adherence to decent values. I searched the inside of the café and discovered the soft drinks cabinet almost empty. This tells me the officers were thoughtful enough to take drinks and refreshments out to the privates and non-commissioned officers forming the guard perimeter on the main road.

I must be honest and admit that I have given consideration to leaving Jess here and seeking a vehicle to use so I can close the distance between us. But I say with honesty that the very idea was quickly discounted. Jess may be slower than army trucks but in her senses I trust and again she showed the same response as we neared the main road by snorting and throwing her head.

It is still very hot and now very humid. I fear another storm is brewing.

NB

CHAPTER EIGHTEEN

The battle for Brookley

'Yes. Yes,' Reginald nods while thinking, 'yes.'
'You agree?'
'Yes. Yes.'

'I mean they haven't worn masks or eye protection since they started, no protective clothing at all and every single one of them is covered in cuts with broken skin.'

'Yes,' Reginald says again, 'indeed. Cuts. The possibility of blood or fluid transference will be very high. And tell me again what happened with Mr Howie?'

'Nick was on the floor, everyone was leaning over him and Mr Howie, Blowers, Cookey and Marcy were all rubbing their cut hands into him and we all heard Mr Howie offer himself instead of Nick.'

'And you heard this internally rather than externally?'
'Yes. Mr Howie did not speak yet we all heard it.'

'Perhaps he did speak but given the tension of the moment it merely appeared as though he did not speak.'

'No. As soon as I heard his voice I looked at him and most of the others did too. Marcy was right next to him and she was staring at him. Clarence was facing Mr Howie, Cookey and Blowers were opposite and of course Nick was lying down. They all had a clear view and Mr Howie was not speaking.'

Reginald nods again and listens intently as the air in the van cools rapidly from the air conditioning on maximum, 'telepathy is a form of extrasensory perception cognition through which information can be passed but it is fiction. It does not exist. It is not possible therefore if something is not possible then there must be another explanation for it.'

'But...'

'Having said that,' Reginald says cutting her off, 'that was my belief only three weeks ago but having been subjected to an advanced organic state of telepathic control in the form of a hive mind collective intelligence I would suggest that whatever variance of infection or virus you are all infected with has meant that, at times of extreme emotion, Mr Howie has gained the ability to broadcast his thoughts in the same way the infection transposes its will upon the host bodies.'

Charlie does as Reginald did and listens intently until the full realisation of his suggestion hits home, 'oh,' she says dully, 'oh dear.'

'Yes, my dear,' Reginald says softly, 'oh dear indeed.'

'So we are *all* infected.'

'I am not a doctor,' Reginald says holding his hands out with the palms facing Charlie, 'and I can only make suppositions based on the very limited information I have. But, given the fact that we know the infection can use such a technique and coupled with the fact that at least four of the group appear to be immune to the virus in its current known state then yes, indeed it does appear that way.'

'Five,' Charlie says, 'five are immune. Six including Meredith.'

'I was not counting Marcy or myself. Marcy and I turned. That we later turned *back* could suggest that whatever variance of virus within us is different to the one inside you, or inside the four we know are immune.'

'But Mr Howie was kissing Marcy,' Charlie says thinking hard, 'in Maplin.'

'It was only a matter of time,' Reginald says with a low groan, 'but perhaps that does not change anything. If Marcy and I are carriers it could be that the type of virus in you stops you taking any further infection from us, or indeed from them.'

'We really need to find virologists.'

'Indeed we do but our course at this time is to seek ways to cull their numbers which is a futile act and one likened to bolting the proverbial stable door after the horse has ran very far away.'

'You think this is futile?'

'Charlie, anything less than an arsenal of nuclear bombs being dropped is futile. They are like cockroaches and rats. Millions of them in the country and no doubt billions of them worldwide. What can thirteen people do? Our efforts should be as you say and directed at finding a virologist to understand why we have variances within our small group and what can be taken from us to create either a vaccine or a cure.'

'You think they can be cured?'

'In truth no. I think the best we can hope for is a vaccine to prevent anyone else being turned and then waiting for them to die out naturally.'

'That would take years.'

'Yes.'

'And even then it would only take a few to survive and...' she trails off at the long bleak future ahead of them.

'Yes,' he says and lets the subject drop at seeing the range of emotions cross her face. He looks at the monitor and the view of the countryside coming at them on two images and the other showing the view of the countryside being left behind. The future and the past shown almost as representation of what they are discussing. Ahead are the possibilities. Behind are the facts of what they can prove. Ahead could be anything but behind there are only trees.

Charlie's radio squawks on the desk, *'Howie to everyone...we're passing through the next village now...Brookley is only a few minutes after that.'*

A few houses go by on the monitor. Then a few more until they are passing what is attempting to be the main road complete with one shop. Turning to the matter at hand, Reginald stares down at the map on the desk and the village of Brookley followed Flit-combe and finally Stenbury. Smaller towns between them but those are the ones to be leap-frogged.

They should be seeking professional experts who can under-stand this but unless Mr Howie is ready to listen to that sugges-tion then they have no choice but to stay the course and plan to stay alive until he is ready. The village passes by plunging then once more back into the open countryside as they head to the spot allocated on the map to be used to deploy the drone. Thinking such a thing makes him shake his head in disbelief, that he would be in the back of an armoured van having been turned into a crazed monster and now working as a military strategist for what is possible the only functioning resistance group in the country is beyond comprehension and best not to be dwelled upon.

'We should be close,' Reginald calls out to Roy who transmits the same on his radio, 'look for an opening to the field on the right side.'

'Howie to Reginald, you there?'

'Reginald here, please do go ahead Mr Howie.'

'No fields here, mate. There is a bloody big industrial estate though.'

Charlie leans forward to check the map as Reginald checks is and peers over to look at Charlie's. 'The maps must be old,' Charlie says, 'do they look new?'

'*Reginald to Mr Howie, does the industrial estate look new in appearance?*'

'*Er...yeah I guess so...they're all metal instead of the old brick things.*'

'*Then we suggest they have been built since the maps were completed and this is the correct location.*'

The vehicles had slowed down as the communication was held and now with them moving on again Reginald and Charlie check the monitor as the opening entry way into the industrial zone comes into a view complete with a large sign board indicating the names and trades of the various business located within. The Saxon leads the way down a broken concrete road running between the units to a wide open patch of wasteland complete with puddles left from the intense rain and thick weeds growing through the cracks.

Half a mile from Brookley and as Roy's van comes to a halt next to the Saxon so Charlie opens the rear door and jumps down to turn back and carefully lift the drone out to rest on the ground. Reginald switches the monitor to the live feed and activates his handset as Roy climbs into the back to watch him.

Everyone armed and ready, guns up and aiming out with Meredith running in a wide circle round the group sniffing the ground.

'Ready?' Nick gets to Charlie and check the drone as she turns the handset on and nods, 'go for it, nice and high remember.'

The insect-like machine comes to life with four sets of blades whirring with a rising pitch as she starts a gentle press of the stick. Up it goes, straight into the air and banking gently backwards.

'Forty metres,' Reginald calls out from the readout on the display.

'That's enough,' Nick says knowing that although they can see it they can't hear it and unless you're actively looking it will be almost impossible to spot.

'Here goes then,' Charlie says stepping carefully to the back of

Roy's van and using the monitor instead of her naked eye to chart the course. An instant view of the industrial unis seen from the air and she pushes the direction to force the blades to tilt and propel the aircraft towards the village.

'Amazing,' Roy mutters as Howie, Dave, Clarence, Paula and Marcy gather at the back of the van to watch with Blowers keeping watch on the perimeter. The fields below the drone glide gently past. A farmhouse and outbuildings. A fishing pond and wooded copses all seen in real time high definition. 'Tilt the camera up a little,' Roy says and watches the view subtly change and there, ahead in the near distance is the edge of the village green coming into view.

'Main road,' Reginald says more to himself, 'there, it splits and goes round the green.'

'I see it,' Howie says, 'looks empty so far.'

The green is highly recognisable with both the northern and southern road have houses butting up but only the northern side shows a far greater mass of dwellings, side roads and buildings beyond with near on open land behind the houses on the southern road. Maintaining the height the drone seems to glide through the air and with the monitor showing visual only and the craft being far enough away to be out of earshot they watch mesmerised at the vista opening up.

'Reggie,' Clarence says, 'speak out what you can see.'

'Pardon?'

'Say what you can see, like a commentary.'

'Oh. I see. Er...well the roads are there and the green is there, yes indeed. I am not entirely sure what to say at this present juncture but...'

'The green is empty,' Roy takes over smoothly, 'no fences by the looks of it. Er, looks like a cricket pitch in the middle and what's that?' He asks pointing to a small building at one end, 'maybe a bandstand or something? A structure anyway. Er...the southern side houses are smaller than the northern side but the gardens are bigger. Charlie can you go over the southern side houses first.'

'Which way is that?'

'Oh, right, go right...'

'Okay,' she watches the screen and moves a stick as the craft banks right and heads towards the houses on the southern side.

'Keep the height,' Clarence says quietly, 'and do one fly past on the southern then back along the northern side.'

'Will do,' Charlie mutters.

'Detached houses,' Roy says pointing at a series of buildings in turn.

'Access from the rear gardens then,' Clarence says.

'There!' Marcy says leaning in then clambering up to point at the monitor, 'see...' she points to a house and the back garden.

'Fuck yeah,' I say at the objects now so clear at being pointed out. People standing still and all facing towards the backs of the houses.

'More,' she says, 'can we go lower?'

'We can't risk them hearing the drone,' Roy says, 'but we can see they've got some in nearly every garden...not the first what...five or six houses? But then I guess they are figuring we won't be stopping at the beginning of the road.'

'Waiting for us though,' I say, 'that thing is bloody brilliant.'

'Yep, every garden all the way to the end,' Marcy says as the craft reaches the end of the line and starts the turn to cross the green and commence the return journey along the other side.

'These houses are semi-detached by the looks of it so every other building will have a side access,' Roy says, 'yes, see two gardens but only one building. Can you see?'

'We can see that, Roy,' Clarence says.

'I worked it out from seeing two gardens but only one house.'

'Yep. Got it,' Howie says.

'The gardens are split down the middle.'

'Moving on from the gardens,' Clarence says, 'can you see any infected?'

'I can't,' Roy says shrugging, 'anyone else?'

'In the houses then,' Howie says his words cutting off abruptly as the first side road comes into view and a stack of people standing inert behind the first natural bend, 'or maybe not...how many is that?'

'Over a hundred,' Clarence says, 'tightly packed in. They must be roasting,' he adds as an afterthought.

'Fucking hope so,' Howie says, 'one hundred there so they must have some decent numbers in the houses too...'

'And we've got Flitcombe to go yet before we get to Stenbury,' Clarence says with a smile.

'Thousands then,' Howie says with a return smile.

'And you appear to be happy with that,' Reginald observes drily, 'which is most disconcerting.'

'Ah, we'll be alright,' Howie says with a beaming smile, 'we've got you, Reggie.'

'What?'

'Another side road,' Dave says nodding at the screen, 'more.'

'More there is,' Howie mutters.

'Gardens too,' Roy says pointing out the figures waiting out of sight by the side gates as Reginald leans closer to the monitor, 'but remember the gardens are separated by a fence because the houses are semi-detached so it looks like one building whereas in fact it's...

'We get it, Roy,' Paula says, 'the way I'm looking at it...I mean they're all concentrated across that middle section of the northern road.'

'I agree,' I say. Side roads leading from the northern road are clogged with bodies tucked up and the only one in gardens that we can see are in the middle section of houses.

'Indeed yes, one can assume that upon entering the village you would naturally gravitate towards the only commercial premises and in this case it is the village post office.'

'Southern road then?' I ask the group but glance to Clarence then Dave.

'I don't know,' Clarence says thoughtfully, 'if we've got to do what's expected of us then we should go for the post office and wait there. That's what we would do if we didn't know any of this.'

'You think by taking the southern road we'd let them know that we know what they know?' Howie asks with a frown, 'is that likely? I mean, we're completely incompetent and slapdash at the best of times. Why don't we just drive straight into the middle of the green and wait for them to come to us? That *is* something we'd do.'

'Agreed,' Clarence says with a nod.

'Everyone happy?'

'Happy is not a word I would use to describe this situation in any capacity,' Reginald says, 'in fact I would go so far as to say I am at the extreme and polar opposite of being happy.'

'Noted, everyone else?'

'Happy with that,' Paula says, 'aim for the middle and hope for the best.'

'Spot on,' Roy says standing up straight to stretch his back with a wince that makes us all hold our breath as we wait for the inevitable self-diagnosis that he's now got incurable back disease, 'bent over too long,' he says twisting side to side completely oblivious to the weighted silence.

'MAY I BRING IT BACK NOW?' Charlie asks.

'Indeed you may,' I reply, 'please bring our drone into a safe landing if you would be so obliged.'

'I will kindly bring our drone back to the very best of my abilities.'

'Jolly good, everything is jolly good.'

'What's got into you?' Paula asks at my cheery countenance.

'Tally ho, chucks away.'

'Chocks,' Clarence says, 'not chucks.'

'Chocks away,' I beam round at the confused faces, 'I think we should go into the next fight in the theme of world war two airmen. Tally ho!'

'Fuck yes!' Cookey shouts from a short distance away, 'roger that, Sir! We'll feed it to the boche.'

'They don't like it up 'em,' Clarence booms, 'let's give the rotters what for eh chaps!'

'Bombadier Blowers?'

'Yes, Captain Howie?'

'Oh my god,' Paula groans rubbing her face.

'Are we ready to move out, Bombadier Blowers?'

'All present and correct, Captain Howie!'

'Now now chaps, listen in, come on gather round, that's it, we're going into a fight now with the enemy and I want you to know how bally well proud of you all I am. Yes, that' right. Bally well proud excusing my French,' I say with a wink at Marcy who can't help but smile, 'and I know we'll stick it up 'em today.'

'They don't like it up 'em,' Clarence booms.

'No they don't like it up 'em!' I say.

'Not up 'em,' Clarence bellows with a shake of his fist.

'But we'll have a good clean fight and stick it in 'em.'

'They don't like it in 'em,' Clarence says.

'In 'em or up 'em,' I roar.

'Not up 'em or in 'em,' Clarence says deafening everyone within a few feet.

'Leftenant Charlie, is the drone safely back?'

'Sir! The drone is coming into land now, Sir!'

'Make way for the drone!' My shout is taken up by all the lads affecting world war two posh voices.

'Drone coming in now, Sir,' Nick shouts, 'like an angry Spitfire she is, Sir.'

'Make way for that Angry Spitfire,' I jump down and stride out to the side.

'Angry Spitfire coming in now!' Blowers calls out, 'make way, make way now.'

'Making way,' Cookey says moving back.

'They don't want it up 'em,' Clarence booms again.

'I say chaps,' Roy stuns us all with the best yet, 'isn't it rather spiffing that we're going to stick it in 'em.'

'They don't like it in 'em,' Clarence says, 'lads, what don't they like?'

'They don't like it 'em, Sir!'

'There's my lads, good lads.'

'Angry Spitfire descending now, Captain Howie.'

'Prepare for descent,' I call out.

'Descent preparing underway,' Bombadier Blowers says.

'Commander Cookey, is the ground clear?'

'I say the ground is jolly clear, Captain Howie.'

'Here she comes,' I say watching the drone lowering through the air, 'round of applause for the Angry Spitfire.'

We all clap politely, even Paula and we watch as the drone bounces down to muted cheers.

'Well done, Leftenant Charlie.'

'Thank you, Sir.'

'Navigator Nick, are we ready to pack the Angry Spitfire away?'

'Packing away now, Captain Howie.'

'Jolly good!'

'Jolly good!'

'I say chaps, shall we load up and get ready to go stick it up 'em?'

'They don't like it up 'em,' Clarence growls shaking is fist again.

'Yes let's,' Commander Cookey says.

'Major Mohammed? Are you ready to stick it up 'em?'

'They don't like it up 'em, Sir,' Major Mohammed says laughing, 'innit, you get me, bro?'

'Nice touch, Mo,' I laugh, 'chocks away then, everyone load up and we'll go stick it up 'em.'

They all reply with shaking fists that they don't like it up 'em and into the Saxon we load with Paula, Roy and Charlie going with Reginald.

'I say chaps,' I say getting into the front next to Clarence, 'shall we give them what for?'

'We'll show them rascals,' Clarence says.

'Damned boche,' Cookey shouts, 'for Queen and country.'

'For Queen and country!' We all shout back and the mood rises with a sense of buoyed up jubilation as rifles are checked, magazines are checked, bag straps are checked, hand weapons are checked until Clarence starts humming the Dam-Busters theme tune and we're off, all joining in to the one of the most iconic pieces of music to ever come out of British cinema history. Someone, probably Cookey, presses their radio button and our earpieces fill with the noise that transmits to Roy's van.

A straight road runs to the green and with the plan to aim for the middle I keep the speed and power on knowing the Saxon can take the high kerb edge with ease and we bounce up and onto the grass with a cheer with Roy's van to our right side with Paula waving with a huge grin and Roy tapping the steering wheel in time to the music still being sang.

I feel it before I see it. A loss of traction that makes the steering wheel in my hands wobble strangely and were slewing to the right into the path of Roy's van. The ground sodden from the rain looked normal but the weight of the vehicle sinks it down into the slippery mud and the big tyres lose traction.

'FUCK,' I shout in alarm glancing across to see Roy fighting to control his vehicle as we both fishtail and slide through the grass.

'BRACE,' Clarence shouts with a grim expression as he grips the dashboard in front of him while we aquaplane along the grass from the power, speed and momentum gained from the entry into the green. On course to impact and I know there is nothing that can be done. The wheels aren't gripping and no amount of power or brakes applied will make any difference. The front jerks round and we go side on down the green with Roy desperately trying to steer away from our path. His van shoots away to the right but a second later comes back towards us. Silence in the van as everyone clings on and I catch glimpse of Paula shouting something over her shoulder to the two in the back.

Our back end spins round until we're turning dizzyingly as we slide across the green and the view outside spins round as my stomach lurches from the sensation. My head loses its position in time and space and a wave of nausea hits me so I clench my eyes shut and grip the wheel. The Saxon is heavier and the weight of gravity does the work to slow us down faster than Roy's lighter van and we spin to a giddying stop facing back the way we came and looking at the wake of thick churned up mud.

The second van keeps going, spinning round and round as it slides further down the green and through the roped off area of the cricket pitch.

'Shit,' I grit my teeth as my mouth fills with saliva in the pre-curser to puking. Engine off, engine on and I force my movements to go easy and apply gentle pressure to the accelerator and the engine thrums but we stay still. I ease off and try again and the wheels spin on the spot digging us deeper into the mud. The Saxon is four wheel drive so the engine is giving power to all the wheels at the same time and it would only take one of them to gain purchases to drag us out but they spin and churn to throw thick gloopy mud into the air. No traction control and no engine management system that would kick in to drive power to one wheel at a time until the vehicle gained grip and we wallow deeper as I slam into reverse and hope to fuck we start moving. A glance up and Roy's van has come to a stop at least two hundred metres away and I can see the mud flying into the air as he too tries to drive out of the quagmire.

'Fuck...fuck...come on,' I growl in prayer and force my movements to remain controlled. 'Nick, get up top and keep...'

'INCOMING...' A blast of voice from the radio and Paula shouting the alarm.

'*Which side?*' Clarence asks pushing the button under his shirt.

'BOTH...'

I twist round in my seat and spot the figures pouring from the houses and side streets on the northern side, 'they're all coming,' I say.

'Same on the southern side,' Clarence shouts.

'Everyone out,' I push my door open and look down at the thick wet mud before lunging out to land with a splodge that spurts goo all up my body and face. Rifle in hand and I shove my axe down my back under the bag and start wading to the rear of the vehicle as they drop out one by one into the mud.

'*We're stuck,*' Roy's voice calm and controlled in my ear and although he can be a pain in the arse he never flaps.

'*Same, we're coming to you,*' I radio back and catch sight of Nick falling over with a loud shout and Clarence bending to grip his arm lifting him back to his feet.

We trudge and slip, falling and sliding with curses as we try to keep our rifles free from the mud and suddenly Roy's van seem impossibly far away across an expanse of sticky wet earth.

On both sides the hordes reach the green in thick lines and they do the same as the vehicles and go too fast for the conditions and slide across to fall head over arse in a jumbling tangle of limbs that buys us time.

'Two teams,' Dave says, 'Simon, your team is alpha, everyone else is bravo...is that clear?'

'Yes, Dave,' a chorus of replies.

'Staggered fire teams, alpha will fire into the northern side while bravo move...bravo will fire into the southern while alpha move...is that clear? Alpha...DOWN AND FIRE...'

Blowers, Cookey, Nick, Mohammed and Blinky drop to one knee, aim and burst fire across to the northern side. Bodies drop instantly but the distance is too great to see if they fall from being shot or from slipping on the mud. While they fire we push on, grunting with exertion and trying to move by planting our feet wide and allowing for the slide. Small steps works best but it's taxing and within seconds my legs are burning.

'MAGAZINE,' Nick is the first to shout.

'BRAVO DOWN AND FIRE,' Dave shouts and we do the same, dropping to one knee, aiming across to the lesser numbers on the southern side and firing bursts across the green. The air fills with gunshots from assault rifles and there's no doubt we get kills, not with Dave and Clarence firing. Thirty shots each and a few seconds later we're up, moving and changing magazine as Blowers and his group drop down to fire. The hordes make gains by simply throwing themselves into the field without concern for personal injury. We don't have that luxury and a wrenched ankle now could be catastrophic so we have no choice but to go slower.

Shots ahead from three rifles firing into the bigger northern line pushing on into the green. The fact that we are meant to win this battle now seems a moot point and it's clear the infection is taking advantage of our mistake by separating into lines and groups that surge across the ground with increasing speed and agility.

'BOTH TEAMS FIRE,' Dave shouts and we all drop to pour bullets into the mass on the northern side but with our focus diverted so the ones on the southern side make better progress as they too learn how to move fast across the mud and it's obvious both hordes are aiming straight towards the three from Roy's van.

Several break free from the horde on the northern side and sprint ahead with alarming pace as they howl into the air. Roy's rifle clicks empty and he lets it drop on the sling, pulls his bow round, nocks an arrow and looses into the closest with a head shot that sends the male flying back into the mud. Already the second is nocked and loosed and the second infected is taken down.

'Dave, southern side,' I pant and watch as he twitches over to aim and fires single shots into the ones breaking free from that horde.

Arrows fly. Dave gets head shots and the rest of us run towards Paula and Charlie expending magazine after magazine into the charging lines. Thighs burning and chests heaving but we drive on slipping in the mud while we ram fresh magazines home. I drop and fire mine into the northern side, get up and start running again but the ground is so sodden my feet slide out until they sink down inches into the gooey mud. My knees hurt and my ankles ache as much as my thighs and the sweat pours down my face as a black streak goes flying past me with Meredith showing what four wheel drive with built in traction control really looks like. She stays low, her paws barely touching the ground and any slips made by the paws hitting the ground are compensated by her perfect poise and centre of gravity.

'Meredith is loose,' Nick shouts, 'watch your fire.'

'Dave and Roy northern side, everyone else southern,' I shout knowing those two will get perfect shots every time with no risk of hitting the dog. The rest of us adjust and fire a devastating volley down the green into that smaller group but still more pour from the gardens, houses and side streets on the topside.

Meredith reaches them and after slaughtering one on her way in, she disappears from view to cause carnage within their dense ranks and as amazing as she is even she can't take down enough to lessen the risk of them reaching Paula, Roy and Charlie before we get there and we can't risk firing into them now.

'We're gonna have to go in,' Clarence shouts as he changes magazine.

'Yep, Blowers...sort the southern side out then join us.'

'On it, you heard Mr Howie...FIRE INTO THOSE FUCK-ERS... FASTER...'

'Marcy, stay with Blowers,' I sling my rifle and pull the axe free.

'I'm immune I can...'

'Do not question me, Marcy,' I snap her words off leaving no room for discussion, 'Dave, get to Meredith, Clarence with me. Ready?'

'Yes, Mr Howie.'

'Go,' Clarence and I side by side with our double headed axes held ready. Dave going ahead drawing his knives as he goes. 'Roy... protect Meredith.'

'I am,' he says as calm as ever firing into an undead lunging towards her broad back as she sinks down to rag a female's neck open. The arrow strikes sending the undead spinning away as he nocks and aims tracking the dog who is completely unaware of the cover she's been given.

'Meredith, here,' I call out between gasping breaths, 'here... come on girl...'

'She's zoned out,' Clarence gasps.

'NICK...Try calling her back.'

'MEREDITH...HERE GIRL....COME BACK...'

'Fuck it,' I mutter at the distinct lack of response watching her whip about as arrows fly inches from her body.

'More arrows,' Roy shouts, 'Reggie, bring me more arrows.'

Carnage. Filthy muddy bloodied sweaty carnage. Spread out with assault rifles firing, undead howling, hissing and screaming and the dog snarling amongst them and Dave seemingly gliding over the wet ground and the natural born killer uses the environment to his advantage as he speeds up then simply drops and slides on his back in the mud through a group that each find their Achilles tendons cut. They fall like comical dominoes one after the other to land splatting in the mud.

Dave is up, running flat out across a short gap and drops down to slide between the legs of a male still turning to get him. The calculation of the speed, distance and angle needed are perfect and the two blades flick up to open the arteries in the groin. He rises, spinning on the spot and waiting for a circle of infected to fall in on him and again his eyes take everything in. The speed of approach, the distance to each and the way they will fall and beyond them to

Roy taking aim. He pauses and ducks at the last second as the closest lunges in to be taken away by the arrow embedding in the throat and he simply side steps into the gap created and steps on the fallen body to gain traction underfoot. Then he lets them come to him, remaining static but leaning from the waist as he bends and lashes out to cut throat after throat. The blades whisper across jugulars and by the time the blood is spraying out he's onto the next one until the blood arcs in the air are synchronised in harmonious order. Cut spray. Cut spray. Cut spray. The immediate area cleared but now he has more bodies to use and stepping stones they become as he treads on stomachs and backs to cut them down.

The trust he shows Roy is incredible and the arrows fly past his head as close as they do to Meredith. Roy is a machine. Nocking. Pulling and loosing without apparent aim and the more he does the faster he gets until two are in the air at the same time. A blur of motion and Reginald at his side holding the arrows out for him to take to lessen the range of motion needed.

Never in my entire life could such a thing be witnessed or believed. Dave ballet dancing with such poised grace that it belies the violent death he gives. Meredith ragging legs out to tug them down, a twitch of a movement and she's at the neck opening it quickly and ragging to the side with a wrench and off to the next one and anything that gets close to touching her is shot through with an arrow fired by Roy who watches Dave and Meredith alike. The silence of the three strikes me more than anything. Behind us are assault rifles firing repeatedly with explosions of cordite or whatever propellant is used to make the bullet fly at sub-sonic speed through the air but in front the deaths are given as equally if not greater and with silence. The knives make no sound. Meredith snarls but it's lost in the noise of the kills and the bow gently kisses the air. Christ, if we had five Dave's, five Roy's and five Meredith's we'd have won already and now be resting on a beach eating burgers and drinking cold beers.

Except we ain't got five of them. What we have is a bloody

great big bloke planted on tree trunk legs swinging a double bladed axe as he stomps a direct path through to the dog and me running in his wake killing what I can get at. Heads lunge and get removed. Arms lopped off and the blades bite deep into necks, shoulders, torsos and spill sticky blood into the sticky mud. An arrow swooshes an inch from my nose to strike a lunging female through the eye and I yelp out and spin to see Roy already loosing the next one, 'I'll work round you, Mr Howie,' he says as calm as anything, 'pretend I'm not here.'

Pretend he's not there? Fuck me this is as surreal as it gets.

'KEEP HER BACK,' Clarence bellows at the sight of Charlie running towards us with a long bladed knife, 'CHARLIE GET BACK NOW.'

She stops and hesitates as Paula catches up and pulls her back with a hand on her shoulder, shaking her head and saying something with Reginald behind her feeding arrows to Roy.

'GOT HER,' Dave shouts with one hand gripping the scruff of the dog's neck while his other flicks out to slice into the flesh of anything stupid enough to get near him.

'SOUTHERN SIDE CLEAR,' Blowers roars from behind.

'SIMON, SUSTAINED FIRE ON MY COMMAND,' Dave shouts back-stepping with the dog.

'READY ON YOUR COMMAND,' Blowers shouts back.

'DOWN,' Dave roars and drops at the same time as Clarence and I plant our faces down into the mud, 'NOW.'

Assault rifles firing over our heads withering them back as Blowers paces forward with his team in a solid line. I glance back to watch them walking with small steady paces. Six of them firing bursts into the packed horde that gets cut to pieces. Paula and Charlie joining to them as Roy snatches his rifle up to add his own intense fire rate.

'CHANGE MAGAZINES,' Blowers shouts.

'UP,' Dave adds his order and we're on our feet back-stepping and facing the recovering horde coming at us. A small skirmish and a few get through our gaps only to be taken down by Roy back on his bow as Reginald changes the magazine in Roy's rifle.

'READY.'

'DOWN.'

'FIRE.'

Again we face plant and I risk a glance back to see Blowers is much closer now and leading a disciplined line that fires steadily into those still charging towards us. Paula and Charlie weave back to fall in at the end of the line and keep pace as Roy goes back to his rifle.

'YOURS.'

'UP.'

We're up and closing that gap between us as Dave drags the dog back and Clarence and I slice down the bodies either attacking us or trying to run past. Metres now between our line going back and Blowers' line coming forward.

'READY.'

'DOWN.'

'FIRE.'

Fucking hell this is amazing. The line headed by Blowers look brutally efficient stepping as one with grim determined expressions from Paula at one end to Mohammed at the other end, 'HOLD,' Blowers calls out to stop the progression a couple of metres back from us, 'YOURS,' he shouts and we pause as each rifle is lowered before lurching up and falling back into the gaps made ready for us. Axes tucked down, rifles pulled round, magazines changed.

'FIRE,' I shout and now we all do so, organised, disciplined and killing the shit out of them. They drop like flies now with every weapon firing solidly and Dave standing with the dog between his legs gripping her tight so she doesn't run off again.

'CHANGE,' we all do it heedless of regard to any that have a remaining round or two left but it shows something to the other side. It shows unity and the strength in that unity. That we are misfits, oddballs and a collective bunch of weirdos that are wholly incompetent at most things apart from this. This we can do and we do it well. Hundreds are slaughtered and although we know this was a move on a chessboard we also know the infection would have taken us here if it had the chance.

'CEASEFIRE,' I shout and the guns fall silent as the last one drops, 'Dave.'

'Yes, Mr Howie.'

'Release the hound,' I look round with a grin, 'I've been dying to say that.'

He steps away and she's off, itching to get stuck back in and snaking through the bodies to sniff out anything that still lives. Snarls sound out as she closes in on them and rags the necks open.

Our line remains solid and unmoving. Changing magazines again and looking, scanning, always looking and always scanning. We check behind but the ground is littered with bodies.

'Good work, Roy,' I call down the line.

'Thanks,' he says leaning forward to nod at me.

'You too, Blowers.'

'Cheers, boss.'

'Everyone okay?'

'Fuck yes,' Blinky says then bends double to puke on the ground, 'sorry,' she waves a hand in the air between retches.

'Charlie.'

'Yes, Mr Howie.'

'I appreciate you coming to help but don't do that again.'

'Of course, my apologies, Mr Howie.'

'No need to say sorry but we'd shout if we needed help.'

'I understand.'

'Bloody brave though,' Clarence says looking over everyone's head to her, 'and I mean that.'

'Thank you.'

'Did she run in to help you?' Blowers asks.

'She did,' Clarence says, 'like I said, bloody brave.'

'Yeah,' Blowers says, 'well done, Charlie.'

'How the hell do you do that, Roy?' Nick asks, 'you were like an inch from hitting Meredith.'

'And us,' Clarence says.

'I can calculate your movements,' Roy says, 'but not if you're trying to compensate for my aiming. If we do that again ignore me and let me work.'

'Understood,' I reply, 'Reginald, nice to see you out of the... where is he?'

'Gone back in the van,' Paula says.

'Fair enough, so,' I say slowly looking round, 'we chose a good place to fight then. How the fuck we gonna get out?' I ask as everyone turns to stare at Nick who chuckles self-consciously.

'We'll find something the wheels can grip on...old carpet from the houses or...'

'They're too heavy for carpets to work,' Roy says, 'we'll need industrial matting...'

'Or chains,' Mohammed says.

'Chains might work,' Nick says.

'We've got chains in the Saxon haven't we?' Roy asks.

'Yeah,' Nick nods, 'thick fuckers too.'

'Like you then.'

'Funny, Cookey.'

'I try.'

'I thought chains worked in the snow?' I ask, 'won't the mud sink through the links.'

'We only need a few inches,' Nick says.

'That's what she said.'

'Cookey you dick,' Nick groans, 'or we can stick some planks of wood down but the risk is she'll sink straight back in once we move off, and finding planks of wood in a hurry might not be easy either.'

'Use doors,' Paula says, 'from the houses, 'they'll do it won't they?'

'Yeah, yeah they will, internal wooden doors,' Nick says looking down the line to Roy, 'will they do it?'

'Solid wood doors will, not the cheap things.'

'Bloody hell,' Clarence says with a heavy sigh, 'and I wonder who'll be ripping them off and carrying them down.'

'We all will,' I announce at the sight of his sweating red face, 'how many do we need?'

'Two at the least but as many as we can carry,' Nick says.

'Right,' I give my own heavy sigh and start trudging through the mud towards the bodies, 'let's get on with it then. Vehicles rescued. Clothes changed. Fluids and on we go...er unless that is anyone wants to stop and have a poo or anything?'

'Why do you keep asking that?' Clarence asks walking past, 'I had one this morning.'

'Me too,' Blowers adds.

'I don't need a shit, Mr Howie,' Blinky says helpfully.

'I asked,' I say with a shrug to Marcy.

Work to be done. Always work to be done and we tread through the bodies still being checked by Meredith apparently content in her work and head towards the semi-detached houses. You know, the semi-detached houses that are really one building but they have two gardens with a fence running down the middle. Roy is a genius but very bloody weird but then I guess that goes hand in hand. Reginald is as odd as they come but then he's spot on so far. Charlie is reticent to the point of being tight-lipped about anything to do with her history but she's clearly very intelligent.

At the houses we switch on for a few more minutes and do clearance of the rooms before taking it in turns at the kitchen and bathroom sinks to rinse the filth and mud from our eyes and faces. Pouring cooling water over our heads and drinking until we feel bloated. Meredith is given a huge bowl and she lies down with her front paws either side to lap thirstily as Nick, Mo and Blinky use pots and pans to pour more water over her coat. She pays no heed and drinks for a long minute before bringing her head up to pant for a few seconds then dipping back down to carry on.

Roy retrieves his arrows, well those that can be retrieved as a few are ruined from being jammed into eye sockets and bones. With that going on Clarence sizes up the first door, a nice solid stripped pine thing leading into a nice lounge with a stripped pine floor. A brief grunt and the door is being walked out to be stacked outside. It doesn't look that hard so I go for the next one, which is another stripped pine solid thing leading to a downstairs toilet. I grasp the edges, tense and strain trying to pull it free but I might as well be trying to push a house over for the effect it has.

'May I?' Clarence asks waiting for me to step aside so he can grasp the door in exactly the same places I was holding it and grunting with the most minimal of effort as he snaps the hinges and walks off down the hallway with an apologetic nod. He walks back in, trudges upstairs and walks back down carrying another one which he stacks outside. Blowers and I go for the kitchen door and work together straining and grunting to try and pull the thing free. Cookey joins in, then Nick and Blinky until we're all huffing and puffing to and most likely working against each other.

'Last one?' Clarence asks from behind us leaning against the wall.

'Yeah,' I step back and wipe the sweat from my eyes as the others give up and let him get past, 'fuck's sake,' I mutter when the door comes away in his hands.

'You weakened it,' he says and walks off again.

Outside we work in twos carrying the doors over the road and onto the green as we navigate back through the bodies towards the Saxon and Dave keeping watch like the sentinel he is. Already covered in mud so getting more covered in mud hardly seems to matter as we work to jam the doors under the edge of the wheels and work them up and down like levers to push them harder under the wheels. We slip, slide, curse, sweat and become mud monsters until finally Nick and Roy announce it should be enough.

'We'll have to push from the back,' Roy says examining the front wheels again, 'if we all do it we might get onto the doors.'

'Who wants to drive?' I ask out loud, 'ladies?'

'Don't be sexist,' Paula says with a glare at me, 'but okay,' she darts off to the driver's door and clambers up, 'hard or slow?'

'That's what she said,' an exhausted Cookey shouts.

'Slow,' Nick says wading to the back with the rest of us, 'Charlie can you stay at the front and shout when the wheels get purchase.'

'Why can't you do it?' She asks pointedly.

'Because I'm stronger and can push more,' he says walking off while wiping the mud from his face.

'That is a fair and reasonable answer,' she says after a brief pause, ' yes you are indeed stronger,' she adds in a thoughtful tone with a glance at his backside which makes us all take notice and she notices us noticing and blushing furiously she leans down to examine the wheels and look occupied. I share a glance with Marcy who lifts her eyebrows questioningly.

'Ready?' Roy asks, 'Paula, dear. Can you start now please?'

'Not if you call me dear again I can't.'

'Fine. Paula, can you start now please....dear,' he mutters under his breath.

'I heard that!'

'She did not,' he says looking round.

'No way,' Clarence says shaking his head, 'she's guessing you said it.'

'I am not guessing, Clarence.'

'On your own, Roy,' Clarence says planting his heels into the ground and bracing his shoulder against the edge of the Saxon.

The engine starts with a solid thrum that vibrates through the chassis and we all throw our bodies against the rear of the vehicle as she starts to apply gentle pressure to the accelerator.

'PUSH,' Clarence shouts straining with his face flushing an even deeper shade of red, 'COME ON...'

We strain and push with feet sliding out from underneath as the wheels spin in the mud with the inevitable shower of shit flying back to marinade us all.

'Almost,' Charlie shouts, 'little bit more...just a little bit more...'

We cry out from the energy sapping work as Marcy slips to land face first in the squelchy mud and I burst out laughing as she jerks back up wearing a facemask. The Saxon jolts, bites the doors and is off chugging away over the adhoc road we laid down as Paula takes advantage of the motion and pushes on.

'STOP,' Roy shouts knowing full well she'll sink straight back into the mud once she leaves the last door laid down. Only she doesn't stop and the Saxon doesn't sink but fishtails, bucks and slews but it keeps going as she aims for the closest bodies and uses them as rubble to drive over.

'Ooh,' I wince as the first head pops like a melon and the sound of twigs snapping reaches us clear above the sound of the engine. Bodies being crushed, exploding, imploding, bursting apart as the Saxon bumps and jolts over them.

'Argh,' Clarence gives his own wince at another head popping apart with a spray of blood and brains flying out.

'Nasty seeing it from this side,' Blowers says.

'Yeah right,' I agree at the limbs and torsos being snapped and squashed as she rally drives over them.

'Oh fuck,' Cookey's turn at the sight of the female undead getting her legs caught in the wheel and being dragged along going round and round with the motion of wheel, smashing into more bodies as she pulverises herself into a sloppy wet mash of bones and gore.

I turn away and shake my head then burst out laughing again at the two wide eyes staring at me from a face of mud.

'What?' she says, 'have I got something on my face?'

'Seen this?' I call out as Marcy turns to proudly display her facemask.

'Actually feels quite nice,' she says stretching her jaw, 'like a proper mask.'

'Really?' Charlie asks.

'Try it,' Marcy urges, 'seriously, it's really nice.'

Charlie stares with that same hesitation showing through as though she wants to do it but is holding herself back.

'Fuck it,' Cookey says and bends down to scoop a big handful up which he smears into his cheeks and forehead, 'what does it do?' He asks.

'Same as a mask,' Marcy says, 'let it dry and wash it off to unclog the pores.'

'Ah okay, I think my pores need unclogging,' he says rubbing it in, 'try it, Blowers.'

'Are you fucking...' Blowers goes to snap the reply off then instantly changes his mind, 'yeah fuck it,' but instead of copying Cookey he simply drops down and shoves his face into the muddy ground and slides his head side to side before standing back up, 'has it done it?' He asks looking round at the laughs from the sight of him, 'try it, Charlie. Feels really nice...like cool and weirdly refreshing.'

'Yeah that's it,' Cookey says, 'it's cooling.'

'I will,' Mo Mo says laughing, 'Blinky?'

She's already down and splodging it over her face as Charlie watches and tentatively drops down to one knee and scoops a handful up to sniff before making a decision and rubbing it gently into her cheeks.

'Here,' Marcy says waddling through the mud, 'let me,' she scoops a thick double handful up and starts working it into Charlie's cheeks, 'your complexion is gorgeous,' she says, 'you haven't got a blemish on you.'

'That has got to be the best thing I have ever seen,' Cookey says as we all watch Marcy rubbing mud into Charlie's face.

'Perverts,' Marcy tuts.

'Clarence?' Cookey asks.

'No.'

'Aw come on...'

'No. I am hot. I am thirsty.'

'Aw come on, want me to do it for you?'

'Touch me with that mud, Cookey and...' time freezes as Cookey reaches out and splodges a great big handful of wet mud on Clarence's left cheek who freezes in disbelief, 'you little shit,' he explodes out as Cookey screams and tries to run but gets caught with a vice like grip and is dragged backwards. Clarence laughing at the temerity of Cookey to actually do it and he upends the joker to dunk his head up and down in the mud, 'apologise...apologise...'

'I'm sorry,' Cookey gasps between laughs while he spits mud and grass, 'sorry...I said sorry...'

'Er...I made it,' Paula says in our ears as we watch Clarence beating on Cookey instead of the progress of the Saxon, 'what are you doing?'

'Face masks,' Marcy transmits the reply, 'try it, feels lovely.'

'Not up here thanks,' Paula says at the edge of the green and the squished up dead bodies in front of her.

'It is cool actually,' Clarence says after dropping Cookey face first into the mud and rubbing the mud on his cheek.

'Yeah?' I ask and get my own handful to try. He's right. The mud is refreshingly cool on my hot skin and instantly I feel a soothing sensation like a cold flannel is being draped on my face.

'Load it on boys,' Marcy says turning with a wolfish grin of teeth showing through the face of mud, 'we've got another one to do yet,' she looks past us to Roy's van sat in the midst of the green with the rear wheels sunk over halfway down into the brown gloop.

So it begins. A Journey of mudmen and women sliding and crawling through the quagmire to reach Roy's van.

'DOORS!' Clarence stops and thunders the word out and so we return to the place the Saxon was stuck to collect the doors and so re-commence the journey of mudmen and women sliding and crawling to Roy's van. The doors are slid, prodded and levered into position and with Paula back with us and behind the wheel we try again, gathering at the back to heave and strain as we lift and push while getting caked in mud being flung up from the spinning wheels.

Every mouth grimaces and sweat pours through the mud on our faces. Muscles burning, legs shaking and bodies slipping from our feet giving out to send us splatting down but no laughter now and those that fall get a breath of air and lurch back up.

'STOP,' Charlie appears at the back shaking her head apologetically, 'it's not working.'

'What's not working?' Clarence growls spitting a clug of mud from his mouth as we stagger round to stare down in dismay. The front wheels are on the rapidly sinking doors but the slickness of the mud on the sheer polished surface of the doors have created a virtual ice rink with nothing for the tyres to grip.

'Ideas?' I ask round, 'the chains in the Saxon aren't long enough.'

'Ropes?' Paula asks leaning out of the passenger door.

'We don't have any long enough.'

'More doors?' Cookey asks.

'Ditch the van and get another one?' Paula asks and quickly winces from the dark look given by Roy, 'or not,' she adds quickly.

'Bodies,' Clarence says, 'we'll have to use them.'

'Yeah, yeah might work...pretty fucking gross though.'

We stare over at the corpses littering the ground with limbs splayed out and the sickening grey flesh stark against the filthy blood flecked mud.

'Come on,' Clarence says bunching his shoulders and stepping out. We fall in behind him stooped and with heads bowed and the cooling mud packs soaking back through with the sweat dripping from our pores.

Into the carnage of the battlefield we stalk. Clarence grabbing two bodies by their ankles and setting off with the cadavers dragging behind him. I reach down, grab a thin wrist and start to tug the body of a middle aged woman over the mud. It feels awful and wrong. Her wrist is so thin in my grip and still warm too. The weight of her, the drag I can feel, the way her head lolls with the bumps and drags and her legs splaying out. The heat builds. The mud clings and I slip down losing my grip on her and the mud underfoot. Nick and Charlie working together heave a big male by the ankles. Cookey and Blowers grasping a wrist each. Mo Mo and Blinky, Charlie and Marcy, Paula and Roy and Dave, the smallest of the group yet he drags a big female behind him with ease but I notice even his face is starting to flush.

Clarence stays at the front of the van picking the corpses we leave and shoving them down into the mud before stomping and kicking them into position. Bones snap, ribs crack and gases escape from mouths and arses that spew shit from voided bowels. The air is rank, full of death, faeces, bad breath, stale odour, blood and the stench of innards.

I get back to the bodies and wait for Dave to come back so we can work a body between us. We don't speak but then neither does anyone else. Not Clarence as he takes the bodies from the couples working or the couples as they walk back to get another one.

Bending over and I reach out to grab an ankle and stop dead. A butterfly tattoo wrapped round a slender ankle with rose vines and flowers leading down onto the foot. The colours are so vivid against the grey skin and I glance up to see matted once blond hair atop a face that would have broken hearts in life as she has tried to do in death. I look round at the corpses nearby and see more signs that speak of the people they once were. A golden bracelet on a wrist that glints in the sun and a plain wedding ring on a finger and as soon as I see that I can't help but look round at the other hands and the wedding rings showing.

I squat down and rest for a second with the fight gone from my body. The woman with the butterfly tattoo has a small round hole in her forehead marking the entry point of a bullet that could only have come from Dave simply for the precision of the placement. No doubt the back of her head is gone but she's on her back and I can't see it, only the once blond hair fanning out and matted with blood, gore and mud. The rest of her body looks remarkably intact, filthy, emaciated but intact, apart from the flesh torn from her inner thigh from the infected mouth that sunk it's teeth in to pass the deadly virus. Another festering wound to become a haven for flies and maggots, but then this wound looks quite clean. The skin has started to heal with a scab forming within the layers of epidermis. The skin near the bite is clean too with no obvious signs of infection.

'Clean wound,' Dave says standing over me.

'I was just thinking that,' I say quietly, 'check that one,' I nod at the closest male and watch as Dave toes the body over and drops down into a squat searching for the bite mark. He lifts the left arm and shows me the wound on the bicep, 'clean,' he says.

'Scabbing?'

'Yes.'

'No maggots,' I say looking down at my woman again.

'Anyone see any maggots anywhere?' I ask out loud.

'Maggots?' Marcy asks, 'why you asking that?'

'Normally see maggots in the wounds,' I say, 'but this one is clean...like, not infected...'

'She wasn't infected?' Marcy snaps striding towards me.

'No,' I wave her to slow down, 'I mean the wound isn't infected...like all red and nasty...look,' I motion down at the girl, 'scabbing and clean.'

'Yeah I see,' she says, 'what's that one like?' She asks Dave.

'Same,' he replies and drops the arm to roll the next body over, 'face,' he says, 'no maggots, clean wound, scabbed.'

'They still stink like dirty fucking wankers,' Nick says darkly tugging at the ankles with Charlie, 'here, let me...'

'I can do it,' she says pointedly.

'Yeah but he's got shit all over his legs...'

'I'm fine,' Charlie says firmly.

'Evolution,' Marcy says resting a filthy hand on my shoulder, 'worrying,' she adds with a muddied frown.

It takes time. Everything takes time and it takes energy too. More than we have and this heat saps it straight from our guts and bones. We could have drips fitted and still struggle with not getting enough fluids. Clarence works the hardest with his strength never ending as he bends, scoops the bodies and flings them down before using his feet and legs to drive them into position until there is a rolling log road of corpses in front of the van stretching from the green to the battlefield where more bodies lie ready to be used as traction.

'Paula,' Clarence waves tiredly at the front of van urging her to get in and drive as the rest of us get to the back.

'Ready?' I ask between teeth gritted in preparation of the pain to come.

'NOW!'

We push. My god we push. Several tons of armoured metal on a solid chassis and with limbs straining we inch the bastard thing across the doors and into the first human form that will give traction except the human form is a few inches higher than the level of the door on which the front wheels rest so an even greater application of force is required. Grinding ourselves into the earth from whence we came and to which we shall return and we pit strength and sinew against something we could just ditch but fuck that, you don't give in, you dig deeper and drive on until the blood drips from your nose and the elements of heat and pain become just another enemy to defeat. Willpower overcomes everything. Sheer stubborn minded fools pitting themselves against and for the same object.

A rhythm starts to form, an organic motion of movement done as the van rolls back from the lip of the body the front wheels are trying to crest. We push harder, shouting and driving it forward into the human remains but gravity overcomes us and the van sinks back. We push it forward, hit the bodies and hold it for the briefest of seconds before it rolls back. We do it again and again. Forward, hold and back, forward hold and back and as that motion becomes more apparent so we let the thing roll back instead of fighting to hold it in place. A sawing manner of back and forth and so the combined strength of inertia and force starts to show and as that happens we feel a hint of victory being within our reach so we dig deeper still and push harder. One action feeds the other until instead of shouting with pain we are roaring with determination and heaving the slick front wheels into the body that caves in with popping squelches noises. We get across the first body onto the second row then the third until the rear wheels hit the door and get onto the sheer wet surface, but a sheer wet surface is better than a gloopy one and we feel less resistance in the push until suddenly, as though no effort was ever required, the rear wheels hit the mashed up body and find traction within the shards of bone, muscles, sinew and matter. The van chugs, bites and Paula, sensing the grip is being given, applies pressure which turns the rear wheels faster which grip harder and away she goes, bouncing and jolting over a carpet of bodies as we stand back giving cheers to the gods of pushing vans that we finally bloody did it.

CHAPTER NINETEEN

M ud monsters we are. Beastly apparitions from a child's nightmare. We emerge from the gloopy field with mud soaked clothing chafing against our bodies and with feet becoming heavier with every step.

'Every half an hour,' I mutter to myself, 'something happens every half an hour...we can't even drive across a field without it turning into a bloody disaster. I mean...what the fuck happened?'

'It was the rain...'

'Rhetorical, Roy,' I groan and try to wipe some of the mud from my face but just end up smearing more of it about.

'We need to clean off,' Clarence says shaking his head at the state of us all.

'Really? You think?' Marcy asks him. 'Seriously though, is it like this every day with you lot?'

'Yep,' Blowers says leaning against the side of the Saxon, 'this is an easy day so far.'

'Easy?' She asks nodding as though refusing to believe it, 'this isn't easy.'

'It's not even lunchtime yet,' Nick says.

'Lunchtime? Do we get lunch today?' Cookey asks with what I

think is a hopeful expression but you can't really tell under the facemask.

'Do we fuck. We never get lunch,' Nick says.

'Right,' I say standing upright to stretch my back with a big groan as Paula jumps down from Roy's van and strides over.

'Everyone get cleaned up,' she says as I blink at her.

'Was just about to say that,' I say.

'I said it,' she says with a shrug, 'Dave, have these two houses been cleared?'

'Yes.'

'Sure?'

'Yes. We took the doors from them.'

'Did we?' She asks staring round, 'completely lost my bearings then. Right, everyone inside and get washed, changed and take some fluids on. Come on,' she claps her hands like a teacher ushering us all towards the doors, 'girls on the right, boys on the left. Come along now. No dilly dallying you rascally rapscallions.'

'What the fuck?' Nick says.

'Reginald,' Paula calls out, 'we're going in to get cleaned up. You're on watch.'

'I beg your pardon,' he blusters appearing at the back door of Roy's van.

'Keep watch,' she says, 'you know,' she waves her arms around at the surrounding area, 'look out...you're on look-out.'

'Me?'

'Yes you,' she says walking behind the girls heading towards the semi-detached house on the right side.

'But...'

'Just bloody keep watch and shout if anything moves.'

I would smile at the exchange but I can no longer move my face due to the mud drying on my face.

'Hose...garden,' Clarence says going straight through the kitchen into the garden, 'where's Meredith?'

'With me,' Nick says chucking the cups and plates from the

washing bowl onto the side with a clatter. He twists the tap letting it run for a few seconds before filling the bowl as Clarence pulls the hose free.

'Crisps?' Cookey asks holding a cupboard door open.

'What they got?' I ask.

'Quavers.'

'Cheese?'

'Yep.'

'Go on then,' I say as he throws a bag over to me.

'Clarence, you want some Quavers?' He calls out.

'Yeah,' he shouts back, 'I'll get washed first. They got anything else?'

'Just Quavers.'

'S'fine, Cookey,' he says dumping his rifle and kit bag on the ground next to his axe and starting to undo his pistol belt.

'Ah she's happy now,' Nick says standing back and watching Meredith drop to the floor with the bowl between her front legs and tongue going like the clappers into the clear water.

'Quavers, Nick,' Cookey asks holding a bag over, 'like I need to ask,' he adds muttering to himself.

'Cheers,' Nick says taking the packet and leaning back against the side.

'Mo?' Cookey asks, 'Quavers?'

'Cheers.'

'Blowers?'

'Yep.'

'Dave?'

'Yes.'

'Roy?'

'Please.'

'Oh that's so bloody nice!'

Seven men armed to the teeth with assault rifles, axes, knives, pistols, a sword and a bow and arrow all eating Quavers with mud covered hands watching a huge bald man standing under a running hose in the garden of a semi-detached house after killing hundreds of zombies that used to be people. It doesn't get weirder than this. Oh and a killer dog drinking water from a bowl. Weird as fuck.

'You using the hose?' Marcy calls out from over the fence.

'Yep, very nice,' Clarence says in ecstasy, 'try it.'

'Can you see through?' She asks.

I lean out to stare at the six foot high fence panels, 'no,' I shout, 'can't see anything.'

'What are you eating?'

'Quavers.'

'Cheese?'

'Yeah.'

'Are they nice?'

'Really nice.'

'Is Dave there?'

'Yeah.'

'Dave?'

'Yes, Marcy.'

'We're going to strip down and wash under the hose.'

'Okay.'

'Will you stop the others from trying to look?'

'Okay. Alex that means you.'

'Too tired, Dave.'

'Any Quavers left?' Blinky shouts.

'Dunno,' I shout back, 'Cookey?'

'Two bags, here,' he goes to hand them over then stops with a grin, 'Blinky you want me to bring them round?'

'Yeah.'

'No,' Marcy, Paula and Charlie shout in chorus.

'Worth a try,' he says stepping out the back door, 'incoming,' he launches them over the fence, 'you checked your cupboards?'

'No,' Blinky shouts, 'I'll do it now.'

I look back to see Clarence now in his underpants scrubbing

the mud from his body with a pile of filthy garments at his feet. 'Having fun, mate?'

'Yep. I'm done. Who's next?'

'I'll go,' Nick says dumping his kit next to Clarence's.

'We haven't got any crisps,' Blinky shouts, 'just some health food shit.'

'Ah well,' I say as Nick starts stripping his clothes off, 'don't get the cigarettes wet.'

'In my pocket, here,' he chucks his trousers over so I can fish the battered packet out.

'Who's using the hose on your side now?' Cookey asks.

'I am,' Charlie shouts back.

Silence from our side.

'Who's doing it your side?' Marcy asks.

'I am,' Nick shouts.

Silence from their side until a low chorus of giggles comes floating over the fence making us all look round at each other shrugging and pulling puzzled faces.

We get through one by one until it's my turn and I strip off before standing under the gorgeously cold water running down my head and shoulders sending shivers down my spine. The heat is taken away with the mud and my body starts cooling down as the ground runs filthy from the mud and gore washed away.

Flitcombe is next then we go for Stenbury but a seed has been planted and this hose appears to be giving water to it. My intentions were clear. Attack and kill as many as possible but now I'm not so sure that's the right thing to be doing.

Reginald said the intelligence within the infection is increasing so fast that within a short space of time we'll be fighting an enemy that can outthink every move we make. So what do we do?

Do we use this time to kill as many as possible or something else? What else? A cure. How? That would mean London and finding the people we need but we've already been to the hospital where Doc Roberts worked. We saw the devastation first hand. There won't be anything left.

The urgency starts humming in my gut again. That pull to get going and keep moving. I drop the hose down and nod for someone else to take a go while I grab my bag and start sorting out new clothes to wear.

Cull the numbers. Yes, that's the best way forward. Kill as many as possible and keep going to give everyone else a chance at survival. Is that my motivation? For the good of mankind or for my own personal desire at getting back at them for what they have done? Both I guess.

The scale we're operating on is too small. Too tiny. We are playing at being soldiers fighting a child-like enemy that pretty soon will become more intelligent than us and with millions of soldiers to use. Fuck me, we could have planes and tanks and it wouldn't be enough. We could detonate a nuclear bomb in London but that wouldn't stop the other forty million spread about the rest of the country.

We should do something else. We should take what we have, with us being immune and work out what to do with it. Yes, that's the way forward instead. We leg it and stay low trying to find experts and scientists who know about this sort of thing. Yep. That's a plan. We leave and sneak into London.

Argh no. No no no. That's not right either. It's common sense and it's a logical plan but something in my gut is telling me to keep attacking them and take the fight to it. To the infection. Spank it up and down the country while we still can. Cull and kill. Slaughter them in every way possible and don't stop until the last one drops dead. Find guns. Big guns. Bigger guns. Find an army. Build an army. Keep going and do not stop.

Right. Common sense and logic is saying we bug out and find experts. My heart is telling me to fuck 'em up with sheer over-whelming violence. Which one? A battle of mind over heart. Clinical thought processes over passion. Passion is what makes us human. Passion is what drives us. Passion and heart and feeling love and hate. Those are the things that have either propelled mankind or held us back.

Logic and find experts to use what we have. Heart and fucking kick the shit out of them. Logic. Heart.

My left hand is logic. My right hand is my heart. What the hell am I doing? They both look the same. So, in this hand I have intelligence and a logical decision making process that is telling me to deal with the overall picture of an infection that is attacking the human species and thereby rendering the same species obsolete. We will be eradicated and made extinct. Got it. That's the left hand.

The right hand is violence. We fight and kill. We show the infection what it is to be human by having that drive and will to live. We make a stand and by doing that we send a message to every other survivor to stop hiding and get out and fight while they still can.

Left hand logic.

Right hand passion.

Cock it.

I don't know. I clench my hands into fists then splay the fingers. Which one?

'Left or right?' I mutter, 'Dave, left or right?'

'Left or right what, Mr Howie?'

'Left hand logic. Right hand passion. Which one? Choose.'

He stares at me suddenly clean and dressed in new clothes. They all are. 'When did you get in here?' I ask Marcy and the girls standing at the back of the house watching me.

'Few minutes,' she says.

'Oh. So...' I ask the group as a whole, 'left hand logic...right hand passion...which one?' I hold my hands up opening and closing them into fists.

Mo looks down at his own hands copying me by bunching them into hard fists, 'right,' he says firmly.

'Mo,' I nod at him sensing his need for vengeance.

'Logic over passion,' Paula says, 'left.'

'Paula,' I nod at her respecting her way of thinking.

Marcy stares at me with a slight tilt to her head as though she's trying to work something out. A wry smile crosses her features and she walks slowly towards me watching me closely.

'Left or right?' I ask her.

'Me?' She says as though the answer is obvious, 'right. I'll always choose passion.'

'Hmmm, this is isn't actually helping.'

'No?'

'No.'

'Funny thing is,' she says coming to a stop in front of me and reaching out to take my hands, 'is that hands can do this,' she pushers her fingers through mine interlocking and drawing my hands together, 'see? My right goes to your left and your left is with my right...but...they also do this,' she pulls her fingers from between mine and presses my hands together in prayer and gently pushes my fingers so my hands interlock themselves, 'passion *and* logic can become passion *with* logic.'

'Cor blimey,' I say staring at my own hands, 'that's clever. Right fuck it. Move out, we're gonna go spank some zombies.'

'Or just completely ignore what I just said.'

CHAPTER TWENTY

'Reginald, how far to Flitcombe? What do we know about it? How many can we expect and what's the best point to attack them from?'

'Mr Howie,' he says looking up from the monitor with a start.

'And where will they be expecting us to attack from?'

'Oh gosh...'

'Charlie.'

'Right here, Mr Howie.'

'Flitcombe. How far? What do we know and...'

'I heard the questions,' she says politely climbing up into the back of Roy's van and heading to the maps folded on the desk, 'let me see.'

'So we're ignoring the whole logic discussion then?' Marcy asks walking across the road towards the back of Roy's mud smeared van.

'Nope, not at all,' I say with a grin, 'so, how far to Flitcombe?'

'About ten miles?' Charlie asks Reginald who looks from her to me and down to the map.

'I er, gosh I would say yes, about ten miles.'

'Ten miles. Got it. How big is it?'

'Got a plan?' Clarence asks moving in beside me.

'Yep.'

'A plan is always better than no plan,' he says.

'I said that,' Dave says.

'Oh did you?' Clarence says winking at Mo, 'don't think I heard you, Dave.'

'I said that.'

'How big is it?' I ask again.

'About the same size as Foxwood,' Charlie says.

'Foxwood? The one with the duck pond right?'

'Yes, that's correct,' she says.

'Howie,' Paula says in a warning tone, 'I know that voice. What are you planning?'

'And Stenbury? How far to Stenbury?'

'Gosh I would say about thirty miles,' Reginald says tracing his finger over the map on his desk.

'And Stenbury's big right?'

'Stenbury is the main town for this rural area. It is substantially larger than the small villages we have seen thus far and therefore it will have a greater population and not forgetting of course,' he says blinking at me, 'that the infection will be drawing more in while we go through the aforesaid villages.'

'How many can we expect?'

'At Stenbury or Flitcombe?'

'Both.'

'I would hazard that Flitcombe will see numbers the same as this god forsaken place, perhaps a few more given the closeness to the greater population zone.'

'Few hundred then?'

'Mr Howie I am not confident in making accurate predictions of this nature.'

'Answer the question to the best of your ability. Can we expect a few hundred? More? Less?'

'How many were here?' He asks.

'Couple of hundred?' I say looking at everyone gathered near me, 'about right?'

'Maybe a bit more,' Clarence says using his height advantage to peer over at the corpses lying on the green.

'Dave?'

'More than three less than four.'

'Between three and four hundred then?'

'Yes.'

'Reginald?'

'Gosh, right...well that is a considerable number. Indeed it is. For a small place and the other player knowing you will win which in turn tells us the other player is willing to sacrifice those pieces. Hmmm, I would say we can expect perhaps a slightly larger number at Flitcombe...'

'Okay, so maybe four to five hundred?'

'Mr Howie I cannot specify to the degree you require. There are too many variables. For instance, look at this map,' he holds it up towards me, 'every grey section represents an area where human beings occupy and you can see just how many there are. We do not know how many still held infected persons...'

'Charlie,' Clarence says leaning into the van, 'check the guide books and see if they give a population of Stenbury.'

'So let's say we had three hundred and fifty here,' I say, 'and we're looking at four hundred and fifty at Flitcombe...how many is that?'

'Eight hundred,' Paula says.

'Eight hundred sacrificed, plus the few we've already done before we got here. So call it a thousand? Everyone happy with that?'

'I'd say a few more,' Clarence says, 'more like twelve hundred.'

'Okay, call it twelve hundred. That's one thousand two hundred host bodies the infection is prepared to sacrifice to get us into Stenbury. How can we use that figure to represent the numbers they have *in* Stenbury?'

'Christ, Howie,' Paula says rubbing her face and thinking, 'say it used ten percent of its total force? Clarence, Dave? Would an army do that?'

'This isn't an army,' Clarence says flatly.

'Okay well let's say it used ten percent of its total mass which would be twelve thousand...so bloody hell! That's over ten thousand...'

'So we could be looking at ten thousand in Stenbury?'

'Fucking ten thousand,' Paula says again, 'ten thousand people to kill...'

'What's ten thousand divided by thirteen?'

'Er...about seven hundred and er...oh Christ...seven hundred and sixty nine or...yeah about that.'

'Okay, we've each got seven hundred and sixty nine to kill. Dave, you happy with that?'

'Yes, Mr Howie.'

'Whoa hang on,' Paula says, 'I'm guessing at the ten percent thing. What if it's used five percent? That could be over twenty thousand people.'

'So fourteen hundred each then?' Blowers says, 'is that right?'

'We've got to get those numbers down,' Paula says.

'Population of Stenbury,' Charlie says holding a tour guide open, 'as of two years ago at the time of this publication...was twenty three thousand.'

'Fuck!' Paula says.

'Too many,' Marcy says shaking her head, 'that's too many.'

'Plus the others it's pulling in from the other towns and villages,' Reginald says.

'No hang on,' Clarence says folding his arms and looking massive, 'there wouldn't have been twenty three thousand er...of the er....the infected people in that...'

'Zombies,' I interrupt him, 'just say zombies.'

'I'm not saying that word,' he says stiffly.

'Why not? Say it. Zombies.'

'They're not...they are not those. Those are made up in films. These are real. Anyway, there wouldn't have been twenty three thousand people there. How many people would have lived here? Maybe a few thousand? We didn't have a few thousand waiting for us.'

'No they've all buggered off to Stenbury that's why,' Roy says.

'No no, you're missing the point,' Clarence says, 'the point is that many would have been killed. Some more would have run off or are hiding.'

'Yes. Hiding in Stenbury,' Roy says.

'No, Roy...'

'Either way,' I say watching Clarence getting flushed in the face and pre-empting an argument, 'that's a lot.'

'Fifty million,' Dave says in his flat tone.

'Where are they then?' Clarence says staring round.

'In Stenbury,' Roy says.

'Okay. Moving on from that but we can all agree Flitcombe is going to have a few hundred and Stenbury is likely....I said likely... to have several thousand or possibly in excess of ten thousand... sound fair?'

'Who you asking?' Paula asks, 'if you're asking me then I'd say no that's not fair. They've got more than ten thousand and we've got fourteen.'

'Don't count me,' Reginald says.

'Thirteen,' Paula says, 'against ten thousand...'

'Fuck 'em, we'll win,' Cookey says with a grin that sets most of the rest of us off smiling.

'Too many,' Marcy says more firmly, 'you've got pick your fights and this one is too big...even for you.'

'We can't even sneak in and lay traps,' Paula says, 'the whole place will be crawling with infected.'

'Can't we?' I ask her, 'you've done it before haven't you?'

'Yeah a few times but not against ten thousand and not against ten thousand that were expecting me...not like that...'

'Can we lure them out to somewhere else?' Charlie asks.

'Would they follow us?' I ask.

'If we made it look like we were running away they would,' Clarence says, 'like yesterday. We ran and they gave chase.'

'Reginald,' I say turning back to face him, 'distance from Flit-combe to Stenbury?'

'Approximately fifteen miles.'

'We could prep Flitcombe?' I suggest, 'get in, kill everything, get it ready...go for Stenbury, run back to Flitcombe and...er...kill everything...again.'

'Classic double bluff right there,' Clarence says rocking on his heels.

'Bluff,' Dave says.

'Soooo,' Marcy says quickly, 'let's not get into the bluff conversation again. How do you propose we do it?' She asks me.

'Me? Fuck knows. That's Paula and Dave's bag...' I pause at Clarence clearing his throat, 'and Clarence's bag. I was going to say Clarence.'

'Course you were,' he mutters.

'Reginald, you and Charlie get thinking...think dirty and cunning...think like right nasty bastards of ways we can use Flit-combe to our advantage. Study those maps and the area once we get there.' I turn round to face everyone else, 'we're going to taunt it...like goad the shit out of it...we need to make it think we're as cocky as hell and so consumed with self-belief that when it sees us running it thinks we're real. Everyone happy?'

'We should stay fluid,' Paula says in that tone of easing back the inane eagerness, 'in case Flitcombe is no good.'

'Don't forget we're leapfrogging,' I say, 'so there will be other places we can use...'

'No I'm with you,' she says nodding, 'but let's think things through properly from now on.'

'Agreed. Load up and we'll move out. Reginald and Charlie, find us a place we can use about a mile from Flitcombe for the drone.'

CHAPTER TWENTY-ONE

'Find us a place he says, find us a place. How many, how big, how far...find us a place. Oh my good lord I really need some tea. You know, Charlotte, I haven't had a nice cup of tea for days. Days. Weeks. Probably more. No wonder I'm a bag of nerves. Find us a place he said...'

'This farm?' Charlotte asks holding her finger over the map then reaching over to point at Reginald's map.

Reginald rolls his eyes again at the injustice of it all and looks down at the farm and quickly calculates the topography, the gradient and the distance to Flitcombe.

'Yes a good location but the distance is further than a mile which I believe is at the maximum range of the drone. Yes... perhaps here,' he says tapping a finger on the map, 'open ground by the looks of it with a good thicket of trees to provide visual cover but the range is under one mile.'

'Yep, got it,' she says in admiration at the way he went from nervous wreck to switching on and reading the map like it was a book.

'Ah now the village of Flitcombe,' he says pushing his glasses back up his nose, 'yes yes, the village of Flitcombe. What can we see? What can we see indeed? What does the map tell us? Really,' he says tutting again, 'the pressure is unbearable and would it really hurt them to find some Darjeeling or Camomile? Would it? Hmmm? Out there gallivanting about throwing axes at one another and they can't look in some wretched kitchen cupboards for some tea...'

'Have you asked them to find you some tea?'

'Of course I have not asked them. A gentleman does not ask. A gentleman suffers in silence and does not ask.'

'I'll find you some next time we stop.'

'Ah that is most kind of you but alas I would also require a manner in which to heat water and a receptacle within which to make the tea.'

'Fire and a cup?'

'Well yes, to be so blunt and straight talking. Fire and a cup.'

'Some of the houses still have gas supplies and I dare say if you asked Mr Howie he would make a fire for you.'

'My burden upon this team is already such that I feel most ungracious. I could not ask for such a thing.'

'I can,' she says politely, 'Paula?'

'Gosh no,' Reginald blusters in panic at the social faux pas about to take place.

'Yep?' Paula asks leaning in through the doorway.

'We found a place for the drone to be used.'

'Great stuff, how far?'

'Er, stay on this main road and we'll say when we get close.'

'I'll tell Howie.'

'Er, Paula?'

'Yes, love?'

'Do you think Mr Howie would mind if we looked for some Darjeeling or Camomile tea when next we stop?'

'You have a lovely way of speaking you know,' Paula says smiling warmly at the younger woman, 'sure thing, we'll check the kitchens. For you is it?'

'Er...yes, although I should imagine Reginald would also like some tea.'

Paula smiles having taken in the terrified look of shame coming from Reggie and ignoring it by looking only at Charlie, 'sure,' she says, 'we'll find some.'

'Paula to Howie?'

'Hey Paula. It's Marcy, go ahead.'

'Hey, tell Howie Reginald and Charlie have found somewhere to stop before we get to Flitcombe. For a toilet break...you know...Roy is droning on about it.'

'Haha, yeah got it.'

'Also, and I'm sure the lads are listening to this but Charlie just said she loves herbal tea. Darjeeling and Camomile.'

'On it,' Cookey's voice booms over the radio, *'herbal tea will be found.'*

Paula grins into the back, 'I think they'll get you some.'

'Thank you,' Charlie says.

'Tell them not me, you've got a radio.'

'Oh yes, of course...er...Hi, it's Charlie, er thank you for saying you'll find some tea.'

'Did you hear what I said?' Paula asks Roy, 'I said you were droning on.'

'Yeah I heard.'

'Droning? Get it? Somewhere to launch the drone.'

'Er, yes, yes I understood that.'

'It was clever wasn't it?'

'Er yes, very clever.'

'Don't patronise me.'

'I wasn't!'

'So were. Do you like herbal tea?'

'Earl Grey.'

'Oh I love Early Grey. *Marcy it's Paula, do you like herbal tea?'*

'I like the fruit teas, you know like the hot lemon and ginger ones you can get. What about you?'

'Earl Grey. What about Howie?'

'Er he's shaking his head and pulling a face like he wants to vomit. Clarence says he likes Earl Grey.'

'Really? I'd never of thought of him as an Earl Grey man.'

Smiling at the conversation Charlie looks at Reginald and slowly the smile fades at the pensive look of irritation on his face. 'Reginald?'

'I do not need mothering,' he says tightly, 'you do not need to ask for me.'

'I'm sorry,' she says quickly, 'I thought you wanted some...'

'Yes I would dearly enjoy some tea but what I do not enjoy is the fact of someone thinking I am incapable of asking for myself.'

'I apologise.'

'Indeed. Perhaps we should be focussed on the task at hand.'

'Of course,' she says bending over to focus on the map and inwardly chastising herself for the awkwardness created, 'I am sorry, Reginald.'

'Let it be,' he says stiffly, 'but thank you all the same,' he adds in a slightly softer tone, 'now...Flitcombe...'

The irritation at the momentary embarrassment eases the nerves and he looks down at the map forgetting the gravity of the situation. People are just insufferable. They really are. And Mr Howie can ask all the questions he wishes but must realise he may not get the answers he requires. However, it is answers he wants so answers he shall get. Yes. If he wants ideas then ideas shall be presented.

'Main road,' he says tracing a finger along the map. 'We have a straight section of road going into the village with what appears to be a square or central meeting point to the right side of the road bordered by buildings which one can assume are shops and stores. Yes, that must be right. Buildings on the left which could also be stores but a village of this size will only have a few stores unless the rest are boutique stores, cafes perhaps, hair salons...yes I should imagine they are. What do you think?'

'I agree,' she says studying the same thing on her map, 'there is a road circumventing that central location on the right side although it appears the road is narrower than the main road it runs from.'

'Have you seen the road after the immediate heart of the village?'

'No why? Oh. Oh I see.'

'Indeed. Most interesting,' he says.

'Is that an S bend?' She asks examining the curving road direction.

'More than an S bend,' he says, 'from the village the road bears a tight left bend with a collection of buildings on the right. Then it veers into a tight bend on the right with another collection of buildings on the invert of the S on the left...then the road goes left again and in the invert we have yet another collection of structures before the road straightens out. Indeed,' he says nodding eagerly, 'yes indeed the town of Flitcombe is more than it appears to be.'

'How so?' Charlie asks glancing over at him.

'We have a standard ubiquitous village but immediately after we have three distinct sectioned off areas each within the invert of the bend. If you were to walk in a straight line from the village you would cross through the middle of each. We need to know what each section holds...I can hazard a guess but...'

'Industrial estates?'

'One of them yes but given the closeness to Stenbury I am hazarding that the price of land to rent and develop in Flitcombe is far less than that of Stenbury. I would calculate therefore that one of those sections will be an industrial unit, one will be a modern business park and the other...well, it could be commercial, light industrial, manufacture or any such thing of a similar nature. Paula,' he calls with a glance at the monitor and the live camera feeds shown, 'we are nearing the area to be used for drone surveillance, 'on the right there should be a gate or entry way leading into open land adjacent to a thicket or copse of trees.' He stops talking and listens as she transmits the same on the radio before continuing.

'To the immediate area and the immediacy of the confrontation awaiting,' he says nodding to himself again, 'and remembering we want to lure Mr Howie into Stenbury...I would place my pieces within this central meeting location with more held in reserve within and behind the buildings bordering the same. Would you agree?'

'I would,' she says in awe of his ability to take in such detail so quickly.

'Yes,' he says sighing deeply, 'here will be the fight and the sacrifice,' he taps the area of the central meeting point bordered by the building line, 'but post battle we must ensure these three sections are cleared,' he sweeps his fingers over the three defined places within the bends of the road, 'and then Flitcomebe will be ours, or rather Mr Howie's.'

'Okay,' she says staring at him with wide eyes.

'But remember,' he says finally glancing up at her, 'the other player wants us to win here but if it spots an opportunity to take us it will do so. Mr Howie was right, he must show confidence to the point of the extreme but without complacency.'

'We're here,' Roy calls out as the van bumps softly from the road onto a rough track following the Saxon into a field of scrub.

'Confidence. That is the key,' Reginald drifts off with eyes glazed as he plans, counter plans, thinks and counter thinks of the way ahead. The infection is still gullible to a degree. That is clear and that gullibility is a weakness in the armour to be used to their advantage.

Around him the vans come to a stop. Doors open. Light comes in. Voices talking and joking. Cigarettes being lit with the foul odour permeating his now personal area. His mind stays within the game thinking of the words spoken by Mr Howie. Lure them back here. Yes that can be done but the infection will only chase what it believes it can take. It must believe Mr Howie's self-belief that he is undefeatable. The other player must see that Mr Howie will be his own undoing, that is the way. That is the key.

'Reginald?' The man himself at the back doors leaning in staring straight at him with a deep gnawing hunger evident in those dark eyes. Reginald looks up, locking eyes for a second that drags as he sees this man will do what it takes to win. 'Where will they be?' He asks with a tone indicating that Reginald will know the answer.

Reginald swallows feeling a strange pulse of energy in his gut, 'the main road runs straight through the village. On the right is a central meeting area bordered by buildings.'

'There? In that central bit?'

'Yes,' Reginald says with a firmness to his voice that surprises even himself, 'there. They will be within the buildings and perhaps behind too depending on how many they can get into that open central area.'

'Understood,' Howie nods.

On his feet and Reginald crosses to the back door watching Howie move back towards the others setting the drone up,' Mr Howie.'

'What?' Howie says turning back as Reginald clambers down and into the strong light of day and the wall of humidity.

'You were right,' Reginald says as the others all stop talking to listen, 'what you said about confidence. You were right. You must show confidence.'

'We will.'

'No you don't understand,' Reginald says taking a step forward, 'confidence is the key. I think perhaps you said it without realising the impact of your words but indeed I have thought it through and yes, confidence is the key. Confidence to the point of extreme. The other side *must* believe that you have absolute self-belief in your ability to win. You must not only act but project that confidence.'

Howie listens intently as Reginald stands straight and looks nervous but holds that eye contact which is something he doesn't normally do.

'You see, Mr Howie, after the village there is a series of bends in the road and within each invert of the bend is a defined area I would suggest is being used for business and industrial units...'

'I don't understand,' Howie says shaking his head.

'Which part?'

'All of what you just said.'

'Map. I will get the map, please stay here.'

'I'll get it,' Charlie says jogging past and jumping easily into the back of the van. She comes out unfolding the map as she walks towards Howie.

'See here,' Reginald says pointing to the series of bends, 'the invert is the inside of the bend, you see?'

'Ah got it now.'

'Within these sections are most likely industrial units. To walk a straight line from the village towards Stenbury will take you through these three sections which in turn means anyone on the road will not gain a clear view of ahead.'

'Got it.'

'Industrial units are good,' Paula says walking closer to the map, 'they're full of things we can use.'

'Yes,' Reginald nods eagerly, 'yes yes, this is what I meant. This ground may be ideal for the placing of battle.'

'The placing of battle?' Howie asks smiling gently as Reginald starts to withdraw into himself again. 'No mate that's brilliant. Spot on. Good work.'

'But the confidence is the key,' Reginald says again, 'the other side is still naïve with a certain gullibility and that is a weakness you can use to your advantage. If you can bring the pieces from Stenbury back through these three sections you may have a chance to reduce the numbers to an amount you can cope with. Do you see?'

'I see,' Howie says nodding.

'But to do that, oh gosh...to do that Mr Howie you must show the infection you believe you can win by yourself...I mean with your few numbers...it must see you as strong so when you show the weakness of retreat it believes that weakness is real.'

'Will do,' Howie says simply.

The confidence wanes with the sudden realisation of everyone staring at him and into himself he withdraws. Taking the map from Charlie he offers apologies stammering and nervous before retreating back to the safety of his van and into the blessed relief of the shade.

What was that? He knows what it was. Reginald knows exactly what it was but to experience it first hand is still unsettling. The energy of Mr Howie that swept him up and along on a tide of false hope and confidence that they can win. Of course they cannot win. What was he thinking? What are any of them thinking? Oh dear. This isn't good, not good at all. But still, now he perhaps understands why they follow this man and can see why Marcy follows him so closely.

CHAPTER TWENTY-TWO

D *ay Eighteen*

UPDATE No 5

I HAVE STOPPED to record my observations although I do not wish to. I do not want to. I wish I could take away what I have seen and given the chance I would return to my sanctuary, close the gate and never again leave.

FOLLOWING the route behind the soldiers, Jess and I happened first upon Hydehill and another scene of carnage. The centre of the battle was evident from the shell casings and with some greater understanding I scoured about and could determine where the lines of soldiers were formed across one junction and also facing the buildings on both sides.

. . .

MY TREPIDATION COMMENCED IN HYDEHILL. The sheer brutality of the slaughter. That every single infected was killed outright and left to rot. I hold no allegiance to the infected hosts but I could not view upon human forms so damaged and not be moved by it.

THE MOST DISTURBING sight within Hydehill was a single body lying near to the smashed in entrance to Maplin electronic store. The body was an unrecognisable lump of meat. The head had been removed by their attack dogs that had then apparently feasted on the corpse. The legs were broken, the arms too. It was sickening, cruel and barbaric.

THEN WE FOUND BROOKLEY. A small village dominated by a large green that is now forever tainted with the death given here.

THIS PLACE IS something from a nightmare and so horrific that it almost looks false. Like a giant movie set designed to invoke a reaction no matter which direction you turn to look.

I have gone from abject admiration at the professionalism of these people driving through the countryside ridding the land of the infected to harbouring a sensation of wariness and fear towards them. The killing, the sheer amount of killing is beyond anything that a human should ever do. This is not cleansing or taking back the land from the infected hosts but bordering on genocidal actions of people driven by an undeniable thirst for violence.

THE GREEN HAS tracks of vehicles carving paths through the thick mud. Those vehicles must have become stuck and it appears the ingenuity of the soldiers has prompted them to use wooden doors from the houses in an effort to build a road of sorts.

It is obvious the doors have failed and so they have used bodies. Hundreds of dead bodies that lie slaughtered in the heat and already the stench is abominable.

The mud is no longer true brown but red from the blood spilled. Gunshots within those corpses but many of them were hacked apart by bladed weapons and again the attack dogs were sent in. That I observed the surgical precision wounds only served to increase my fear.

THE ROAD of bodies was the very worst thing. I cannot describe it. Mangled, broken, filthy and saddened beings used as filler to enable vehicles to get from the mud and then left to lie forever where they fell.

THE ROAD WAS MARKED with the position the vehicles broke free from the green due to the excess mud. Next to that position was a house which I entered and at the rear I found the soldiers had used a garden hose to cleanse themselves. I find this troubling. That they could kill so many and then stop to wash so close to the scene of their slaughter.

I KNOW they are doing the right thing. Every single infected person that now lies dead gives a greater hope for our species to survive and I must steel myself against these horrors as I use the judgment and knowledge of my formerly peaceful life. This is not that life and nor will it ever be.

But still. It concerns me.

. . .

I WILL CONTINUE but cautiously and with fear cementing in my stomach. Jess however is fine and still seems to be enjoying our grand adventure.

IT IS NOW VERY HOT.

NB

CHAPTER TWENTY-THREE

I watch the screen as the drone lifts off and a second later we see ourselves from above as the aircraft gives near silent flight into the air and starts the journey to Flitcombe.

Marcy close to my side watching over my shoulder with everyone else gathered in tight as Charlie operates drone and Reginald works the camera.

The drone sails over the trees showing us a bird's eye view of fields and scrub land before we glimpse the boundary of the village in the distance.

'Go higher,' Nick says standing behind Charlie, 'bit more... yeah perfect.'

'Main road,' Reginald says pointing a finger to the screen and the distinct line of the black tarmac running towards the village, 'we'll focus on the immediate village first I think and yes, this area is the central meeting place I was referring to...'

'Fuck me,' Cookey mutters, 'well done, Reggie,' he adds at the sight of the undead gathered in that same section just to the right of the main road.

That whole section is thick with them. Hundreds all waiting in the heat and spilling out over the road.

'Reginald,' I say leaning closer, 'how long is that straight section when you first go into the village? I mean how far away will they see us when we go in?'

'Ah yes, I see...I would say no more than three hundred metres.'

'Okay.'

'Backs of the buildings are clear,' Roy says.

'They'll have more inside the buildings,' Clarence says.

'Still a few hundred by the looks of it,' Paula says quietly, 'Dave?'

'Over three hundred on view,' he says dully and I notice his right hand dropping to the hilt of a knife in his belt and he looks over at me as my own heart rate starts to increase. I drum my fingers on my leg feeling the tension in the back of my neck so I twist my head to the side grimacing as something clicks.

'The man said we've got to show confidence,' Clarence says stretching his back out.

'Aye, he did,' I say as that tension grows.

'Plan?' Blowers asks.

I shrug, 'straight in?'

He nods, 'works for me.'

'Hand weapons?' Nick asks.

'Yeah why not.'

'There's three hundred in sight and more in the buildings,' Paula says quickly, 'we can't fight that many with hand weapons.'

'...'

'I said we can't fight that many with hand weapons. Are you listening to me?'

'The man said we've got to show confidence,' Clarence says again.

'We've got guns,' she shouts, 'guns that fire bullets...'

'We'll need those for Stenbury,' Blowers says.

'Are you being serious?' She turns to face us all, 'don't be so fucking stupid.'

I look to Blowers seeing his hard eyes and Nick standing tall and Mo staring with hatred at the screen. The left hand is logic. The right hand is violence.

'Howie, I cannot fight hand weapons against so many,' Paula says.

'You're not going to,' I say with a voice that comes out low and hoarse, 'Marcy, Charlie, Blinky, Paula and Roy stay with Reginald. We'll call when we need you to start firing...'

An eruption follows but one I was expecting and I hold my hand up as something in my eyes brings them to silence.

'I'm coming,' Blinky says urgently, 'like fuck I'm staying...I'm coming.'

'Me too,' Roy says staring levelly at me.

'Roy,' Paula says but cuts off when he simply ignores her.

'Blinky, we've done this before many times,' I say but she cuts me off shaking her head.

'I was born for this,' she says urgently, 'I was fucking...'

'Blinky we know how to move with each other...' Clarence says.

'I'll learn,' she shouts, 'I'm coming. I'm fucking coming. I can fight...'

'Blinky...' I say.

'No,' she shouts again looking furious, 'I kept getting sent off for being violent...I'm violent...I'm fucking violent...'

'You don't have a hand weapon,' Clarence says.

'She will use Mohammed's Axe,' Dave says staring at her.

'What will Mo use?' I ask.

'Knife. With me,' Dave says not even looking at Mo who clenches his jaw but shows no other reaction.

I nod at Blinky, 'with us then, Mo, give her your axe.'

'Yes,' Blinky hisses showing the rage in her face.

'Roy?' I ask.

'Sword.'

'Sure?'

'I've earned my right to defend my team.'

The right hand is violence.

'Fair enough.'

'You'd be better on overwatch, Roy,' Clarence says.

'Overwatch?' I ask.

'Sniper, with his bow,' Clarence says, 'like he did in Brookley.'

'Roy?' I ask.

'I'll do overwatch,' he says with a nod.

'Nick,' Clarence says, 'fancy using my axe?'

'Fuck yes,' Nick blurts, 'what you using?'

'Got something else in mind,' he says darkly, 'my axe is heavy mind.'

'Fucking best day ever,' Nick says.

'What?' Clarence says when I look at him, 'you'll see.'

'Any point in trying to talk you out of this?' Marcy asks, 'no I didn't think so. Okay, we'll be waiting...'

'I can fight,' Charlie says firmly.

'You're staying with us,' Marcy says equally as firmly, 'they know how to move with each other...'

'Blinky is going and I can learn just as well...'

'You've not seen it,' Marcy says looking from face to face, 'you'll see what I mean when you see it.'

'I saw it yesterday.'

'Yesterday wasn't the same,' she says, 'yesterday was...'

'Small,' Paula says, 'this isn't small. And this isn't sexism either...Lani was right there with them before she died...she was one of the finest up there with Dave.'

'Load up, my team with me in the Saxon, Marcy you drive Roy's van. Everyone get their rifles into Roy's van with bags and ammunition. That's our fall back point.'

CHAPTER TWENTY-FOUR

The battle for Flitcombe

The right hand is violence with which we shall show confidence to the point of extreme.

'Everyone ready?' I ask slowing down before the last corner while my hands grip the wheel so tight my knuckles turn white. There they are. Spilling out across the road in all their perfect undead glory.

'*Marcy, reverse in so the back doors face them.*'

'*Got it.*'

'*We'll see you in a bit.*'

'Blinky, stay with Nick. The dog always stays close to Nick so she'll give you some protection. Dave, you taking Mo?'

'Yes. Mohammed stay within sight of me at all times.'

'Yes, Dave.'

'Do not try and copy what I do but do as I told you and focus on the cuts I taught you.'

'Yes, Dave.'

'I will protect your flanks and rear, focus only on what is in front of you.'

'Yes, Dave.'

'We stay close to Mr Howie at all times. We protect him. Do you understand?'

'Yes, Dave.'

'I'll be fine,' I call back, 'you worry about yourselves.'

'Do what Dave tells you,' Clarence says, 'and everyone stay away from me.'

'Why?' I ask.

'You'll see.'

'Roy, I'm guessing you need height. Top of the Saxon the right place for you?'

'Yes and please it is important that everyone listens to this. Do not try and compensate or do anything you think aids my firing. I will work round you as you move naturally.'

'Understood.'

'I really cannot emphasis that enough.'

'Yep, got it, Roy.'

'And we need to be closer than three hundred metres.'

'Okay, how close?'

'One hundred and fifty metres will be good.'

'Tell you what, I'll drive in and you tell me when you want me to stop.'

'I'll do that.'

'Roy,' Clarence says, 'be ready to use that GPMG if we start running back.'

'I'll do that.'

'Fucking hang on,' Blowers says quickly, 'Roy is going to be firing at us running back towards him? Fuck that...'

'Run to the sides then,' Roy says.

'The sides? How the fuck do we get to the sides?' Blowers asks.

'Ah we'll be alright,' I say nonchalant, 'Roy, don't shoot anyone.'

'I'll try.'

'Try!' Blowers sputters, 'do more than fucking try, Roy.'

'Nick,' I shout back cutting Blowers off, 'I know you're immune but don't get cocky with it...they can still rip you apart.'

'I won't.'

'Yeah, Nick. Don't get cocky.'

'Fuck you, Cookey.'

'Are we there yet? I'm gonna spew in a minute.'

'This is fine, Mr Howie,' Roy says with a hint of horror at being trapped in a metal box with Blinky about to puke.

We come to a stop facing the horde now all turned and staring down the road towards us. Roy's van pulls up alongside with Marcy at the wheel waving at me. I grin back then laugh as the reversing warning beep starts sounding in the street as she pulls back to start the turn.

'What's that?' Cookey asks from behind me.

'Roy's van. Right, everyone out and get ready.'

I open the door and drop down into the incessant heat. A bottle of water opened and I force the whole of it down as the others do the same.

Axe in hand and I walk round to the front while the others jump down and stretch with curses at the foul humidity.

'Meredith had water, Nick?'

'Loads.'

'Everyone alright?' I ask as they file towards me with Nick resting Clarence's double headed axe over his right shoulder.

'Perfect,' Roy says getting to his feet on the roof of the Saxon. He nods with one hand on his hip staring at the horde and moving a step left then a step right as he gauges the distance and angles. 'Can't see the far corner of that square area...see the monument?'

I look round seeing the stone cross six feet above the heads of the infected, 'yeah I see it.'

'Don't go more than seven or eight metres to the right of that. The building line cuts my view.'

'Blinky, did you hear that?'

'Yep,' she says tightly.

'You ready then, mate?' I ask staring up at Roy arranging his arrows at his feet.

'I'm ready...and remember,' he says again as Blowers tuts and rolls his eyes, 'do not compensate for...'

'Fuck's sake, Roy. We heard you,' Blowers says.

'I'm just saying.'

'Yeah like a hundred times.'

'Three actually.'

'More than fucking three...'

'Alright,' I call out, 'Clarence, where are you?'

'Coming,' he says hidden from view at the back of the Saxon.

'What was that noise?' Nick asks following a chink of metal clear and audible. Another rattle and something being pulled with a long drawing sound.

'You waiting for me?' Clarence asks.

'Yes, mate.'

'Be right with you, just choosing the best ones.'

'Best ones what?'

'Ah yeah, these two...perfect...'

Heavy metal hitting concrete then the sound of dragging as Clarence comes into view dragging two long heavy link chains behind him.

'Seriously?' I ask looking at the chains looped over his huge hands.

'Yep,' he says, 'saw it on a movie.'

'What fucking movie was that?'

'Can't remember,' he says with a shrug, 'we going then or what?'

'Fuck,' I mutter looking past him to the chains stretched out on the ground, 'they're really long, Clarence.'

'I said everyone to stay away from me,' he says stiffly.

'Yeah like where?' I ask.

'Ah fuck,' Blinky shouts before bending forward to vomit on the ground with chunks of digested food splattering the road.

'Oh we look fucking awesome,' Cookey groans, 'Roy's van sounds like a rubbish lorry, Blinky spewing up and Clarence looking like a serial killer...'

'I don't look like a serial killer.'

'You do,' I say, 'you just need some denim dungarees.'

'And a straw hat,' Blowers adds.

'Look are we chatting or fighting?' He asks with a huff.

'Finished?' Nick asks as Blinky stands up.

'Yep,' she announces, 'let's fuck these cunts up.'

'Okay then,' I say slowly, 'ready, Dave?'

'Yes, Mr Howie.'

We start walking. One foot after the other while keeping our eyes fixed on the horde ahead and two big chains scraping noisily behind us.

'Are those chains?' Marcy asks over the radio.

'Yeah,' I reply thumbing the switch under my shirt.

'Does he know he looks like a serial killer?'

'I do not look like a serial killer,' he says bluntly.

'He said yes and he wants some denim dungarees...and a straw hat.'

'You'll be laughing in a minute when I'm lopping heads off with these bad boys...oh shit...'

'Did you just call them bad boys?' I ask as we all start laughing, 'you did...you called them bad boys.'

'Fuck off,' he groans.

'He just called his chains bad boys.'

'No way!'

'So did. We all heard it.'

'Can we just focus on the bloody fight please,' he snaps.

'Better go, we're getting close.'

'Howie, remember what I said...about tonight...don't die today.'

Oh fuck. 'Yes. Thank you Marcy for broadcasting that.'

'Tonight?' Clarence asks grinning at me, 'what's happening tonight then?'

'Nothing.'

'Mr Howie?' Cookey says laughing, 'you and Marcy got a date night?'

'Are you blushing, Boss?' Clarence booms.

'No. I am hot.'

'Tonight then,' he says, 'don't die today, Boss.'

'I won't.'

'Mr Howie.'

'Yes, Cookey.'

'Don't die today, Mr Howie.'

'Thank you, Cookey.'

'Mr Howie,' Nick says, 'don't die today, Mr Howie.'

'Very funny, fuck off the lot of you.'

'One running,' Blowers shouts snapping our attention back to the horde. A hiss of air and the arrow goes into the eye socket of the eager zombie with such force it rips him from his feet and the first blood of the battle of Flitcombe weeps red on the ground.

They watch us. Standing still. We watch them equally as still and the banter is gone now. The jokes and the comments all vanished. We are here and so are they.

'Mr Howie.' The voice crackles in our ears so polite, clipped but distinct and surprising for Reginald's use of the radio, *'you must show confidence. It is of the upmost importance you make them think you know you will win. You are a humble man. You all are humble men but this is not the time for humbleness.'*

'Give me five minutes,' I say and walk step out from the line with my axe resting across my shoulders. Easy. Casual. Calm. Eyes watching. Always watching. Tension mounting. I roll my shoulders and move my head side to side to stretch my neck. I spit to the side.

IN THE VAN they stare at the image in the screen captured from the camera in the left side rear light cluster. Reginald seated with the other three standing behind him and the tension so thick you could spoon it out. Clutching the radio Reginald watches Howie then flicks his eyes up to the horde. A player on a board and Howie is his best piece. The trap. The lure. Howie must play it perfectly. Reginald is in the game now and as absorbed as any other. Slowly he lifts the radio to his mouth and presses the button before speaking softly.

'THAT'S IT, Mr Howie. That's it.'
I keep walking knowing Roy will be stood proud on the top of Saxon with the arrow nocked and ready and inside Roy's van they will be clutching rifles ready to come out and behind me on the line will be a small man resting his right hand on the butt of his pistol.

'CONFIDENCE. Arrogance. You defy them, Mr Howie. You offend them. You and your team.'
Reginald lets go of the radio switch and watches Howie ambling in perfect control towards the horde knowing everything must be done with perfect timing and he notices his words make Howie stand more erect as though generating an arrogant swagger.

HALFWAY NOW AND each step brings me closer to three hundred or more infected owned and occupied by one entity that wishes to do us harm. Sunken faces drawn tight across skulls with hair hanging limp and greasy. Hands clawed sharp as daggers and not human anymore. The humanity has gone from what these once were. Fetid decaying death that smells abhorrent with rancid breath and eyes blazing red. So many eyes. All red and bloodshot and the saliva drools from their mouths dripping thick on chins and chests. Naked some of them. Naked and evil for they feel no shame and have no emotion. Some are clothed and greater the offence is given for those clothes worn. Clothes are for the living. For those that need shelter and nurture.

I come to a stop fifty or so metres from them and listen to the low moans emitting from their throats. I tilt my head showing no fear and look from face to face seeing what they once were and what they now are as I lower my axe from my shoulder so the head rests on the ground and the shaft upright in my right hand while my left hangs loose at my side. Easy. Calm. Controlled. Contained. Ready. Waiting. Watching.

'OH PERFECT, YES MR HOWIE,' Reginald mutters staring unblinking at the monitor. Holding still like this is an act of pure arrogance by making them come to him as though they want him more than he wants them.

'You watch him,' Paula whispers to Charlie, 'keep your eyes on Howie and watch.'

MY HEAD LOWERS AN INCH, an inch more and in so doing I widen my peripheral vision feeling that first proper pulse of rage starting to tug at my insides.

'Come on,' I mouth, 'come on...COME ON....'

The rage shows. Pure and beautiful and that spark from me ignites them and they come. Oh they come. They come fast and charging with mouths snapping open and limbs working smoothly in synchronicity with their bodies. They flow and surge faster and faster building pace and speed with intent showing clear in their faces.

'FASTER,' I vent my incessant desire to kill them into the charged air. Fury burns my hand that holds the axe but still I do not move. I let them come and hold my position.

. . .

'NOT YET, NOT YET,' Reginald mutters with his thumb brushing the switch ready to press down. Let them come. Let them run and show no fear.

'Shit,' Charlie balks at the sight. Hundreds of infected charging towards one man standing with his axe head resting on the ground and not a flicker of movement in him.

'Just watch,' Paula mutters feeling the thrill of knowing what she's about to see.

'One more second,' Reginald says to the monitor and gets ready to press down.

'NOW FIGHT. FIGHT THEM....'

The voice whispers soft but I can feel the hunger within it as Reginald starts his journey towards this need for violence the rest of us have.

The right hand is violence.

I am violence.

I charge. Unable to contain myself from the need to inflict harm and on legs that stride fast with the axe rising to be gripped in two hands and it goes high above my head as the first one closes me down with a full on sprint and we lock eyes and roar our venomous hatred of each other.

I win. I cleave the fucker in two from skull to groin with a downward slice of sharp metal going through bone and sinew and muscle. It splits in half with innards and bowels falling to the ground but I'm gone and spinning round in a circle as another one is taken in half through the stomach.

'OH YES, YES YES YES INDEED,' Reginald shouts as Howie breaks to sprint and thereby showing the other player he is full of pride and rage and therefore fallible. 'Indeed,' Reginald says again turning round to look at Charlie staring open mouthed at the screen.

It was the speed of it. The way Howie went from standing to moving and suddenly a fully grown man was split in half from top to bottom. A second later and another is cut in half and Charlie feels the hand squeezing her arm as Marcy reaches out without knowing she's doing it.

THEN I'M in amongst them feeling more alive than I have ever felt. More real. More...fuck I don't know what it is but I'm here doing this. A head cut from the body and I spin launching the blade through a leg. Stop dead. Reverse thrust and up into the groin opening an artery. Half a turn and I ram the blunt end of the shaft into a stomach making the body fold in two as I step back and slice down. Around I go in a tight circle with the shaft sliding through my grip that tightens on the last few inches so I can make use of the length of the weapon. Cleaving and killing. Slicing and killing. Death rains on the ground with blood pouring and bones snapping with crunches. I don't hear it. I don't see it but only what I can do and what I am.

I get faster. They get slower. I gain speed until through them I go with my lips pulled back and my heart drumming a beat that my body thrives to keep pace with.

Faster. Legs detached. Arms cut. Heads removed. Innards spilling. They die and I live but still it's not enough and that furious demand grows building pressure in my head.

I dominate them. I control this place but still I cannot satisfy and feed what is desired. I am addicted but like an addict there is no shut off. The hunger gnaws and despite the blood taken so I cannot spill enough.

I need more. I have to have more. Give it to me. Give me what I need. I start to growl deep in my throat. I want more. I am angry.

Give me more. The growl increases in volume to a snarling intensity that takes me one step further away from being human and like Meredith I see only the target and the target that must be killed.

I scream into the air and stand still with my head turned up feeling that energy pulsing like nothing I can ever feel again. Why can't I satisfy it? Why can't I feed my hunger this time?

CHARLIE EDGES CLOSER. Enraptured by the sheer sight of one man ripping through hundreds of others and every step he takes there seems to be a spray of blood or a limb falling or a body crumpling to the ground.

'What is that?' She asks quietly trying to keep track of the movements and slowly realising a pattern is forming as the infected charge at him then at the last second they seem to wilt as though trying to get away.

'They're scared of him,' Marcy says, 'of being able to do this.'

'This isn't real,' Charlie says blinking hard then staring again, 'this isn't real.'

'Ha, look at Meredith,' Paula says as the dog breaks from Nick's gasp, or maybe Nick let her go. Either way she streaks over that ground in a flurry of legs and tail.

A BLUR of black shoots past me with a set of teeth clamping onto a skull as the body is taken down under the weight of Meredith and the sight spurs me on. Two of us now. Two of us fighting side by side and she whips about using her size to smash them from their feet. With a snarl her jaws close on the throat and she's off, away and leaping high to rip another one to shreds. I follow in her wake watching her work feeling the energy between us and her heart beating in her chest. I feel the strength flow into her muscles that bunch and explode and taste the blood on her tongue and runs free from her mouth. She cannot be defeated. She is skilled in this and together we fight as I drop the axe and desire what she has. That contact from her to them. I want that. I want that now. I use my hands gauging skin from necks and letting my teeth rip arteries open until the blood sprays high. I grasp arms snapping them at the elbow and driving my feet into the sides of legs breaking the joints. I grip heads and twist to feel the spine snap and by my side she snarls with a fury that builds with every passing second.

'SEE?' Marcy says watching catching glimpses between the bodies of Howie now fighting with his bare hands and the sight of him clamping his hands on a face and sinking his teeth into the neck that gets torn away with a ragged clump of flesh spat to the side.

Charlie squeezes her eyes closed at the sight and turns away. The dark eyed man that was so polite and friendly now biting into infected flesh with a dementia that is too sickening to watch. She knew he could fight, she saw it first-hand yesterday and saw his power but this? This is something else. Sickening but her eyes are drawn back to the screen almost against her will and there is another feeling, like a pull.

ANOTHER BLUR and two more join our fray as Dave flits past me into a solid pocket of undead charging towards me. I stand up with blood pouring down my chin feeling that hunger finally being satisfied. One charges from my side and I turn almost lazy in execution of the movement as an arrow takes him through the ear. Another from the other side and he too is killed with a barbed arrow through his neck.

'Mr Howie,' Dave says nodding in greeting with the blood dripping from his blades and he looks alive now. He is animated with eyes that seem to shine. He stands stock still unmoving as an arrow embeds into a head lunging at him. Without looking he reaches out and grips the shaft of the arrow pulling it free as the body drops.

He turns, casual and easy and stabs short and powerful driving the arrow into the neck of another one. A grunt. A nod and he goes back to work with the blades of his knives turned up against his forearms.

Mo Mo fights with an intensity that rivals how Lani fought and the rage shows clear on his face. One knife in his right hand and he uses those cuts taught to him by Dave to deadly effect. Stab and slice. Slice and stab. Move quick and plan ahead. He cuts a throat but already his eyes are on the next target as he drops and spins to sink the point through the throat and uses his left fist to punch the body away freeing his blade. He drops and back steps with a sweeping kick that trips one running past him sending it into the jaws of Meredith waiting for the kill.

They know how to move with each other.

He comes up standing fully with an arrow flying not an inch from his nose but he doesn't falter and not a flinch shows as he tracks and works his next kill.

'BETTER GET the rifles and bags ready,' Paula says moving to the back of the van where she stops and rolls her eyes at the other three glued to the screen.

'Mo's fast,' Marcy says in commentary, 'wild but fast.'

'Blinky,' Charlie gasps at the sight of her friend charging into the fray.

'CUNTS...' Blinky charges in screaming hell for leather running low with the axe held like a stick. The girl is demented and consumed with a thirst to hurt and cause pain but she's on our side and so the pain she gives is righteous. She slams out wild and rushed but the delivery is spot on. The axe cleaving through a shoulder so deep she has to boot the thing in the stomach to free the blade. She doesn't fight so much as hack and bludgeon but she's got strength and strong legs that pivot and drive forward.

'Fuckingcuntsfuckingcuntsfuckingcunts...'   She   mutters snarling and beastly with hair slick across her soaking forehead. She chops down but finds one coming in at her right with a lunge for the bite. She twists round letting go of the axe to slam her fists into the face breaking nose and jaw as the thing sags under the blows and as it sinks she stamps down into the skull before twisting back to snatch her weapon back up.

Motion on the other side and Nick ploughing forward with the double headed axe chopping left and right with that wry smile etched on his blood flecked face. The lad is strong and fit and it shows in his movements and manner and that confidence at knowing the blood can't hurt him shows now as he goes harder, faster, pulsing with the energy flowing through all of us.

BLINKY FITS IN PERFECTLY. Charlie sees it now why Dave said she could go. That pure furious desire for violence and to unleash hell on anyone in her way. She was always being sent off on the pitch but here she is perfectly designed to the work and now, watching Nick move into the circle she understands what they meant by they know how to move with each other.

COOKEY AND BLOWERS stomp through raging together side by side, always side by side. Always together with axes working deadly and strong. They are incredible. A team of intrinsic thought as they flow around one another. Flanks protected, rear guarded and always in sight of each other.

Oh it grows. That energy and the need to do harm. It feeds the addiction as we few slaughter them down using their greater numbers against them for they can only ever present a front line against us and with so many pressing behind they have no place else to go. So they fall and die and the ground runs with thick blood red and metallic in the air that stifles us all.

Arrows fly through us. Seemingly round us. I raise my arms to chop down and feel an arrow whizz under my wrists taking one through the eye.

AROUND HOWIE THEY FIGHT. He is the core that holds them and that pull grows stronger. That desire to be with them and in that circle killing. Marcy feels it and stares with hard eyes locked always on Howie. Charlie flits her gaze from one to the other wishing to watch all of them and not wanting to miss a thing. Dave is beautiful and she recognises the grace with which he moves. Like water flowing round them, so poised and always being where he needs to be. Reginald watches too and for something so gruesome he doesn't see the blood or gore but watches for the actions and reactions. How the other player uses the pieces and the arrangement of the board and outside Paula arranges the rifles and bags while glancing up to see Roy firing his bow.

IN THE MIDST of this carnage a new noise comes to the fore, permeating my head for the novelty of the sound. A hissing with solid pops and bones being snapped. I look round locking eyes with Nick as we both seek to find the source.

'DOWN DOWN DOWN,' Clarence booms the order and we obey with instant obedience dropping to lie within the corpses as the man strides from the edge on legs like tree trunks. His right hand above his head circling clockwise. His left also above his head but anti-clockwise and in each the chain spins long and thick. Hissing through the air as he stomps a path to our centre.

The effect is incredible. Death is given but faster and bloodier than anything yet. Chains striking heads with such force it snaps them over breaking necks. Skin ripped from bones that break and splinter. Round and round they go striking anything stupid enough to be in the way and with the rest of us down the infected charge at him. One after the other bang bang bang and they go down or flying off as his muscles warm up to the movement. He gets faster spinning harder. Whirling chains that render the forms lifeless and the blood rains down on us as we lie staring up watching. Still the arrows fly and still Meredith works. Tens are killed within seconds, or mangled so badly they crawl and writhe on the ground to be stabbed or chopped by us.

They charge in with a message clearly sent through all of them. The chains whip but snag and wrap round bodies. Clarence loses grip of the right chain and instead works the one in his left hand but that too snags from the bodies pushing at him and it's over, done. Clarence loses his chains so reverts to what he knows best, which is breaking things. We rise up axes and knives going back to what we know.

'DO YOU SEE NOW?' Marcy asks in a hushed whisper. 'That's why we couldn't go with them...we can't do that.'

'I might,' Charlie says just as hushed.

'Howie knows what he is doing,' Paula says from the back doors leaning in, 'if he wants you here with us then that's what you do. I know I'd be more of a burden in there...anyway, get ready they'll be falling back in a minute. Roy, you'd better get on the GPMG...'

'How does she know?' Charlie asks watching as Paula moves away towards the Saxon.

'It's Paula,' Marcy says, 'she knows everything.'

'FALL BACK,' I shout feeling my limbs starting to drain from the exertion in this heat. 'Dave...repeat...'

'FALL BACK...'

There is no denying his voice and together we fight a retreat into a solid line that starts back stepping as they rush on sensing we're giving ground.

I push my hand into my chest pressing the radio switch, 'Roy...' I gasp the word out, 'ready?'

'*Ready,*' his voice is clear and calm as ever. I glance back to see him now inside the hole of the Saxon as Paula, Marcy and Charlie stand aiming at the back of Roy's van.

'SIDES NOW,' I shout, 'SIDES NOW...'

We peel away to the verges on the left and right while still running back down the road towards our vehicles. An instant later the GPMG thuds to life firing into ranks now exposed from our sudden retreat. Assault rifles join the noise a fraction later slaughtering them down with rounds slamming through bodies and flesh.

We sprint hard clinging to the edges with Nick gripping Meredith's neck forcing her to stay with him. Back we go running past a hail of bullets whizzing into the undead behind us.

'CEASEFIRE,' Paula shouts as we close that final gap. The three stop firing and change magazines as we rush in to our rifles and kit bags already lined up and ready. With heaving chests and faces streaked with sweat and blood the rifles are taken up and on our knees we drop and aim down the road.

'Fire,' I shout and we open up. Assault rifles now numbering eleven and one general purpose machine gun firing sustained and controlled. They are withered. Ripped apart and once again they lose and we win.

Hand in hand. Violence and logic and as the thought enters my head so I look down the line to see Paula glancing at me with a quick smile and nod before we go back to killing those that are left.

CHAPTER TWENTY-FIVE

'Twenty seven minutes,' Reginald says from behind us as the last shot is fired by Dave.

'What was?' I snap from being jarred out of my focus.

'The battle took twenty seven minutes,' he says ignoring my rasping tone. 'Less than half an hour to kill nearly five hundred infected persons.'

'Oh,' I say changing magazine and putting the empty one next to the other empty ones I've already used. So many. Christ, I look down to see empty magazines propped on the ground. Each one of them representing thirty bullets. We just killed five hundred people in less than half an hour. 'Seems about right,' I say in a distracted voice then tut at the state I'm in again, 'just got bloody changed too.'

'Wash it off, you'll dry in no time,' Marcy says propping her rifle down, 'Charlie, you got that case of water there?'

'Right here,' Charlie heaves it out and slits the plastic membrane before walking down the line letting us each take a bottle.

'Got any Lucozade?' Nick asks stepping out a few feet to pour the water over his head. 'Your axe is awesome,' he says turning back to Clarence.

'Chains didn't work though,' he says ruefully.

'Too long,' Paula says, 'and one would have done the job. Brilliant weapon to clear an immediate space so I'd recommend you keep one with you.'

'Was good,' I say adding my thoughts.

'Fucking brutal,' Blowers says, 'can you loop one over your shoulders or something? If we get caught in a tight spot it would work very well.'

'Yeah don't see why not,' Clarence says thoughtfully and looks up as Roy walks over from the Saxon, 'good work again, mate.'

'Cheers,' Roy says nodding, 'seemed to go alright,' he adds looking round at everyone, 'you all okay?'

'You's missed my nose by like this much,' Mo says holding his thumb and forefinger apart by a fraction.

'I would never have hit you,' Roy replies, 'and I got the one lunging at you.'

'I lifted up to chop down,' I say holding my axe up in replay, 'and the arrow went under my wrists as I lifted...incredible...absolutely incredible.'

'May I give feedback?' He asks me.

'You don't have to ask, mate.'

'Blinky,' he says, 'don't over extend the axe when you lunge forward, you left yourself wide open a few times.'

'Got it,' she says between thirsty sips from the bottle, 'on my left yeah?'

'Yes, I had them but they were close,' Roy says.

'Okay, yeah will do.'

'How did you find it?' I ask her.

'Fucking awesome,' she blurts, 'Mr Howie, Sir. Fucking awesome, Sir.'

'You did well. Dave? Mo do alright?'

'Good.'

'You're very fast,' Paula says smiling at Mo, 'you'll be as fast as Lani was soon.'

'Yeah?' Mo asks, 'feels slow when I look at Dave and everyone else...like everyone got their thing going on, you get me?' He asks looking at her then back at me, 'like Mr Howie uses the axe but he can go without it...and Dave got two knives and like Nick is just fast man, like...fucking quick...and you's two,' he says looking at Cookey and Blowers, 'so tight.'

'You're good, Mo,' Clarence says, 'very good, just do what Dave says and you'll get faster naturally.'

He snorts a dry laugh, 'ain't nothing natural about this.'

'How do you mean?' I ask.

'I been fighting for years,' he says, 'estate kids, cops...men...ain't no fighting like this though. This isn't natural.'

'Suppose not,' I say with a shrug, 'so Reginald, twenty seven minutes yeah?'

'Indeed, twenty seven minutes from the first kill to the last.'

'Roy's arrow or the one I chopped in half?'

'The one you cut, Mr Howie. I counted from that point.'

'Went okay did it?'

'Yes I believe we gave a satisfactory performance. I do hope you did not mind me speaking to you on the radio but I had the benefit of being able to see the bigger picture.'

'No problem at all, I think it worked well.'

'So far yes, we have gained the board for now and the time to set our pieces where we require while the other player believes we are celebrating in victory and gathering ourselves for the next attack. However, I would most strongly suggest we are being watched as we speak and so we...or rather you undertake to clear this area to the best of your ability.'

'Yep, will do. You heard the man, house clearance down the main road. Kill any crawlers and shout if you see anything.'

'Who wanted Darjeeling?' Blowers asks, 'was it you, Charlie?'

'Yeah like you even need to ask,' Cookey says with a laugh, 'and fuck off, I've already said I'm getting it.'

'Not if I find it first,' Blowers says.

'You won't be looking for tea,' Cookey says assuredly.

'No?' Blowers asks.

'Nope. Butt plugs yes, tea no.'

'Funny.'

'I try.'

'The tea is for me,' Reginald says, 'I can't think properly without tea.'

'Fuck me, you're like this now without thinking properly?' I say in awe, 'what are you like *with* tea then?'

'Sharp, Mr Howie. I am sharp,' he says with a firm nod before disappearing back in the van and leaving a stunned silence in his wake.

CHAPTER TWENTY-SIX

We clear the houses first. Front door to front door. Every room is checked. Up narrow staircases and into bedrooms, bathrooms and we check back gardens, sheds and every single place that could hold a single living person.

The last house on the left side of the road at the village end and a few metres back from the first bend in the road and I pause to wipe the sweat from my face then nod to Blowers who leans over to push the door handle down.

'Wait,' Mo hisses staring at the door slowly creaking inwards. We all freeze, staring at the young lad who tilts his head to one side and nods once before lifting his rifle and walking past all of us into the house. Blowers goes in behind him up the stairs and out of sight.

'Boss,' Blowers calls out. I go up with Dave right behind me to see Mo holding one finger up and pointing it at a closed bedroom door.

'In there?' I ask.

'Yeah, one.'

'You saw it?'

He shakes his head then shrugs, 'one in there.'

'Okay,' I step to the door, twist the knob and give it a push before stepping back with my rifle raised. Guns bristling and eyes glaring but nothing obvious so I edge forward and gradually peer round the door to see a single adult female undead standing by the window and staring out through the thick net curtain.

'One,' I say lowering the rifle a few inches, 'female.'

Dave comes in and I edge over as Blowers and Mo follow suit.

'What you got?' Clarence calls up the stairs.

'Single infected in the bedroom staring out the window,' Blowers shouts.

We hold still and something about the sight holds me frozen to the spot and I lower the rifle down to my waist. She doesn't turn round, or rather *it* doesn't turn round but stays looking out the window to the street below. She's dressed too. In jeans and a black top. They're a bit torn and dirty but otherwise she looks normal, too normal and for a second I think I'm looking at the back of a human.

'Oi,' I call out and glance back to the others still holding their rifles aimed and ready.

She doesn't move so I take a step closer to the edge of the double bed, 'hey,' I snap.

When she does turn it's with poise and dignity. Standing erect with head held high and still. She doesn't drool either and the hands appear relaxed and normal instead of clawed. Her eyes are fully red and bloodshot though and all the more terrible for the normalcy of the rest of her. We lock eyes. Me and her. Me and it.

I walk round the bed closer to the woman, to the thing, to the infection that stares back at me through a pair of red bloodshot eyes. I can't see any injury either. Not a bite mark or cut on her visible skin. No blood and her skin, although deathly pale, isn't the sickening grey pallor we've seen so much.

'What?' I ask shrugging my shoulders as though waiting for her to say something, 'something you wanted?'

'One race...'

'Back to that yeah?'

'What's going on?' Cookey asks pushing into the room, 'oh hiya,' he says cheerfully to the female infected, 'is this your house?'

'One race...'

'Yeah we kinda heard you the first fifty million times,' Cookey says, 'ooh who is coming by the way?'

'He is coming.'

'Yeah. Who?'

'He is coming.'

'One what?'

'One race.'

'When is he coming?'

'He is coming.'

'One coming?' Cookey asks scratching his chin as though confused but his questions get faster with a rally going back and forth as everyone else crowds in the room and round the door to listen.

'One race.'

'He is racing?'

'He is coming.'

'He is coming in a race?'

'One race.'

'He is racing to come?'

'He is coming.'

'Coming now?'

'He is coming.'

'Has he come?'

'He is coming.'

'In a race?'

'One race.'

'One face?'

'One race.'

'Will he come in the race?'

'He is coming.'

'Are you helping him?'

'One race.'

'Helping him to come.'

'He is coming.'

'He comes a lot.'

'He is coming.'

'On his own face?'

'One race.'

'On your face?'

'One race.'

'He race.'

'He is coming.'

'One coming,' Cookey steps closer speaking faster while smiling evilly.

'One race.'

'He race.'

'He is coming.'

'He is one.'

'One race.'

'He is one race....FUCK!' Cookey shouts jumping back as Meredith rushes past him and slams the female against the wall with her two front paws pressed into the chest while barking furiously. She holds the woman there for the briefest of seconds barking with huge noises into the face of the infection before clamping her jaws on the throat and tearing the flesh away with a sickening wet ripping noise.

'Fuck's sake,' Cookey says sighing as the body slides down the wall, 'I would have won that.'

'And we'll never know,' Blowers chuckles.

'Jesus, how desensitised are we?' Cookey says staring down at the body, 'we just watched her throat being ripped out.'

'Fuck 'em,' Nick says from the bedroom door, 'we going then or what?'

'Yeah,' I say as we start filing back down the stairs, 'Mo? How do you do that?'

'Dunno, Mr Howie,' he says from in front of me.

'What does it feel like then?'

'Dunno,' he says again, 'like I just know...like a fact.'

'Uncanny, mate,' I say walking out into the sunshine to see Paula and Roy have brought both the vehicles down, 'right, what's next? Paula?'

'Well,' she says, 'we can either have a quick break now or go through the three industrial areas and see what they've got to offer....or we can go on and use the drone to grab a look at Stenbury and then check on the way back here.'

'Er...I think grabbing a look at Stenbury first would be the best idea. Everyone happy with that? Quick look then back here for a brew...fuck me, you all look knackered,' I say looking round at the slumped shoulders and faces flushed red, 'this heat,' I add nodding, 'okay, quick advanced reconnaissance pathfinder recce scouting ahead sniper sneaky ninja commando secret trip to have a sneaky peaky at Stenbury then back here for coffee and cake.'

'Cake?' Nick asks, 'we got cake.'

'No cake,' I say, 'just coffee. And some Camomile tea for Reginad. Or Darjeeling tea...but no cake.'

'Unless we find some cake when we look for Reginald's tea,' Nick suggests, 'like boxed and sealed...'

'I like the cut of your jib m'lad,' I say, 'keep that up and you'll go far in the apocalypse...eh Paula? We're always looking for bright young people to be made into managers.'

'Supervisors,' she says.

'To be made supervisors,' I say to Nick, 'have we got a supervisor management apocalypse living army training package?'

'Er yes, yes we do,' she says with a big smile, 'it's very extensive and includes an evidence based monitoring programme within which you will be given one on one training with Dave on the best ways to kill people with a knife and also personal instruction from Clarence on the best melee weapons...'

'Good word that,' Clarence says approvingly.

'And Roy takes you through the basics of caring for your bow and through to the applied theory of modern warfare with Reginald and not discounting the input from Marcy on how to look your very best for the end of the world.'

'That's important,' Marcy says seriously, 'appearance matters.'

'Then of course you will have map reading and advanced theory with Charlotte and then you'll be paired with me on how to organise a bunch of coffee drinking caffeine pumped misfits and making sure they've each got clean pants to wear...'

'I'm down to my last pair.'

'Noted, Simon,' she says without losing pace, 'and finally you'll be with Mr Howie who will give you personal and guided instruction on how to lead said living army through the waste lands of southern rural England in a thoroughly polite and rather humbling way while biting the throats out of infected people when he's got a perfectly good axe to use.'

'Noted,' I say with a wince.

'An axe, I might add,' she says looking at me, 'that was given to Dave for sharpening prior to the battle and the handle of which has since been scrubbed with antibac...'

'Yep,' I mutter again nodding in apology.

'As have all the axes,' she says staring round.

'Thanks, Paula.'

'Cheers, Paula.'

'So how about it?' She says breezily to Nick, 'signing up to the management programme?'

'Er...'

'I'll do it.'

'You are banned, Cookey.'

'What? What for?'

'For ever,' she says, 'and ever and ever...'

'So unfair.'

'Your mum is,' she says with one hand on her hip and one eyebrow perfectly arched as Blowers mouth drops open and the rest of us stare in shock.

'Paula made a mum joke,' Cookey whispers staring at her with an expression akin to fear, 'nobody move...I think she may have lost it.'

'So, Nicholas,' she says turning back to Nick, 'fancy it?'

'Nah I'm good ta,' he says politely, 'wouldn't mind the cake though.'

'Cake,' she says, 'cake...I'll add it to my list of things to do. Along with getting Simon some new pants. You had new pants,' she says turning to him, 'in the shopping centre. I packed them myself.'

'I've used them,' he says with a shrug, 'it's hot.'

'I need some more knickers too.'

'Yes, Blinky,' Paula says taking it all in, 'anyone else?'

'Socks,' Clarence says, I can only find one pair.'

'Who stole Clarence's socks?' She asks glaring round, 'check your bags and hand them back if you've got them. We will not have sock thieves in our team. Anything else? Marcy? Need some mascara?'

'You know I do. I already told you.'

'Really?' I ask Marcy, 'make-up?'

'Hey,' she says mock serious, 'girl's got to make an effort these days.'

'Actually I've been wearing mascara,' Paula says, 'not that anyone would notice.'

'I noticed.'

'Course you did, Roy.'

'I did.'

'I noticed Paula, and I thought you looked very pretty.'

'Thank you, Cookey.'

'Such a creep.'

'Fuck you, Blowers.'

'Come on then,' she says clapping her hands, 'load up and we'll get moving. Nick, there's Lucozade in the Saxon by your seat. I've put the original in there, you prefer that one right?'

'Ah cheers, Paula.'

'And there's some tinned peaches in there too. Eat some fruit. Dave, can you make sure they eat the fruit.'

'Yes, Paula. You will all eat the fruit. Is that understood?'

'Yes, Dave.'

'Yes, Dave.'

'Yes, Dave.'

'Nicholas?'

'Yes, Dave.'

'Reginald,' I call out as I walk towards the Saxon, 'we'll need somewhere to launch the drone...'

'I've already asked him,' Paula says with a grin.

'If humanity survives this it will be because of you, Paula.'

'Yep, probably.'

CHAPTER TWENTY-SEVEN

W e leave Flitcombe behind and drive through the series of bends out of the village and onto a wide main road bordered by high hedgerows. Puddles steaming and still deep at the sides but the water is evaporating fast in this incredible heat. It's so close and muggy, like the weather you get before a big storm only far worse.

Tins of peaches are opened and one passed up to me to eat while I drive the vehicle, which is tricky and messy and only just about accomplished.

'Marcy with us?' I ask realising Clarence is up front with me and turning while eating a slice of slippery peach and navigating the bendy road ahead.

'In Roy's van,' Clarence says reaching out to grip the wheel, 'she swapped with Charlie.'

'Charlie in the back here?'

'Behind you, Mr Howie.'

'Oh okay, just checking. You alright then?'

'Fine thank you, Mr Howie.'

'Going alright with Reggie?'

'Yes fine thank you, Mr Howie.'

'He's switched on. All those things he said.'

'He is deceptively intelligent,' Charlie says, 'really very intelligent.'

'Yeah?' Clarence asks half turning to look round at Charlie, 'he just needs some confidence in himself.'

'And a tie.'

'A what?' Clarence asks smiling.

'A tie. A neck tie. In fact he needs a shirt and tie.'

'We offered back at the shopping centre didn't we?' Blowers asks.

'Yeah but I think it offended him,' I say.

'Reginald is very aware of social structures,' Charlie says diplomatically, 'and would actively seek to avoid any social situations that would render him to be seen as a difficulty.'

'But he told you he wants a tie?' Clarence asks.

'No. He keeps moving his hands to adjust the tie...I kept seeing it and...'

'He does that all the time,' Cookey says, 'like this,' he adds mimicking Reginald's hands going to his neck.

'That's it,' Charlie says, 'he does it as a stress reliever, something for his hands to do. Like a smoker?'

'Well,' Clarence says deeply, 'best get him a shirt and tie then.'

'Wouldn't that offend him?' I ask, 'like...you just said about social awkwardness.'

'Yes and yes it would,' she says, 'but perhaps the having of the shirt and tie would be the lesser of two evils in comparison to his needing that reassurance of himself against the difficulty he would suffer in asking.'

'Er...' I say.

'She said we can get him a tie,' Blinky says.

'Ah cool,' I say.

'I speak Charlotte,' Blinky adds, 'when she's being all posh and shit.'

'I am not being all posh and...'

'So are,' Blinky scoffs, 'you get soooo posh in front of Mr Howie and Clarence.'

'Blinky!' Charlie says sharply, 'that is not appropriate.'

'Ah stop blushing,' Blinky snaps.

'Then stop drawing attention to my faults.'

'You? You don't have faults.'

'I do and can we cease this discussion in front of the others please.'

'Whatever.'

'Charlie,' Blowers says, 'don't worry about it, mate. We're living on top of each other, we'll get on each other's tits all the time.'

'You said tits to Charlie,' Cookey says slurping a peach slice down, 'that's not appropriate.'

'Sorry, Charlie,' Blowers says seriously.

'It's fine. I am not posh.'

'Yeah you are,' Cookey says laughing, 'it's awesome.'

'Really I am not.'

'Fuck it, be you,' Nick says, 'you've got a lovely way of speaking. Wish I could speak like that.'

'Yeah me too,' Cookey says, 'you finished, Mo?'

'Yeah, was nice. I like the way you's talk, Charlie. Maddox could do that when he needed.'

'Do what?' Charlie asks politely.

'Like switch to talking nicely, he spoke like we did to us but the bossman made him learn how talk properly, you get me?'

'I think so.'

'So's like, how do you do it?' Mo asks.

'Talk properly?' Charlie asks.

'Yeah, so like I wanna talk properly. What do I do?'

'Pronunciation is a big part,' Charlie says, 'and avoiding the use of slang phrases or colloquial expressions and of course not abbreviating everything you say.'

'So like, I say every letter in every word?' Mo asks saying every letter of every word as everyone else chuckles.

'Yes, that is a start,' Charlie says, 'and speaking to your audience.'

'What's that?' Cookey asks.

'As Blinky so awfully pointed out. One may adapt their way of speaking depending on the company the person is in. For instance, I may choose to be more polite and formal to Mr Howie, Clarence and Paula as I see them as leaders within this group thereby giving respect to the structure in place.'

'Do you swear like a trooper when you're with Blinky then?' Nick asks.

'No I do not.'

'She does,' Blinky says, 'says cunt and everything.'

'I do not say that word.'

'I will hereon and er...speak properly,' Mo announces.

'Wherewithal,' Nick says, 'that's a posh word, you should use that.'

'Wherewithwho?' Mo asks.

'Wherewithal,' Nick repeats.

'What does this word mean?' Mo asks in his new polite voice.

'Fuck knows, I heard someone posh use it.'

'Charlotte? Mo asks, 'please do tell me what this word means.'

'Money,' Charlie says, 'it's a reference to having money for a specific purpose.'

'Really?' Nick asks, 'thereby, that's another posh word.'

'Henceforth,' Cookey says.

'Thus,' Blowers adds.

'Vagina,' Blinky says, 'instead of cunt.'

'Yes, thank you, Blinky,' Charlie groans.

'What? I was just saying you can say vagina instead of cunt.'

'And you don't have to keep saying it.'

'What? Cunt?'

'Patricia.'

'Sorry, Dave.'

'OH THAT'S SO NICE,' Marcy says lying on the floor in the back of the van and feeling the temperature climb down from the air conditioning on full blast.

'It is.'

Lifting her head a few inches Marcy stares for a second at Paula leaning her back against the bulkhead next to the hatch door, 'you okay?'

'Me? Paula asks opening her eyes, 'fine. You?'

'Fine,' Marcy says.

'This conversation is riveting,' Reginald mutters at the desk examining the map again.

'Pah,' Marcy says, 'just because you found your testicles again.'

'Marcy!'

'What, Reggie?'

'Reginald. My name is Reginald.'

'You'll always be Reggie to me.'

'Be that as it may and yes I admit we have known each other for a time longer than the others...'

'Shush now, you're making hot air.'

'You are insufferable.'

'Am I? Really? Aw thanks, Reggie.'

'It is not a compliment.'

'You saying I'm ugly then?'

'What?! I never said anything of the sort. I merely pointed out you are insufferable.'

'Yeah but you said it wasn't a compliment.'

'Just because something is not a compliment it is not automatically rendered as a criticism of your physical being.'

'So you're saying I'm not ugly?'

'I am not saying anything about the way you look...'

'Oh leave him alone,' Paula groans, 'don't rise to it, Reginald.'

'Yes, yes you are right, Paula. I shall not rise to it.'

'You will,' Marcy says grinning up at him, 'my little Reggie, it's nice to see you smiling again.'

'I do not smile.'

'Well talking again instead of being all grumpy.'

'Indeed.'

'I have a question, Reggie.'

'Reginald, Marcy. My name is Reginald.'

'Can I ask my question?'

'Is it a real question?'

'Yes it is actually,' she says rolling onto her side and propping her head up on one arm and her serious tone makes the small fastidious man turn in his seat.

'Everyone has a role,' she says glancing at Paula, 'I mean look at everything Paula does...which is everything.'

'Ah,' Reginald says steepling his fingers, 'yes you are questioning your reason for being within this group.'

'Yes I am.'

'I was contemplating this same thing and I knew it would be concerning you.'

'How?' She asks staring up at him.

'Because you are vain,' he says matter of fact, 'you will always therefore be seeking to question your place in anything.'

'I'm not actually vain,' she says in a quiet voice, 'I think that's got a bit out of hand.'

'If I looked like you I'd be vain,' Paula says not unkindly.

'I don't just want to be judged on how I look...'

'You play to how you look,' Paula says gently, 'we all grow into who we are.'

'Hmm, so why am I here?'

'Because you turned then turned back,' Paula says.

'Reginald did the same and he's now got a reason for being here. Blinky can fight, Charlie is like super intelligent and super pretty...'

'Marcy?' Paula asks with a warning tone to her voice.

'I'm not jealous,' Marcy says, 'but she is. She's lovely. Roy can do that with his bow...I mean of all the people in the world to bump into and Roy finds this group?'

'Reginald?' Paula asks with a heavy sigh, 'this is your field.'

'This is not my field at all but yes, there will be a reason.'

'Really?' Paula asks quickly snapping her eyes back open.

'Without doubt. Marcy is correct. Every person here plays a role. Perhaps to a degree some may find themselves fitting into a role as a conscious or even unconscious way of fitting into the group thereby securing their own safety. I for one only spoke up today because I could foresee the dangers presented...'

'And going back to me again,' Marcy says smiling wolfishly, 'why am I here? What can I do?'

'Lure men with your boobs.'

'Paula,' Marcy tuts but smiles over at her, 'seriously?'

'Perhaps that is yet to be known,' Reginald says, 'I confess there are...' he stops to blink with his hands going to his tie knot that isn't there, 'variables? No...that is not right. There are *things* happening which we do not know.'

'You're so different now,' Marcy says looking intently at Reginald, 'like a completely different person.'

'Indeed,' he says ignoring the comment for the lack of intellectual value it contains, 'in truth it must relate to your draw to Mr Howie.'

'Pardon? You've changed because I fancy Howie?'

'No,' he says slowly rolling his eyes, 'your role within the group must be connected to your draw to Mr Howie.'

'You do fancy him then?' Paula asks.

'Yeah,' Marcy laughs as Reginald rolls his eyes again.

'Good Lord,' Reginald says, 'you asked a question. Perhaps we should focus on that rather than who we fancy.'

'Who do you fancy then?'

'Marcy, I do not fancy anyone. There are people in this world that operate above a base state of who they find physically attractive. I am giving consideration to the fact you have previously told me about your intense draw to Mr Howie. Indeed, I recall the days we spent in the houses by the bay opposite the fort while I begged for us to leave and you insisted we stay because you knew he would come.'

'So you don't fancy anyone?'

'Oh for the love of...I am ending this conversation.'

'Reggie, I'm only playing,' Marcy says sitting up and reaching out a hand to rest on his knee, 'don't be weird with me.'

'Weird?'

'We've always been like this,' she says, 'I mess about and you nag.'

'I have known you for a matter of days,' Reginald says staring down into her eyes and seeing the woman he followed without question changing day by day, 'you are changing,' he says studying her eyes.

'We're all changing,' she says, 'your eyes are almost back to normal too and yeah, it's only been days but Paula said this morning that time is magnified now...so it feels like I've known you for years.'

'Yes,' he says with a gentle sigh, 'it does feel like that somewhat. Truly, Marcy. I do not know the reasons but I am thinking on it, along with many other things.'

'How am I changing?' She asks as Paula watches on with interest.

'You were powerful,' Reginald replies quickly with an answer given without hesitation, 'you commanded. You had focus and intent that went hand in hand with your physical beauty. That power is diminishing and I am afraid all that will remain will be the physical beauty.'

'Harsh, Reginald,' Paula winces.

'No, no I asked,' Marcy says looking pensive, 'maybe that's all I am then. Something pretty to look at.'

'Ah, you're more than that,' Paula says trying to force some belief into her voice.

'What then? Lani could fight *and* she was beautiful. I can't fight...I can't plan like you do...I can't think like Charlie...'

'What happened in Maplin?' Paula asks lifting her head an inch.

'Maplin? Nothing...I just spoke to Howie.'

'About what?'

'I told him to calm down.'

'What happened then? When you were inside?'

'He was huffing and puffing and making everyone else stressed and poor Nick just found out he was immune but he was tapping his foot and muttering so I took him inside and made him relax a bit.'

'Dave went flying in,' Paula says with a look of knowing etched on her face.

'I slapped Howie. He threatened me, saying I was trying to hold him up then accusing me of doing it on purpose...you know how he gets...all angry and brooding.'

'So you slapped him?' Paula asks chuckling, 'did it work?'

'Too right it did. I slapped him twice and then kissed him and he relaxed.'

'Oh,' Paula says lifting her eyebrows and glancing over to Reginald, 'okay...so you kissed him...and then what?'

'Well nothing. He calmed down and...'

'And since he walked out of Maplin he's been calmer,' Paula says giving voice to the point she was building towards. 'Marcy, Howie wouldn't stop for a piss when he's like that and the others would go with him simply because he's Howie.'

'Oh,' Marcy says blinking, 'so that's my job then? To keep Howie calm?'

'I'm not saying it like that...Reginald? Do you see where I'm going?' Paula asks.

'I do. Indeed. Mr Howie was intent on pushing forward but by your actions he stopped and allowed others, such as myself, the time to plan and calculate ahead.'

'Oh,' Marcy says again but duller this time as she deflates, 'so it does come back to how I look. Howie fancies me so I can calm him down...I even promised to show him my arse tonight.'

'You did what?' Paula asks bursting out laughing again.

'I did, he was like angry so I said I wanted to take the watch with him then we got talking about my arse and I said I would show him but he had to stay alive today if he wanted to see it.'

'Oh that's what that was about,' Paula says.

'So I'm just tagging along now and my job is to give Howie something nice to play with.'

'Hey,' Paula snaps, 'don't you dare say that,' she pauses as Marcy looks over sharply, 'Howie isn't like that and I think his attraction to you goes a bit beyond how you bloody look, Marcy. There's a power to you two when you're together. Jesus, you are vain. Everyone can see it so stop seeking reassurance.'

'I only...'

'I don't care what you only did or didn't say,' Paula says scathing in her rebuttal, 'Howie...no...we risked everything to get you and Reginald. Lani died for fuck's sake. We follow Howie and Howie followed you. Is that enough for you?' She stands quickly glaring at Marcy, 'how far until we're there?' She asks Reginald.

'A few minutes,' Reginald replies quietly.

'Fine. Tell me when we're close.'

'Paula,' Marcy says standing up.

'Enough. Pull your head out of your perfect arse, Marcy,' she says closing the hatch behind her plunging the back of Roy's van into a deep weighted silence that stretches out as Reginald turns back to studying the map.

She goes to the back doors folding her arms and staring at the road behind realising she has no idea where they are. What town they are in or where they are near. Have they been through another town yet? Aren't they leap-frogging or something? She looks down at the drone on the floor feeling like shit for not knowing how it works and not taking the interest to find out.

She was something. She was powerful and she commanded. She had an army and a purpose too. She was going to prove this infection was intended to cure not to kill but something went wrong. Everything went wrong. Did it? Is it wrong? Confusion in her mind and the same confusion everyone feels at the nagging idea they are not following the right path.

'Reginald,' she says quietly, 'what should we be doing?'

'Seeking a cure,' again he answers without hesitation with a reply of utter belief.

That's it. That's the reason for being here. Together, between them all collectively, they hold a cure, or at least a vaccine but without the experts to understand it they are floundering about killing hundreds within a land now dominated by millions.

She turns back to Reginald and watches him tracing his finger along a thick red line on the map while his other finger remains static an inch or so away from the first. His lips move as he calculates time and distance before glancing up to the monitor and nodding as though seeing what he wished to see.

She calmed Howie down earlier so she has that ability to get through to him. She can ease that biting urge he has to kill and destroy them one by one. It's manipulation but not evilly done.

'I'll talk to him later,' she says.

'Who?' Reginald asks without looking up.

'Howie. About changing our direction.'

'You will?' Reginald says looking up with a look of surprise.

She nods, 'yeah, I'll get through to him. We should be going for a cure.'

'Yes,' Reginald says blinking again before turning to look down once again, 'perhaps that is your role. To drive us in the right direction and give Mr Howie focus where no other can.'

'Now?' She asks, 'should I talk to him now? Maybe we shouldn't go to Stenbury but...'

'Marcy,' Reginald says sitting upright inhaling deeply, 'as much as I desire to avoid any confrontation and to be seeking a way to end all of this...we cannot, with any conscience, leave such a number of infected persons in one place. The consequences could be catastrophic beyond anything we could imagine. Look at what you were able to do with hundreds. This town may have thousands or indeed upwards of ten thousand.'

'Reggie,' she balks at his words wide eyed and not recognising the small man in glasses, 'you want to fight them?'

'We have no choice. We are committed to this game. The other player...the infection has massed thousands in response to our course of conduct and the actions we have taken. If we do not see it through they will be left to commit destruction on a scale that is staggering in comprehension and in so doing they could get larger and far increase the level of threat they pose. They must be killed. This game must be finished.' He stops and looks at briefly at the monitor, 'Paula? Two minutes ahead there will be a junction on the left leading to a farm.'

'Okay,' Paula shouts and Marcy listens as the information is relayed while feeling ten steps behind everyone else.

CHAPTER TWENTY-EIGHT

D*ay Eighteen*

UPDATE No 6

FLITCOMBE.

    I have counted in excess of four hundred corpses.

    Hacked apart by blades. Cut with scalpels. Chains were used to smash them down and their dogs used to rip them apart while arrows were fired to kill with brutal precision. Assault rifle shell casings show the line they fought from and larger calibre bullets too.

    I do not understand what I am seeing. Why fight hand to hand if you have guns? This is the first time I have seen the larger calibre bullet casings and even now, with so many killed they still stopped to have target practise with their bows. Perhaps that is the reason they chose to fight hand to hand...for practise?

    Water on the ground where they drank. Every door to every house forced and every house searched. You can still see the blood smears on the walls as the soldiers have walked through and I know I am close as the blood on the ground still runs wet and glistening.

Do I want to find these people? I am no longer confident that this is the right thing to do but I also know I must continue and find them. One of them is immune.

The List. That is all that matters now. I must harden myself.

Jess grows weary. We have covered a great distance and this heat and humidity are unbearable. She keeps working though and it's almost as though she has her own determination to find these people.

I will go on but I now dread the next sight I will encounter.

NB

CHAPTER TWENTY-NINE

'That must be it,' Clarence says pointing to the open gated entrance leading to an unmade road. I slow down and take the turn easing the vehicle onto the bumpy road. The village we passed on the way, the leap-frogged town, was small with barely a main street with a village shop. Still, if nothing else it will help funnel them and there were plenty of abandoned cars left about that we can use.

'So,' Charlie says to Mo, 'what are we going to do now?'

'We are going to a farm to launch a drone I say,' Mo says still trying to speak posh.

'You don't have to say *I say* every time, Mo,' she says with a laugh.

'Do Mo's voice again,' Cookey urges Charlie, who in the interest of fair play, had tried speaking *street* as Mo tried posh.

'Gosh no, once is enough for me.'

'Ah go on,' Nick says.

'Innit,' Charlie quips, 'brother.'

'Bruv,' Mo says laughing, 'not brother.'

'Oh I thought it was brother.'

'Bruv you get me yeah?'

'You get me,' she says.

'Deeper,' Mo says.

'You get me bruv?' She says deeper.

'Nah like rougher, like...you get me bruv?'

'You's get me bruv innit...'

'Perfect!' Mo shouts clapping his hands, 'totally spot on I say.'

'Yeah I is speaking street now,' Charlie says holding that deep raspier voice.

'Yes that is very good,' Mo says lifting his voice up a few notches and pronouncing every letter.

'We's the feds yeah?'

'We are the authority,' Mo replies.

'Yo gangsta innit,' Charlie reels it off quickly, 'yo's gonna bump a hat in yo kneecap.'

'What?' Clarence asks bursting out laughing, 'what was that?'

'Street innit bruv,' Charlie says, 'yo's bumping hats in yo kneecaps.'

'I say,' Mo says between laughs, 'I do think you mean you are going to pop a cap in someone's backside.'

'You's what? I mean what? I mean pardon?'

'Pop a cap in your ass,' Mo says still laughing, 'not bump a hat in a kneecap.'

'Oh did I get it wrong?' Charlie sighs, 'damnation. You say it,' she says to Mo.

'Nah.'

'No do, you say it.'

'You's want me to talk street bruv?' He goes full on raspy and deep, 'you's dissin' me yeah? You's disrespectin' me? Yo pop a cap in yo ass motherfucker.'

'Oh yes!' Cookey shouts in the din, 'bloody brilliant.'

'Oh that is so cool,' Charlie says.

'Is it cool is it I say?' Mo asks switching back to posh.

'We're here,' I say driving past the farmhouse and staring round at the barns and outbuildings, 'switch on now, we've got a farm-house, a barn and two old shitty looking sheds.'

'Mr Howie, I will take Mohammed and do the farmhouse.'

'Righto, mate. Blowers, you take Cookey and do the barn. Nick and Blinky on the sheds. Charlie, you start getting the drone set up while Clarence and I do management stuff and have a meeting about forecasts and such like.'

'It's hot and will stay hot but it might rain,' Clarence says looking out the window before opening his door and feeling the wall of heat, 'yep, it's hot.'

We clamber out with weapons held ready scanning the vicinity and slowly easing away from the vehicles. Roy brings his van to a stop and is out and scanning within a second or two with his rifle gripped and ready.

'Dave, you doing the farmhouse?' Paula asks seeing them walk towards the main door.

'Yes, Paula.'

'Call me if the gas supply is still on, we'll brew up here.'

'Yes, Paula.'

'Howie...'

'Ssshhh,' Roy waves at her then touches his ear before motioning round.

'Sorry,' she whispers and we wait while Blowers gets the barn clear and Nick tentatively checks the big sheds that look like they'll fall down any second.

Charlie stands her ground on one side holding her rifle while Marcy holds at the back of Roy's van.

'Mo,' I transmit quietly into the microphone, 'you feeling anything?'

'Nothing, Mr Howie.'

'Cheers, Nick? What about Meredith? She with you?'

'Same. She's taking a piss at the moment.'

'We're clear in the barn.'

'Cheers, Blowers...Charlie, you can start getting it ready.'

'*Dave, did you check the gas?*' Paula asks into her radio.

'Give him a chance,' I say with a smile.

'*Yes.*'

'*Yes you checked it or yes the gas is on?*'

'*Yes.*'

'*Which one yes?*'

'*Yes.*'

'*Dave, is the gas on?*'

'*Yes.*'

'Ha, it's funny when it's someone else,' I say as Meredith comes bounding over wagging her tail like she hasn't seen anyone for days on end. She gets a big fuss while we drift over to the back of Roy's van and watch Charlie and Reginald setting up.

'Boss,' Nick says handing me a smoke.

'Cheers, you're quiet,' I say to Marcy standing nearby.

'Thinking,' she says.

'Oh, what about?'

'Things,' she says, 'Paula, do you want me to make the coffees?'

'You can help me if you want,' Paula replies in a clipped tone that has the rest of us looking everywhere but at her.

'Want a hand?' Nick asks starting to walk after them.

'We'll be fine thanks, Nick,' Paula says.

'Okay then,' Nick says turning back round pulling a face.

'What happened?' I ask Reginald, 'Reginald? What happened?'

'Hmm?' He asks engrossed in the monitor on his desk.

'Fuck me, did Marcy and Paula fall out?'

'Minor disagreement,' Roy says, 'I am sure they'll sort it out.'

'What was it about?' I ask staring at the two of them going through the open farmhouse door then seeing Dave and Mo come out.

'I didn't hear it all,' Roy says, 'but something to do with Marcy wondering what role she has here.'

'This heat makes everyone fractious,' Clarence says.

'Mr Howie, can I use the toilet please, Mr Howie?'

'You don't have to ask, Blinky.'

'Okay,' she says standing there.

I sigh again and rub the back of my neck, 'yes you can use the toilet.'

'Thanks, Mr Howie,' she says turning smartly.

'I'll use the barn,' Clarence says heading off.

'Yeah good idea,' Blowers says. Nick, Cookey and Mo walk after him as Roy heads off to the shed leaving me watching Charlie and Reginald with Meredith trying to work out who to follow.

'Come here,' I click my tongue and she trots over as I drop to a crouch and start rubbing the top of her head, 'good girl, who's a good girl?'

She snaps her mouth open and closed a few times making little excited whining noises before suddenly deciding getting fuss from me isn't as important as being near Nick and the lads.

I move to the back of Roy's van and sit on the ledge of the open rear door smoking my cigarette and shifting uncomfortably as the sweat starts seeping out my forehead to roll down my nose. If this was normal times the news and weather people would be going nuts at this weather. It's so fucking hot and humid, like there's no air and the sky is pressing down giving me a low dull headache in the back of my skull.

Five hundred killed in twenty seven minutes. Clarence reckons we got about twelve hundred before that so that's one thousand seven hundred people we have killed today. Not people. Things. Infected things. Don't think of them as people. Don't think about the lives they had and the love they felt. Don't think about the children and the homes. Not people. Things and I will kill every last one of them.

'Are you okay, Mr Howie?'

'Eh?' I look up startled to see Charlie staring over at me, 'yeah miles away, you ready?'

'Battery was drained. We've just put the charged one in and starting again.'

'Reginald, it's Marcy. Do you want Camomile or Darjeeling? We've got both.'

'Can you tell her I would like Camomile please?'

'He said he wants Camomile,' I transmit.

Charlie and Reginald chat quietly while I rest in the shade and listen to the others filing back from the barn and shed. It's only afternoon and we're on track for a bloody good result today. I think ahead to Stenbury and although I don't know the layout or the numbers I feel comfortably confident that we'll win. We've got Dave, Clarence and Paula to plan and the rest of us to execute. Reginald is coming into his own and Charlie is great the way she watches and questions things thereby making us think.

In my head a plan is already forming. Of me and Dave walking into the town side by side as cocky as you like and chopping a few down before appearing to become overwhelmed and dropping back to a firing line. If we get the width right and prevent them flanking us we'll be able to cut hundreds down within a few minutes before another tactical retreat that looks like we're falling back under pressure.

We'll lead them back through that tiny village and find another pinch point to use as a firing line then back down the country roads to Flitcombe and through the industrial estates or whatever those three sections are. With luck we'll find gas bottles and trucks, fuel and an electric supply from generators and some barbed wire. Dave can cook up some nasty bombs with a few basic ingredients. Proper guerrilla tactics. Hit and run and wither them down as we go. Ammunition we've got lots off. Grenades too and if the worse comes to the worse we'll tell Dave they all called him a twat.

Then what? Get through today first then find somewhere for the night to rest and worry about everything else later. One day at a time.

'Mr Howie, the drone is ready.'

'Thanks, Charlie. We'll wait for the others.'

'We're here,' Clarence says looming over me.

'Paula and Marcy are still brewing up,' I say.

'Fair enough.'

I stand up and yawn with a big stretch and stare idly at Reginald at his desk in the van, 'you okay, mate?'

'Pardon?' He says looking round quickly, 'are you talking to me?'

'I am, you okay?'

'I am fine, Mr Howie.'

'Seems to be going well so far today.'

'Indeed, yes. Yes so far it appears to be working. Perhaps after this victory we should give consideration to the next course of action.'

'Yep, worry about that tonight. Let's get through today first.'

'Yes of course.'

'Aye up chuckies,' Cookey says, 'there are two beautiful women walking towards us.'

'Eh?' I turn back to see Marcy and Paula carrying trays of mugs from the farmhouse, 'coffee...coffee...coffee,' I stride towards Marcy staring at the tray in her hands, 'any?' I ask.

'Just wait and let me put them down.'

'Nah can't wait...any?'

'Howie, just hang on a second,' she says moving out of my reach. I follow close behind her muttering the word coffee over and over.

'Reggie, your tea is here,' she says carefully lowering the tray down ono the ledge at the back of Roy's van.

'Coffee...which one?'

'For the love of...yes this is yours...' she says handing me a mug.

'Cheers,' I grasp the mug, offer a grin and move away passing Nick holding a cigarette out for me. 'Righto my chaps, we launching the drone then?'

'Let Charlie have her coffee first,' Paula says giving me a reproving stare.

'Can I do it?' Marcy asks, 'Nick? Will you show me how?'

'Sure,' Nick says.

'Can I do the camera?' Cookey asks.

'You going to mess about?' I ask.

'If I say no can I do it?'

'Go on then but don't piss about and drain the battery.'

'I promise.'

'Seriously, Cookey,' Nick says, 'the batteries take ages to charge.'

'I said I promise. I'll be proper serious. Reginald?' He says getting into the van, 'will you show me how to do it?'

'You have permission from Mr Howie?'

'He just said I could.'

'I was not listening. I was drinking Camomile tea.'

'Oh. Is it nice?'

'Yes it is very nice.'

'What's it do?'

'Soothes my mind.'

'Oh. Does your mind need soothing then?'

'Yes. I have a troubled mind at the best of times.'

'Wanking is good for that.'

'Alex!'

'Alex!'

'Cookey!'

'What? I was just saying.'

'Such a dick,' Blowers snorts turning away to laugh quietly, 'wanking...'

'It is,' Cookey protests, 'like scientists said so and everything.'

'It is actually,' Roy says seriously which just sets Blowers off even more. 'Ejaculation releases endorphins into the body which... are you okay, Blowers?'

'Fine,' he gasps bending forward trying to keep his coffee from spilling.

'Does it work for women?' Blinky asks.

'I don't know but, but well I should think it probably does,' Roy says thoughtfully.

'Yes it does,' Marcy says staring down at the controls in her hands, 'this looks really complicated...what?' She asks looking up to everyone staring at her, 'it does look complicated.'

'Cookey close your mouth, lad, you're almost dribbling,' Clarence mutters.

'Roger,' he says snapping back to the present, 'what am I doing in here?'

'Camera, drone,' I say trying to rid the image in my own mind as much as everyone else.

'Ah yeah, Reggie? That okay?'

'Not if you call me Reggie.'

'Sorry, Reginald.'

'Thank you and yes, sit down and please do not move the maps.'

'Nick? Charlie?' Marcy asks, 'what do I do?'

They explain the controls going through each button and stick while Reginald does the same to Cookey.

'Move to the back of the van so you can hear Cookey and Reginald,' Nick says guiding her over, 'okay, press that and you'll hear the motor rising...'

The drone starts to whir with all four propellers spinning to life then it shoots up a few inches and drops down with a clatter.

'It's okay,' Charlie says, 'the legs can absorb the landing,' she adds with a quick smile at Nick, 'try again.'

'Gently now,' Nick says, 'ease it straight up. That's it...keep going...keep going....Reginald? You should have vision now.'

'Eye in the sky is live,' Cookey says then adds quickly, 'that wasn't pissing about...sorry yes we have visual feed, Nick.'

'You can hold it in one place now,' Nick explains, 'just maintain the height but don't touch the direction stick.'

'Wow,' Marcy says staring up at the drone buzzing like a big angry insect a few metres above our heads, 'I'm flying it...'

'Yep, Cookey...have a go at the camera before we move off,' Nick says, 'Marcy just try and hold it still.'

I turn round to see Cookey holding the other controller and being watched closely by Reginald.

'Rotate the camera down,' Reginald says, 'the focus is automatic.'

'Yep got it,' Cookey says focussing hard.

I watch the feed going from open sky to the brown earth of the ground as Cookey turns the camera down then zooms in too much. He pulls back gently as the drone starts a gentle glide before holding static again as they both learn the deft touches.

'What's that?' Cookey asks peering at the black and brown blurs on the screen.

'Zoom out,' Reginald says.

The camera pans back with tiny increments until Marcy's shoulder comes into view with the black of her top contrasting against her tanned skin, 'fuck me,' Cookey says, 'this camera is awesome...have you seen the detail?'

'What are you looking at?' Nick asks.

'Marcy's arm...you can see the hairs and everything.'

'Really?' Marcy asks turning to watch the screen in the van, 'is that my arm?'

'Yeah your er...right arm? Yes your right arm,' Cookey says.

'Hang on,' Marcy says, 'how do I lower it?'

'With this stick, gently pull it down...you can hear the motor changing pitch as it drops.'

'Okay,' Marcy whispers staring up at the drone and working with gentle touches to drop it down lower towards the earth. With the drone a few feet above her head she eases the direction making it move away a foot or two before bringing it down lower first to head height then lower again until she's facing it. 'Try it now,' she says to Cookey grinning widely, 'how do I look?'

'You are so vain,' I laugh finally realising what she was trying to do.

'Oh wow,' she says staring into the van at the screen filled with her own face, 'zoom in on my eyes...bit more...oh look,' she says happily, 'the red is nearly all gone now,' she blinks at the camera focussing in on her eye. 'Okay, that's filled my narcissistic need for now. Up we go.'

The drone shoots into the sky whirring loudly as Cookey works to pan out and show everyone in the group all staring up.

'Which way?' Marcy asks.

'North,' Reginald says.

'Doesn't help.'

'That way.'

'Again, Reggie that does not help.'

'That way,' Nick says pointing north, 'and er, you don't have to watch it all the time...I mean it's in the air so...'

'It is my first time and I wish to do it properly.'

'Yep,' Nick nods sucking air in while motioning at Charlie to say something.

'Marcy you will lose sight in a minute,' Charlie says in that ever so polite way, 'at which point you will have to use the screen to observe your direction.'

'Okay,' Marcy says turning quickly and nodding at Reginald before fixing her eyes on the screen, 'stop shaking your head, Reggie. I can see you doing it.'

'Reginald,' he mutters rolling his eyes instead.

'Reginald, commentary,' Clarence says as we start climbing into the van to stand closer to the screen and getting tuts and huffs from Marcy as we block her view.

'Indeed,' Reginald says spinning round on his chair to look down at the map then back up at the screen. 'Ah yes, yes indeed. Marcy can you see that main road?'

'On the left?'

'Yes. That is the main road into Stenbury. Follow that road but...'

'Don't go right above it,' Roy says interrupting.

'I was about to say that,' Reginald says.

'And don't drop down too much either.'

'Cheers, Roy,' Marcy mutters gliding the drone through the air.

'A roundabout should come into view any second. This will be large with three main roads feeding into it. Our road comes from the south and the others lead east and west. The exit road runs north and directly into Stenbury High Street which is a one way system designed to allow vehicular traffic through the main...'

'Too fast, Reggie,' Marcy says staring at the screen, 'roundabout?'

'Yes, indeed that is the aforesaid roundabout. See the main road you are following runs south to north and there we can see the roads...'

'Yes I can see the bloody roads.'

'These are important,' Reginald says bristling at the sharp tone, 'they both connect to side roads leading into the main town centre and effectively form a dual ring road of sorts. This is something we need to know.'

'Okay. Sorry.'

'Over the roundabout and we go into Stenbury High Street. Note the first building on the left, this square edifice here,' Reginald taps the screen with the end of his pen at a squat looking grey building with long white antennas on the roof. 'This is Stenbury police station, hold the drone still please, Marcy. Thank you. I should imagine it holds an armoury as my research tends to suggest Stenbury is the main town for this county therefore it might be feasible for the police armed response units to deploy from this central location.'

'Fuck me, Reginald,' I say in awe, 'where did all this come from?'

'Excuse me, Mr Howie,' Reginald says in apology for not answering, 'opposite the police station is the fire station and again one could surmise that in addition to the general pump appliances they may also have possession of an extendable ladder in case you are in need of height.'

'Reginald,' Clarence says widening his eyes, 'this is fantastic.'

'Well done, Reginald,' Blowers says respectfully.

'Fucking brilliant,' Nick adds quickly.

'Indeed,' Reginald says shifting uncomfortably at the praise, 'the High Street is a straight road through with various retail and commercial outlets bordering the road and as you can see the main road is very wide with ample parking spaces either side. This may create issues if you were considering a pinch point tactic or narrowing of the enemy forces if we were to draw them back down this main road towards the roundabout.'

'Saying that,' Paula says, 'where are they?'

'There is a large public square in the centre which we shall come to in a moment. Move on please, Marcy. This building here is the post office,' he says tapping the screen at the bird's eye view of the deserted High Street as the drone glides on. 'Post offices and banks have secure areas which may be something to keep in mind should one be in need of a secure area.'

I listen intently as he reels off shops and stores, highlighting a café that should hold stocks of water or at least running water. The man is in his element and transformed from the nervous bag of bones twitching and wailing at every bump and bang. Clarence flicks his eyebrows up when I glance over and I catch sight of Blowers gently shaking his head in disbelief at the way Reginald shows just how much thought he's put into this.

'Now,' Reginald says bringing my attention back to him, 'the main road we're following runs north going through to the end of town and into the industrial and business districts. However, please note the crossroads just coming into view. The road running east to west is also part of the town centre and I would suggest this crossroads *is* the centre point of the town's shopping and retail zone. To the left is the public square complete with a fountain, war memorial and various benches. To the right are more stores and that road to the right runs, through a circuitous route to join with the main road connecting with the roundabout. Do you understand?'

'So let me get this right,' I say, 'the road north is the main road through and the crossroads connect to both of the main east and west roads that join the roundabout? Right?'

'Yes. You are correct. You can see how this is important because it allows the other player to flank you should you get drawn into the town too deeply.'

'Still can't see any infected,' Paula says.

'They will be within nearly every building we have viewed so far,' Reginald says, 'hidden and out of sight and I will estimate we will see a sizeable force within the public square intended to lure you in before those secreted within the buildings can enclose you.'

'That's the trap then,' Clarence says, 'we'd get into the town and think it empty before finding them in the square...at which point we'd get flanked and circled.'

'Clever fuckers,' I say quietly.

'Not yet, Mr Howie but given time they certainly will be,' Reginald says seriously.

'Marcy, please go left so we can gain a view of the public square.'

The town looks gorgeous and serene with a blend of old style Victorian architecture mingled with modern facades of High Street retails stores. With the sun shining it looks picturesque, like something you'd see on a television advert. We watch chimney stacks glide beneath the camera and the dizzying multiple roof patterns of slopes and diagonals from the buildings being enlarged and developed over the years.

'Movement,' Nick snaps the word out bringing our attention back to the intersection below the drone and two children running hell for leather from the direction of the square. An older boy maybe twelve or thirteen and a younger girl that can't be older than six and she clutches his hand as he drags her sprinting down the road. The way they run, the movement and panicked manner of legs pumping and arms flailing and we instantly recognise them as people. A man runs into view several metres behind them and even from the distance of the drone above them we can see him yelling to the children and motioning with his arm for them to run. Panic etched on his face then movement behind me as several undead surge into the shot after the man. He tries running, pumping his arms and legs while glancing behind him to the four or five infected chasing. He shouts again to the children and as one we hold our breaths in the van. Not a word is spoken but we lean closer, edging towards the screen. The little girl cries out trying to break away from the boy and fighting to turn back to the adult male. The boy jerks her on shouting at her with soundless words that we cannot hear. The man shouts again, waving for them with desperation in his face but he knows they're too fast. At the last second he stops and turns running back into the infected.

'Oh fuck,' I gasp watching as he barrels into the first two sending them sprawling with what must be the bravest thing I ever seen. He takes them down hard but the other three react quickly and dive onto his body. Legs thrashing and arms hitting out while he fights to keep them busy. Mouths sink into his flesh, biting his legs, arms, hands and face. That he screams is obvious.

'Run...' Clarence whispers watching the children, 'run...RUN...'

'Oh no no no,' Paula covers her own mouth with her hand as several more undead sprint past the murder being wrought on the ground. Four, then five, six and more that surge into view until a dozen are sprinting flat out towards the children still running down the centre of the road.

My heart ramps with increasing beats per minute. My fists

clenching so hard my nails dig into the wounds across my palms where Dave cut them.

'Please...' Clarence begs, 'just run...'

It's too late. The boy might have stood a better chance but trying to drag the girl and they don't stand a chance against the pumped up infected adults that close the distance no doubt screaming in primeval blood lust.

'Fuck,' Clarence, despite the fights we've been in, the blood we've spilled and the death we've given, snaps his head round away from the screen with pain etched into face as the infected swarm the children tearing them apart with a frenzy I have never seen before. They don't even try and infect them and preserve the body but act like wild animals fighting over a fresh kill to be eaten.

Tears fill my eyes and my breath comes faster and harder. My jaw clenched and I cannot speak, cannot talk, cannot react.

The drone moves on. Gliding silently over the square swarming with infected raging in motion. I expected them to be still and waiting but they're not. They're pumped and running with snarls and absolute lust warping their features.

The square is bordered on the sides by buildings. The base of which are all retail or food places. On the fourth side is the road and more buildings on the other side.

'There,' Paula shouts pointing at the screen. I scan the view trying to make sense before seeing a determined movement as several undead turn on the spot catching sight of an adult woman sprinting from a doorway. Red hair flying wild as she runs as fast as she can but she's panicked and wild, paying no heed to her direction. They close in from all sides forcing her to try and veer and weave and it's like watching a sport. Like an American football player running with the ball trying to dodge the opposing team members who lunge and dive. She's taken from the front while looking to the side. A heavy built male slamming into her with such force she bounces back sagging with the wind driven from her lungs. Again they swarm descending like hyenas for the kill and the light grey paving beneath her runs red from the blood coursing from her flesh bitten away.

'Look,' someone in the van shouts. I don't know who for my mind races with the sight I'm seeing. A man running from a doorway turning hard right and going down the building line with several hundred infected instantly snapping about and starting after him. He sprints hard then a sharp left and he slams into a red doorway to the side of a shoe shop hammering his fists on the wood. The door opens and he falls in before it's slammed shut as the infected reach the spot and start throwing themselves against the door.

'Marcy, give me the controller,' Nick reaches past me taking the controller from her hands, 'Cookey, 'I'm lowering...get the camera on the building line where the bloke went in.'

'Got it,' Cookey breathes the words out as Nick glides the drone lower towards the mayhem unfolding below the drone.

The camera tilts, swivelling to gain a view of the red door then working up towards the windows on the first floor.

'People,' Blowers says at the sight of a man edging closer to the window from inside the room. He peers out, tentative and grimacing at what he can see below. He backs away saying something into the room behind him. Figures moving, more men coming into view. A woman holding a baby walks in and gets waved to go back. Cookey zooms in giving us a fleeting but clear view of the terror on her face as she clutches the baby closer to her breast and the large kitchen knife held in her hand.

'Go along,' Nick says pushing the drone deeper into the square. Cookey pans out showing the large stone blocks of the building until we see the first bay window of the next building and more people inside the room. Men women and children. The adults showing signs of intense stress with some holding their hands to their heads while others sob clearly. Children are held tight or stand-alone crying with fear.

'We gotta go in,' Clarence gasps turning his great head to glare at me.

'Get ready, we're moving in thirty seconds. Reginald, stay here with the drone...Paula, Marcy and Charlie...'

'I can fire a gun I'm coming,' Paula snaps.

'Me too,' Marcy says swallowing.

'Everyone move now,' I say as they start dropping down from the back of the van. 'Bags loaded with ammunition. Hand weapons ready...Nick, take Clarence's axe, Blinky take Nick's axe....Charlie...'

'I've got my stick,' she says rushing towards the Saxon.

'Stick?'

'Hockey stick...'

'That's no good. Lads, get into that farmhouse find weapons.'

'On it,' Blowers sets off sprinting with Nick, Cookey and Mo on his heels.

'Clarence?'

'I'll find something,' he shouts racing off towards the sheds and outbuildings.

'Mr Howie,' Reginald calls me from inside the van.

'What?' I get the back and peer in to see him still glued to the screen.

'There are too many,' he says, rushing the words out, 'far too many.'

'No choice. Dave, I want you on the GPMG as we go in.'

'There are simply too many,' Reginald blurts, 'the town could hold thousands.'

'Reginald,' I snap facing back into the van, 'we're going in and that's it. You will stay here and keep that drone up. Find us somewhere to take the survivors.'

'It cannot be done. There are too many, Mr Howie. Please, I implore you to listen to sense. Those survivors are already dead...'

'Not yet they ain't. Paula, can you fire the GPMG?'

'Never done it but I will.'

'Soon as we get in take over from Dave...Dave, show Paula and Charlie how to reload it now. Be quick. *Lads, Clarence...find a sledgehammer we can use to beat the walls down between the buildings...*'

'Oh gosh, Mr Howie...please...'

'Reginald! You will stay here and find us a defensible position to take the survivors. Am I clear? EVERYONE HURRY UP WE ARE MOVING OUT NOW. Charlie, you will protect Paula on the GPMG. Can you drive?'

'I can, Mr Howie.'

'Charlie is a better shot than me, I'll drive she can shoot,' Paula shouts back.

'Fine. Be ready to drive it. *What the fuck is taking so long?*'

'*Nothing here, Boss,*' Blowers pants down the radio.

'*Axe...sledgehammer...on way back,*' Clarence snaps the words out through the radio.

'*Lads, back here now.*'

'*On way.*'

'Reginald, you've got your rifle but we can't leave anyone here with you. If it all goes wrong then get back to the fort.'

'Wrong? Oh my...'

'Reginald,' I force calmness into my voice and lock eyes on him, 'we will not leave survivors to face that lot. We've never done it. We will never do it. Search those windows, find out which buildings have got survivors in.'

'Oh gosh this is very dramatic.'

I turn round to see Meredith waiting at the back of the Saxon with ears pricked and eyes flitting in every direction as she senses the change in energy. I wish I could communicate with her and tell her to get to the survivors. Find them and protect them. Instead I head over and pour more water into her bowl knowing she'll need every drop for what we're about to do.

'Dave,' Clarence shouts running back towards the vehicles, 'need a blade on this axe.'

'Pass it,' Dave says jumping down from the back of the Saxon.

I look over to see Clarence passing him a long handled single head axe similar to the ones the lads use.

'You want your axe back now?' Nick says running back with the lads.

'Keep it,' Clarence says, 'I'll use this,' he adds hefting the sledgehammer.

Three, maybe four minutes since we came running out of the van, 'load up, we're moving out.'

CHAPTER THIRTY

I slam the door closed and start the big engine while the others cram into the back. The sweat is already pouring down our faces so we drink while we can. Passing bottles of Lucozade around to guzzle the sugary glucose. Dave's hands blurring as he scrapes the blade of the new axe to something like a scalpel.

Clarence in the front with me gripping the composite material shaft to the bloody great big sledge hammer. His knuckles white and I don't think I've ever seen him so angry. He seethes but quietly. Dangerously. Eyes fixed on the road ahead and his nostrils flaring.

One mile from the farm to the town. Only a couple of minutes but time becomes stretched with every second feeling like a minute. The image of the two children burnt into my mind and that man turning with the ultimate sacrifice giving his own life that his children may live.

This day just became sinister and my soul starts burning with incandescent rage that is pure and makes my heart race faster and that darkness that threatens to swallow me whole is now off the scale. As my hands tighten on the wheel so my right foot pushes harder forcing the Saxon to roar defiant and loud. The big engine deep and throaty as though desperate to be in amongst it now.

I clench my jaw feeling tears stinging my eyes as I see the face of the little girl and the disbelief she showed at being caught like that. The way she looked up into the faces of the demons with an expression of utter incomprehension. I press my foot harder feeling the tyres rumbling over the road surface while a tear runs down my cheek but I'll take that sorrow and turn it, use it and force it into every muscle of my body and deeper into my gut so the hatred for them builds to drive me on.

'Plan?' Blowers shouts.

'Plan?' I hesitate for a second easing the speed off to navigate the roundabout as we start the final push into the town proper, 'red door. We clear that and get inside. Dave and I will hold them off. Get everyone together and wait for Reginald to tell us where to go. Clear?'

'Yep,' Clarence nods once and firm.

'If we get separated we go back through the towns we've been through. Aim for that golf hotel or worst case the fort. Bags on. Weapons ready. We're going in.'

We scream past the roundabout and into the main road going past the squat police station building on our left and the fire station on our right. Past shops and stores with windows smashed but up close now and I can see some efforts have been made to secure some doors and entry points with wooden planks hammered in place. Spray painted symbols on doors that speak of a system developed by survivors doing the best they can until thousands of infected descended on their town. The fact we brought them here weighs heavy in my heart. That if not for us those people would not have been killed. Our vanity, our pride and thirst for death. My vanity. I did this. I made this happen with cocky arrogance that burns my cheeks in shame.

Towards the crossroads we go. Still accelerating as Clarence reaches for the mouthpiece of the public address system. He presses the button down, tapping on the plastic grill as a dull thudding sounds outside. That it's still working after everything we've done is testament to the engineering of this vehicle and the army that used it. Organically that thought whirs instantly into images of the army and soldiers while I realise that so few of us crammed into the back of a now obsolete armoured personnel carrier are all that's left. Just us. We have to clear them away and get those people out. There is no one else coming. No rescue for us. No army or police now. The desperation is profound and deep.

'Reginald...we're going in now...' I thumb the button under my shirt seeing the crossroads coming rapidly towards us.

'Mr Howie...yes I'm searching now,' Reginald's panicked voice comes back earning a sharp glance from Clarence to me. I shrug. Nothing we can do to help him now.

THE SILENCE HITS. Three minutes ago everyone was crammed into the van staring at the screen but now they're gone and the noise of the Saxon's big engine fades until all that's left is the sound of his own heart pounding.

Reginald looks round feeling suddenly vulnerable and isolated. His eyes fall on the assault rifle propped against the desk with his bag of ammunition left beside it. With one hand holding the drone steady in the air he reaches out to draw the rifle closer. Both hands on the controller but the worry builds so he pulls the rifle closer then lifts the heavy thing up to rest across his lap with the barrel pointing to the still open back doors.

The next problem presents itself. Two controllers are used for the drone. One for the drone and one for the camera. How can he operate both? He has to fly the blasted thing, gain the position and sweep the buildings for survivors then somehow find a safe route which will mean examining the maps. How long will the battery last? What if it fails? What if he makes a mistake and gets everyone killed?

He places the camera controller on the desk then quickly gets his hands back on the flight controller and curses inwardly at trying to figure out where he is. He goes higher, forcing the drone engine to increase to gain height before reaching out and trying to rotate the camera directional function on the other controller to pan down for a bird's eye view.

As that's it. The square is right below him still showing in full high definition quality. Infected swarming in what looks like every direction. Chaos and from that chaos he is expected to find order and come up with a plan? How? How can anyone look at that lot and find and sense of cohesion within it? This is absurd. Bloody ridiculous. Still, he watched with horror at the two children being killed and despite having seen the same thing many times before under the power of Marcy he still feels the incredible shock and innate sadness of such an awful tragedy. It was different back then. The infection that held his mind desensitised him to those horrors and took away the personal connection to what pain and suffering are but now he felt it. He saw it and felt it. Not just the fear for himself either or his own disgust at seeing such gore but the unfairness of it. The loss of life of two so young and innocent. That's it. The innocence. There must be an opposite though. In order to feel happy one must know sadness. To know innocence is to have guilt in the world so the infection is that guilt. It carries that guilt for doing what it is.

An intelligent man and those thoughts pour through his mind in a matter of seconds until he reaches the conclusion that he must do what he can. After all, he is relatively safe here and not crammed into the back of the Saxon going into a battle they cannot hope to win. Or can they? Is it about winning now or about surviving? Get the survivors and get out. That's the objective.

He stares harder at the screen. Resolute and determined not be outwitted by a crass infection still mastering the ability to form words.

There is always a method. In chaos there is always order for nothing is ever truly random. Isn't that the point in principle for this day? Therefore if nothing can ever be random then those infected must be running for a reason. He looks harder trying to find sense in the lines and groups sprinting in all directions within the square but feeling the urgency to be searching the buildings and seeking survivors.

No. These infected will show him the survivors. Of course! Closer again he leans towards the screen staring and seeing the order taking shape. Each door is a point of entry and towards those doors the infected run but they don't run to the closest but somehow groups within the mass all go towards one location while others run past them towards yet another. Yes. Groups within groups. Like Blowers leading his team within the larger team under the direction of Mr Howie.

The doors then. The points of entry. He examines the thickest parts of the dense crowds realising there are set distances between the nucleus of the densest part of each section. They gather thick at the door pushing in. Stragglers hanging back almost as though waiting for runners. Then a short distance down and again a thick nucleus heaving towards the doors.

Each nucleus must represent where the survivors are. He guides the stick back on the controller gaining height to see the whole length of the building line running the side of the road bordering the square and infected running towards each door.

Time is precious so method must be applied. He must start at one end and go along the whole building checking each window. Yes. One sweep along on the first floor then up to the second floor and back down.

He banks the drone to the side gliding it along the building line towards the crossroads and the first building. He has to reduce height now which means adjusting the camera but reducing height while changing direction requires two hands. Gosh, this is hard. He drops the height first bringing the drone to a hover before reaching out and trying to tilt the camera but the drone drops a few feet plunging too close to the infected below. With a snort he pulls up, overcompensating and shooting too high into the air and losing his sense of placement as the camera is now swivelled up too much and is facing the sky.

The Saxon will be there any second. He must hurry. He snatches a breath and pans the camera down again before moving his hands back to the drone controller and starting the drop back down to first floor. He goes a few feet then a camera adjustment. A few more feet and another camera adjustment but it's taking too long and the pressure builds as the sweat beads to fall down his face.

'Hello?'

Reginald screams out spinning in his chair as he snatches the rifle from his lap. A man at the back door lurching away into the front of a horse stood a few feet behind him. The horse snorts and tosses its great head sending the man back towards the van as Reginald screams again.

Neal Barrett had followed the road from Flitcombe seeing the signposts for Stenbury and dreading finding the larger town and the inevitable death within it. From his last diary entry in Flitcombe he had felt the urgency within Jess to keep moving. If she was exhausted from the great distance and the awful heat she didn't show it. She sweated and drank water but kept pushing on. Even when he tried to slow down and ease the pace, part in need of rest and also because of the building fear at what they will find she ignored him and kept on and if anything her pace got faster.

The sound of an engine then greeted them. Something big and throaty that was increasing in speed. He followed the noise down the main road and tried correcting Jess when she started to veer towards the farm track but she was having none of it. She was going up that track and nothing he could, short of shooting her, would change her mind.

They got closer to the farmhouse until he finally slipped from the back of Jess and started walking steadily into the open parking area, pausing on sight of the armoured van. Edging closer he strained to listen while scared witless at what he will see. Jess again pushed on, impatient and annoyed at going so slow. She nosed his back, lurching him closer with heavy snorts until he reached the back door and clapped eyes on the man wearing glasses staring at a monitor on the desk.

As Reginald lifted the rifle in panic so Neal tried running backwards but again Jess had other ideas and with a firm shove of her nose she sent him back towards the van while he scrabbled to bring his own assault rifle round on the sling. Both Reginald and Neal gibbering and yelping at the sight of the other wrestling with an automatic rifle. Both of them panicked and fumbling. Neal not having the presence of mind to go left or right but repeatedly trying to go backwards and getting pushed forward. Reginald trying to heft the rifle and seeing a terrified man running forward and backwards while shouting out. A few seconds and both of them hold rifles aimed and shaking with the barrels wavering round in circles.

'Who are you?' Reginald squeaks rushing his words out.

'Don't shoot me...don't shoot me...' Neal gasps closing his eyes in fear then remembering he has to open them to see where he is firing.

'Who are you?' Reginald says again, his voice high pitched and terrified.

'Neal!' Neal Barrett shouts matching the other for tone and pitch, 'don't shoot me...I'm a scientist...'

'A scientist?' Reginald squawks.

'A scientist,' Neal squawks back, 'don't shoot me...I won't shoot you...'

'You won't shoot me?'

'I won't shoot you please don't shoot me.'

'I don't want to shoot you.'

'I don't want to shoot you either...'

'A scientist?' Reginald asks again.

'Yes!'

'And you won't shoot me?'

'I don't want to shoot anyone,' Neal says still rushing his words out, 'oh God, Jess...stop pushing me...'

'Gosh...eyes! I think I need to see your eyes...no, I know I need to see your eyes because....because the infected have bloodshot eyes and...'

'I know! I'm a scientist...'

'Yes yes, you did say...er...may I see your eyes.'

'Yes,' Neal says twitching as though wanting to move forward but feeling the need to run away, 'er...so...I have to come closer?'

'Yes...come closer.'

'But...your gun is pointing at me.'

'Oh I am so dreadfully sorry,' Reginald says automatically and lowering the rifle before realising the other man still has his raised so lifts his back up.

'Oh God don't shoot me,' Neal yelps seeing the other man lift his rifle back up.

'I won't but...yours is still up.'

'Mine is up because yours is up.'

'You go first then.'

'Me? You'll shoot me.'

'Gosh no,' Reginald says feeling a rush of sense permeating his head with an instant recall of the task he was meant to be doing and with another yelp he drops the rifle and rushes back to the drone gliding gracefully down through the sky towards the infected in the square. He jabs the stick once again forcing the drone to go back up.

Neal stands frozen staring in confusion at the other man dropping his rifle and rushing back to his desk. He goes to move then stops, twitching and about to say something but then seeing the other man suddenly becoming very focussed and feeling an idiotic reluctance to disturb him.

'*Reginald...we're going in now...*'

'Oh gosh...' Reginald says snatching the radio up, '*Mr Howie... yes I'm searching now...*oh my, oh my they're almost there...I can't do the camera and the drone...gosh...'

'Drone?' Neal asks finally lowering his M4 assault rifle with the folding stock.

'Ah yes, Reginald shouts turning towards the back door at the man, 'Scientist...can you operate a drone?'

'A drone?'

'Yes a drone?'

'What drone?'

'This drone. It has two controllers,' Reginald says holding both of them up then cursing again as he struggles to hold the stick steady and therefore keep the drone hovering, 'I cannot do both controllers. Mr Howie left me here but I cannot do both controllers.'

'A drone?' Neal says again shaking his head.

'Oh my yes, indeed...you see the drone has to go to the first floor windows to find which buildings have survivors so Mr Howie can find them...but I can't operate the camera and get the drone in position *and* study the maps *and* find a safe exit route all at the same time! Really I can't. I wish I could but I cannot. Oh my this is catastrophic,' Reginald flops back down into the seat setting the controllers down before going back to operating the drone and taking it down towards the windows. 'Do forgive me for ignoring you but many lives are at stake and...'

'May I come in?' Neal asks tentatively still twitching as though ready to flee but slowly understanding that something important is happening.

'Yes. Yes do,' Reginald says struggling to adjust the camera angle, 'this is...DAMN AND BLAST...right, you must come here and take this,' Reginald says ordering Neal into the van who responds by stepping up and walking slowly forward towards the controller being held out. 'Quickly now,' Reginald snaps, 'take it, man. Watch the screen.'

Reginald shoves the controller into Neal's hands and sinks back down into his chair, 'I operate the drone...'

'Oh my god!' Neal sputters staring in shock at the screen and the mass of infected raging within the square, 'where is that?'

'Stenbury. I don't have time to explain. There are survivors in these buildings,' Reginald says quickly tapping the screen, 'Mr Howie is taking his team in a fools attempt at rescuing them...'

'There's bloody hundreds...'

'Thousands. Not hundreds. Tilt the camera...'

'But...oh my...what...'

'Tilt the blasted camera,' Reginald shouts, 'too high...bring it down...gentle movements on the stick.'

Neal flusters pushing the stick on the controller too hard sending the camera panning up into the sky then back down to the ground. He steps closer to the screen staring in awe at the sight and feeling the urgency shown by the other man. 'Where?'

'Up...take it up...slowly! Yes....that window,' Reginald says quickly, 'hold it on that window....now zoom in.'

'Zoom?'

'The other stick.'

'Oh, yes. I have it. Ah zoom...there are people inside,' he says blinking at the sight of terrified people inside the room seen through the window.'

'First building,' Reginald says rushing to make a note, 'I will go along to the next window...'

Neal nods feeling his heart hammering in his chest while his mind struggles to keep up with the change of events. Instead he focusses on the controller operating a camera on a drone hovering above the heads of thousands of infected host bodies.

'Second building....' Reginald jots it down, 'next one...we have to go faster now.'

'Yes of course,' Neal says with the first signs of the panic easing down. He zooms out gradually as the other man glides the drone on towards the next building until the window of the first floor comes into view. Zoom in, adjust to the left, zoom in again and there, more people inside.

'Third building....I am going up. Pan down to see them all. I think we've established the pattern now.'

'Pattern?' Neal asks.

'Yes. Pan down...zoom out. Now see the nucleus of infected clustering at each dense point?'

'Yes. Doors?'

'Yes. Entry points. They know there are survivors inside each entry point...' Reginald snatches the radio back up, '*Mr Howie....every building on that side has survivors. You must clear the front of that building line...*'

'*Yep. Clear the front...we're going in. Find a way out.*'

'*Yes working on it now....good luck...*'

Dropping the radio Reginald pulls the stick back sending the drone higher into the air opening the view of the Saxon barrelling into the crossroads and turning towards the square.

'Where are the others?' Neal asks stepping closer again.

'Others?' Reginald says darkly, 'there are no others.'

'*MR HOWIE....EVERY building on that side has survivors. You must clear the front of that building line...*'

'*Yep. Clear the front...we're going in. Find a way out.*'

'*Yes working on it now....good luck...*'

Fuck me. With the square laid out clearly in front of us we gain the first real view of the infected swarming thick and angry and numbering thousands.

'DAVE,' I shout fixing my eyes on the building line where the infected are massing at the doors. I didn't need to shout his name for the second I straighten up he starts firing with a couple of short bursts that I can only guess are for him to gain aim and distance. After that and it becomes a sight to see.

I accelerate hard aiming to mount the pavement and sweep along the front and not every shot by Dave is a headshot, but the effect is just the same. Heads exploding like melons hit by bats. Pink mist after pink mist and scores are gunned down with that solid drumming beat of the heavy machine gun so reassuring and solid.

We bounce up the kerb with the big wheels absorbing the bump and I steer over to just inches from the front of the building line. At once the direction of the infected changes from attacking in towards the doors to facing and charging at us. Thousands and they less than human with every fight we greet them in. Animals or aliens or something horrific, warped and disgusting.

Graceful sweeps by Dave cut them down as he holds the aim at the average head height. Dozens killed instantly and more blown back off their feet as the heavy rounds strafe through their bodies.

Clarence braces. Extending both his hands to push hard against the dashboard while shouting for everyone else to do the same. Faster now and the Saxon builds with power that closes that distance until we slam into the first dense pocket running towards us. Destruction is given instant and messy. The Saxon bucking over the bodies that get mangled under the wheels and more slammed aside or killed by the solid metal sides hammering into them. On we go deeper into the hordes as I snarl through the bloodied windscreen at them. I can hear them now too. A primeval screeching howl emitted by thousands of voices that works to compete with the machine gun firing above us.

A twitch of a change and instead of charging without focus they switch to charging and then launching themselves at the wheels in an attempt to either ground us out or jam the wheels up. They've done this before and it almost worked but their numbers were nowhere near what they have now. They can afford to sacrifice hundreds at a time and still have so many left.

On they come faster and harder as we sweep down battering them away from the front of the buildings. The sides ping from the impacts as they swarm in greater numbers towards the passenger side desperately trying to use sheer weight of bodies to grind the Saxon into the wall. I can feel the pressure being applied and just see a blur of bodies coming in so fast I can't do anything but try and hold a straight line. Corrections on the steering wheel forcing the Saxon out from the wall but still the engine roars and we sweep them away with brutal efficiency to burst clear on the far side and I turn hard easing the power off and coming round in a wide circle as Dave twists on the gun to keep firing into heads that pop and explode.

Straightened up now and I go for another run but hold a course just away from the building line and build the power back up accelerating hard but even I can see they've rallied and become too dense to get through. I steer right aiming to the edge and they follow suit to surge into my path. I steer harder right but they keep rushing over. Hitting bodies again now and I ease power, turn hard left and slam my foot back down forcing a path through the incredibly thick hordes.

Meredith barking like crazy. Clarence still pushing his hands against the front and Dave firing controlled bursts. We kill so many but what we gain is insignificant in terms of what they have. We carve another path following a veering snaking route through the square and wrenching a solid metal bench from its fixtures that gets pinned to the front and acts like a bladed scoop that snaps legs with ease.

'GO ON,' Clarence booms slamming a hand down urging me to punch on. The longer we can keep this up the more the vehicle and Dave can kill and the more time we buy for Reginald to find us a way out.

We snake, power on, turn hard left then hard right but they get organised and again start coming in with frightening power slamming into the sides so hard one after the other that it affects the steerage. They come again for the front diving head first and bodily into the front wheels. At one point the Saxon loses grip as the front passenger wheel is taken from the ground from the press of bodies but I steer hard the other way and with my foot down to the floor we grind out and away. This time I aim for the crossroads and the chance of any empty road. Everywhere I look more are pouring from buildings into the streets. Heads bursting apart but not enough. I gain the crossroads punching free of the dense packed hordes and driving down then slowing to start the turn in the road. About face we come until we're aimed back at the square.

'Be ready,' I shout knowing this is the last run before the Saxon gets grounded out.

'You can't leave Paula and Charlie in here against this lot,' Clarence says as I start accelerating back towards the square.

'Yep, agreed.'

'Hear that?' Clarence says twisting round, 'Charlie and Paula with us...Dave get that GPMG down...'

'Barrel is too hot,' Dave shouts, 'it cannot be touched.'

'Bollocks,' Clarence curses, 'lads get some water up to Dave, cool that barrel and find some thick rags to hold it with.'

'No time,' I shout.

'Make time, we need it.'

'Easier said than done, mate.'

NEAL STARES dumbly at the screen watching the swathes of infected being killed by the army vehicle ploughing crazily along the building line. His own mind trying to make sense of the things he is seeing. Driving into such a thing is the first thought in his mind. How brave does someone have to be to do that? But it punches through killing so many but the sight that holds him frozen with his mouth gaping is the small man firing the machine gun on top the vehicle. It took Neal a few seconds to make sense of what he was seeing. Pink explosions puffing silently into the air one after the other until suddenly the penny dropped and the connection was made. That man was firing into their heads. Which is not possible. It is beyond possible. Therefore, if something is not possible then it is impossible. This is fact. This is science. But no, right there, in front of his own eyes there are heads exploding with a burst of brains, bones and blood hanging in the space where the body was before it either slumped down or flew back.

Is this it? Is this what they do? Drive into the infected and shoot them through the head? No. He saw the firing lines and the use of bladed weapons and attack dogs but that vehicle doesn't look big enough to hold scores of troops. So many thoughts mingle and merge with a sight taken in and one that evolves too quickly to keep up with.

'Exit route...exit route...' Reginald mutters, 'safe place...'

'What er,' Neal goes to speak but finds his mouth suddenly very dry. Coughing he tries again, 'what are they doing?' He asks meekly.

'Hmmm? Oh right, yes...they're clearing that building line so they can have safe ingress into it. From there they will group the survivors together and...damnation,' he says staring up at the screen and watching the formations taken by the infected persons flinging themselves at the Saxon.

The visual effect is staggering. Human bodies moving faster than thought possible with cohesion and purpose and throwing themselves in deathly sacrifice at the wheels that churn them into mangled corpses.

Neal feels his stomach heave and churn at the sight of limbs being sheered and bodies torn apart. Blood everywhere that pools thick on the ground before being stomped through by the next horde surging on.

'No no no,' Reginald mutters to himself again but knowing

deep inside there is now another person with him so falling back into the habit of verbalising his thought processes, 'see, see that...'

'See what?' Neal asks.

'The formations and methods they are using. They're too fast and charged. No no no, this will not do. The second that vehicles comes to a stop they will be swarmed. What to do? Think, Reginald, think.'

'Where, I mean, sorry. Where will they stop?'

'I should imagine I will direct them to aim for that first building, once inside they can work through to the other end but not like this. Are you seeing this? Look at the speed they are moving at. I tell you now they will swarm that vehicle the second it stops.'

'So...you...' Neal stares at the screen switching his mind to the immediate task and problem presented. Cling onto that one problem. Forget the hundreds of other things and focus on this one thing now. 'Clear them away,' he says dumbly, 'I see. The army truck will stop but you are worried the infected host bodies will swarm them *before* the soldiers get into that door?'

'Correct. They may have to draw them out before they can even attempt such a thing,' Reginald says reaching for the radio. *'Mr Howie, I am watching the formations they are using. Do not stop yet. I repeat do not stop yet. They are too many. You will get swarmed. Lead them away.'*

'Yep heard that. We're going in now.'

'Mr Howie! You cannot see what I can see. You must draw them out...Mr Howie...'

'Find a way out, Reginald. We'll get inside.'

'Oh good God the man does not listen!'

'Yeah I do and I heard that...'

'If you must go now then go for the first door. First door...'

'FIRST DOOR IT IS THEN,' I mutter darkly. We're facing the

way we need to go but reversing down the road away from the square while the lads pass bottles of water up to Dave who pours them over the barrel of the machine gun.

'He's getting it down,' Nick shouts.

'Eh?'

'The GPMG, Dave's got it down.'

'Give it to Clarence, is it loaded?'

'Yep, fresh one in.'

'Everyone ready?' I shout taking the Saxon out of reverse and bringing her to a stop, 'hard now,' I say quietly, 'hard....hear me? Hard in...get inside that first door. Fuck it, here goes,' I slam my foot down and feel the instant pull of the engine thrumming louder with increasing pitch until it's screaming out as we charge at the infected charging at us. Human matter against hard steel. Organic against man-made and fuck the lot but we mow them down with barely a jolt on the chassis. Bodies splatting with sickening squelches and the sounds of bones snapping as we gain speed aiming for the first building on the road bordering the square.

'HARD,' I shout and feel that burning energy banging to be released. It wants out. It wants carnage and destruction. It needs violence and to be satiated with the death of these foul things that we plough through like a hot knife through butter. The Saxon ramming them down and to the sides. Up the kerb and I anchor on the brakes slewing the back end in a fishtail slide that kills more infected from the momentum gained.

We come to a lurching halt with the rear doors bursting open and the sound of assault rifles firing on full automatic. Clarence heaves the GPMG over the seat, kicks his door open and drops down with a roar that is blotted out by the sudden drumming of the heavy machine gun fired from the hip and I'm out into the chaos and it's like being hit by a train. An overwhelming surge of infected charging with such deranged violence we instantly get pushed towards the building line. Eleven assault rifles emptying thirty round magazines and a heavy machine gun blatting through a belt of large calibre bullets but all we do is gain seconds by the bodies that fall and impede those behind. Into a circle we fall back getting pushed towards the door and there isn't time to form cohesion or a plan, there isn't time to shout orders or get organised but we fight to stay alive and the size of this force finally hits home. Meredith pinned between Nick's legs but she seems to understand now that it's not her time to fight but to wait with Nick.

Seconds into the battle and it's already desperate. We cannot change magazines fast enough. We cannot fire enough bullets. Scores are killed and gunned down but for every infected shot ten more are ready to take its place. We can't break position or even make for the doorway not ten feet behind us for fear of being over-run. All we can do is fire and fire but God only knows we've got seconds before they surge so hard we'll be annihilated.

'Dave...do something,' Paula screams as she changes magazine and once again we pin all our hopes on one small man. The GPMG expends the final rounds in the belt is dropped on the spot as Clarence pulls his rifle round to use and instantly just that fractional reduction in firepower shows as a fresh energy pulses through them.

'HOLD THEM,' Dave shouts and he's away, running low to the side and into the dense ranks where his true home of close combat is and where nothing can touch him. Again the loss of his rifle firing into the oncoming hordes shows and back we go again stepping as one with a carpet of dead bodies already stretching in front. Our shots are wild and panicked. Not aimed for head shots but hoping the sheer volume of bullets thrown will hold them back but crawlers are made and they inch towards us forcing us to divide our attention from the standing to the sliding.

'MEREDITH,' I roar knowing she can't understand, knowing there is no way of communicating our desperate need for her skills but by fuck she responds and the shock is enough to make me double take as she whips out from between Nick's legs and staying low she slaughters the crawlers with ease as the hairs on the back of my neck stand on end and a chill runs down my spine.

'WE DO NOT YIELD,' I roar changing magazine to slam a fresh one in, 'WE HOLD...'

'Charlie, change the magazine in the GPMG,' Clarence orders taking her rifle from her to fire both his and hers with ease. She drops down heaving the gun towards her while avoiding the piping hot barrel and working quickly to feed a fresh belt into it.

Something in our manner. A stiffening of resolve that shakes off the immediate shock of the ferocity of the attack and we become the thing they hate so much. A unit that works as one with every angle covered and every person holding their space with grim determination showing on their faces.

An explosion rips through a dense pocket not twenty feet away but the sheer weight of bodies between us and the sound means we have no idea of the source or reason. Then another, a huge bang that sends a ripple of percussive shockwave through the undead in front of us. A second, maybe two seconds then a third blast and they come faster until Dave appears on the opposite side of where he ran off.

With almost casual movements he bites the pin from a grenade and lobs it into the crowd then spins as ever graceful and slides into a space created and again bites a pin and lobs the bomb before slinking out of view into the ranks.

Grenades explode one after the other creating gaps and holes which in turn cause confusion. Bodies and body parts fly into the air. Bang. Bang. Bang. Blood and guts showering down as he works a line about seven ranks back knowing the human forms between him and us will protect our group from the shrapnel.

The hive mind reacts. We all see it. Hundreds of infected in our view and as one they abruptly turn and start pushing the other direction.

'They going for Dave?' Cookey shouts.

'Must be,' I say.

He snorts and changes magazine, 'good luck with that you dumb fuckers ah fuck's sake, Blinky that went on my bloody boots.'

She retches again puking down as Cookey hops away before standing upright and wiping her mouth with the back of her hand, 'don't stand so close then dickhead.'

'Door,' I say to Clarence.

'GET IN...QUICK GET IN.'

We spin round pointing our weapons at the man holding the door open who yelps and runs back in fright at our sudden explosive turn towards him.

'In, go...DAVE...'

'Coming, Mr Howie,' his dull voice sails clear and unhurried, almost relaxed as he goes about his work.

We continue firing into the backs of the infected all trying like idiots to get to the same place that Dave is at. Or that he was at. Or where they think he will be next except it doesn't work that way with Dave. With the pressure eased we aim better and with such close proximity we get clear head shots and outright kills. Paula goes first, running into the doorway with her rifle aimed and sweeping as the petrified man goes back further into the hallway and trips on the base of the stairs. Marcy after her as we fall back. Charlie heaving the heavy machine gun up and running back with Blinky. One by one we get through until just Clarence and I remain outside.

'DAVE...NOW...' I hold my aim and shout while scouring the ranks for a glimpse of him.

'Yes, Mr Howie,' he says softly from my immediate right as he walks smartly between Clarence and me through the door.

'Gotta love him,' Clarence mutters rolling his eyes.

NEAL WATCHES the Saxon slew to a stop then the small group burst from the doors already firing into the infected host bodies.

His heart in his mouth and despite being one mile away sat in a van in a peaceful location outside a farmhouse he feels a release of adrenalin, fear, terror, hope and utter shock all mingling into one incredible rush of emotions that renders him mute and unable to do anything other than gawp.

'Gosh,' Reginald tuts disdainful with a dramatic roll of his eyes, 'really they do not listen. I said this would happen. I really did. It is exactly as I predicted but do they listen? No they do not. Now what will they do? I ask you? Hmmm? What are they going to do now?'

'They'll be killed,' Neal whispers unable to draw his eyes from the small group now holding a tight horseshoe shape with their backs towards the buildings. The drone shows perfect clarity but no sound so without the explosive bangs of the assault rifles and the heavy thud of the GPMG he has but one sense to view them in and his eyes work hard to take it all in. Instantly he spots a giant of a man standing with legs planted apart firing a huge machine gun one handed while clutching a sledgehammer in the other. The man is enormous with shoulders like boulders and a gleaming bald head. Not like a body builder with defined muscle but just big, very bloody big. A dark skinned young man possible Arabic in ethnicity and young too, maybe eighteen. Slight build but the expression on his face is one of utter violent intent and the way he holds the assault rifle is like watching a professional soldier. They all do it. The speed they fire, adjust aim and fire then shout something as they work with almost blurred speed to change magazines. A tall lean man standing close to a pretty woman with dark hair. A squat looking young lady mouthing what he can only assume are obscenities at the infected. Three young men, one dark haired with a stern expression and a blond haired lad beside him and the third has an enormous German Shepherd held between his legs. The dog is going back, lunging tiny motions while barking with her lips pulled up to show big teeth. Two very attractive women, one younger with a slimmer more athletic frame and the other with a fuller more curvaceous figure. Then a small man and unlike the others that all show expressions on their faces this man is flat. He shows nothing but somehow looks very calm like this is something he has done thousands of times before.

'HIM!' Neal shouts finally resting his eyes on the dark haired man he saw in the village of Finkton.

'Hmm? That's Mr Howie,' Reginald says, 'who doesn't listen to the advice I give.'

'He's immune,' Neal blurts.

'Yes indeed. They probably all are.'

'What?'

'What? They probably all are.'

'But...I mean...what?'

'Er, see the three young men stood close to each other? They are immune. In fact Nicholas only found out today which was nice for him.

'What!?'

'Oh yes, he got bit and scratched. Very alarming and I'm given to understand it was a momentary loss of focus but I should imagine he was excited at the time due to the prospect of getting into Maplin.'

'Maplin?' Neal whimpers.

'Yes, Maplin. Er, shall I point them out to you?'

'But...they're...oh my god! They're going to get killed...'

'Gosh no, they'll do something in a minute. I don't know why I get so worked up really I don't. Let me see, the big one is Clarence, very nice man but he does get somewhat cross at times. That is Paula, lovely lady but can be very patronising and she's like a mother hen to this group. That is Charlotte and Patricia who goes by the name of Blinky because, well she blinks a lot. Hockey players. Indeed, very athletic young ladies that were trialling for the England hockey team. We only met them yesterday but they seem to be fitting in very well. Charlotte in particular is highly intelligent. The four young chaps are Simon, Alex and Nick... they are known as Blowers, Cookey and er...well Nick respectively and the last one is Mohammed who prefers to be called Mo Mo. That small man is Dave. Er, gosh how to describe Dave? Well he is...he is er... well I am sure you will see for yourself momentarily. The last two are Marcy, the woman here and Mr Howie who is the leader of this band of intrepid, foolhardy, immature, caustic, sarcastic, unlistening people that collectively are, without doubt, the most stupid but also the most dangerous people in this country I should imagine. Oh and that's Meredith. She's a dog.'

'Dog.'

'Yes. A dog. Oh see here,' Reginald says pointing at the screen, 'Dave is moving off. Let's watch him shall we and you will soon see what I mean.'

It's too much. The whole of it is too much. From the bird's eye view Neal can see thousands of infected host bodies pushing and driving towards a very small group of people but somehow that small group are holding them off. How? His mind needs to understand reasoning and causality. To glance and it appears impossible but that is not the case. Thousands against a few. Thousands pressing forward. The small group holding them off. Thousands against a few. Ah yes, yes a pattern shows. The size of the numbers attacking is almost irrelevant for the front line they present to the few can only ever be of a finite size and yes, now he looks he starts to see order within the chaos. The infected that get killed drop down which in turn cause obstacles to those still coming forward.

He blanches in shock as the dog whips out from between the legs of the man holding her and starts racing between the crawlers snapping her jaws onto their throat before giving a very fast wrench and away to the next one.

'Watch Dave,' Reginald says tapping the screen lightly. Neal looks but immediately pulls an expression of puzzlement at what he is seeing. A line of falling bodies within the horde. Falling down. Yes, like dominoes falling one after the other. He leans closer seeing sprays of blood shooting into the air and catching glimpse of the small man weaving through them with a speed that defies what a person should be able to do. He goes to the army vehicle and disappears inside. Some of the infected go in after him but then fall back out just as quickly as they enter. The small man, Dave? Yes Dave. He appears at the back doors holding a bag and staring for the briefest of seconds up at the drone before dropping back down and once again weaving through the dense lines.

He zooms in operating the controller to adjust the camera as he tracks Dave and watches as the man pushes his hand into the bag, pulls something out and appears to take a bite from it before throwing it away. A few seconds later and several bodies explode up into the air.

'Ah yes,' Reginald says knowingly, 'Dave is using grenades.'

One after the other the man takes a bite, lobs the thing away and pushes on as explosions detonate holes within the horde. Confusion is created with infected trying to turn in towards the man slipping through them. Then they all turn. All of them. With precision and absolute purpose of movement they turn in to the direction of the man and start pushing towards that location. Except the man keeps moving through, round, under and over them until finally breaking free on one side and strolling towards the two left outside the building and walking between them like nothing happened.

Neal releases the breath he had been holding. Exhaling long and noisily still unable to bring his mind to accept the things he has just seen.

'Just them,' he croaks.

'Sorry, what was that?' Reginald asks feeling somewhat more confident now there is someone else more panicked and flustered than he is.

'Just them,' Neal says again nodding at the screen.

'Well yes,' Reginald says unsure of the comment, 'did you think there were more?'

Neal nods, shallow but then firmer as he recalls the scenes of carnage while following the route through the towns and villages.

'How many?' He asks still in that croaking voice.

'Fourteen of us including myself and Meredith.'

Fourteen. Immune. Some? All? One dog. Not the army. Not officers and soldiers with order and structure. Again it is not possible that so few can kill so many.

'This must be very shocking,' Reginald says staring at Neal with what he hopes is a sympathetic look, 'but I'm afraid we don't have time to delay. We must find them a way out.'

Neal blinks and draws a deep steadying inhalation of air, 'how can I help?'

I'M the last through and dive forward while Clarence slams the door closed and starts ramming the newly fitted heavy-duty bolts home and Nick hefts a big strip of iron that he clangs down into brackets bolted into the wall that form a solid bar across the door.

'Up,' I give the order as Blowers takes point and charges up the stairs with his rifle aimed and ready. We thunder up with our solid boots drumming on the wooden boards. A hard turn and we push through a doorway into the main room with the large bay window full of people cowering in fear. Men and women holding children and more coming from other rooms.

We sweep into their lives with the fury of battle in our movements and quickly assess the layout of the room. Large and open plan with a doorway leading to a kitchen area and another going into a bedroom at the back. In the hallway the stairs lead down and another set go up to the second floor.

'Everyone stay calm and do exactly as we say,' Paula comes into her own staring face to face and nodding reassuringly, 'we'll get you out but you must stay calm and listen. Is that understood?'

Nods all round. Relief mingled with terror and complete shock that renders them silent and almost witless.

'Anyone upstairs?' She asks. I watch the responses as they glance to each other still too stunned to respond.

'Nick, take Mo check the top floor. Bring any survivors down. Blowers, get everyone at that window ready to stop them coming in...'

'Coming in?' A man asks in horror backing away from the window.

'Yep, they will,' I say quickly, 'Clarence, internal wall.'

'On it,' he says striding into the hallway with the sledge-hammer gripped in his hands.

'Who is in charge here?' Paula asks.

'You are,' the man backing away from the window wails as Cookey snorts in laughter then promptly apologises at the glare sent his way from Paula.

'I think they've realised Dave isn't with them,' Blowers says peeking down.

'Drone is there,' Cookey says waving through the glass

'Reginald, we're in,' I say into my shirt while pushing the button down, 'Paula, get everyone together in the hallway.'

'Mr Howie, yes I can see Alex waving at me. How many are there?'

'Charlie, head count them.'

'Eight, Mr Howie,' she replies having already done it.

'Ooh she's quick,' Cookey quips.

'Quick as fuck,' Blowers mutters.

'Upstairs clear,' Nick says jumping the last few steps with Mo behind him, 'hi, I'm Nick,' he says politely to the terrified people being ushered into the hallway.

'Smooth, Nick,' Blowers shouts.

'Enough,' I say, 'Reginald, we've got eight in here. Clarence is going for the internal wall.'

'Understood, Mr Howie.'

'What are you doing?' The same man asks Clarence and thereby offering himself up as the spokesperson.

'Listen, mate,' I say striding over, 'Blinky, get glasses of water to everyone while we've got the chance. Bowl for the dog. Nick, Mo, find missiles to throw down...lads, get that window smashed out and shoot the fuckers while we've got the chance. Dave? You got any grenades left?'

'We should save them.'

'Yeah good idea. Right, mate. Listen in, we've got a drone outside and we saw this whole row of buildings have people inside them. Is that right?'

'Yes,' he blurts.

'Good. You been here since it began?'

'Er, yes we have. Er...we lived here, well some did and some... well some left and some others arrived but...'

'Excuse me,' Marcy says butting in politely, 'this is Mr Howie, you might have heard of him?'

Clever woman and that one question changes everything as every head snaps to look at me then at Clarence as realisation starts to dawn.

'We have,' the man says staring at me, 'you have a fort...we were thinking of going there...'

'Howie, I'll take care of this with Paula. You go...' she says nodding to the window.

I don't know why but just having that one less thing to worry about and *not* having to try and prise information from terrified people seems to take a great weight off my shoulders and with an instinctive response I lean in and plant a kiss on her cheek, 'you are bloody awesome, listen to Marcy and Paula,' I say to the man before striding off towards the window, 'righto, that sofa looks heavy...'

'Yeah no problem,' she says taken aback from the display of affection, 'er...well,' she says blowing air out through her cheeks, 'that's got me all flummoxed.'

'Huh?' The man whimpers again.

'Oh right, yes...so there are eight of you in here. That big man is Clarence, he's going to beat that wall down and we'll go through the buildings to the end.'

'Okay...yes okay. What, what should we do?'

I get to the window zoning out from the conversation between Marcy and the man and Paula in the hallway doing the same to the others.

'Starting,' Clarence booms a split second before a dull thud vibrates the walls as he starts whacking the sledgehammer into the wall.

Below us the infected certainly have realised Dave is no longer blowing them up and have turned back towards the building line and commenced the surge towards us.

'Smash these windows out,' I say and get to the sofa that I start pushing towards the window, 'get anything heavy we can launch down.'

'Boss,' Nick says opening a dark wood cabinet to reveal bottles of spirits.

'Yep, do it...but throw them deep.'

'Fuck yes,' Nick grins grabbing the first bottle, 'need rags, cloths...anything we can shove in the top.'

'You making Molotov's?' Mo asks.

'Yeah.'

'Let me,' he says taking the bottle from Nick, 'I done loads of these.'

'I bet you fucking have. Blinky, get some bedding from the bedroom.'

'What for?'

'For the...just get it.'

'Alright,' she snaps rushing into the bedroom, 'get some water, feed the dog...get some bedding...'she mutters grabbing the duvet off the bed and pulling it back into the front room, 'this do it?'

I jump away from the sound of breaking glass and turn to see Blowers, Cookey and Roy raking the windows out with their rifles.

'Charlie,' Blowers shouts amidst the craziness of everyone shouting and running about, 'where's the GPMG?'

'Out here, I'll bring it,' she runs into the room carrying the machine gun that Blowers props on the window sill and aims down.

'Mr Howie? Okay?'

'Yeah go for it.'

The gun fires up with strafing bursts slamming down into the packed hordes now raging at the bottom of the building as cloth is torn into strips and stuffed into bottle necks before being lit by Mo and carried to the window with thick black smoke coiling up.

He pauses to lean out and throws the bottle down which bursts apart with flames spreading as the alcohol ignites.

'Next,' Nick says handing him a bottle of whiskey. He slams them down spreading his shots to cause the most effect while Blowers fire into the horde.

'Mr Howie,' Roy brings my attention round to him pointing at the sofa.

'Yep,' I get over and grasp the other end. Together we lift and run it the last few steps to launch through the window snapping through the thin wooden frames. A heavy three seater Chesterfield no doubt worth a few grand but it does the job and several are taken down. We burst back into the room grabbing everything with weight and throwing it out. It doesn't do much and maybe we get a few kills but a lot more get broken legs and snapped bones which reduces the massed ability to push forward so fast.

'COMING UP,' Mo shouts launching the next bottle down. I get over and lean through to see them doing what I feared and piling by throwing themselves into mounds that get higher as they climb up.

'Clarence...we've got to move...'

'He's almost through,' Marcy says running into the room, 'survivors in every building along this line and one family opposite.'

'Fuck it,' I snarl looking over the heaving expanse of square to the buildings on the other side, 'we'll try.'

'They've been here since it began and have had little contact,' she says quickly, 'altogether there's about forty five.'

'forty five survivors?' I ask in shock.

'Children, and er...some not so able bodied too.'

'Cock it. Fucking day just gets better. Right, we'll do what we can. Fuck, they're making a pyramid,' I say leaning out to look down again, 'clever fuckers.'

'WE'RE THROUGH...'

I run from the window into the hallway to see Clarence coated in a film of dust that hangs heavy in the air and a big ragged hole beaten through the brick and plaster into the hallway of the next building.

'Fall back,' I shout, 'Blowers, bring up the rear with the...'

'Oh god why did you say that?' Clarence groans as Paula shakes her head at me and even Dave turns to offer me what is probably a withering glance for him.

Silence. Nothing. I lift my eyebrows thinking we got away with it until Cookey appears in the doorway grinning like a Cheshire cat, 'did you really just say that?'

'Well done,' Paula tuts at me.

'Boss,' Blowers says disappointedly walking past almost bouncing on the spot with happiness.

'Cookey,' I say fixing him with a glare, 'we're busy okay? Very busy.'

'Yep.'

'I know what I just said but...'

'Yep. Blowers bringing up the rear.'

'Yes I said that but...'

'You said,' he says adopting a quick thoughtful pose, 'that Blowers likes it up the rear.'

'Oh god, no I did not say that.'

'Oh okay, you said Blowers likes bringing it up the rear?'

'Almost at the top,' Nick shouts, 'and did you really have to say that? He'll be going all fucking day now.'

'Fucking yes I will,' Cookey announces promptly and proudly, 'Mr Howie said it so I can use it...for ever and ever and ever...not even Dave can tell me off.'

'Ooh pushing it,' Marcy winces, 'bit excited, Cookey.'

'Blowers pushes it. When he's doing it in the rear.'

'Fucking hell,' I groan, 'sorry, Blowers.'

'Look can we stop pissing about now?' Paula snaps.

'Blowers likes pissing...'

'Oh for fuck's sake,' Blowers sags on the spot.

'When he's at the rear.'

'Right enough, say it as we go,' I say, 'Clarence, you go through first. Blowers...er...'

'Yes, Mr Howie?' Cookey asks.

'Not you, Blowers...actually. Fucking give that gun to Cookey.'

'Eh?' Cookey says stepping away.

'That's an order. Cookey take that machine gun and bring up the rear.'

'No...Blowers does the rear...'

'Haha fuckhead,' Blowers nods smugly pushing the heavy gun into Cookey's arms.

'Touché,' Marcy says, 'nice touch there, Mr Howie.'

'Since when did you call me Mr Howie?'

'When you do smart things.'

'Not very often then,' Paula mutters then smiles sweetly, 'we'd better go...everyone through that hole,' she says urging the still cowering people to get through after Clarence.

'Dave, keep an eye on the back and stairwells.'

'Yes, Mr Howie.'

'GO GO,' Nick, Mo, Charlie and Roy all shout running

walking backwards from the room firing their weapons at the window now out of sight.

I hold off waiting for everyone else to get through and sling my rifle to my back and tug the axe free, 'Cookey, get into the next flat and be ready to fire when Dave and I drop through.'

'On it,' he snaps into work mode running past me.

'Charlie first...' I shout and pull her back to guide through the hole, 'get some water while you can. Mo, you next...get through and get some water, Mo. Roy, you next...get a drink...'

'Yes I heard you thank you.'

'Nick...ready? Run straight through me and Dave...one... two....THREE...'

He turns and runs full on across the hallway and through the hole as Dave steps smartly in front of me with a knife in each hand.

'You go through, Mr Howie.'

'Fuck that, mate,' I say stepping in beside him, 'budge over a bit you're taking all the room up.'

'I can go in there,' he says pointing a knife at the front room.

'No because then none will get through to me.'

'I can let some get through.'

'You cheeky fucker,' I say then come to focus as the doorway fills with the charging infected pouring up and over the pyramid and into the room. I nudge Dave over and step in front closest to the doorway and meet them head on with the axe swishing up to drive through the groin of a female undead that gets battered back into her comrades behind. Adjusting my grip I get ready for the next one and get yanked back by a hand pulling on my belt as Dave steps in front and takes the next two down with frenetic speed.

I stand stunned for a second not believing that just happened. Dave pulled me back so he could get in front but not angry or trying to protect me. It was play. Dave just played a trick.

'DAVE STAIRWELL,' I shout mustering some panic into my voice and instantly he leaps round towards the stairs as I take his place and slam my axe into the undead coming through cleaving down through his skull that bursts apart. I fight gloating and feeling smug at outwitting him and keep the doorway clear but they're building in numbers on the other side as more come through that window. The longer we can hold them here the more time Clarence has to beat through the next wall.

'Mr Howie...Marcy has taken her clothes off...'

'Eh?' I step back turning then cursing a second later when Dave glides past me, 'oh you sneaky shit.'

He holds position swishing his arms back and forth and spinning on the spot to gain greater momentum. Heavy thuds in my ears but not from Clarence beating the next wall down but coming from the door at the bottom of the stairs as a concerted effort is made to force it open but the heavy duty bar and bolts do their job.

I look round trying to think of what to say or use to get in front of Dave then grinning mischievously. I go through the hole to see Cookey lying prone with the GPMG aimed towards me and him grinning at our antics. I grin back and step to the side of the hole, 'Dave, we're falling back. Dave...seriously we're falling back...'

He turns quickly seeing the hallway behind him now empty and through the hole to Cookey ready with the GPMG.

'MR HOWIE?' He shouts running through the hole towards Cookey.

I time it just right and wait for the first infected to come barrelling across the hallway and through the hole before I strike hard with a blade deep in his belly that severs him almost in two. I kick him back and step out to cover the hole as Dave stops and stares back at me.

'*Howie, you're needed,*' Marcy's voice in my ear.

'Dave, did you make her say that?'

'No.'

'Promise?'

'Yes, Mr Howie.'

'*Coming,* all yours,' I say first to Marcy then to Dave and break to run across the hallway and into the door to the apartment on the other side and Cookey on the floor, 'how's the rear?' I ask quickly.

'Not funny,' he mumbles.'

'What's up? Shit!' I come to a stop in the main room so full of people. 'How many?'

'Eight from the first building and another seven in here,' Marcy says.

'Mr Howie, they're already...' Roy starts to say.

'Mr Howie, it's Reginald. Are you aware they are now building the climbing bases beneath every window?'

'Yep, got it,' I say into my shirt, 'Roy, is that what you were going to say?'

'Yes, they're fast,' he says profoundly, too profoundly and it sends a ripple of silence through the room.

'We'll be fine,' Marcy says working quickly to recover the moment, 'nothing we can't handle, right lads?'

'Reginald, have you been told how many we've got?'

'Not yet, Mr Howie.'

'Approximately forty five. We've got fifteen with us already. We're in the second building.'

'That is understood.'

'We'll need a vehicle to load them into...a bus or a coach...see if you can find one.'

'I will do my best, Mr Howie and will add that to my ever growing list of things to do.'

'Sorry, Reginald. Listen, can one of us get to the Saxon?'

'No. Absolutely not.'

'We've got to clear those bases away before they get through...' I pull my hand away from my shirt and listen to the thuds of Clarence beating the next wall down while feeling like we're about to get trapped.

WITH THE TEAM safely through the door and Neal recovering himself enough to apply thought to the problem at hand they start examining the ordnance survey maps of the town.

'What are we looking for?' Neal asks.

'A way out,' Reginald replies. 'A route we can take them down. Preferably a route that is narrow at points...'

'To create a bottleneck right?'

'That is correct. A pinch point greatly aids their ability to cull the numbers but we must also be mindful of the other player flanking them.'

'Other player?' Neal asks abruptly.

'What? Oh gosh, forgive me. It's my terminology. I was fretful you see and I felt that if I treated it like a game of wits it took some of the pressure away.'

'I see,' Neal says politely, 'that does make sense. You say you were fretful?'

'Oh very.'

'Me too.'

'Really?'

'Terrified if I may be so honest,' Neal admits.

'You may be honest and I too was most terrified,' Reginald says glancing at the scientist and starting to recognise a kindred spirit. 'Do you know how to read a map?'

'Yes I do,' Neal says recovering some pride.

Reginald nods about to say something then stopping at the sound of slurping and sucking coming from outside.

'Oh my horse,' Neal says getting to his feet, 'I do apologise, I left Jess without a thought.'

He rushes outside and over to Jess drinking water from the big bowl left for Meredith and works quickly to untie the straps and strips to lift the saddle and bridle free. A case of water left on the ground when the Saxon went off and he pulls a bottle free, twists the cap off and pours the contents over her broad back using his bare hand to sluice the sweat and grime away. More bottles get emptied into the bowl and yet more poured down her flanks, legs and neck. She seems content enough to stand in the shade drinking water.

'Sorry about that,' Neal says getting back into the van and chastising himself for leaving his assault rifle propped against the side of the desk.

'Of course,' Reginald says politely, 'I may have identified a suitable route, or at least the start of one,' he adds glancing up to the screen and reaching out to push the stick of the drone back up to increase the height for a couple of minutes allowing him to focus on the maps.

'Oh right,' Neal says pulling his chair into the desk and looking down at the map.

'Here is the last building,' Reginald says tapping a grey square section on the map, 'this is the square,' he motions to the black line marking the edges of the public square. 'There is a service road at the rear that runs this direction through these streets which appear narrow on the map until we reach this large building here and given the layout I can only think this must be a supermarket and these marking here are for the petrol station...are you okay?'

'My god can you see that?' Neal asks having glanced up at the screen and now unable to remove his eyes. 'What are they doing?'

'Oh gosh, they're building bases to climb up...see they're already through the first window and will get through the others very shortly.' He reaches for the radio thumbing the switch on the side as he brings it to his mouth. *'Mr Howie, it's Reginald. Are you aware they are now building the climbing bases beneath every window?'*

'Yep, got it.'

'What will they do?' Neal asks in a whisper.

'I do not know,' Reginald says trying to think.

'Reginald, have you been told how many we've got?'

'Not yet, Mr Howie.'

'*Approximately forty five. We've got fifteen with us already. We're in the second building.*'

'*That is understood.*'

'*We'll need a vehicle to load them into...a bus or a coach...see if you can find one.*'

'*I will do my best, Mr Howie and will add that to my ever growing list of things to do.*'

'*Sorry, Reginald. Listen, can one of us get to the Saxon?*'

'*No. Absolutely not.*'

'*We've got to clear those bases away before they get through...*'

'What's the Saxon?' Neal asks trying to keep up with the frantic turn of events.

'The army vehicle,' Reginald mutters staring at the screen, 'there must be a way to clear them away from that building line but they cannot get out to the Saxon.

'What about this vehicle?'

'Good Lord are you crazy! We cannot go into that square. We wouldn't last two minutes and this vehicle is not heavy enough. No, there must be another solution.'

'They will be through those windows in minutes,' Neal says watching the human mounds growing steadily as more climb up and fling themselves down and trying to swallow the shock of every single thing he is seeing. 'These people must survive.'

'That is what Mr Howie is trying to do but we must clear those bases or suggest a way for them to be cleared.'

'No you do no understand. Mr Howie and your group must survive. The ones that are immune anyway. They have to survive.'

'I told you they are all immune.'

'No, you said they are *probably* all immune.'

'They are immune. We do not have time to explain and go through it but please be assured I have calculated that they are *all* most likely holding immunity.'

'Then they must all survive. You have to order them to get out.'

'My dear chap. Do you think for one second that I could give such an order and it be obeyed? You do not know these people. They do not listen.'

'My friend, the infected hosts will get through those windows very soon. We cannot allow so many immune people to perish in this way...not in anyway...I do not comprehend how so many immune are together but those reasons can be gained later when it safe to do so but for now we must assist them in any way we can.'

'I understand and that is what we are doing. Now think of a way to clear those bases away from the windows.'

'They must be driven at in the same manner they did before.'

'We do not have a vehicle heavy enough for that task,' Reginald counters.

'What do we have? We need something that will propel them away, weaken the base, knock it aside...'

'I understand that,' Reginald says again, 'but short of having a water cannon which are banned on UK soil then I do not know what we can suggest.'

'Water cannon, is there a fire station?'

'Good Lord,' Reginald balks slightly offended that this strange man made the connection *and* the suggestion before he did. 'Well yes, there is a fire station that I am sure holds appliances but it is down the end of the High Street therefore completely beyond reach of even their fastest runners.'

'Then we must go,' Neal says rising to his feet.'

'What? Are you mad? I do not know how to use a fire engine and...and besides, they haven't been used for eighteen days so the batteries will be flat and...'

'No,' Neal scoffs, 'they maintain their vehicles to a very high standard. We must go. We must clear those bases.'

'I...No...Please we cannot...'

'I am scared,' Neal says quickly, 'scared out of my wits but I know those people must be saved. We must help them. We have to go right now. Shall I drive and you operate the drone? Jess will be fine here, she can rest. Does that door lead into the front?'

Reginald gibbers and balks at the idea but also knowing there isn't another suggestion or idea in his mind. Mr Howie and his team have been brave enough to go into that enemy knowing what risks were against them and this man is right, several of them are immune and most likely all of them. They must be protected or at least assisted to whatever tiny amount can be given.

Any suitable time for forming a valid argument evaporates as Neal rushed to slam the back doors closed and crosses past the desk towards the front while Reginald rushes to secure the maps and controllers.

Neal gets into the front and after a brief examination of the control he gains the understanding that this is just an ordinary van. He starts the engine dreading the thought of going anywhere near that square but also knowing what the costs would be if so many immune were killed. He is not a brave man and clearly Reginald is not either but together they must do what they can.

As the van pulls away so Jess lifts her head and watches. Content in the shade to rest for a few minutes and her body temperature is working down from the cooling water poured over her body. This day has been hard going but the pull is so strong it cannot be ignored. The pull to keep moving and follow that scent and that feeling. It is intrinsic and organic. She is intelligent but lacks conscious thought so she simply gives into the pull and sets off in a gentle trot after the van and down the track towards the main road that leads to the town.

CLARENCE SLAMS the head into the wall again and again. His huge shoulders bunching and exploding with energy while the sweat pours down his face stinging his eyes.

'Head down,' Marcy says pulling him round to pour a bottle of cold water over the top of his bald head. She wipes the sweat from his eyes quickly and efficiently. 'Want Nick or Roy to take over?'

'I'm fine.'

'Go then,' she steps back and away from the hammer being slammed again into the wall and the sounds of bricks tumbling the other side but it's hard going. Old houses built strong when only the best materials and workmanship were used with thick blocks to deaden the noise transference.

The situation is critical and everyone knows it. Cookey firing into the hordes pouring into the hole with Blowers knelt at his side feeding the belt and ready to give cover when it needs changing.

Dave at the window with Howie firing down into the infected crawling up the pyramid of human forms and Roy at the back of the room arrow nocked and ready to fire his bow should any get through. Nick and Mo making Molotovs with Blinky tearing rags up while Charlie and Paula form a guard on the petrified people cowering low against the wall in the room Clarence works.

Marcy walks back into the main room pausing to look through the hallway to Cookey and Blowers working the machine gun. She drops her bag and draws a bottle of Lucozade that's warm and flat but full of glucose. To the lads she goes dropping to a crouch and holding the bottle to Blowers' lips first and letting him guzzle the drink.

'Cheers,' he says pulling his head back, 'do Cookey.'

'I wish,' Cookey still jokes knowing the situation is becoming desperate and feels the bottle being pressed to his lips. A turn of the head and he angles to slurp it down, 'cheers, Marcy....tell Mr Howie we'll need some rifles on this section in a minute when the belt runs out.'

'Will do,' she pats him on the shoulder rising to her feet and rushing back into the room, 'Howie, the belt's almost out. They need more guns.'

'Take Charlie and go,' Howie shouts firing his rifle down.

'With you,' Charlie runs from the bedroom following Marcy back to the lads.

'This is fucking nuts,' Howie snarls the words taking a second to lean out and look down the road to the mounds growing larger and higher by the minute and the square still full to the brim of infected.

Something has to give. Something has to be done. They're already through the first window and almost at the second and only being held off by Dave and Howie firing sustained into them. The third window will only be a few more minutes then they will be pressed in on three sides plus the danger of the infected getting through the street door.

Howie grimaces trying to think of a way and knowing there must be. There is always a way but right now the hopes are diminishing as fast as the heat is rising.

'MOLOTOVS,' Mo shouts the warning joining Howie at his side and launching the bottles down at the base of the pyramid. Another one goes down thrown by Blinky and more follow as the street comes aflame with acrid smoke billowing up. The infected pass through the flames unhindered as they catch alight. They cough and retch as humans would but do not feel the pain or discomfort as humans should. Instead they push on aflame and ignited to climb up and dutifully lie down while inside the rooms of the buildings people scream and cower clutching knives and meat cleavers as they prepare to defend their loved ones against the thousands of infected that have infested their town this day.

NEAL GOES FAST. Pushing his foot and feeling the power of the diesel engine driving the wheels. A heavy vehicle but designed well and he stares ahead at the road wishing he'd had time to make a diary entry. What would he say? That he'd found the professional soldiers and not only discovered they were not professional soldiers but they were all immune and only numbered fourteen which included a dog.

No matter. They must survive but even he could see the hopeless peril they were in. Even if only one can get out it might be enough. There will be more and it will mean scouring the land searching through the list but he must try. After all, isn't this why he left the project and took refuge from the world? Isn't this the reason he turned himself into a fugitive knowing they would be hunting him? To do this. To be prepared and try and right the wrong so inflicted on this world.

In the back Reginald operates the drone holding it static in the sky while using the camera to zoom into the mounds as he tries to detect a weakness but the mounds are thickly layered at the base and only getting narrower towards the top and he gives a reluctant nod of respect to the infection for the shape it has chosen to use. Fear grips him. Downright and outright terror at what they are doing but there is a grim determination there too. That suddenly he can fend that fear off and stop it gripping him completely. Seeing Howie and Marcy and those few go into something so awful yet doing it willingly with smiling faces. Maybe some of that has rubbed off and left a mark on him or maybe deep down he knows his species is threatened and so even he, an abject coward, rises to the challenge. Well, maybe not rising to the challenge but at least not turning round and running the other direction while gibbering in fear.

Fire engines. How do they work? They hold water that must come out at volume so there must be an internal pumping system that sucks the water from the tank and drives it into the hose. He thinks hard to anytime he has seen a fire engine on the street or on television and the fact they always leave the engines running. That must provide the power to pump the water but surely there will be a complicated set of dials and buttons?

'Roundabout ahead, Reginald.'

'Go straight on, er...the fire station is on the right. You'll see the yellow cross hatching on the road in front of it.'

What about the drone! Oh gosh he frets now at the small details of what to do with the flying object. A roof. Yes land it somewhere and let it wait there. Where though? He scours the rooftops knowing they will be at the fire station any second and spots a wide gully between two gently sloping roofs. Gently now and he guides the drone over and down, dropping height as he brings the thing into land while remembering Charlie repeating Nick's words that the legs on the drone are designed to withstand impact.

'We're here,' Neal calls out bringing the van speed down, 'er, how do we get in?'

'No idea,' Reginald mutters smiling to himself as the drone is brought down safely into the gully. He powers the camera off remotely to save power and puts the drone into sleep mode.

'The doors unlocked,' Neal shouts through the open driver door that Reginald didn't realise had opened.

Reginald goes to leave rushing to the back doors before pulling up short and rushing back to grab the two assault rifles and then back down and out through the doors into the appalling heat. Huffing and puffing he runs over cursing his own bad luck and lack of fitness but secretly glad he's still wearing the wicking top and not a shirt and tie in this heat.

He pushes through the gap left in the sliding door by Neal and faces the huge monstrous red gleaming fire engine that stands so tall and so wide and so...just so big. How on earth do they even drive something like that?

Neal gets to the side and fumbles for the release catch on the metal shutter that slams up to reveal a gleaming clean array of dials, small wheels and levers. A thick spout in the middle must be where the hose is connected. Where is the hose?

'Hose?' Neal mumbles staring at the sides of the vehicle.

'Yours I believe?' Reginald says politely holding out the M4 assault rifle.

'Oh thanks, I must stop leaving it about. Have you seen the hose by any chance?'

'The hose? Is it not there?'

'Well, I've found this control panel and I can only assume this thick spout is where the hose connects but damned if I can actually see a hose.'

'Oh there must be one somewhere,' Reginald says standing back and spotting the release lever on the next shutter that he grabs and releases. 'Ah we have tools,' he says nodding respectfully at the neatly ordered way the tools are all stacked, 'it's very clean,' he remarks.

'Yes I thought that,' Neal replies, 'what about that next shutter?'

'Oh this one? Oh yes, er, this appears to be a hose or several hoses in fact. Do they come in different sizes?'

'Do you know I have no idea,' Neal says, 'the spout is one size so perhaps they are to increase the length?'

'Oh now that is a wise suggestion,' Reginald says, 'and looking at the remarkable way this is organised I would say the first hose on the left is the main connecting one. Does that sound right to you?'

'Well it makes sense to me,' Neal says. 'How do we get the water out?'

'Ah now I was thinking this same thing on the way here. They always leave the engine running don't they.'

'Oh yes they do, yes of course. So the main engine must provide the power for the pump mechanism. What about the facility to actually draw the water from the tank?'

'Well, I may not know but I know two men who will,' Reginald says reaching for his radio then remembering he's not at his desk and the radio is inside the van, on his desk, which he isn't at. 'Oh, well let's have a look shall we?'

'I think this one must be the display for the tank er...level? Is that the right word?'

'Yes I know what you mean, as in how much water is left in the tank?'

'Yes.'

'Yes, indeed I would agree,' Reginald says, 'what about that next one? What does it say?'

'Er, it says pressure. Ah so that must be the pressure and the wheel underneath must be turned to increase or decrease the pressure.'

'Wow, we're doing really very well,' Reginald says, 'is there an on switch?'

'Well I don't know. What about this lever? Shall I pull it down?'

'Yes, pull it down and see what happens. Ah nothing happens. Perhaps it's only activated when the engine is on.'

'Ah yes we said the engine should be on,' Neal says, 'right well, shall we then? Would you like to drive?'

'Oh I'm not a confident driver,' Reginald says, 'perhaps you would care to take the wheel.'

'I will certainly try. It's a steep climb up.'

'It is somewhat,' Reginald says scurrying round the other side and clambering up the step to open the door.

'Well at least they've left the keys in the ignition,' Neal says, 'what a relief, it's automatic. You know I was worried about how many gears there would be. Well, here goes, fingers crossed.'

The engine starts first time. A whir, a cough and it rumbles to life proving the high safety record and maintenance of the fire service.

Neal releases the handbrake, eases forward and hits the side of the engine on the side of the sliding doors that get ripped clean from their hinges and dragged into the road, 'damn it,' Neal curses, 'I do apologise.'

'Wait!' Reginald shouts knowing he must get his radio. He drops back down and runs to the back of the van, steps up, rushes across, grabs the radio and rushes back through the heat and up into the cabin where he slumps into the seat breathing hard, 'do go on...straight up this road and turn left into the square.'

WE ARE FUCKED. Royally and completely fucked. We shoot down and drop heavy things and set them on fire but still they come getting faster and meaner every bloody shitty pissing minute. This is fucking hopeless.

'Get everyone in here,' I shout, 'quickly, they're almost at the window.' I lean out and see the next window is near on ready to be breached and hoping the infected at the bottom of the mounds are getting squashed flat.

No way out. Trapped on three sides. The window. The hole we came through and now the other building we've just punched into. People come screaming into the bedroom to get ushered into the kitchen and lounge. Men and women, boys and girls, young and old that were getting by in their little town until we decided to fuck it up for them. We did this. I did this. I made the infection come here to meet us without ever thinking there might be people here.

There is no divine intervention now. There is no back-up or escape plan. There is no fall back point. All the exits are blocked with numbers so vast that not even Dave could stop them and that single thought sends a shiver of fear through me. Dave is unstoppable. He is beyond human in what he can do but even he cannot salvage this. He'll survive and if he chooses he could walk away unscathed except I know he won't. He'll either put a bullet through his own brain the second I drop dead or he'll just keep going until eventually even he will tire.

I search for an answer where there is none. If Dave, Clarence and me went down we might be able to clear this mound but that won't stop the other mounds from getting to the windows.

With a sudden change in pace the infected surge faster and harder up this mound. Thick lines scrabbling up the newly formed stepping stones of broken bodies and such is the wave coming at us that as one we step back. A roaring howl comes with them. Like a signal that passes through their ranks until the whole of them are charging with unabated malice.

'CLARENCE,' I scream his name at the last second as the light is blocked from the window by the infected pouring through and this is it. This is the final stand. They've gained this window.

I just have time to drop the bag from my shoulders and lift my axe as the first one comes lurching at me. He goes down easy with his head rolling across the floor and the screams of the survivors behind me only add to the incredible din inside this room.

We fight plunged into a darker, muggier, super-heated space that is confined and dangerous.

Clarence runs into the room slamming the sledgehammer into four grown adult male undead with such force it sends all four of them back out through the broken window giving us a brief flash of daylight. Dave lunges left and right refusing to any let get past him. Roy runs into the fray with his sword out and starts slashing wildly.

Blowers, Nick and Cookey run in and thank fuck they do because right now we need every pair of hands just to keep them back and as I get thrown back I glance down the hallway to see Blinky firing the GPMG with Charlie at her side.

'ON ME,' I bellow and push back into the fray, 'FORM A LINE ON ME...'

Mo at my side fighting like a demon and doing what Dave told him by protecting me and the surge of admiration I feel for him gives me a greater strength to rally and push back. Blowers and Cookey get to the other side. Nick beside them. Meredith at his side. Clarence next to Mo and then Dave at the far end completing our straight line.

'ON...PUSH ON...' I drive forward slamming my axe into them again and again, 'DO NOT YIELD...'

'BLINKY...get in here,' Paula runs down to take over the GPMG allowing another brutally violent fighter to join us and the stocky woman comes sprinting with her axe held ready as she finds space to fight forward. We hack and cut and slam. We punch and headbutt and get hit. We get struck and we bleed but like bastards we fight that line and with snarling grunts of exertion we start trying to force them back but still they come through that window adding weight to those opposing us.

Tiny movements now in this restricted space and the axe is no good so I ditch it behind me draw my knife and start stabbing anything in front of me. I hear the clang of our longer shaft melee weapons being ditched and it's down to this. Dirty fighting with knives in closer combat than we have ever known. Our hands and wrists become saturated with blood and mouths snap at our faces. A female sinks her teeth into my hand as I stab the one next to her. I lash out breaking her nose with my other hand then headbutt the one I stabbed to drive him back.

Blood everywhere spraying into my face and soaking me bodily. Mo moving so fast with his right arm a blur of frenzied stabbing as he puckers stomachs and chests. Blowers loses his knife in the skull of a body that drops and instantly his hands come up and he drops into a boxers stance slamming hard jabs and swings into faces breaking jaws and noses.

Meredith lunges and slams them back able to use her body weight and the power of her legs. I see her drop down, bunch and spring forward and each time she does so they go back a foot. She does it again. Down, bunch and tense then explode and as her head reaches their neck so she bites and removes the flesh.

Fuck it. Works for her so I try it. I drop back, tense and explode into them with a snarling fury and into the neck I sink my teeth and wrench back. I do it again, down and explode up and into them. I do it again getting more explosive and gaining more power with each try. Back they go. Just my few in front of me but I get them back. It's only inches I gain but right now inches are all we can hope for.

I drop down sensing Mo at my side and together we slam up and into them and he digs his knife into the neck as he impacts. Down we go and back out. Working in time with Meredith. Drop back, bunch and explode. Blowers next and he drops with me, Mo and Meredith and we shoot forward driving them back harder. Again we do it and while Mo stabs, Blowers and I bite. We bite. We bite their fucking throats out and feel the blood filling our mouths and it's dirty and sordid but this is how much we refuse to yield.

'TOGETHER,' I spray blood and flesh screaming the word as Cookey realises the action and drops down with Blowers at his side and on Meredith's cue we go up and forward gaining another inch or two. Back and up. Down and up. I retch hot blood and puke on the spot. My eyes sting and my throat burns but we do it again and again until I look down the line and see Nick doing the same.

We do as Meredith does. All of us. We drop back and go out. We bunch and explode into them driving knives into throats or mouths into flesh.

'HARDER.'

Dave's booming voice permeates all of our minds giving us something to cling to as we explode back up in time with Meredith.

'DOWN....UP...'

Like an overseer beating a drum to slaves working the oars so Dave gives time to our motion.

'DOWN...UP...'

That voice is so loud and so powerful that in the chaos of this filth we retain some order.

'FASTER...DOWN..UP..DOWN..UP...'

My thighs burn from the constant crouching and bursting up but that pain is nothing to the knowledge that so few of us can hold back so many of them.

'HARDER..DOWN..UP..DOWN..UP..DOWN..UP..'

From Meredith we fight. Around her we form and do as she does. Clarence gets the best gains with his body weight and power driving them back a foot at a time and catching sight of his face I see him relishing this. In his element pitting strength against mass.

'DOWN UP DOWN UP. HARDER. WE DO NOT YIELD. DOWN UP DOWN UP...'

Clarence's voice joins Dave. I add mine. We all do and it gives us more unity. We shout down and drop. We shout up and slam into them. They rally and drive us back a step then Marcy is pushing into my side and dropping as I drop and bursting up as I go to clamp her teeth into a throat that gets ripped out and spat aside as we drop. Her voice joins ours and in this she can fight. Doing this is something she has done many times before and it shows. That she even knows how to do this speaks of her bloodied past and the awful things she did but right now, in this place at this time I am thankful.

Side by side. All of us. On Meredith we time our movements synched by Dave and joined by the rest.

'WE WILL PUSH THEM BACK. DOWN UP. ON THREE WE WILL PUSH. ONE. TWO. THREE! NOW PUSH PUSH PUSH.'

This is it. On three we go up and we stay up and drive our legs against theirs. Grunting with the pain burning through our bodies and more people slam into my back as the survivors finally take responsibility for their own lives. They join and we push. We push and strain and heave with feet driving into the ground. Mo and Marcy to my sides pressing shoulder to shoulder.

'MORE PEOPLE.'

Dave's order cannot be ignored and the crushing weight behind me increases as every man woman and child joins the push. Bodies underfoot snag and trip but we stomp them into mangled things.

'DIG IN.'

We listen to Dave for Dave knows and every time he shouts so we gain a tiny fraction of more power to use.

Gasping for air. People screaming with the exertion. Children driving in pushing their arms into the legs of adults.

'ON MY TIME...LEFT FOOT...RIGHT FOOT... LEFT FOOT...RIGHT FOOT...'

The man is a genius. He beats time telling us when to plant our left foot and then our right. For long seconds we simply pace on the spot but then something starts to give. The generation of collective force in a culmination of every left foot slamming down at the same time and driving in while the right foot does goes next. Stomp and push. Stomp and push. We gain. We gain millimetres. Left. Right. We feel them sag back then rally and push but we've got timing now and Dave's voice gets louder giving us the will to keep going and ignore the pain and despite the thrill at knowing we're holding them back I know we cannot sustain this.

In the press of bodies I feel Marcy's head butt gently against mine then Mo on the other side and give thanks for that contact. In that crushing weight I jerk and heave to get my arms out and stretch to reach across their shoulders.

'We'll be okay,' I wheeze the words out with my chest getting crushed by the people pushing into us from behind, 'just hang on... we'll be okay...'

God. If you can hear me and I know you must be busy right now with the whole end of the world thing going on, that by the way you let happen in the first place. Prick. Anyway. Now is a good time. Anytime now would be good. Right now. Because we're sort of fucked and we can't hold on. But you're still a prick. But we need some help. Prick.

'She's not going to help if you call her a prick,' Marcy gasps.

'Eh?'

'God isn't a woman,' Nick shouts.

'She so is,' Paula's ragged voice from somewhere.

'You can't call God a prick,' Cookey wheezes, 'more of a twat.'

'Don't blaspheme,' Clarence shouts grunting to push forward.

'I hate you all,' I mutter under my breath.

'Nah you love us, Mr Howie...Hey Blowers...are you enjoying being a meat sandwich between sweaty men?'

'Yep. You?'

'Loving it...might get a reach around if we're lucky.'

'Alex!'

'Sorry, Paula.'

'TURN LEFT DID YOU SAY?'

'Yes, turn left into the square,' Reginald says gripping his rifle to his chest and still forgetting that he hasn't radioed the others to tell them what he's doing.

'What is the range on the hoses would you say?' Neal enquires still as politely as before.

'Oh gosh, well they cannot get close to fires so I would surmise the range is good but of course the power will lessen the greater the distance. Be that as it may however, it is the second pyramid we need to aim for. The first has already gained entry and I should imagine are being held back by some form of pinch point.'

'Well I was thinking,' Neal says thoughtfully, 'this vehicle is really very heavy and I should imagine it is also very powerful.'

'Are you thinking of driving into them?'

'What do you think?'

'I think we don't want to get too deep otherwise we won't be able to access the hoses without being killed. That is what I think,' Reginald says stiffly.

'Good point,' Neal concedes, 'how about we hit the first mound and try to shift it then back up and do the whole hose thing? Would that be okay? The first mound is quite close to the edge of the square.'

'Hmmm, yes okay. That is an agreeable suggestion,' Reginald says glancing at his companion and taking note of the politeness in his tone. 'Oh gosh,' he says Neal starts the turn into the square.

From above it looked bad but from here it looks much worse and the noises are just incredible. An absolute din of bedlam with infected persons all pushing towards the visible mounds that are now reaching the window levels and by far the largest concentration is at the window of the second building. The top of that mound is thick with bodies trying to push inside while something is obviously holding them back. A desperate situation that becomes ever more desperate as Neal pushes his right foot down and accelerates hard towards the first mound.

Several tons of vehicle and water gain momentum while being driven by powerful diesel engines and both the men cry out in fear as the reality of what they are doing strikes home but it's too late to do anything else now. There is no going back and the fire engine closes the gap from the intersection, into the square and straight into the human mound built thick to the window.

The impact is immense with the enormous wheels gaining grip and driving up for a few feet before the weight of the vehicle has it sinking down into the soft tissue of the infected bodies. Blood sprays out in all directions and the mound disintegrates from the many parts falling away as the solidity of the base is compromised.

The engine powers on. Forcing the mound either aside or under the wheels and the success of the strike is far greater than anything they could have hoped for.

Screaming in panic, Neal keeps his foot down while yanking the wheel a hard left to start the turn through the square and much like the Saxon the solid front of the fire appliance gives instant death to anything stupid enough to be in the way. The wheels bump and bounce over corpses as the fire engine drives through the square in a long turning circle to face back the way they came in. With the speed still high the vehicle slews and slides almost losing control but pure luck sees them mowing a path through the carnage and back out into the intersection where they scream down the road.

He slams the brake on too hard sending poor Reginald sliding forward onto his seat with a hand snatching out to stop himself slamming into the dashboard. Buttons get pressed. Blue and red lights flash and the sirens warble clear into the air. Panic ensues with Neal fighting to turn the vehicle round and taking out walls and fronts of buildings as Reginald jabs his fingers at the control panel changing the sirens through their set array of tones.

The turn completed and they start back up the road towards the square as Reginald finally presses the siren button enough times to make it turn off. The emergency red and blue lights still strobe and reflect off the buildings and any glass still remaining in frames.

'STOP STOP,' Reginald begs before they go too deep and again the brakes are applied bringing the fire engine to a juddering stop with a final twist of the wheel so the side faces into the square.

Neal goes first dropping into the wall of humidity and racing round the front of the engine while Reginald gibbers and blusters while trying to hold his rifle and his radio and open the door at the same time. Somehow he does it and drops down to run and join Neal.

'The hose...get the hose,' Neal squawks getting to the water pump control panel.

Dropping the rifle and radio on the ground, Reginald snatches the first hose and drags the metal end out from the slot and over to Neal. With shaking trembling panicked hands they shove and screw and twist the metal fitting onto the cup of the spout while all the time trying to stare round at the square.

Finally it slots on and seems to lock in place and both pairs of hands start turning the wheels and pushing buttons until Neal remembers the lever and drags it down which instantly causes the big engines to get louder as something mechanical inside starts rumbling. More levers and buttons get pressed and wheels turned. Frantic and unfocussed but the hose suddenly stiffens to life pinging straight as the end goes out deeper into the square with Reginald running behind it like he's trying to catch a fleeing chicken.

Too late. They've been seen and some of the infected are

charging towards them. Reginald's rifle on the floor next to his radio and he starts running for them while Neal runs past him towards the end of the hose both of them still whimpering with wild panicked looks on their faces.

They have seconds. Just seconds and in that absolute point of crisis Reginald goes for the radio instead of the rifle, diving down and snatching it up while fumbling to press the button on the side.

'OVERWATCH...OVERWATCH...OVERWATCH...'   He remembers the word they used and screams it over and over while Neal grabs the hose and starts wrestling as he struggles to understand how to make the water come out the end then it does and he gets knocked on his arse from the power of the spray jetting out the end. Clinging on for dear life he gets dragged across the ground from the hose pinging left and right with the pressure on the pump at maximum flow and still Reginald screams the word into the mouthpiece as the infected gain speed towards them.

'IS THAT SIRENS?' Nick shouts.

'Yay, the police are coming,' Blowers shouts.

'Mo...quick run...' Cookey shouts to a few squashed sounding laughs.

'Funny.'

'What the hell is going on out there?' Paula shouts as we listen to the sound of a big engine driving nearby.'

'Dunno...just bloody push,' I gasp feeling my feet starting to slide as the infected drive in harder from the window.'

It gets worse. The pressure. The heat. The sheer amount of energy required to hold and keep pushing but it's not enough and slowly we start losing ground and not even Dave's shouts can rally us now.

'MR HOWIE...' A man shouts from the hallway, 'they've stopped coming through the hole...'

'WHO SAID THAT? NEVER MIND...KEEP ON IT,' I shout back thinking it to be some foul trick so they can come through again.

'One of the people here took over the machine gun,' Charlie's voice from somewhere, 'and whomever is touching my bottom can they please stop.'

'Alex!' Paula shouts.

'I am nowhere near her,' Cookey shouts, 'wish I was though,' he adds.

'*OVERWATCH...OVERWATCH...OVERWATCH...*'

'That's Reginald!' Marcy lifts her head up, 'must be him outside.'

'Roy...go,' I hiss, 'get down to the first building...'

'Yep,' he gasps back struggling to free himself from the press of bodies and finally breaking free to lunge and grab his bow and arrows, 'keep that gun trained on this hole,' he says to the man gripping the GPMG, 'IT'S CLEAR THROUGH HERE NOW...'

'What the fuck is Reginald doing?' Clarence asks, 'can anyone get to their radio?'

'Not a chance,' I wheeze, 'you?'

'Nope...'

'HEAVE,' I shout feeling the urgency in the infected ramp up again.

THE RADIO DOESN'T WORK and feeling that last flutter of panic Reginald ditches it and finally takes the assault rifle up before shakily rising to his knees. He lifts the rifle trying to recall what Dave said and checking the safety is off and the bolt has been yanked back. He aims. Shaking, trembling, whimpering and while Neal gets thrown about still trying to fight the hose pouring gallons of water over the ground he locks on to the nearest infected male running towards them. His finger tightens on the trigger. He braces, holding his breath and wishing something else would happen that would take this madness away. He blinks and the man is gone. He blinks again trying to understand what just happened but more are coming. A female with wild hair flying behind her is the next closest and he locks the sights and again starts to squeeze the trigger but she goes flying away to the side with a violent action and again he blinks and stares down at the barrel of his rifle.

'Reginald. Get up and help that man with the hose. Overwatch is on. You are safe.' Roy's voice blurting through the radio so calm and measured and he springs up staring at the first window and Roy leaning out firing down into the infected charging towards Neal.

'Now Reginald,' Roy says again still calm and perfectly composed. Reginald gets his wits and rushes to aid Neal fighting with the hose. He dives in, grasping the writhing end as they battle to gain supremacy of the inanimate object that bucks and weaves like a snake on acid.

Two men suited to science and study work with their hands and bodies to force the hose up as they get to their feet and direct the spray at the oncoming runners. The result is brilliance. Pure brilliance and a flow of super-powered water that jets from the hose blatting every running being away. They are knocked back, knocked over, sluiced and swept away.

'The pyramid please,' Roy's voice again guiding them to adjust the aim as they force the end of the hose into the second mound of bodies, *'go closer, you are safe.'*

Words that any coward needs to hear and they walk forward as though walking into a great wind. Bent over and straining to push the hose on. Together they aim up and focus the jet on those infected stood on the top of the mound and still trying to get through the windows. They are taken away. Instantly. Not there. The power of the water simply removes them from where they were and sends them sailing through the air to land in crumpled heaps. They start working down aiming the jet at the top narrower section of pyramid and watching as the bodies get loosened and swept out one by one until the whole thing is crumbling and falling away.

'Now, Mr Howie,' Roy says into his shirt, 'mound removed... push now...'

'YOU HEARD HIM...FUCKING PUSH...' we heave and dig our feet into the floor feeling the pressure on the other side lessen. We gain a step then two then three and suddenly the momentum is ours and we race towards the window sending them falling out in droves to land splatting on the corpse covered ground below.

'FUCKING YES!' Nick leans out watching them fall then dropping back inside to slump down as everyone else bends over or sits where they are to gasp air and ease the lactic acids in our muscles.

'Well done,' I say breathing hard and looking round at the red flushed faces, 'good work...ROY? WHAT'S GOING ON?'

'LOOK OUT THE WINDOW.'

I do as told and peer out to see Reginald and another man using a hose connected to a fire engine to water cannon the infected mounds away and Roy giving them cover. He's joined at the window by the man using the GPMG who starts firing down.

'Who is that?' I ask round the room and get shaking heads back at me, 'Marcy?'

'No idea,' she says, 'maybe it's God...'

'You said God was a woman.'

'Yeah I did didn't I? Not God then. Reggie, it's Marcy, who is that with you?'

'I think he's a bit busy, Marcy,' Charlie says after a pause.

'Reginald, it's Cookey...you are one brave bastard for doing this... cheers mate.'

'Nicely said, Cookey,' Clarence says.

'Yep,' Cookey says stepping back, 'now who was groping Charlie's arse? I want names...'

'And just as quickly he becomes a dick,' Blowers says.

'Yeah you like di...'

'Can we deal with this first?' Paula says exasperated and looking round at the people still trying to recover their breaths, 'it's like this all the bloody time you know. Right,' she stands straight stretching her back, 'can you all arrange getting some water handed round and make sure those children drink plenty. Howie? What's next?'

'Dave and Roy keep an eye on Reginald and his new friend, make sure they can get away because that lot will switch attention any second now. Clarence, we need to get into the next building. Nick, check the street doors...everyone else gather your kit, get water, check weapons and make ready. Did anyone get bit or scratched? Check yourselves and each other...'

'Can I check...'

'Cookey you are not checking Charlie.'

'Wasn't gonna say that actually.'

'You can check me for bites, Cookey,' Charlie says.

'OH MY FUCKING GOD...did you hear that? Best day ever I swear it is...no no no nobody speak and ruin this moment...I haven't been this happy since April got her head chopped off by Dave.'

'Alex!'

'Sorry, Dave.'

'Hang on, you just said you were happy Dave chopped her head off,' Blowers says.

'Whatever,' Cookey shrugs, 'soooo Charlie,' he says with a wink.

'You're a pest,' Paula says.

'If Charlie's bit can I kiss her to pass my immunity?'

'Oh for fuck's sake,' I walk off with Clarence leaving Paula to handle it.

'You're immune?' Someone asks standing up. An adult woman

clutching the hand of a young child, 'can you make others immune?'

'Er...'

'Immune?'

'He's immune.'

'He said he can pass it with a kiss...'

'My children...'

'Whoa,' Cookey says stepping back and immediately looking to Paula.

'Now hang on,' Paula says holding her hands out.

'He's immune,' the woman with the child blurts.

'We're not sure if he is immune or not,' Paula says trying to wave everyone to be quiet, 'please, he was just joking about...'

'Joking? He can't fucking joke now...'

'He said he was immune.'

'Are you immune?' A middle aged man demands, 'are you or not?'

'Oh fuck,' Cookey says backing away.

'Make my children immune...do it...'

'And my son...please, do something for him.'

'Enough,' Marcy snaps striding into the centre of the room, 'that is enough. Most of us are immune and no, we do not pass our immunity by kissing or touching or doing anything...'

She gets drowned out by voices clamouring to be heard that get louder with shrill panicked demands for her to do something. Some turn on Paula throwing questions thick and fast while others still shout at Cookey then at Marcy.

'Dave,' Marcy says.

'SILENCE.'

Wow. That did it. The whole room drops into sudden quiet broken only by the pop of Dave's rifle as he protects Reginald and the other man using the hose.

'We do not have time for this,' Marcy says, 'do as Paula said.

Get water and be ready to move and believe us, if we could make your children immune we would. But we cannot.'

I glance at Clarence who lifts his eyebrows, 'can she?' He asks in a low voice.

'Pass immunity?' I ask back keeping my voice down, 'probably not.'

'She did Lani who turned back to normal.'

'Yeah then went mad and tried to blow me up with a grenade while we were having sex.'

'Yeah,' he says rubbing his chin, 'that's a good point. Wall then?'

'Go on,' I go behind him as he heads back to the wall he was beating down before we got distracted by climbing zombies.

I leave him to it and head back into the main room noticing the staggering difference between us and the other people. How we just did something so horrible and nasty yet we're back on our feet and already preparing for the next issue that will no doubt arise. The survivors cry and sob, some remain stunned and stare into space. Others talk fast nodding and shake as the adrenalin wears off and I notice the compartmentalising in my own head. They are survivors and they fit into the box marked survivors. We are the team. They are survivors. We rescue them and they should be quiet. Fuck. That ain't right but right now it's the option we use because we need focus and a few minutes to breathe and gain some normalcy before it starts again.

I move into the room getting ready to say something and explain what we're trying to do but Marcy cuts me off rushing in front of me and pushing me back into the room with Clarence.

'Nick, Blowers and Cookey with me please,' she says over her shoulder pointing for me to go through.

'Yeah what's up?' Nick asks handing me a cigarette.

'Cheers, Nick.'

'You were all biting them,' Marcy says turning Nick on the spot and taking a bottle of water from his bag, 'you look like monsters, get cleaned up.' She turns Nick back round to face her, 'mouth closed,' she tells him pouring water over his face and using her hand to rub and sluice the blood and gore away. 'Blowers,' she says moving over to him, 'close your mouth,' she does him next then Cookey and finally onto me rubbing the blood away with another bottle of water before standing back and checking each of us, 'that'll have to do.'

'You were biting them,' I say looking at her clean chin.

'Er yeah but I washed it off,' she says obviously, 'I can't believe we just did that.'

'What biting them?' Nick asks, 'Mr Howie does it all the time.'

'I do not do it all the time.'

'Well, you done it a few times now.'

'Yeah but like...yeah I have...but only when I needed to do it.'

'Well yeah,' he says.

'Not like I want to bite them. It's fucking gross.'

'Telling me,' Blowers says, 'that hot shit spurting in your mouth...oh fuck off, Cookey.'

'What? You said it,' Cookey laughs.

'Can we get diseases from doing that?' Nick asks.

'What other than catching zombie, dickhead?' Cookey asks.

'No, fucktard. I mean other diseases.'

'No. You can't,' Marcy says firmly.

'Okay,' he says accepting her answer without question, 'cool, can we smoke now?'

'Go ahead, Paula do you want one?' She calls out.

'Bloody right I do,' she says walking in, 'and I give it two minutes before someone moans about us smoking near children.'

'Could open a window,' Cookey says.

'But, I thought diseases were carried in blood,' Nick says after inhaling his first drag.

'They are but. No. You will not catch anything. I promise.'

'Okay,' Nick says accepting the next round of argument in his usual chilled way but clearly going back to thinking about it.

'*Reginald...time to go...go now...GO NOW.*' Roy speaks into our ears urging Reginald to leave.

'Let's go,' I follow the others back into the now destroyed main room and over to the window to see the infected have turned like a school of fish and are now charging wholly across the square, 'fire into them,' I bite the cigarette between my teeth, tilt my head to keep the smoke from my eyes and fire into the square. Still so many of them and we are far from safe and the last few minutes of pissing about now stings my pride. This day is far from done and that pressing urgency is right there as we go back to work.

———

THEY DO NOT NEED TELLING TWICE and in unison they drop the hose and run back to the fire engine having seen the instant turn and charge of thousands of undead switching direction at once.

Neal rushes to the driver's side while Reginald gets to the still open passenger door and throws his rifle in before clambering up and slamming the door closed. What he sees when he looks back out the window are hundreds of dead bodies but yet many more alive and on their feet still raging and the knowledge that they have bought only time and not saved the day settles heavy on his heart.

'Which way?' Neal says slamming his door.

'Into the square,' Reginald says hardly believing the words just came from his mouth. Neal doesn't reply but slams the stick into drive and jolts forward to turn in the crossroads and heads back into the square for one final run.

Having dropped the hose it automatically stopped spraying as the shut off sprang back into place. Now rigid and the hose sticks out from the side acting as a whip that slams through the infected as they speed back onto the square driving through and over the infected in one frantic run to the end before they turn and head back. They kill scores and take more out with broken bones but still it's not enough.

On the way out and Reginald watches via the big wing mirror as they give chase streaming behind as the fastest ones make the best progress. His hand snaps out jabbing the sirens that warble to life in that long sad cry of high then low.

'Go slow and straight down this road,' he says cursing this new found sense of bravery, 'perhaps we can draw a few away.'

Neal looks to his own wing mirror that is bloodied and dripping gore with a chunk of hairy scalp flapping in the wind hanging down. Such a day. A day of days and he only hopes that what little they have done helps those inside. With that thought in mind he slows down easing the power off until the big engine glides to a gentle stop. He waits with his left hand easing the stick into position and judging the timing from the view in the wing mirror.

'Now?' He asks still ever so politely.

'I would say so,' Reginald says.

Into reverse and foot hard down. The engine screams and jolts back mowing another score down that impact on the hard metal end of the frame and get squashed under the wheels to be dragged bleeding and broken. Stop, forward gear and again they move off with the siren now the cry of an ice cream van drawing the hordes to the promise of the snack inside.

'Shall we do that again?'

'Oh I don't see why not,' Reginald says winding his window down to lean out, 'we got a good few that time.'

'Do you want to tell your comrades we'll try and lure some away.'

'Good suggestion, *Mr Howie. It is Reginald. Can you see what we are doing?*'

'*Yep, good work, Reginald but don't go too slow, you've got several hundred right behind you...and who is that with you?*'

'Neal. He is a scientist.'

'*A scientist? What kind of scientist?*'

'*I do not know,* what kind of scientist are you?' Reginald asks.

Neal glances over and smiles a tight smile, 'may I explain later?'

'*Mr Howie. Neal wishes to explain later.*'

'*Right. That's er...yep whatever. Keep them after you and we'll do what we can this end. Did you find us a way out? Oh and a bus. Did you find a bus?*'

'*No I did not. I was rather busy doing practical rescuing rather than theoretical strategy formation...*'

'*Ah you did well, Marcy said she's proud of you.*'

'*I did not say that, Reggie. I said you've finally grown a pair of bollocks.*'

'*Ah yes, as always you are as poetic as you are beautiful, Marcy.*'

'*Is that a compliment? Howie, was that a compliment?*'

'*Mr Howie, there is a supermarket north of your location with what looked to be a fuel station within a large parking area. That is as far as I was able to view. It may be of use to you.*'

'*Cheers, Reginald. Don't risk yourselves. Draw them out as long as you can but do not put yourself at risk. Is that clear?*'

'*Yes, Mr Howie. Understood. Good luck.*' He slowly lowers the radio as the fire engine comes to another gradual stop that serves to entice the infected towards the back. A pause, a longer pause and reverse is taken with the pedal slammed down and the following jolts, bumps and pings speak of another decent set of kills given and onwards they go. Doing what little they can.

'WEIRD FUCKING DAY,' I mutter to myself and find a big glass of water being held up by a young boy, 'thanks,' I say taking the water, 'how old are you?'

'Ten,' he replies quietly while I down the glass.

'What's your name?'

'Darren.'

'Yeah?' I ask taking care not to spray the water from my mouth, 'not Darren Smith is it?'

'No,' he says staring up at me, 'are you immune?'

'Yes I am.'

'Can you make me immune?'

'No, Darren. It doesn't work like that. Sorry, mate.'

'What about my sister?'

'No mate, if I could I promise you I would.'

'How did you get immune?'

'I don't know.'

'Was it medicine?'

'No, mate. I think I just am immune. Like naturally. I'm not sure.'

'Will we die?'

'Not today.'

'Do you promise?'

'Yeah. Yeah I promise.'

'I helped,' he blurts as though afraid the conversation is over, 'I pushed with everyone and helped.'

'That's good. I felt you pushing, you're strong.'

'Howie,' Paula says from the other room, 'Clarence is almost through.'

'Okay, I have to go back to work but you stay with your mum yeah?'

'My mum died.'

'Shit, really? I'm so sorry. Er, you with your dad then?'

'He died too. Mum bit him.'

'Fuck! Sorry, I shouldn't swear. Who are you with then?'

'Lorraine, she was our neighbour.'

'Oh right, well stay close to Lorraine then...er...good lad,' I nod and go to pat him on the shoulder then flounder for a second and rush off giving him another manly nod instead then blush from my own utter crass stupidity.

'MIND OUT THE BLOODY WAY,' Clarence shouts at the wall.

'I don't think shouting will make it fall down.'

'Very funny,' Clarence says turning to look at me, 'they're on the other side.'

'Yeah that's the whole point isn't it?'

'You turned into Cookey?' He asks gripping the sledgehammer.

'Sorry, just hit it. They'll soon move.'

'You're the boss,' he grunts and hits the blocks which explode out into the hallway of the next building then steps back and starts booting the remaining wall down.

'Hello chaps,' a clipped voice sounds out followed by a dusty head poking through the gap made in the wall, 'it's all going on isn't it. Need a hand do you?'

'Er no I'm fine, just step back so I can get this wall down.'

'Right you are. Carry on then,' the man says brightly pulling back and out of view, 'all clear this side.'

Clarence pauses closing his eyes for a second at the surrealness of this day before exploding out and attacking the last few blocks with unrestrained malice.

'GO ON!' The voice shouts from the other side, 'have at it.'

'Mr Howie, they're coming back,' Charlie says leaning into the doorway behind me.

'Okay, we're going straight through. Get everyone ready and keep people posted on the windows.'

'Sir,' she says rushing off.

'Not Sir,' I shout after her, 'just Howie,' I mutter to myself.

'We're through,' Clarence says pushing his body through the hole.

'Mind out, grab some water I'll check ahead.'

He pulls back as I hear Paula and Marcy urging everyone to their feet and the sound of assault rifles firing sustained bursts from the windows. Through the ragged gap and into a communal hallway of the next building. A quick look down the stairs shows me the main street door is bolted and barred so I rush into the open door to the first floor apartment and into the main room to find a dozen or so people stood at the back of the room in two neat lines. All of them quiet and although they look terrified there is a calmness in the air and not one of them starts screaming or throwing questions.

'Major Hawthorn,' the man who stuck his head through the hole steps smartly in front of me and snaps out an even smarter salute, 'retired of course,' he adds with a stiff nod.

'Wow,' I mouth at the difference from this room to the last, 'er... how many in here?'

'Twelve,' he says in a deep voice so clipped and precise, 'all watered, fed and ready to move out.'

'Mr Howie?' Nick shouts from the hallway, 'you in there?'

'In here,' I call out.

'Everyone's ready,' he says rushing into the room and doing the same double take at the neat lines of people, 'fucking hell, oh shit, sorry for swearing,' he adds quickly with an apologetic nod to the man stood with me.

'Pah! Don't apologise to me,' the man booms heartily, 'reassuring to hear the colourful language from the troops I always say. Rank?'

'Eh?' Nick asks, 'oh...er?' He looks at me quizzically.

'We're not the ar...um...'

'Private, Sir,' Nick says standing straight, 'in a way.'

'Backbone of the army, good for you,' Major Hawthorn states to everyone in the room.

'Boss,' Clarence shouts coming through the hole in the wall, 'few hundred gone after Reginald the rest are going for the street doors,' he bustles into the room blanching at the sight that caught me and Nick out then clapping eyes on the Major.

'Major Hawthorn,' Major Hawthorn booms.

'Sir,' Clarence booms bringing his feet together and snapping out a salute as smart as the one Major Hawthorn did, 'Sergeant. Parachute Regiment.'

'Parachute Regiment you say, by damned I knew it would be my old lot, either that or the Marines. Damned bloody Marines.'

'Damned Marines,' Clarence replies smartly, 'bastards.'

'Rotters the bloody lot of them. Bloody navy boys.'

'Easy now,' another old man at the head of the two lines adds his own booming voice to the fray.

'Thompson was a Marine,' Major Hawthorn explains, 'isn't that right, Thompson? Eh? Joined the wrong bloody lot. Must have been drunk when he signed up I say.'

'We saved your backsides enough bloody times,' Thompson retorts striding over, 'Captain Thompson. Royal Marines. Retired. At your service,' he says gripping my hand firmly then swapping to Nick and Clarence. 'Who is commanding?' He asks.

'Mr Howie is,' Clarence says nodding at me.

'Regiment?' Major Hawthorn asks.

'Tesco,' I reply watching them both become instantly confused, 'I wasn't in the services.'

'Mr Howie is the finest leader I have served under,' Clarence says brusquely as though in defence at my own self-effacing explanation.

'Reserves?' Captain Thompson asks.

'Nope, just Tesco.'

'Mr Howie,' Blowers shouts coming into the room with Cookey, Mo and Blinky right behind him, 'can we set up at the windows?'

'Go for it.'

'Get on it,' Blowers orders, 'get the glass out and start firing down. Nick, you with us?'

'Yep,' Nick says joining the others as they start smashing the windows out.

'Mr Howie,' Blowers says to me, 'that bloke is still on the GPMG with Roy feeding the belt but he needs to come off, he can't aim for shit and he's wasting ammunition. I've told Roy to take over but we need Roy with his bow if any break through and get past Dave.'

'Where is Dave now?'

'Still firing from the windows in that last room.'

'Howie, we clear to bring them through?' Paula shouts.

'Get them in here quick as you can. Clarence, you okay to do the next wall?'

'Yep,' he strides off with the sledgehammer.

I press the talk button under my shirt, *'Roy?'*

'Go ahead.'

'Straight down behind the survivors and into this apartment, I'll find someone to take over from you. Paula?'

'Here,' she says coming into the room.

'I need someone else on that GPMG to free Roy up.'

'What about the bloke that's with him?'

'He can't aim for shit,' Blowers shouts from the window, 'he's wasting too many rounds.'

'Er, Charlie?' Paula asks, 'can she do it?'

'She can but I want every rifle at the windows firing down while Clarence gets the next wall down.'

'Fuck me they're going for the street door,' Nick shouts, 'it won't hold.'

'Keep the fire aimed at that door,' I shout as the room starts filling with the survivors from the last two buildings pushing in.

'Major,' I say to ex-army officer, 'I need all of our people firing. Can you get these survivors organised at the back.'

'Leave it with me,' he booms striding off.

'May I make a suggestion, Mr Howie?' Captain Thompson asks as I take a breath, 'that chap that can't fire can feed a belt and I can bloody aim a heavy machine gun. Might I assist?'

'Thanks, go now.'

'Right you are.'

Bedlam again. Chaos and noise everywhere. Guns firing.

Major Hawthorn's voice booming to get everyone at the back and down low. Clarence beating the shit out of the wall in the next room.

'Mr Howie?' Charlie asks running in.

'Window, fire down.'

'Sir,' she says rushing over.

'Not Sir,' I mutter again with my voice lost in the din, *'Reginald, It's Howie. How many buildings in this line?'*

'Five, Mr Howie.'

'Thanks.' Three down, two to go then we've got to find a way out and get a shed load of people away from several thousand screaming ramped up psychotic infected fucking zombies. Fuck me I need some coffee. 'Nick...'

'Here,' he says throwing his packet across the room.

'We're all in,' Paula says as Marcy brings the last few in. 'You two,' she says pointing at two people that look only a bit less terrified than everyone else, 'get water to those firing at the windows. They've each got a bag. Open them up and fill their empty bottles. Do it now. Go.'

I walk past leaving her to it and into the hallway to see Captain Hawthorn setting up the heavy machine gun with the other bloke kneeling at his side getting the belt ready.

'Where do you want me?' Roy asks.

'Window firing down but be ready to drop back if we get breached. Dave?'

'Coming, Mr Howie,' he says jogging lightly into view. He gets through the hole and stops to look at the two men on the GPMG, 'who are they?'

'Er, Captain Thompson was in the Marines, dunno who the other bloke is.'

'Sir,' Dave nods politely to the ex-officer ignoring the other man.

'Mr Howie, in here please,' Blowers on the radio and I get back into the room and over to the window.

'What?'

'Look,' he says pointing out the window and down the building line. I lean out grimacing at the sheer numbers still howling below and see a thick mound of gunned down corpses around the door to this building but a distinct lack of fresh infected trying to rush it. Instead they're going for the doors back along the building to the apartments we've already cleared. Clever shits. They know we're all in here which leaves those buildings safe to enter. I look down the building line in the other direction and see they're doing the same to the last two buildings too and a fresh mound of bodies is starting to grow pyramid fashion underneath the last window and fuck me backwards if this day doesn't just get worse by the hour. Speaking of which the afternoon is rapidly turning to evening which will inevitably turn into night. Fuck it. Fuck it fuck it fuck it.

What to do? I look down the building line to the left then to the right and watch the concerted effort as they throw themselves bodily at the doors at the end of the line thereby dividing our firing capability into two and across a much greater distance.

'Paula.'

'Yep,' she runs over to join me and takes in the view without a flicker of panic.

'What do you think?'

'I think we're fucked.'

'Yep, me too. Ideas?'

She bites her lip thinking hard, 'no.'

'Seriously? You're Paula. You always have ideas.'

'What have we got,' she says staring round, 'big square...lots of shops...Reginald is busy being chased...we can't get out. Yep, I'm fresh out,' she says smiling at me.

'Awesome.'

'Ah, you'll think of something,' she says placing a hand on my shoulder, 'you always do, right, back to it.'

'Reginald?'

'Yes, Mr Howie.'

'*How you getting on?*'

'*I take it by that you mean have we finished yet because you are getting stuck again and need some assistance.*'

'*Maybe. Yes.*'

'*We are still somewhat engaged with our followers and are currently working to draw them away from you.*'

'*Okay, mate. No worries.*'

Right. I am fresh out of bloody ideas and getting irritated because of it.

'*Reginald.*'

'*Yes, Mr Howie.*'

'*Was there a fuel tanker at that supermarket?*'

'*I do not know. I did not see it.*'

'*Where's the drone?*'

'*On the roof above your head but we left the feed in the van.*'

'*Okay, mate. No worries.*'

I release the radio button and stare out trying to think of the next move and it's like Reginald said, this is a game. Life and death maybe but still a game. We move and they counter. They move and we react.

'Damned mess if you ask me,' Major Hawthorn falls in next to me at the window staring out with his ramrod posture and firm jaw jutting forward, 'civilians are in order,' he reports briskly.

'Thanks, what would you do?'

'Me? Against this lot? I'd call in a bloody airstrike and be done with the lot.'

'We don't have an airstrike.'

'Shame,' he says deeply reminding me of General Melchett from Blackadder.

'It's just us.'

'Pah. Bloody rotters.'

'We don't have enough ammunition. The GPMG will probably run out during the next attack then we'll be down to assault rifles and pistols...after that it'll be axes, knives and fists.'

'Humph,' he snorts full of disdain, 'damned mess. How many men do you have?'

'Twelve of us plus the dog, and four are women by the way.'

'Twelve eh? Against an enemy that size?' He says nodding at the infected in the square, 'don't try and fight 'em. That's my advice. Get the hell out of it and live to fight another day.'

'We can't get out and protect the survivors at the same time.'

'THEY'RE THROUGH,' Blowers shouts pointing down the building line to the first door at the edge of the square. I lean out to see the infected pouring through the door into the building.

'MAKE READY ON THAT HOLE,' I shout.

'WINDOW, MR HOWIE,' Mo Mo shouts making me turn to face down to the other end of the building and the mound of bodies now reaching the bottom of the window.

'Howie, Clarence is through,' Paula calls from the bedroom. I push away from the window running into the room as the GPMG starts firing sustained bursts.

'Get them in here. Major, we've got more survivors coming in. Clarence, they're almost at the window of the last building...'

'THEY'RE THROUGH...'

'Fuck,' I sprint back to the window to see the top of the mound explode to life as they swarm up and throw themselves bodily through the glass of the bay window. Instant terror grips my heart and the sounds of people screeching in pain comes a split second later.

'No...no...no...NONONO...' I go to lunge for the window intent on jumping down to attack the whole fucking lot of them. Hands grip my shoulders and body dragging me away as Mo's face screws up at the sounds reaching us. Every one of us can hear it. The unmistakable noise of people being killed. Of woman screaming and children crying out and the deeper tones of men trying to fight but getting ripped apart as they do.

The shock comes quick and ripples through us. We failed. Our cocky swaggering defiance failed and because of us more people have been killed. No, they are being killed right now because of our stupidity and the blind reckless actions of what we've done. We can defend ourselves and fight and we accept the death if it comes but we've put others in the line as a result of what we did.

I look round wildly and see Blowers at the far end of the window with tears streaming down his face and Cookey still firing into the square with his own tears dripping. Nick grimacing with glistening tracks sliding through the grime on his cheeks. We all know it. In that instant we know what we've done.

A silence descends that stretches out from this apartment right across the square and like a drunken man I stagger to the window and see every single infected standing still and inert. My heart pounds harder and my stomach grips as I begin to realise what they're doing and I beg them not to do it. I beg and plead shaking my head as my heart breaks and shatters into a thousand pieces.

When it comes it's worse than I could ever have imagined. The most terrible sound floating down from that last building of a single solitary female voice screaming in agonising pain. The infected wait, letting that sound stretch out and break our hearts one by one. That scream slowly fades to a death that I was praying would be delivered swiftly and for one second I try and cling to the hope that it's done. But it isn't. The sound comes again from another voice that wails and screams for a mother that cannot help. A child crying and sobbing high pitched and full of despair. *Mummy. Daddy. Stop them.*

Cookey sinks onto his knees sobbing openly. Blowers sags against the wall shaking his head in desperation with his bottom lip trembling. Nick and Mo dripping tears where they stand and I turn to see Clarence just standing with his head bowed.

It goes on and on. Those awful terrible screams that fill the air. Begging and pleading but the words cut off with the pain coursing through that body. It's more than I can take. More than I can hear. I want to die and end this and give in. Let them know they've won and if I thought it would make a difference I would offer myself to them right now but they won't stop. It will never stop and that evolution comes more human by the second as it gives over to the torture of innocents.

I circle on the spot rubbing my face and pushing my hands through my hair with hard movements. I pant and struggle to draw breath as my chest tightens but still that solitary scream sings out giving a glimpse into a world full of pain.

'Stop stop stop,' I mutter over and over, 'please...PLEASE STOP,' at the window I scream at them, roaring the words, 'PLEASE STOP...' but they pay no heed to me for I am nothing and they have the power to do this. To inflict pain and hurt. To give hurt and take the innocence of a child and the thought, just the sickening thought of a child being hurt while her mother and father are made to watch pinned and silent and unable to even give words of comfort is a thing so bad. So very bad.

A hand on my shoulder and I lash round to see Marcy reaching out with tears tracking down her cheeks and every line and pore on her face burning with pain at what we're hearing but my hand is on her throat squeezing as I drive her back.

'You did this...you...' I see what she did now. I can hear it. I can hear the pain she caused and the misery of the lives she ruined. She did this to people. She took life and hurt and I can't get to the infection but I can fucking hurt her except the person I hurt now is not the person that was. Figures move as though to pull me away but Marcy waves them back and locks eyes on me urging me to kill her, urging me to do it because she knows what she did and nothing will ever take that away. I close my eyes and relax the grip that was cutting the blood and air and she comes to me. Fast and into me with an embrace that holds me close and I cling to her as that sound keeps coming. It keeps coming and cannot be unheard. She presses hands against my ears trying to blot the screams but still they come and I pull away.

It gets louder. It gets worse. It becomes inhuman and the noise of an animal suffering unimaginable agonising pain at the hand of another. It becomes a real tangible thing that can almost be touched and seen. It fills my heart that breaks over and over and we'll always be here in this room listening to this. This is what we deserve. This is our hell. To listen and to know and to be unable to stop it.

Despair grips and mutates into a thing that renders me unable to think and like the rest I sink down onto my knees weeping and the room fills with the mournful howl of a dog giving voice to a little one she cannot save. Meredith sinks next to me. Lying flat with ears pressed down but her head raised and facing up as she sings into the air. Long drawn out and high and it gets louder as the child once more screams out. Meredith scrabbles forward howling and pushing her nose into my face. Pawing me. Do something. Her voice in my head but not a voice but an image of a fleeting idea. Pack leader. The essence of leading. Of what the pack do. I am he. I am pack leader and she is pack. Pawing me and that image grows. The idea of that image of something being willed into me. Little one. Protect the little ones. We are pack. We are strong. She howls and pushes her nose into my face raking my bare skin with her claws. Do something. Pack leader. We are pack. We are strong. Do not cry. We rise up. We fight. We rise up and fight. The noise of the little one. Pain. Rise. Fight. End it. RISE UP. BE PACK LEADER. WE FIGHT.

Thirteen on their feet. WE FIGHT. Thirteen running. HOLD ON. Thirteen moving as pack as a feeling is willed into us. Thirteen down the stairs with our biggest at the front who makes the door not be there. Thirteen running into the square. Thirteen charging with snarling fury. WE ARE PACK. HOLD ON. PAIN. LITTLE ONE. WE COME. WE ARE PACK. HOLD ON.

All thought is gone. All conscious thought ends as thirteen reach the door and let our strongest take it away but I am pack leader. I am he. I go first and I go up to the sound of the little one and into that place where the scent of them is strong and I see them. Little one on the floor held down by many that hold her. She bleeds. I smell it. We are pack. I come for you. No thoughts. No images. No weapons. Hands. Teeth. Enemy. Kill. I see those that hurt this little one. I kill them. We are pack. Pack kills. Pack fights. Pack protects.

She bleeds. They infect her. The badness of them goes into the little one but she lives. End the pain. End it. Kill for mercy. Pistol out. Aimed. Fired. Dead. The pain is gone and I stand over the body of the child with the gun in my hand as her parents scream and rush over the broken corpses to lift their girl from the dirty ground.

Death all around me. We killed so many so quickly. Every one of us dripping blood and gore from our fingers that were used to rip throats out and our teeth that bit into flesh. We broke necks, backs, severed arteries and we did it bare handed but there is another image being willed into us.

More little ones.

I look round to see children pressed against the wall with parents holding them tight who look upon us as though we are monsters.

The silence ends as the infected give voice to the air and gunshots from our dropped rifles boom from the windows as those inside take the weapons up.

'Move now,' I shout to the men, women and children at the back but they cower away from me, 'GET UP AND MOVE...'

Still they cower and scream so I grab arms forcing them onto their feet as the others wade in beside me. We have to get them out of here. We push and pull, we order and shout and bully them down the bloodied stairs and into the square and force them to run down that pavement to see Major Hawthorn leading a group of men outside with our axes held and ready to defend the door.

We have to go now. Going back in that building is to invite death. 'GET THEM OUT...EVERYONE OUT...' I run ahead and snatch my axe from the hands of a man before spinning and cutting through the neck of the first infected coming at us.

'I THINK it will be dark soon,' Neal says leaning over the steering wheel to stare up at the sky.

'I think you may be right,' Reginald says leaning out the open window of the passenger door on the fire engine, 'they're almost here,' he says staring at the infected host bodies still chasing after them.

'Right you are, say when,' Neal says selecting reverse and getting ready.

'Not yet, not yet,' Reginald says watching them run and wondering if they ever get tired then remembering he once was one and he never got tired, 'now please.'

Neal pushes his foot down forcing the engine to drive back-wards and once again slamming into the undead charging head first into the back of the appliance. More thuds, bangs and pings sound out as the wheels thump over a few more bodies until the engine comes to a stop as Neal changes gear and starts going forward again.

'Many left?' He enquires politely trying to see the rear from his wing mirror that is covered in blood and filth.

'Only a few,' Reginald remarks, 'but we've done our bit,' he adds looking over at the scientist, 'Mr Howie cannot moan that we did not join the battle or that we stayed safely at the farmhouse. No no, he cannot say that today. We have joined the fight and even reduced the numbers by at least two hundred.'

'Hmmm, I would say less than two hundred. A few did turn back for the square.'

'Be that as it may, we still joined the battle at the front line and if not for our quick reactions and diligence they would surely have come unstuck. Yes, when we gather tonight I shall be able to add my own tale. Not that I would of course,' he says quickly, 'not one to boast.'

'Of course not,' Neal says agreeably, 'but we have endured

through a skirmish of our own. Tell me, this Mr Howie. Decent enough chap is he?'

'Mr Howie? Oh yes, very decent chap. Apart from the undeniable thirst for killing the infected hosts that is. Other than that yes, he is a very nice man.'

'And open to reason is he?'

'Oh gosh yes, very reasonable man. Impetuous but catch him at the right moment and he will listen. May I ask why?'

'I should perhaps explain to you first who I am and then you can guide me on how best to broach the er, the subject matter with this Mr Howie.'

'I would be glad to help,' Reginald says feeling a prickle of pride at the thought of being confided in. 'Oh hang on,' he adds leaning out of the window, 'could you slow down for a minute? I think we've got them all...yes, can't see a single one now.'

'Really?' Neal asks bringing the fire engine to a stop, 'that would be interesting,' he opens the door to lean out trying to see the whole of the road behind them, 'you know, I think you might be right, Reginald.'

'Yes, I think I am. I can't see any.'

'Nor me. Well would you look at that,' he says smiling, 'we appear to have been victorious.'

'Victorious indeed,' Reginald replies, 'I rather think we can safely return to the farmhouse and partake in a cup of Camomile tea. Do you like Camomile tea?'

'Prefer Darjeeling if I am honest.'

'We have Darjeeling.'

'Do you? That would be nice. I have Earl Grey in my bags somewhere.'

'Oh an Earl Grey would be splendid.'

'We can trade,' Neal laughs, 'a cup of Darjeeling for a cup of Earl Grey.'

'I should get that drone back in the air and find them an escape route. That is if they haven't killed them all by now. Which they most probably have.'

'Which way from here?'

'Ah now, I think we stay on this road which takes us back to the roundabout and from there we can find our way back to the farm-house. Do you have a base you work from?'

'Me?' Neal asks, 'I did but that's some distance away now. No I am now nomadic as it were while I undertake my quest.'

'Quest? That does sound interesting.'

'Yes I was about to explain. It is a long story but one of vital importance and you would not believe the relief I feel at having found someone I can tell it to. I have had this burden on my shoulders for a long time now.'

'Gosh,' Reginald says sadly, 'hmmm? What was that?'

'What?'

'You said something.'

'No. No I don't think so. I said I felt a great burden at...'

'What?'

'Pardon?'

'What did you say?'

'Reginald? Are you okay?'

'What?'

'I said are you okay?'

'Pack.'

'I beg your pardon?'

'What?'

'You said pack. You just said it. The word pack.'

'PACK.'

'What? Why are you shouting pack?'

'I do apologise, what did you say?' Reginald says shaking his head at the fleeting image that swept through it, 'oh dear, I think I came over all funny.'

'Must be the heat,' Neal says warily, staring at the strange expression on Reginald's face.

'Little one? What little one?'

'Reginald? Are you becoming delirious?'

'What? Who is delirious?'

'I think you need some water and some shade.'

'WE ARE PACK.'

'Good Lord!'

'PACK. LITTLE ONE.'

'Reginald?' Neal says pressing the brake in alarm at the booming shouts and staring in horror as Reginald twitches to stare round then stares hard into the sky, 'Reginald? What's wrong?'

'Go back,' Reginald says quietly, 'we have to go back. Right now.'

'Now? Back?'

'Go back. Pack. Pack fight. GO BACK.'

'You really want to go back?' Neal asks gently thinking the man has lost his mind.

Little one. Pain. Images and feelings whirl through Reginald's mind with an instinct to be pack. Be together. Not words or thoughts but just the essence of the suggestion as sure as day follows night. 'Go back...we have to go back...'

'To the square?' Neal asks.

'GO BACK,' Reginald roars. WE ARE PACK. WE FIGHT. PACK FIGHT. HOLD ON.

'Reginald, I really think you should stop and rest for a moment.'

'Go the fuck back,' Reginald snarls lifting his rifle to aim across the narrow gap between them. Pack fight. Little one. Pain. Fight. Pack leader. Be pack.

'Of course,' Neal gibbers turning the wheel to bring the big truck round to face the way they came.

'Faster...go faster...' Reginald gasps, 'they're in trouble...no...I don't know. Please go back.'

'I am!'

'Faster. We must go faster. PACK. FIGHT. MOVE...'

'Reginald? What are you saying?'

'I don't know,' Reginald wails, 'but we have to go now...go faster...'

'We are but please don't point that thing at me.'

'What? Oh gosh I am so very sorry.'

'Please tell me what's wrong with you?'

'JUST FUCKING MOVE,' Reginald explodes slamming his hand on the dashboard and filled with a desire to be there right now. He has to be there. They have to move. The pack move. The pack fight. There is pain. Protect the little ones.

Neal blanches back from the ferocity of the words being bellowed from such a polite and well-spoken man. His whole manner now animated and consumed with burning energy that pulses and blazes from his eyes. The speed increases as Reginald beats the dashboard over and over with a fist slamming down.

'Little one...pack...pain...GO FASTER...we fight...'

Neal wants to do anything other than go faster but he does. He pushes his foot down staring at the road ahead and glancing over at Reginald bouncing frantic on the seat almost frothing at the mouth. They go back over the bodies they crushed like a trail of bread-crumbs as Reginald's head fills with images of blood spraying and he bites down as though he can taste it. His hands claw. He snarls feeling the pack fight and the unquestionable fact that he should be there. When he starts kicking the inside of the foot well then stamping down while gnashing his teeth Neal starts and whimpers in fear snatching looks at the assault rifle gripped in Reginald's hand.

'Where?' Neal asks barely a whisper.

'WE ARE PACK,' Reginald screams lifting his head high making the veins in his neck bulge clear through the skin. 'The square...get to the square...'

'Reginald, there are too many,' Neal swallows the fear down and grips the wheel.

The pain. The little one lives. Infected. Bad blood. End it.

Dead. Pain gone. More little ones. Save them. The urgency grows. There is no question. Only certainty of doing what must be done.

'We will go through the square,' he says with such ruthless cold precision that it sends a shiver down Neal's spine.

COMPRESSION. They are so many and they close in so hard that we are forced back but I still shout for everyone to get out. Staying here is no longer an option.

From that street door the survivors flow out to see a darkening sky and into a wall of heat and undead voices howling to feast on their flesh. We take our axes back and Dave draws his knives. Rifles fire and the GPMG clicks empty but we gather those screaming terrified people into one big group herded together by Major Hawthorn and we start moving north to the closest exit out of the square and the hope there might be a petrol station. It's the tiniest glimmer of hope that we can find something to use but it's all we have.

So we fight. We kill and drop them but they are so many that we will surely tire and fade before they even begin to run out of resources but that sound of the little girl screaming in pain rings true in our ears and drives us on. All of us. Thirteen that slash, stab and bite. We hack for the horror we've brought here and in some sickening cruel way we try to make amends.

Paula and Marcy with us. Fighting side by side and flanked by me and Roy. Ranged round in a circle of protectiveness to those behind and in that midst I can hear the voices of Major Hawthorn and Captain Thompson trying to keep them in order. They are old but they do not panic. In the face of the enemy they hold true and steady and when I turn on the spin I see Thompson lashing out with a meat cleaver and Major Hawthorn stabbing a female in the guts before kicking her legs out and rushing on with his group.

Step by step we start to make progress but it's painfully slow and our few have to be everywhere to keep that large circle intact and a big dog runs relentlessly round and through the children working tirelessly to herd them on and keep the things at bay.

That compression grows and I see Mo go down from a flailing hand of a big male that gets slammed aside then cleaved in half by Blinky who drops a hand and wrenches the lad back to his feet. He doesn't flinch, not a flicker of recognition of the pain that must be coming from the welt across his face but he's straight back in stabbing frenzied and hard. Charlie staggers into me and I spin round using my back to protect her from the onslaught of infected coming at her. Teeth and nails bite and rake into me until Clarence batters them away with his sledgehammer. I push Charlie away shoving her towards the survivors but with a snarling fuck you she runs past me and lays straight back in. Blowers and Cookey work to get either side of her but she's so hell-bent on killing that she doesn't realise. We all are. That girl. That awful noise. The sheer brutal sadness of it. We cannot rid that sound from our ears or take away the knowledge from our minds of what happened to her. I shot her too. Through the head at point blank range from the instinct of a dog telling me her blood was now bad and that projected instinctual mind of Meredith lingers even now.

The understanding to focus. The principle of pack. The unity of fighting intrinsically. Don't think. Do. Be pack. Fluid. From the heart. Fight now. Fight. Be leader. The big man needs help. Be leader. Without seeing I turn to strike into the back of a female lunging to bite Clarence's legs. Don't think. Sense. Feel it. From the heart. Pack.

Marcy whips round stabbing one in the neck that was going for Paula. Roy stabs backwards with his sword opening the guts of a male going for Nick. Mo drops and sticks his leg out tripping one that is killed by Blinky and in turn she spins round Mo's back cleaving up into the groin as Mo springs up and pulls her back an inch so Dave can slice the throat of the one about to bite her and I go in killing two that were going for Dave and behind me Charlie kills the one that took my space in an effort to get Marcy.

Little ones. This side. Three of us break away sprinting round the back of the survivors to take out the few that slipped round in the chaos of the battle. Don't think. Do. I run with Marcy and Roy down the side of the group killing and hacking the infected down. Dave goes the other direction coming round the front until we meet halfway amidst a sea of corpses.

Back now. The pack leader female fights unprotected. We rush to aid Paula but see the others already doing it. All of them. Clarence, Blinky, Mo, Nick, Blowers, Cookey and Charlie all moving fluid to encircle Paula. Be pack. You learn as pups. Don't think. Do.

A chastisement and a sensation of wisdom at being taught and shown. Of allowing the heart to open and feel instead of see. Wolves run and hunt with perfect harmony at speeds that defy what they should be able to do. Turning on the spot and sensing the movements of each other but that sense doesn't just come from sight, hearing and smell but from knowing each other. Eating together. Sleeping together. Living together. Shitting, crying, learning, laughing, playing, bleeding. This is pack. We are pack.

The one who laughs. Cookey being charged down but Blowers and Nick are there before the five get more than a step closer to him. The one who farts and blinks. I shoulder Blinky aside and slice up taking the arm off that was about to rake her face. We flow round each other taking gaps that one just left and in turn the space we vacated is filled as those sensations flow through us. Better. Faster now. Little ones.

All for them. All for the little ones and that sensation of love extended is the strongest of all and that is Meredith's sole focus. That the pack be strong to protect the little ones. Yes. Little ones. They cannot fight. We fight. Pups. Protect. Future.

There it is. We see it. Without them there is nothing. Without our young there is no hope, no species, no life, no worth, no value.

All is empty and gone. For them. Not for us. Now you see. Now you understand. Pack.

The speed of it. The sheer unadulterated speed we gain from that single conscious streaming ideology pushed into our small hive mind brought about by something in our blood but it changes the way we are and the way we fight. It changes our perception of us, of the world and all that is in it. What we are singularly is nothing. What we are in unity is everything. We took the good times and fucked them away. We took peace when it meant nothing to us. We did not have respect for pack or for our little ones. We had no vision of the future. We worked when we should have played. We ate when we should have exercised. We slept too long. We were not watchful or alert. We coveted our gains when in fact we needed nothing more than food that day and shelter that night.

It becomes beautiful. We don't relish in the act of killing but seek the harmony of working together only it's not work. It's something else that I don't have words for. Not thinking or reacting but being. As the infected act as one so we too start to learn and open our minds and feel the presence of each other.

Our spatial awareness increases. Our reactional speed at gauging where this one will go and what direction the ones behind him will take when he is cut down. Whole actions broken into tiny movements of component parts. Blinky can kill. She is strong and fast. She is brutally violent. We all are. Clarence is strong. Mo and Dave are staggeringly fast. Charlie thinks. Paula and Marcy are wild. We each of us can kill but what we can do singularly has no relationship with what we can do in unity as pack.

Blinky strikes left slashing her axe and sending an undead falling back who finds his head removed by Nick spinning on the spot and as Blinky extended to strike out so Clarence lashes forward driving two more back who get their throats cut by Dave and Mo. As those two fall they are used as a springboard by Meredith launching high to clamp her teeth on the throat of an infected battered into position by Roy who then turns away as

Charlie rushes past him stabbing hard into the chest and dropping low to give Cookey space to take the head off. Behind Cookey Marcy darts and drives the point of her blade up into the mouth of a male and behind Marcy I slam three away into the axe blade of Blowers striking them down as Paula reaches round him to drive the point of her own blade into the neck of another. I snatch a hand out giving leverage to Marcy who uses my body to right herself and launch past me. Mo ducks. Dave rolls across his back slashing with a blur of motion then he drops to a crouch as Mo launches himself from Dave's back to gain height to kill the tall one punched round by Blowers. Paula opens her legs to let Meredith rush through who bites up into the groin of a male who finds his bollocks ripped off. Meredith low. I go over her. Clarence behind me. Charlie rolls round Clarence giving space to Roy so he can slash out with his sword. Flow and move. Feel. Instinct. Faster now. They attack harder. Pack fight.

We snarl and growl but not a word comes from us. Not a warning is yelled because the time it takes to see the danger, form the word, gain the air and project that utterance is too long. Through, round, over and under each other. We twirl and circle and lunge but each movement is nothing more than it needs to be and for a few perfect minutes we hold our own. Thirteen against god knows how many but fuck we hold them off. We do not gain ground but we do not yield it either. We pit hive mind against hive mind and ours is faster, stronger, more aligned and in tune as we use what skills we have learnt.

But they have more than us. So many more. More than we can fight and the body can only work so hard for so long before the fatigue starts to show.

NO. FIGHT.

We rally and find reserves to keep going. Digging deeper into our hearts and souls. Meredith hurts from nearly every part of her body but she ignores it. It is not important. Our pain is not important. Future. Little ones.

Gasping for air. Sweat burning our eyes as the blood sprays to blind us. Gore in our mouths and the bile rises from the expenditure of energy. Dehydrated. Exhausted and now giving ground. Beaten back. We fight and flow over and through one another but the survivors cannot move ahead now because the infected have worked to circle on three sides pressing us against the building line.

Hold on. Fight.

We do. For her we do. We drain but find the will to keep going as every muscle and sinew screams in pain and burns from lactic acid.

Hold on. More coming.

There are no more. We're it. This. Just us and as quick as that thought forms so the infected press forward splitting us apart and I fall down on my back seeing nothing but legs and bodies over me and now I find my voice to cry out in warning but I feel a relief. A knowing that something comes. Something big that has fresh strength. I gain the essence of temper and fury and speed and muscles that ripple and bunch glistening golden with sweat. Of height and power and by fuck there she is. A glorious thing to behold and for a second I do not move but stare up in awe and if I ever thought Clarence was strong, she is stronger. This is strength coupled with grace and agility. She is Dave and Clarence together and rears up on hind legs spinning round with a snorting furious noise and eyes blazing pure fucking hatred. When she lands those front legs down so the weight of her kills those she lands on. Round she goes on the spot and now I see those golden muscles rippling with power as her back end slams them aside as if they were made of nothing.

She is scared and terrified but more than that she is foul tempered with anger. The smells of the death here offends her nose. She should give flight and run but the pull to be here is too strong so here she will be. She bucks and kicks out with her back legs with such power she launches three fully grown men off their feet and back into several more that get knocked down.

On my feet and I slash as I rise up killing two more and seeing everyone else surge forward with a fresh burst of energy. The horse rears, kicks and spins with her sheer size clearing space which eases that pressure giving us a slight advantage we can exploit. There is no time to think or dwell on where the hell a horse came from. That's it the same horse as yesterday is obvious from the markings and the way she moves and I see Meredith run under her stomach narrowly missing being kicked.

'Blinky...axe...' Charlie shouts running towards the horse as Blinky reverses her grip and holds the shaft out to be taken by Charlie as she runs past. Fluid. Organic and with instinct. Don't think. Do. Charlie lets that instinct take over and snatches the axe one handed runs to the horse and grips the mane, with a vault she's on the horses bareback clamping her legs into the sides as the axe rises up and slashes down clearing three away. The horse rears feeling the weight of the rider and that instinctive pulsing harmony keeps running. Horse and rider. The most harmonious relationship between man and beast and they give a sense of completeness. The weight of Charlie gives balance and direction and the power of the horse extends to Charlie who grips that mane as the beast rears up again giving momentum to the axe coming down.

Heels in and the horse jolts forward gaining amazing speed within a few strides as she runs into the ranks of the infected that get hacked and bludgeoned down by the axe wielded by Charlie. Never still for a second. Always in motion. Running then turning and rearing up before slamming down. Spinning on the spot then a jolt and they're off again causing mayhem and giving chaos within the depths of the horde.

We stop giving ground and once more find we can hold our position. We still can't get out but each spin and turn of this battle means the difference between dying now or living another few minutes. The survivors huddle together with Major Hawthorn working like a demon to keep them as tight as possible. The children at the back protected by the adults at the front and our few in front of them.

We fight and each time that line builds against us so Charlie rides through behind that first line creating just enough space for us to push them back. As the horse goes on so they rally and surge back in and we fight once more to hold what we can until Charlie can bring her back with her axe slashing down left then right left then right. The horse powering on four legs and using her broad shoulders to ram them down and her head swats them aside. She gets as bruised as we do but pain is not important. Our pain does not matter.

Night now and I did not see the transition from day to dusk to darkness but it's here and that night sky takes the infected and turns them into a frenzied suicidal horde that charges as one driving forward for the final kill. The time is now. This is over. They know it. We know it. We stood and we tried but...is that a siren?

Holy shit that's the fire engine. Loud and clear and getting closer with the sirens warbling and the air horn blasting to tell us to hold on. Hold on. Just seconds now. Hold. We grit our teeth and feel the crushing push coming against us. Driven back and pressed into the survivors with infected hands reaching past us to rake the skin and in so doing they infect those behind us. Chaos erupts as the tight huddle implodes with a cacophony of screams and none of us know which way to fight. Blackness from the pressing horde blotting out the moonlight. We're giving. Yielding. Fragmenting as skin is opened and heads get through the gaps to bite into the flesh of the living.

The roar of the engine mingles with the siren and air horn blasting rough tunes. The aim is off and the infected getting hit from behind by the truck are pushed into us making the crush that much worse and there is no way of knowing who we grip and who we fight now. Swept along on a tidal wave of bodies that writhe and howl and scream. No sense, no order. Just random chaos of pressure and pain. I can't breathe. I can't see or do a thing to make it stop.

Metal brushes my shoulder spinning me round and I bounce down the length of the fire engine as it slews a path too close to the survivors. People are killed but the infected are taken away and as I'm dumped face down I gain the awareness of there being space around me. Don't think. Do.

Back up and I run for our group shouting for them to run, get up, run. Go. Go. Go. I kick and push them to get going and some do. They start fleeing for the northern exit road as my team wade in grabbing children and adults alike to their feet. A man is pulled to his feet by Marcy who spots the rake marks down his arms. She pulls her pistol shooting him through the head and discarding him. We can only care for that that live and stand a chance. The older ones are pushed aside. Those too big and too unfit to move are brutally ignored. Blinky shoots a woman taking the back of her head off for screaming in pain at having three of her fingers bitten off. This is war. This is necessary. We must protect those that can live.

The body of Major Hawthorn is spotted lying with his guts around his ankles but his hands are round the throat of an infected that he took down with him. Captain Thompson on his feet staring at the open wound on his arm then looking up into the cold eyes of Blowers pointing his pistol. The Captain comes to attention and snaps a salute. Blowers stands tall, salutes back then fires. A glance and he moves on for there is work to do.

I don't know how many survivors we had to start with but I know we have less now. Adults that limp and gasp for air and water. Children staring dumbly from the horror they've seen but they get screamed at to move and keep moving.

'CHARLIE,' I shout her name casting round to see her riding back towards me with her face streaked with blood.

'Sir?'

'AHEAD, GO AHEAD.'

'Sir,' she snaps her heels urging the horse on and past the survivors being herded and pushed together by every member of our group and Meredith relentless in her care.

As we push on inching towards the road so the fire engine siren comes back towards us and starts another journey through the square killing more and trying desperately to keep a space between us and them.

On we go. Not running but lurching with limbs so weary and I see Marcy and Paula in the middle with the children urging them on. Shouting to keep going and gripping the hands of children left without adults. Clarence carrying a girl nestled in the crook of his left hand while his right grips the sledgehammer ready to defend her to the last.

We stagger and trip. We go down from the debris underfoot and the slickness caused by so much blood. Flies buzz in front of our faces and through something worse than hell we wade and growl.

Charlie rides hard and stops skilfully next to me, 'Mr Howie, clear road ahead. Car park for the supermarket and the petrol station.'

'Nick? Mo? You got legs left?'

'Fuck yeah,' Nick heaves for air not a few feet away looking drained to the point of passing out, 'what do you need?'

'Both of you, run ahead...petrol station...'

'Yep, Mo?'

'On you,' Mo spits to the side and falls in running beside Nick to sprint ahead.

'Clarence, give her to me,' Charlie takes the child from his arms to place in front of her on the horse, 'another one...quickly...'

'Here,' Paula lifts a child into the air that's grabbed by Cookey who runs the little girl to Charlie and up onto the horse.

'Hold on,' Charlie drops the axe to the floor and leans her arms round the small bodies before shouting for the horse to run.

The rest of us run on. Wheezing and we don't sweat now as we don't have enough fluids left to waste with sweating. We get hot, too hot, dangerously hot. Mouths dry up and our throats burn. Legs feeling like rubber but still we yell and get them into the road with a sense of at least getting out of the square. Howls behind us and still they charge but the fire engine goes through the first lines once again giving us space to run away.

The desperation grows but we get into the road and down past houses that look silent and frightening with black gaping windows and doorways. Quieter here but that just makes it worse too because we can hear the awful ragged breathing coming from our own chests. They're still behind us and we have to stop and deal with those that break away to charge in and still we kill and drop more blood. Swaying and lurching but constantly moving.

Seconds go by. Maybe minutes but it feels like hours until Charlie is galloping down the centre of the road towards us.

'TWO MORE,' she shouts ahead as the smallest children are lifted and handed over. Again she leans forward holding them in place before turning and yelling for the horse to go and she does. She flies on powerful legs that hammer across the tarmac racing towards the supermarket.

'Car park,' Nick's voice gasping on the radio, 'go left for petrol... ahead supermarket...'

'Yep,' I pant my own reply into my shirt and push on.

'KEEP GOING.'

Dave finds his voice bellowing at the survivors from behind giving them all a burst of energy as I feel the pace pick up for a second.

The fire engine drives behind us stopping suddenly then crunching into reverse before going back and into the thick lines giving chase.

Some still get past but Dave is our saviour and in him we trust. He drops back giving the rear protection and all the rest of us can do is pound on urging and pushing the children and adults to keep running and dragging them up when they fall or trip.

'NOT FAR,' Charlie shouting as she gallops back down the road, 'TWO MORE.'

Another two children lifted up and away she goes urging the beast to go faster. It takes forever. The road never ends. The fire engine doing what it can and Dave getting busy with multiple kills but they even get past him. Meredith whips round savaging anything that gets too close. We chop and stab and if we injure them instead of killing then we let it be because moving on is the objective now.

Charlie comes back taking two bigger children and away galloping towards the supermarket that surely does not exist because we would have been there by now.

I see it. The entrance to the car park and the oversized signboard for Tesco. *Supermarket straight on. Petrol station is left.*

Through the open vastness of the car park I see Charlie galloping to the side of the building and dropping the two children down before turning and coming back towards us and I wait until she's back with us before drawing breath to shout.

'My team with me...I need some adults too. Anyone without children will come with us...children go ahead...the rest will go left and draw them into the fuel station. *Nick, you ready?'*

'Almost...'

'Be ready. We have to draw them with us...children go ahead....adults with us...' I feel like a bastard. Separating them from their own but the infection has to see enough of us to follow. My lot understand and get into them pushing adults out from the gaggle of children. They leave mothers clutching babies and some fathers holdings sons and daughters but the rest will be bait with us. Little ones. Future. That is all that matters.

'GO...' I wave the rest to go, 'Charlie...get them to the supermarket.'

'YOU HEARD HIM...MOVE,' she screams and uses the horse to make them run on into the car park.

'Form up...spread across the road as though we're making a

stand,' I heave for air, gasping with ragged snatched breaths. *'Reginald, we're going to lead them to the petrol station...understood?'*

'Understood.'

'Nick?'

'Yep, Dave, you got any grenades left?'

'I have a few.'

'Keep one for detonation.'

'Understood, Nicholas.'

'You've still got grenades?' I ask shaking my head in disbelief, 'what the fuck, Dave? We could have used them by now.'

He just shrugs and looks past me down the road, 'I was saving them.'

'What for? The fucking apocalypse?'

'I do not like using them unless we have to.'

'Have to? Oh my God you are insane.'

'I am autistic not insane.'

'Oh low ball,' I say with a tut, 'that was a cheap shot.'

'Focus,' Paula says through gritted teeth, 'how close are we letting them get?'

'Few feet,' Clarence replies for me and turns to look across the car park and the children being urged on by Charlie on the horse and Meredith running beside them, 'at least they've got Meredith with them.'

'Aye, right...game faces on.'

'Fuck your game face,' Marcy says lowering her head and looking exhausted as the rest of us, 'this is the only face I can do right now.'

'And she still looks great,' Paula mutters rolling her eyes.

'What's the plan, Boss?' Blowers asks between his own ragged breaths.

'Plan? No fucking plan. We run through that petrol station and blow it up.'

'Got it,' he says swallowing painfully, 'good plan.'

'Shit plan,' Marcy grumbles, 'all your plans are a bit shit.'

'Moaner,' I say turning to face the road.

'Leg humper.'

They're close now and slowing down to gather up before they rush in for the final battle. I drop down into a crouch holding my axe in a double grip, 'come on...COME ON...'

'FUCKING CUNTS,' Blinky roars at them, 'FIGHT US...FIGHT...'

'Blinky, where is your axe?'

'I gave it to Charlie, Dave.'

'What have you been using?'

'Knife, Dave.'

'Then where is it?'

'It got stuck in some bloke's skull. Lost it, Dave.'

'Take one of mine. Does anyone else need a weapon?'

'I'm good, Dave,' Cookey says.

'We done?' I ask over my shoulder, 'Paula? Any last minute admin?'

'Er...did we ever find out who stole Clarence's socks?'

'Who the hell are you people?'

'Shit, sorry mate,' I say quickly, 'I forgot we weren't alone then. My bad.'

'Forgot? How the hell can you forget...'

'INCOMING,' I shout over whoever is moaning behind me and watch the horde come running down the road and the clever bastards are holding form and rank this time. No ragged charge but together as though ready to use sheer weight of numbers but fuck you, we have a plan.

'Dave...how far do we have to get away?'

'From what, Mr Howie?'

'From the bloody petrol station we're about to blow up. How far do we have to get?'

'Far.'

'Oh.'

'Very far.'

'Oh. Fuck.'

'Great plan, Howie.'

'Got a better one?' I ask her.

'Well you won't be seeing my backside tonight if we all blow up.'

'Whoa,' Cookey blurts, 'nobody told me we were doing this.'

'Children are secure,' Clarence says, 'and maybe we should think about...'

'RUN,' I scream letting them get too close. We burst away sprinting for the entrance to the car park and taking the left lane towards the petrol station. '*NICK....*'

'*WE SEE YOU...STRAIGHT THROUGH THE PUMPS...*'

I glance back to see the fire engine driving up from behind them squashing a few as it goes but we really did leave it too late and they're like just beyond arms reach behind us. Dave, the cocky shit, drops back a bit and kills as he runs. The bodies he drops trip a few more but we're still seconds away from being caught because they can run all day but we can't.

'*Reginald...How...How many...behind us...how...many?*'

'*Oh hundreds, Mr Howie. Possible more than that.*'

My body needs oxygen so my airwaves open wider to draw more in but all I get is the acrid stench of petrol and diesel that has been pumped over the forecourt and the head of a pipe snapped off that spews more out gushing over the hot tarmac. The thought of running into a petrol station flooded with fuel while wearing radios and carrying metal weapons that could clang and spark is not a happy thought.

Our feet splash through puddles of fuel as we get closer to the pumps and I see Nick and Mo Mo running out of the kiosk to join us. I would tell them well done but not one of us can speak. So we run and sprint and go through the pumps that make us want to gag and puke. Everything about this new world causes discomfort and now our eyes water from the fumes and our throats burn even more.

We have nothing left to give. We are on zero. Running on empty through a petrol flooded station that will have huge tanks of fuel underneath us. We get through and start on the exit road barrelling down towards the car park. We have to make distance but we can't get so far that we risk being unable to detonate.

'NOW...BLOW IT NOW...'

Reginald in the fire engine driving into the car park and with his position of height we have to trust what he can see.

'Dave...' I pant. The grenade comes out of a pocket. The pin gripped between his teeth and he bites it away. Stops and throws it high into the air back towards the fuel station.

'RUN...'

Dave ordering us to run and you know when Dave tells you to run that something bad is about to happen.

So we run. We gain speed and sprint while crying from the pain. Some of the adults drop back and get taken down by the infected. One trips and is left where he lies to be devoured.

The first pop is dull and for a second I turn as though to ask Dave what he was going on about. A dull bang and I can even hear windows smashing and the metallic twang of the pumps being blown apart and fragments striking hard surfaces. Then a secondary explosion that ignites the fuel and a third that plumes the flame across the ground towards the pipe still spewing the liquid out. Then a fourth as that pipe explodes and the air starts to fill with flame

Then it goes bang. A big bang. A really big fucking bang that heaves the ground under our feet as the tanks go up sending tons of concrete and steel bursting in every direction. Hundreds of infected killed outright. Simply removed from existence as the air supercharges with heat that flows up into the air with a mushroom cloud of broiling flames that roll and widen by the second. The shockwave takes us off our feet and every single being running on that exit road is knocked down. Flames scorch our backs. Heat threatens to engulf us and for a second or two I cannot draw air into my lungs as the wind sucks back into the vortex of fire behind us.

A wailing screech that becomes a bass filled deafening roar. I get over onto my arse and start scrabbling back and see bodies flying aflame and sailing across the car park. The place where the fuel station was is now the centre of a fierce raging fire that spreads out further and further with every second. That we're not out of danger becomes painfully obvious and those underground tanks must have been full from the size of these detonations and explosions. The flames grow like something alive with such brightness it hurts my eyes. Yellows and oranges mixed with chemical blues. I glance over to see Dave giving a rare smile as he looks up to the magnificent height of the flames eating the sky. It's coming towards us. Almost like something gentle and tentative and I watch transfixed only just about feeling the heat on my face. It's beautiful and in a few seconds it has done what we've been trying to do all day. It's killed them. Hundreds and hundreds now dead. What we suffered in agony to achieve this has done in the blink of an eye.

'You fool, get up,' Marcy grabbing my arm pulling to get me up and I snap back to the now and feel the heat coming ahead of the wall of flame and this beast does not care who it kills. It will take us as easy as the infected and in that last second before I turn and start running I see one of the adults screaming on the floor unable to get up and run. His flesh melts way before the flames get to him. His hair and clothes burst into flame then he's gone. Devoured and taken.

We go back to running but it's worse now than ever. Every drop of moisture is gone from the air in this place and I realise we don't know how many infected are left. There could still be scores or hundreds.

With flames licking our arses we run like crazy bastards towards the supermarket. With a wall of heat pushing us on we run and drive our exhausted legs towards the front of that building as though it will give sanctuary or the blessed promise of water and rest.

Except we cannot have those things. Not yet. There is still work to do and our pain does not matter. Just the future. Just the little ones.

'FORM UP,' I don't know where I draw the spit from to make the words sound but I know it hurts to shout.

Charlie canters over high and proud on horseback and past us she goes as though ready to protect our backs. Meredith runs out to join the line that forms out wide as we come to a stop only metres from the front of the store and we turn back. We drop down with weapons held and blink the mist from our eyes. We make ready for however many are left. Sucking lungful after lungful of air as we try and ease our hammering hearts. The weapons tremble in our hands and we sway on the spot but we stand and wait as Charlie comes to the end of the line and stares ahead.

Adults behind us collapse crying and crawling or limping over to the children still hidden in the shadows at the side of the building. Stars twinkle overhead. The moon silvery and glowing. Orange flames dance and grow higher and we can hear the roaring so loud and the air is full with the stench of chemicals and cooked meat.

What we see is a fire engine, or what's left of one. The panels are buckled and twisted. Dented and hanging off. The front is buckled in. The passenger door is ripped off. The sides are coated in blood and blackened from smoke and flame. It drives slowly across the car park towards us with one single remaining red light flashing weakly.

We don't move. We don't flinch but wait with our own faces blackened so the whites of our eyes show clear. Lips thinly pursed and wishing it to be done. Let them get here and be done with it.

The engine stops with a grinding noise that speaks of things broken. Reginald climbs down from the passenger side with his assault rifle gripped like he should be gripping it in the way Dave taught him.

The driver's door creaks open. The other man gets down and now I recognise him from the bloke on the horse yesterday so I glance down to look at Charlie and in my mind I think it's her horse now and he can fuck off if he wants it back. She's one of us now.

'It's done,' Reginald stops a few feet from us, legs planted apart and he pushes his glasses up his nose.

We don't reply but we wait. Crouched. Ready. With snarls in our throats ready to come out.

He takes another step towards us looking from face to face and that chin of his lifts in pride at what he sees. 'It's done,' he says turning to look over his shoulder at the flaming petrol station, 'they're all dead,' he turns back to face me, 'ten thousand, Mr Howie.'

I shake my head, 'no,' I croak.

'We've been back to the square. There are crawlers but...you have done it. You have won.'

It takes a while to sink in and we all remain where we are as though it's a foul trick and instead there will be another few hundred popping up from behind the flower beds.

'Yeah?' I croak again.

'Yes,' he says politely with a reassuring nod. 'My rifle is empty but if I may have another magazine I will keep watch here while you...' he falters and hesitates, 'I don't know, but I will watch for you...for us...'

CHAPTER THIRTY-ONE

The store has been looted. Shelves ransacked and mostly emptied but in the corner of the store the stacks of water bottles remain untouched. Figure that one out. The world ends and people take face creams, deodorants, make-up, snack food, spices, fish paste but they leave the bottled water.

Their loss is our gain and into that corner we trudge while two strangely polite men stand watch. My team and the adults and children walk with heavy feet and heads bowed. A dog and horse go with us. Panting and hooves clip clopping across the tiled floor.

'Children first,' Marcy whispers rough and low but we abide her wishes and hand the bottles over to watch as those children small and large drink and drink with water sploshing down their chins. They drink to ease the pain in their throats and replace the moisture lost from the tears they have wept. They drink and we watch. Weapons held. Meredith ever watchful and now we have two that can see over our heads for the horse is even taller than Clarence. Not one of us questions why a horse is taken into a supermarket. None of the adults or children do either. We all ran together so why wouldn't we drink together.

The symbolism of letting the children drink first passes but only when Marcy nods do we go for the big five litre bottles and screw the big caps off to turn the bottles up and over our heads. The water is warm but nowhere like the heat we've been used to and we shiver and gasp as the liquid cascades down over our faces. We gulp and gulp. Belching and filling stomachs that gurgle in delight. We stop and take a breath then drink more. We sluice the shit from our skin and tip water until the floor floods.

We take knives and split the big five litre bottles to make bowls for Meredith and the horse and my god they drink. Meredith drops with her front paws either side of her makeshift bowl and sucks thirstily with her swollen tongue lapping non-stop.

We pour water over her back to bring her body temperature down and the children drink.

'Help me,' Charlie says in a voice more normal now and nods to the lads to help her pour water over the back and legs of the horse. They use their hands to rub the sweat away and ease the heat coming off her flanks and body.

I look over at Paula leaning against the end of an aisle with her hair soaked and clinging to her scalp. She draws a deep breath and drinks more as she glances over towards me. We watch each other for several seconds. The leaders. The pack leaders watching their brood. From Meredith we all saw her role within our group and however Meredith viewed us is how we are and once again I give a prayer of thanks that we have Paula with us.

Clarence sits on the floor with his legs stretched out and a cluster of children leaning against him so drawn by the obvious size of the protective bear. His head drips from the water poured down and his eyes cast slowly round. Charlie soothing the horse with firm hands and soft words while the lads and Blinky gently pour water over the long body and neck. Meredith lying close and still drinking. She got us through this day. This day is hers. These children owe their lives to that dog and her refusal to back down. What we did in that room. What we all did with bare hands and teeth. I can't remember it but just see flashes of Marcy tearing an artery open with her teeth and Blowers and Cookey stamping down with feet to break a skull and Mo gouging eyes out. Clarence ripping a throat out with his fingers. Dave breaking necks. Charlie with handfuls of hair as she breaks the face on the floor beneath her. Blinky tearing a gut open then reaching in with her hands to rip the entrails out. Meredith killing and the blood that sprayed on the walls and ceiling. I close my eyes and I can still see Paula ramming a male against the wall and sinking in with her teeth to bite through the neck. I snap my eyes open and stare across at Paula staring at me and the energy ripples through all of us.

'Howie,' I turn round to see Marcy staring at me with warning in her eyes, 'not now. Later.'

'But...'

'Later,' she says softly, cutting me off, 'now is not the time.' She motions with her head towards the survivors.

I walk over to Marcy and drop my forehead to rest on her shoulder then feel her hand reach round onto the back of my neck.

'We got through it,' she whispers into my ear, 'you kept us alive again.'

I try and nod which isn't that easy with my forehead pressing into her shoulder bone so I give up and shrug. I lift my head a notch to whisper into her ear, 'Paula's immune.'

'I know, put your head back down,' she says applying the gentlest of pressure to my neck, 'and stop thinking so much.'

'Don't think...'

'Do,' she whispers back with a soft gentle snort, 'listen, these people don't need to know what we are. We'll keep that between us, yes?'

'Okay.'

'They've been through enough and we can't give them what we have. Understood?'

'Okay. But maybe we can.'

'That's not for now. We'll talk about it later.'

'Okay.'

'Same goes for everyone,' she says louder, 'we'll talk later. Not now. Paula? Are you okay?'

'Dandy,' she says arching an eyebrow, 'right,' she gets to her feet and looks round the group with the eyes of a mother hen, 'where are we going, Howie?'

'You decide.'

'And decide I will. Staying here is not an option but we do need to go back and collect our weapons.'

'And the Saxon,' Roy says.

'And the Saxon,' Paula repeats.

'Farmhouse for my van.'

'Thank you, Roy. After that? I suggest the place we stayed last night.'

'The golf hotel?' Clarence asks.

'Yep, plenty of beds, plenty of food. Running water, showers and open ground in every direction. Everyone happy? Good. Get up we've got work to do. Come on stop your dilly dallying,' she claps her hands striding into the middle, 'are we keeping that horse?'

'Yes,' Blowers says firmly as both Cookey and Nick make it clear they agree.

'And how do we transport a horse?'

'Horsebox,' Nick says.

'Great. And where do we get one of those?'

'The farm where Roy's van is. There's one in the barn.'

'What if the man asks for his horse back?' Charlie asks.

'He can ask me,' Clarence rumbles, 'and I'll tell him to ask Dave.'

'We can't steal a horse,' Marcy says.

'Not stealing,' Clarence says, 'more long term borrowing.'

'Right,' Marcy says, 'and what if he really wants his horse back?'

'Then he can really ask me and I'll really tell him to really ask Dave.'

'I will say no,' Dave says flatly in such a way it brings the conversation to an immediate end.

'Right enough horsing around,' Paula quips looking round expectantly and deflating at the distinct lack of response. 'Come on then. Let's get moving. Nick, Mo and Roy. We will need a vehicle to transport these people. Everyone grab water, fill your bags. Ready?'

It takes effort to get moving again but we trudge back outside to Reginald and Neal standing together.

'Here,' I walk over and hand them both bottles of water, 'anything?'

'All clear, Mr Howie,' Reginald says, 'may I give my rifle to Dave?'

'Dave?'

'None of you have weapons. Dave is the best shot so therefore it makes the most sense for Dave to...'

'Yep fine, Dave take the rifle.'

'M4 with a folding stock.'

'Eh?'

'That man has an M4 with a folding stock.'

'Do what?' I look round to see Dave pointing at the assault rifle held by Neal, 'ah right, you heard it yesterday.'

'Yes, Mr Howie.'

'So that was you on the horse yesterday was it?' I ask Neal.

'It was,' Neal replies, 'how many of you are immune to the virus?'

'We'll talk later,' Marcy says.

'This is of vital importance. You really must listen to...'

'She said we'll talk later,' Blowers says giving his hard glare that silences the poor man on the spot.

'Come with us,' I say, 'we're going to the square...'

'Again? Good God have you not had enough?'

'For our weapons,' I continue, 'and our vehicle...and the

crawlers will have to be dealt with. After that we'll take these people to a safe place we found yesterday.'

'Where is that?'

'I don't know you,' I say blunt and to the point, 'no offence but we've had a fuck awful day. I appreciate your help but right now we've got work to do. We'll talk later when we're safe.'

'I understand, Mr Howie but...'

'They have a hive mind...we will not talk now at the risk of being overheard by one of them pretending to be dead. Oh and can Charlie keep your horse for a bit?'

'Jess?'

'No, Charlie.'

'What?'

'Christ, are you related to Dave too? Can Charlie keep your horse for a bit?'

'The horse is called Jess.'

'Oh right, got it. Yeah can Charlie keep Jess then?'

'My horse?'

'Oh my god! Marcy...'

'Go over there,' she says ushering me away before I get angry, 'Neal, I'm Marcy.'

'Hi,' he says somewhat taken aback at that smile she flashes.

'Charlie is one of us. She used your horse during the fight.'

'Yes I saw.'

'Great. Can she keep using it...her...the horse...Jess...'

'Oh well...I er...'

'Fuck's sake, mate, we're keeping your horse, got it?' Blowers snaps.

'Of course.'

'Sorted,' Blowers nods striding off shaking his head and muttering darkly.

'That is if you do not mind?' Charlie says politely with the horse.

'Do I have a choice?'

'She is your horse, of course you have a choice,' Charlie says.

'No,' Blowers shouts.

'We are not stealing this man's horse,' Charlie says.

'Long term borrowing,' Clarence calls out.

'That is not right,' Charlie says firmly, 'appropriation of property must be done with consent. Sir, I am sure you are aware but your horse is gifted. She did not shy away from the fight but rather went towards it...'

'The police trained her...for riots...'

'Ah yes that explains it,' Charlie says looking up at the long face of the horse staring at her with what looks like abject love in its eyes.

'Watch out, Mo. That horse is a copper.'

'Funny, Nick,' Mo chuckles, 'where did you learn to do that?'

'It comes naturally,' Nick says.

'Not you,' Mo says, 'Charlie.'

'Oh me? Polo.'

'What's that?' Mo asks.

'So posh,' Blinky mutters.

'I am not posh.'

'Posh people play polo,' Blinky retorts.

'Try saying that when you're pissed,' Cookey laughs, 'posh people play polo...'

'I like Polo's,' Nick says, 'I'm bloody starving. Anyone got any food?'

'You're always starving,' Blowers says.

'We'll get some food when we get back,' Paula cuts in.

'What's polo?' Mo asks.

'Mint with a hole,' Blowers says.

'You like holes,' Cookey says.

'Seriously, what's polo?'

'Hockey on horses,' Blinky says, 'for posh twats.'

'I am not a twat.'

'Oh so cool,' Cookey says, 'say that again.'

'What twat?'

'So cool.'

'What is?'

'The way you say twat,' Nick says.

'Twat?'

'So cool.'

'I do not say it differently to you?'

'You fuck...you do,' Nick says correcting himself as swearing at Charlie doesn't quite feel right.

'They are like this all the time,' Reginald points out looking across to a dumbfounded Neal, 'you do adjust.'

'Neal,' Marcy says cutting through the conversation, 'Charlie was good on your horse. Can she continue using her?'

He nods quickly too afraid to say anything else.

'Charlie, you ride,' I say, 'keep watch. Reginald? Neal? You walking with us...I don't think that fire engine will last much longer. Get the children in the middle. Blowers, your team at the back. Clarence and Dave flanking. Roy...shit where's your bow?'

'In the square.'

'Okay, Marcy up front with me, Roy and Paula behind me and Marcy. We keep those children inside our circle at all times. You got any more ammunition for your rifle?'

'M4 with a folding stock.'

'Thanks, Dave.'

'I have one here...the rest are in my bags,' Neal says.

'Load it up and give it to Charlie.'

'You want my weapon *and* my horse?'

'You've got a pistol on your belt. Charlie is higher so she can see further.'

'I see...yes well that does make sense but may I ask to have it back later?'

'Yep, you'll get it back. Everyone ready? Move out.'

Back into it. A sense of heightened awareness but although we're still exhausted at least the water we consumed has taken away that dire thirst. We stay close and tight with the survivors in the middle encircled by the rest of us and Charlie cantering ahead on the horse holding Neal's M4 strapped over her shoulders.

With the fires still raging and the air full of chocking acrid fumes we go wide and have to venture over to the further reaches of the car park before we can get back onto the road that leads to the square. We see bodies flown far and wide from the explosion. Body parts. Torso's smouldering and cooking. Legs, arms and things we cannot recognise. As we get back on that road we start to realise the flames are not just from the burning fuel station. Houses now alight and set on fire by scorching fragments and flaming corpses sent through windows and doors. The back walls of the houses closest to the fires have been blown out leaving huge gaping holes with flames licking out.

We move fast, staying in the dead centre and I notice that Jess doesn't flinch from the pops, bangs and crackles of flames. When a dull thud sounds out inside a house from something bursting she doesn't so much as blink but trots on with Charlie riding bareback scanning the route ahead with Meredith running at their side and that image gets imprinted in my memory.

Night time. A long street full of houses on fire. Bodies strewn everywhere and the ground littered with debris. Smoke billowing and a woman holding a rifle riding a horse down the middle of it all with Meredith right by them. A powerful image that gives representation to what we now are. I look back to see every face staring ahead and seeing the same thing and I hope those children always remember this night. Not for the horror of it, not for the fear but for what was done for them and that image right there will be cemented forever in their minds.

But all things have an end and that image, that powerful majestic mirage of human working with animals picking their way through the apocalyptic waste-land is brought back to the mortal world in which we live.

'She's so fucking fit,' Cookey sighing dreamily that has the rest of us smiling as we scan and watch.

I look over to Marcy keeping pace at my side. She is a different person now. The whole of her has changed in my mind from a thing I detested but couldn't stop thinking about to someone I half-liked and half-detested but still couldn't stop thinking about to just being Marcy. And I still can't stop thinking about her. Like she's always there in my mind. She is so gorgeous and Paula was right, even in this shit hole and after the day we've had she still looks great. Wet hair swept back down her neck and her cheeks flushed from the heat that seems to radiate and reflect the light from the flames around us. More than that though, beneath the physical beauty there is a strength and love. She fought side by side with us. She bit into them. Took their blood and put her own life at risk again and again. She stepped up and worked with Paula to make sure we had water and worrying about the small things that can still make the difference between living and dying. Sexy as hell too and that top hugs her figure accentuating her curves perfectly.

I look ahead with a sigh and try to focus on the now but truth be told Meredith has got this. She runs from crawler to crawler with a quick now expert snap of the jaws to dispatch it and on she goes. Nose down and weaving a path. Charlie keeps her head up staring down the road and while watching them I notice the horse veer slightly to the right to step on the head of an infected moaning softly. The head bursts all soggy and broken and on the horse goes without showing any sign she did it on purpose.

'Did you see that?' Marcy asks.

'Yeah,' I say, 'strange times.'

We reach the square without incident and view the scene of what has been the worst day so far. Thousands of corpses stretching thick and far with nucleuses showing where the individual battles took place. The way the thick line of them are lying over there shows the route the fire engine took. The broken mounds under the windows. The clusters round the door we finally came out from and the trail of them as they tracked and surged against us going for the northern exit road.

Low groans and hisses come from everywhere. So many broken mangled infected hosts that cling to life not feeling pain or discomfort but forever seeking to pass that virus and at the far end standing squat and solid is the blessed sight of the Saxon. How the hell that thing survives and keeps going is beyond me.

'Mo, do you want to bring it up?'

'Yep.'

'Aim for the crawlers on the way back.'

'Fuck yeah,' he says sprinting down.

'Nick, I forgot to say thanks for the petrol station. That was good work.'

'No worries.'

'Everyone remember we are being listened to,' Paula calls out for the benefit of the surviving adults and children, 'stay quiet and stay together.'

'Such a teacher,' Cookey mutters.

'And later we will have a nice cup of tea courtesy of Cookey.'

'Bollocks. Yes, Paula,' he groans.

'Nick, Roy. We'll need a vehicle,' she says.

'I'll get my bow first,' Roy says threading through the bodies towards the open street door to the flats.

'Everyone else look for our weapons,' Paula says.

We move out pulling torches from our bags. The bags that were organised and sorted by Paula and we drink water that Marcy made sure we packed before we left the supermarket. The small things make the difference.

We sift through the rank fetid gore prising assault rifles from underneath the dead. We pull innards from the trigger guards and flick bone shards from the barrels. Slowly, one by one they get found and stacked up ready for cleaning as Mo drives a circuitous route back through the square popping skulls. Meredith ranges wide sniffing and biting while Charlie lets the horse meander her own route with those back feet treading on anything that might still be alive.

Antibacterial wipes are pulled from bags and we get to work cleaning the shit from the weapons. Working into the grooves and field stripping to get the worse of the gore away. Dry firing tests are done before fresh magazines are loaded in. Roy comes back with his bow in one hand as Clarence lifts the GPMG from next to the corpse of Captain Thompson. That too gets cleaned then fitted back on the Saxon with a fresh belt fed into it. We take magazines from the boxes in the Saxon and fill our bags while Nick, Roy and Mo head off into the darkened streets to find a vehicle.

While we do that, some of the adults head into the apartments and come back carrying bags of bedding for the children and clean clothes for them to change into. More wipes are used to scrub little hands and faces and in that place of carnage and death we gain order and structure.

It takes time. Everything always does but eventually we are back to having working rifles slung across our chests and hand weapons tucked away. Neal gets his M4, with the folding stock, back.

Reginald works with us. Sifting, cleaning and grimacing every time he touches anything sticky or gooey but he does it.

'Boss, got a minibus, that do?' Nick asks through the radio.

'Perfect, can you get it started?'

'Mo's already got it started. He's a fucking genius.'

'Great. Bring it back.'

We finish off as the diesel engine of the minibus floats across the square. A battered old thing marked up with a taxi logo but it'll do. Paula leads them all along the building line towards the road as I get back into the Saxon and feel an immense sense of relief at being surrounded by this seemingly indestructible thing. The engine starts and I pull away slowly following the others towards the waiting minibus.

We get the children loaded first then the adults squeeze in and like I said, it ain't perfect but it'll get us the hell out of here.

Once loaded we drive a slow journey away from Stenbury stopping at the fire station when Reginald remembers that's where they left Roy's van. Nick, Roy and Mo in the front of the minibus and Charlie riding to the side. We go slow knowing that the horse must be exhausted but she doesn't show it. Everyone else crams into the Saxon and rests quietly for the mile back to the farmhouse.

Once there we pull up and tell the adults and children they can go inside to use the toilet or get cleaned up, drink water, look for food but stay close and our work continues.

The drone is brought back by Roy operating the controls with Cookey doing the camera. Nick and Mo head into the barn to look at the horsebox while Reginald sorts his desk out folding maps and stacking paperclips. Everyone does something and all under the ever watchful eyes of Paula.

Eventually Roy's van is backed up to the barn and the horsebox fitted to the tow bar and I establish that it isn't a horsebox at all but rather a horsetrailer. Same bloody thing if you ask me.

Netting gets filled with stuff for the horse to eat and she is guided inside seeming happy enough as the horsey stuff is packed away. Saddle and bits of rope and dangly things that look like they should be in a BDSM club. Horse people are weird.

With water in our bodies and spare fluids to use we start sweating again but that sweat adds to the stale sweat from the day and we stink. I mean we really hum. All of us. Stinky pits, filthy clothes, grimy greasy skin and hair that feels like oil has been poured through it.

The minibus is filled with sleepy children lying on adults and Nick asks for someone else to drive it so he can go on the GPMG in the Saxon and smoke. Clarence takes the minibus with Mo. Roy drives his van with Paula, Reginald and Neal and the rest pile back into the Saxon and our small convoy finally moves out to thread a route through the countryside.

Low voices chat in the back and Marcy dozes off in the front with me driving and her hand stretched over the gap resting on my leg. What a day. We go back through the villages. Flitcombe. Brookley, Hydehill and Foxwood. Through the thatched village where we stopped for a drink and it seems like days ago when we stopped here, not hours. We go back through the town we found Roy's van and in the darkness it looks even more foreboding and in the distance there is an orange glow of a town burning to the ground. Stenbury will be pretty much erased from the surface of the planet but that's a good thing. It needs burning to be cleansed and if I had my way I'd burn every fucking town we pass through to the ground. Fire is cleansing and doesn't care. It destroys everything but more than that, what it leaves behind is used. Those ashes form layers of earth that in time will give life. Take away what was and replace with the future.

Aye, a weary tired and somewhat introspective group finally find the motorway that leads to the lanes that thread into the countryside that take us back to the golf hotel and although we were only here for one night it does seem like a home. A sense of coming back to familiarity and a kitchen stacked with food. Clean beds and running showers. We pull up outside and make ready for the final time of being alert and watchful.

'Blowers, you check outside. Dave, you and Mo do the bedrooms. Everyone else search through.'

We drop down with rifles held ready. Reginald and Neal even come out of their van to stand outside and hold sentry while we head in and sweep through with torches shining ahead and low whispered commands.

'*Clear outside,*' Blowers whispers soft into his radio.

'*Bedrooms clear.*'

'*Kitchen clear.*'

'*Rear store rooms clear.*'

'*Dining room clear.*'

'Thank fuck for that,' I say louder as everyone files back to the front reception. 'Charlie? Neal? What do we do with the horse overnight? Does she stay in that trailerbox thing?'

'Horsebox, Mr Howie.'

'Yeah whatever.'

'Well personally I would let her graze,' Charlie says looking politely to Neal. 'I mean, the weather is warm and if anything happens she can run away.'

'Won't she walk off?' Cookey asks.

'She will stay close,' Neal says.

'So?' I ask, 'we let her graze then? We'll have a watch on all night in reception so we can keep an eye on her.'

'She will be fine, Mr Howie.'

'Yeah sorry mate,' I say forcing myself to stay polite, 'is that a yes to letting her graze?'

'Sorry, yes. Please do let her graze.'

'Awesome, get the minibus up the side. We'll put the Saxon and Roy's van either side of the entrance but we'll get the GPMG inside the reception. The survivors can take the bedrooms, all of us will stay in the dining room like last night. Everyone happy?'

'Hungry,' Nick calls out, 'fucking starving actually.'

'Can any of you cook?' Paula calls out to the people clambering from the minibus.

'Is there a kitchen here?' A man asks, 'I was a cook before...well...'

'There is, we need everyone fed. Straight through the dining room. Blinky, show this man where the kitchen is. Lads, go and get cleaned up and changed. We'll go after you. Charlie, do you need help with the horse?'

'I'll help,' Neal says quickly jogging over to help with what used to be his horse before it was appropriated as Charlie called it. Appropriated for the war effort. I snort at the thought making myself laugh.

'Something funny?' Clarence asks stretching his arms out with a big groan.

'Appropriated for the war effort,' I say.

'Like it,' he booms, 'we've appropriated the horse for the war effort.'

'It was an organic transition of events that allowed the present situation to develop to its current system.'

'Nice,' he smiles at me big and toothy, 'surprised you haven't mentioned coffee yet.

'Coffee! Fuck yes. Right, who is making the coffee?'

'Nice one, Clarence,' Marcy sighs.

While the kitchen gets busy we head inside and light candles that are carefully positioned so they won't set anything on fire. The lads shower first and come back with freshly scrubbed skin and wet hair and wearing clean dry clothes that make the rest of us look like the smelly dirty shits we are.

Marcy, Paula, Blinky and Charlie go next and from the kitchen we start getting aromas of food drifting out. I have no idea what the time is, only that it's late.

When the girls come back so Clarence, Dave, Roy, Reginald, Neal and I take our turn and I head into the separate bathrooms to strip off the filthy clothes that get dumped in a pile.

The shower is cold, sending shivers over my body and making me gasp and for a few minutes the water that runs off my body is black and filthy. I scrub and rub my skin and hair using copious amounts of shower gel and shampoo until finally I start to feel clean. After that I stand at the sink and brush my teeth twice and stare at my naked body in the mirror. Not an inch of me doesn't have a bruise or a cut. Bite marks everywhere, some I recall and others I have no clue where they came from. The fat is gone from my frame now and what's left is a man I hardly recognise. A hard face with dark brooding eyes and lean muscles that show under the skin and it almost hurts me to see myself this way so I look away and avoid glancing in the mirror again.

From my kit bag I pull my last clean load of clothes and get dressed. Socks that are dry. Underpants that feel fresh, clean and new. Trousers and a black wicking top and I walk back out and down the corridor to the main room and the air hangs heavy with the scents of soaps and food.

Everyone eating in the dining room. Sat at tables or on the floor. Spoons scraping in bowls. The smallest children being helped to eat and again I notice the way the kids gravitate towards Clarence who holds a little girl on his knee and feeds her with a spoon. Low voices murmuring and we've saved more than I realised. Not everyone of course. Never everyone. A pang of guilt hits me again which is just as quickly chased away by a woman walking towards me holding out a bowl of food. She doesn't say anything but then neither do I. Something about them annoys me. It shouldn't but I feel irritated. Not by the children but by the adults. Like somehow all of this was their fault and how they cower down and cry when bad things happen and take no effort to fix it.

Life is fucked up. I head over to a table with my lot and plonk down in the middle to start eating the food.

'Shit this is nice,' I say after the first mouthful, 'can we appropriate that cook for the war effort too?'

'We were just saying,' Paula says from the other end of the table, 'or rather Nick and Roy were just saying it wouldn't be hard to make this place secure.'

'Do what?'

'Big fence, Boss,' Nick says, 'electrify it and we've got a secure area.'

'Hmmm, maybe.'

'You don't sound convinced,' Roy says.

'We'll see what tomorrow brings. We need to have a chat with Neal. Didn't Reginald say you were a scientist?'

'That's correct,' he says quickly, 'and I really must discuss things with you...for a start I do not understand why so many of you are imm...'

'Shush now,' Clarence says without looking up from feeding the little girl, 'talk about that later.'

'Why not now?' Neal asks, 'we're all here.'

'Because I just said so,' Clarence says softly as though talking to the child, 'and these people here don't know what we have...or if we can give it to them.'

'But I have this list and...'

'List? Give it Paula, she likes lists,' Marcy says.

'Nothing wrong with lists,' Paula says holding her spoon out.

'No I don't think you understand. My list...'

'Mate,' Blowers says leaning forward to look past Paula, 'long day yeah? Can we just eat and drink coffee?'

'And then smoke,' Nick says.

'And smoke,' Blowers adds.

'And have a wank.'

'And wan...oh fuck off, Cookey.'

'Almost had you,' Cookey says, covering his mouth as he laughs.

'I am sorry but this is very serious,' Neal says firmly.

'Serious?' Blowers pulls his head back slipping into that hard glare.

'Simon,' Dave says, 'eat.'

'Thank you,' Neal says mistaking Dave's intentions.

'Do not interrupt my team again,' Dave says fixing him with a look devoid of all emotion, 'they have worked. Now they will eat. Do you understand?'

'I'd say yes Dave if I were you,' Nick mutters which draws a panicked look from Neal who then nods quickly.

'Yes, Dave.'

'Right, I think this little one needs some sleep,' Clarence says rising to his feet and heading off to the adults taking care of the children.

Slowly the room empties as they head off into the corridor with the children and into the bedrooms. With the main doors into the dining room wedged open we keep a clear view of the reception and the entrance doors. The GPMG ready on the reception desk with a belt fed in. Rifles within arm's reach. Bags close by.

'First watch?' Paula asks yawning and looking over at me.

'Me and Howie,' Marcy says before I can say anything.

'Oh yeah,' Cookey says grinning in delight, 'don't die today, Mr Howie.'

'Yeah don't die today,' Clarence says grinning broadly.

'Cheers,' I say shaking my head, 'yeah thanks for that.'

'You didn't die today, Mr Howie,' Cookey says, 'so what does that mean again?'

'Oh pack it in.'

'No I forgot, what did it mean if Mr Howie didn't die today?' Cookey asks looking round.

'I dunno,' Nick says rubbing his chin, 'Marcy? What did it mean again?'

'That is private between Mr Howie and I,' she says primly which just sets them off laughing and jeering.

'Worst reply ever,' I say to her.

'Better than your plans,' she quips back.

'My plans are awesome.'

'Your plans are shit.'

'So vain.'

'Leg humper.'

'You two are made for each other,' Paula says laughing softly, 'and I am sorry to broach the subject but are we going to listen to Neal now or later? I am tired and I wish to sleep.'

'Tired?' Roy asks quickly, 'are you okay?'

'Maybe she's pregnant.'

'I am not pregnant, Cookey. I am just bloody knackered.'

'Know what,' I say to everyone and especially to Neal, 'unless it makes the difference between living and dying right now I don't think I want to know. We've had a day from hell. We're exhausted...everyone needs sleep. Can it wait?'

Neal looks round at the drained faces, at the bags under our eyes and the yawns being stifled and eventually he rests his eyes on Reginald who nods gently, 'they need rest, Neal. Unless of course, as Mr Howie said, it is a matter of immediate risk.'

'No,' Neal says quietly as though to himself, 'it can wait.'

'First thing tomorrow,' I promise him, 'we'll sit down with fresh minds. Sorry, Neal. Look at us...we're falling asleep where we are.'

'No I can see that,' he says, 'we will talk tomorrow?'

'First thing. I promise.'

'We will,' Paula says reassuring him, 'grab a bed and get some rest. Everyone turn in and do the same.'

'I don't need telling twice,' Blowers says getting to his feet.

I stand up and start collecting the empty bowls together as Blinky rushes to her feet, 'I can do that, Mr Howie, Sir.'

'You grab that lot,' I say motioning her end, 'Marcy? Do you want coffee?'

'Yeah go on then seeing as we're on watch for a bit.'

'Enough,' I say smiling at the low calls coming from the rest again, 'get some rest.'

I wait for Blinky to get the rest of the bowls and walk with her to the kitchen.

'How are you?'

'Fine, Mr Howie, Sir.'

'You don't have to call me Sir.'

'Okay, yes, Mr Howie.'

'You did well today, Blinky. I'm really glad you're with us.'

'Really?' She says blinking harder with a look of surprise.

'Definitely, you were made to do this. It might sound lame, but like...well I'm proud of what you did today. You okay?' I ask seeing her face morph into one of abject shock.

'Fine,' she says softly avoiding eye contact, 'that means a lot.'

We head through to find the man washing bowls at the sink and a decent fire burning on the ground in the middle of the kitchen. Everything looks ordered and clean too with no signs of the normal devastation that comes when we make food.

'That was nice, thanks, mate.'

'Welcome,' he says turning round.

'We got much left?'

'Loads, same stuff I'm afraid though. Might be able to knock something together.'

'Great. What's your name?'

'Kyle.'

'Howie, nice to meet you,' I put the bowls down and shake hands.

'Thanks for what you did. Back there I mean,' he says.

'Yeah, bad day I guess.'

'You do that stuff a lot?'

'We do,' I say politely, 'every bloody day unfortunately. Anyway, you got any coffee?'

'In the flasks on the side,' he says pointing, 'help yourself, milk portions and sugar should be there.'

'Cheers,' I get two mugs and fill both with coffee and use the little milk portions to lighten them, 'thanks, Kyle,' I say carrying them to the door and realising Blinky has already left, 'shout if you need any help.'

'I'll be fine, thanks, Mr Howie.'

In the main room I look over to see Clarence already lying flat on his back on his bedding with his rifle and axe in reach. Reginald and Neal talking quietly and the huddled figures of Paula and Roy under their cover. A suitable and decent distance away lie the beds of the others all pushed closer now from that sense of unity and togetherness. Charlie in her bed listening to Cookey then cracking up when he gets to the punchline. Mo already asleep, Nick drifting off. Blinky and Blowers chatting quietly. Meredith lollops into the room from the direction of the bedrooms. She's checked her little ones and makes her way into the den to be with the pack. Whether from instinct or otherwise she heads straight over to Charlie and stops for a fuss. Then to Cookey and on, working her way from each to the other. A sniff. A stare. A fuss and a wag of her tail. She goes round all of them but the striking thing is when she stops at Reginald and now pays him the same respect as she stops, sniffs and wags her tail. He even reaches out to stroke her nose while listening to Neal and off she trots. She shows deference when she gets to Dave. Just a slight drop in the ears and a soft whine. He too reaches out to stroke her and she only moves off when he stops. Back to Charlie and she flops on the end of Charlie's covers with a heavy sigh.

All is well in my world for this night and I look over to see Marcy standing in the reception staring out through the main entrance. I go through and close the doors behind me sealing us in.

Down the corridor I hear low voices murmuring as the survivors start to settle. Someone crying but they do so softly.

'Hey,' I hand her mug over, 'you okay?'

'Thanks, I'm fine.'

'Cool...'

'You can't smoke in here,' she says as I tap one out from the packet, 'it'll stink. Go outside.'

'Okay,' I push through the doors holding it open as she walks out behind me.

'Beautiful night,' she says after a pause.

'Yep, it is,' I exhale the smoke that plumes up into the air and look over to Jess grazing contentedly on the first section of green. The back of the Saxon is close so I stroll over, open the back doors and sit on the back ledge staring out while smoking a cigarette and drinking a coffee.

'Budge up,' she sits down next to me shoulder to shoulder and sips her coffee. Silence. Two people sitting and staring into the night after a day of devastation and utter depravity. The images swim through my mind over and again and I can still hear that little girl crying out so I take another hard drag on the smoke.

'Paula's immune then.'

'Eh?' I ask and that scream keeps on repeating in my head.

'She didn't say a word.'

'Yeah,' I take another draw and inhale the hot smoke into my lungs as if it will somehow stop the sound of that girl.

'Takes it all in her stride Paula does.'

'Yeah,' I flick the cigarette away and take a mouthful of coffee. *Mummy. Daddy. Stop them...*

'Stop it, Howie.'

'I can't.' I really can't either. It replays over and over. The scream. The words. The sight of her pinned down so frail and helpless. I squeeze my eyes closed and twist my head to the side trying to blot the noise out but the images grow stronger. The whole of the battles and fights from today swimming through my mind like a movie on fast forward but overlaid with that scream and those words. That we were too slow. That it took vital seconds for the dog to get us up. Fuck. We waited for a dog to get us moving. We hesitated and wept like idiots too caught up in our own failure to realise we could have acted. We should have moved faster. That girl could be with us now. Tears sting the back of my eyes and my nails dig into my palms from the fists I make.

Pressure against me. Marcy straddling my lap wrapping her legs round my body. I sink my head into the crook of her neck inhaling her scent. My arms loop round and hold on for dear life and when my hands open they feel warm naked skin. She pushes my head up and searches for my mouth with hers until her lips press against mine. Soft and warm. Reassuring and giving tenderness when I am breaking. My hands run down her naked back feeling the ridges of her spine and her own hands drop down to grip my t shirt and pull it up and over my head. Our lips part for the briefest of seconds but go straight back together as I feel her breasts pushing into my chest.

Her breath exhales into me pushing the images and sounds from my mind. Her lips open as do mine and still those images and sounds are driven further back. She takes my hands pushing them down onto her bare arse. Her skin so soft and warm. She lifts up tugging at my belt and rushing to get my trousers down as we kiss harder and longer. Fever builds. Desire and need so deep it aches and slowly I am consumed by her. She makes everything else go away. She chases them into the night kissing and touching me. Naked we become and we lie together touching and feeling. Doing what men and women do. Not killers. Not leaders. Not saviours. Not immune. Not failures. We are but man and woman.

'I love you,' she whispers the words softly as though fearful but those words, those few words that are said so often with such little meaning finally free the last bit of my mind clinging to the day we've had and the things we've done.

I don't know what tomorrow will bring but right now we take the comfort where we can.

With each other.

Printed in Great Britain
by Amazon

50803558R10296